The yellowbacks... classics of popular fiction

The yellowjackets or yellowbacks were a great series of bestselling adventure and crime thrillers that had its origins in the mid to late 19th century following on from the 'penny dreadfuls'. They virtually began the mass market revolution of the early 20th century with a clear standard format and imprint/series livery (what would today be called branding). Hodder & Stoughton published the yellowjackets in two main series with series run dates of: 1923-1939 and later 1949-1957.

As the tagline ('where thrillers really began') on the back cover implies, the imprint and series focused on thrillers that were the bestsellers of their time. This current reissue or retro revival if you will, brings back many of these masterpieces, now classics in their own way and extends it further by including key titles from that period that were either great crime or thriller or even general commercial fiction (including sub-genres of noir, horror, gothic, romance, westerns, etc.) influences of their time. There are some perennial favourites and many rarities either lost or not easily available being revived in the current series. Writers and characters ranged from adventure heroes like Bulldog Drummond, Allan Quatermain, Richard Hannay or the Saint through thriller grandmasters Edgar Wallace and E. Phillips Oppenheim, crime and mystery maestros like Patricia Wentworth, GK Chesterton, Agatha Christie and the Detection club, to western and swashbucklers like Zane Grey, Max Brand, Captain Blood and even romance or general fiction classics like Hermina Black, Denise Robins, Marie Corelli or Stella Morton. These were books that had storytelling at their heart and always entertained.

The yellowbacks had both hardback (with varying design elements) and paperback (which built the series look) versions with the latter still carrying the imprint 'yellowjacket'. The current reissues pay tribute to both and use an amalgam of elements from both editions while retaining the complete yellow (or 'mustard-plaster') livery with the author's name in blue beveled type with a 'simulated emboss' effect and a white outer 'outline', and the book title in black. These reissues retain the distinctive size of the original mass market paperback and follow the three main category variations—the thrillers (crime, westerns, mystery, adventure) had blue lettering for the author's name, while Romance and softer general fiction had red; and other categories like humour had green.

For more detail and a full list of titles visit https://www.hachetteindia.com/home/yellowbacks

THE APOCRYPHA OF SOLAR PONS

THE APOCRYPHA OF SOLAR PONS

August William Derleth (February 24, 1909 – July 4, 1971) was an American writer and anthologist. Though best remembered as the first book publisher of the writings of H. P. Lovecraft, and for his own contributions to the Cthulhu Mythos and the cosmic horror genre, as well as his founding of the publisher Arkham House (which did much to bring supernatural fiction into print in hardcover in the US that had only been readily available in the UK), Derleth was a leading American regional writer of his day, as well as prolific in several other genres, including historical fiction, poetry, detective fiction, science fiction, and biography. Derleth wrote more than 150 short stories and more than 100 books during his lifetime.

THE APOCRYPHA OF SOLAR PONS

August Derleth

hachette
INDIA

The Apocrypha of Solar Pons

Uncollected works. First collected and published in book form by Belanger Books in 2018

This Hodder yellowback edition © Hachette India 2023
(as authorized by the August Derleth Estate and reprinted under licence and with permission from Belanger Books USA for the Indian subcontinent.)
(Registered Name: Hachette Book Publishing India Pvt. Ltd.)
An Hachette UK Company www.hachetteindia.com

1

The texts in these editions in most cases have been reprinted as is, with minimal editorial changes and by and large no bowdlerizing for political correctness; though in some editions, a few words and phrases considered archaic, or those considered offensive now, along with archaic punctuation may have been modified in places to make the text more accessible to today's readers. The narratives, language, beliefs, social mores and/or cultural depictions, in these volumes are a reflection of their times and must be viewed as such. They may also contain certain cultural, racial and gender prejudices and stereotypes that may be outdated or clearly wrong then and wrong today; but their removal would be tantamount to claiming these prejudices never existed. The Publisher does not endorse or support those depictions or stereotypes; and these books have been made available for a discerning audience that will read it for entertainment value and a chronicle/record of popular fiction of past times.

Cover design by Priya Singh adapted from the original classic yellowjacket by Hodder & Stoughton.

Cover illustration by Ishan Trivedi.

Series note: Some of the books in the series (unless otherwise credited) may have cover or inside illustrations from the original yellowbacks or early editions, and while full restoration has been attempted, some images may be grainy or faded due to the condition of the original material. The end notes or bonus material or blurb details may have been sourced from the public domain or free use publications such as Wikipedia and attribution is hereby made also allowing similar free use reproduction from here. Sources requiring further specific attribution may write in and further detailing and/or corrections shall be made in subsequent printings/editions.

Reprint specifications may be subject to change including but not limited to finishes, paper, colour sections.

ISBN: 978-93-5731-181-6

Hachette Book Publishing India Pvt. Ltd.
4th & 5th Floors, Corporate Centre,
Plot No. 94, Sector 44, Gurugram - 122 003, India

Typeset in Electra LT STD 10/12.5 pt by Manipal Technologies Limited

Printed and bound in India by Manipal Technologies Limited

FSC www.fsc.org MIX Paper from responsible sources FSC™ C043100

The Apocrypha of Solar Pons

Original Copyright Information

With a tip of the deerstalker to
Peter Ruber
Ian M. Law
Luther Norris

The Rediscovered Cases

CONTENTS

Foreword

Foreword

PRAED
STREET

THE REDISCOVERED ADVENTURES
BY DAVID MARCUM

From the late 1920's until his too-early death in 1971 at age 62, August Derleth lived, to greater or lesser degrees, in The World of Solar Pons. Already an admirer of Sherlock Holmes when he was a Wisconsin college student, Derleth wrote to Sir Arthur Conan Doyle, asking if there would be any more Holmes adventures. Upon receiving a negative response, he set about creating some of his own – but placing them in (then) contemporary times of the 1920's. Having never been to England – and in fact, he never made it there during his entire life – he relied on travel books and commentaries to fashion a very believable representation. In these stories, Solar Pons made use of the classic methods of Sherlock Holmes. And Derleth made some much-needed money along the way – until The Great Depression dried up the market, and he moved on to other things.

It has been written elsewhere about how Pons was rescued in the mid-1940's by Sherlockians such as Ellery Queen, Edgar W. Smith, and Vincent Starrett. Over the next decades, while also writing many other volumes including historical novels and material related to H.P. Lovecraft's Cthulhu Mythos, Derleth quietly and steadily produced over seventy Pons adventures.

Many were published individually before being collected in handsome volumes published by Derleth's own Mycroft and Moran. But these volumes were limited in number, and not widely available. And there were certain Pons adventures produced during these years that, for one reason or another, weren't collected, and could only be located by diligent efforts of true Pons fans, or not at all, as they lay buried, unknown, in Derleth's papers.

Praed Street Papers and A *Praed Street Dossier*

In 1965, Derleth published a chapbook titled *Praed Street Papers* (1965), one of the rarest of Pons collectibles. It's not very well done – the pages look as if they were photographed and printed directly from typed documents. In the book, Derleth presented several essays, some entries from Dr. Parker's notebooks – more of those in a moment – and Robert Pattrick's Pons unfinished Chronology (which had been published in the 1961 collection *The Reminiscences of Solar Pons.*) It also included two early attempts from the 1930's by Frank Utpatel to draw a Pons comic strip. These two illustrated stories – "The Missing Tenants" and "The Limping Man" – aren't done very well at all, and they tend to sometimes have more text in the very static panels than drawings. It must be said that in Utpatel's version, Parker and Pons, often drawn in puffed dressing gowns, are simply unpleasant to look upon – a mustache-less Parker wears pince-nez with an attached dangling cord in every panel in which he appears, and Pons has a very high forehead and sometimes an almost insect-like appearance.

Utpatel, a friend of Derleth's, was tasked to draw the covers of almost all of the original Mycroft and Moran Pons volumes, as well as to provide internal illustrations for nearly every Pons story in the Basil Copper Omnibus (1981). Sadly, he wasn't the best of illustrators. (Unfortunately, due to quality issues related to scanning the poorly reproduced comics, they are not included in this volume.)

The comic strip is of interest, however, for a few reasons. At the time Utpatel was drawing it in the 1930's, Derleth had mostly stopped writing Pons stories due to a lack of market interest, and he wouldn't resume until the mid-1940's, at the urging of Ellery Queen. Therefore, these drawings represent an interest in Pons by Derleth during a period when he wasn't doing much else with him.

"The Missing Tenants" had originally appeared in *The Dragnet Magazine* in June 1929, and amazingly it wasn't revised and published in any of the subsequent Pons collections until it's inclusion in the posthumous *The Chronicles of Solar Pons* (1973). (The original version of "The Missing Tenants", along with some of the other early published versions of Pons's adventures, can be found in Mark Wardecker's amazing labor of love, *The Dragnet Solar Pons et al.* 2011).

Finally, at the end of the comic version of "The Missing Tenants" is a teaser for the next Pons adventure in the proposed series – and I wish that one way or another it had been written. The last panel states: "*Coming Tomorrow – The Adventure of the Sliding Stick – Solar Pons visits the U.S.A. and attempts to unravel one of the most mysterious cases he has ever encountered – A huge crowd, A man is knifed – Yet no one saw the murderer*" Pons in the U.S.? It was a possibility...

In 1968, Derleth produced several Pons items that were a bit different than what had come before. He published a Pons novel, *Mr. Fairlie's Final Journey*, a standalone chapbook adventure, "The Adventure of the Unique Dickensians" (which was later collected in *The Chronicles of Solar Pons*, and A *Praed Street Dossier*, which contained the essays and stories from *Praed Street Papers*. These would be the last Pons items published in his lifetime.

A *Praed Street Dossier* is a slim hardcover book with a dust jacket, and it's much more attractive and readable than *Praed Street Papers*. Derleth's essays from both books are included in this current volume. They consist of explanations of the beginnings and sources of the Pons adventures, as well as a very short discussion of Parker's background – which was revealed much more thoroughly by Michael Harrison in his introduction to *The Casebook of Solar Pons* (1965), and also Derleth's own favorite pastiches. Additionally, two of the Pons stories co-written by Mack Reynolds were originally in A *Praed Street Dossier*, and they are included here, along with the other two that were found years later in Derleth's papers. (See below.) While the essays in this book are fascinating, and provide some of the only information that we have regarding the facts behind the initial creation of both Pons and some of the adventures, what's important to me is that this book also includes more tales from the pen of Dr. Parker.

From the Notebooks of Dr. Lyndon Parker

In *Praed Street Papers*, Derleth first presented some entries from Dr. Parker's notebooks. One wonders if Derleth was prompted to produce some of these in order to satisfy the curiosity of The Praed Street Irregulars, founded by Luther Norris in 1966. The book is dedicated to Norris, "*Lord Warden of the Pontine Marshes, Godfather to The Praed Street Irregulars*".

The excerpts from Parker's early notebooks begin when he first started making notes about Pons, a few months after they met in June 1919. As Parker states at the beginning of the Notebooks:

> Within a few months of my joining Solar Pons in his quarters at 7B, Praed Street, and before I turned to chronicling his cases at full-length, I began to keep a notebook – not one of daily accounting, but only of random jottings, having become interested enough in his methods to seek to preserve some of his feats. For, in addition to adventures I later set down, there were many instructive moments in his company, and many lesser problems that came and went, that I wished to set down in some fashion for my own edification, and, later, to refresh my memory, since the memory of man is fallible, and time diminishes it or distorts what is locked in it. The entries that follow all date back to my first year at 7B.

The original Notebook entries in *A Praed Street Dossier* run from August 17th, 1919 to January 27th, 1920. Some are just snippets of conversation, or short investigations running for only two to three pages. Others are running entries over several consecutive dates that relate to this-or-that investigation wherein Pons comments on a case or offers help to Inspector Jamison. As they progress, the entries get a bit longer. For instance, there is the service for Reverend Howard Foster on January 7th, 1920, and then the full-fledged story "The Adventure of the Bookseller's Clerk", recorded on January 14th, 1920. One can see from this progression how Parker went from recording brief journal entries to filling in complete narratives with "The Bookseller's Clerk", the earliest chronological Pons investigation to actually be given a title.

The notebook entries mentioned above were not the only ones. In *The Pontine Dossier* (Annual Edition, 1970, Vol.1, No.1, New Series), Derleth contributed some more information from Parker's notebooks, picking up on February 1st, 1920, and running through February 11th. The following year, the *Dossier* published (in the Annual Edition, 1971, Vol.1, No. 2) notebook entries from February 15th to February 24th. Strangely, when Basil Copper's Omnibus edition was published in 1982, it opened with the Notebook entries from August 1919 to January 1920, but he was apparently unaware of the later pieces from *The Pontine Dossier*, because he only included what had been published in 1968's A *Praed Street Dossier.*

The Rediscovered Cases

In 1993, as related in Peter Ruber's introduction to *The Final Adventures of Solar Pons*, a mysterious package was sent to the August Derleth Society with several typewritten carbons of three unknown Pons adventures, "The Viennese Musician", "The Muttering Man", and "The Sinister House", as well as a fragment with two pages of "The Green Stars". Pons scholar George Vanderburgh received permission from the Derleth Estate, who owned (and continues to own) the copyright to these stories to publish them, and they appeared the next year in a small volume, *The Unpublished Solar Pons.*

In 1995, Derleth's daughter April gave Peter Ruber two boxes of Derleth's papers to sort, and these were found to include additional unpublished Pons adventures, including a 30,000-word Pons novella, *Terror Over London* (originally titled *Mr. Solar Pons of Praed Street*, included in *The Novels of Solar Pons*), "The Adventure of Gresham Old Place", and a more complete version of "The Sinister House", now entitled "The Burlstone Horror". Additionally, there were two more Pons adventures co-written with science-fiction author Mack

Reynolds to complement the two collaborations between Derleth and Reynolds that had already been published. (More of that in a moment.)

These discovered adventures were copyrighted in 1998 by Derleth's children, April and Walden, and published as *The Final Adventures of Solar Pons.* Thankfully, as the rights to these stories are still completely owned by the Derleth Estate, currently consisting of his grandchildren, we are able to present them as a part of this volume.

Terror Over London, also an Apocryphal work, is included with the published Pons novel, *Mr. Fairlie's Final Journal*, in *The Novels of Solar Pons.* More about it in the editor's introduction to that book.

The Fragmentary Adventure

As mentioned above, a copy of "The Green Stars", with its tantalizing reference to Baron Ennesfred Kroll, was discovered in the initial package of unpublished manuscripts. However, this fragment was actually first published in the 1977 edition of *The Pontine Dossier* (Annual Edition, Vol.3, No. 2). The editor's comments at the time explain that it was begun but never finished by Derleth in the 1930's. It was promised that a competition to write the best ending to this beginning would be conducted, with a cash prize and the results to be published in the next edition of *The Pontine Journal.*

Sadly, the 1977 edition was the last to be published. If Ponsians of that era offered their own versions of the end of the story, it's likely that we'll never know. However, I do reference it in my own Pons adventure, "The Horror of St. Anne's Row", from *The Papers of Solar Pons* (2017, authorized by The August Derleth Estate). In fact, my story begins at the end of whatever happened in "The Green Stars":

My friend, Solar Pons, patiently concluded his explanation to Inspector Jamison, who had summoned us that morning concerning the death of Peter Pendleton, one of his best men. As Jamison had explained, not an hour before, Pendleton had been sent out to cover Baron Ennesfred Kroll. Earlier in the week, he had broken off all communication with his superiors, before being found just that morning with a piece of paper clutched in his hand, printed with two green stars. The trail had led from where the body had been discovered in Culross Street, off Park Street in Mayfair, across Hyde Park and Kensington Gardens, and thus to Kensington Church Street, just west of Kensington Palace.

Typically, Pons had seemed to know exactly what was going on, identifying the murderer before Jamison and I even realized we were at the finish line. Now they were standing on the pavement in front of the killer's abode, discussing the finer points of evidence against the guilty party, while I looked around at the nearby houses.

Solar Pons Off-Trail

In *A Praed Street Dossier*, Derleth included two Pons stories that he co-wrote with science-fiction author Mack Reynolds. He explains in his foreword that in 1953, Mack Reynolds submitted several Sherlock Holmes stories to *The Magazine of Fantasy and Science Fiction*, but they were rejected because of the fact that they showed a marked lack of understanding regarding Holmes.

Reynold was directed toward Derleth, and his initial stories were reworked and subsequently published as "The Adventure of the Snitch in Time" and "The Adventure of the Ball of Nostradamus". Derleth then indicates that interest in the project withered away. He published the stories in A

Praed Street Dossier, and years later they were included as an Appendix in the Basil Copper-edited *The Solar Pons Omnibus*.

In 1993, two more of the Mack Reynold's collaborations were found in Derleth's papers, and they were subsequently copyrighted by Derleth's daughter and son, and then published in *The Final Adventures of Solar Pons*. "The Adventure of the Nosferatu" and "The Adventure of the Extra-Terrestrial" are included here, along with the first two, through the courtesy of the August Derleth Estate, owners of the copyrights.

There is some question amongst Ponsians whether these stories should be included as part of the Pontine Canon. Personally, the only one that I cannot include is "The Snitch in Time", with its frank visit from a time traveler. The other three, although having certain aspects of the supernatural, can possibly be explained away, or at least accepted with an understanding that "*There are more things in heaven and earth, [Parker], Than are dreamt of in your philosophy.*"

A Sherlock Holmes Adventure

To conclude this volume, I've included a curiosity from the 1940's – A Sherlock Holmes story by Derleth that was later converted into a Solar Pons adventure. "The Circular Room" was originally written for the July 1946 issue of *The Baker Street Journal* – back when the *BSJ* would proudly publish pastiches. (Edgar W. Smith, the original editor, was a great man in that way, understanding the importance of Sherlockian Pastiche, and how it's the third leg of the Holmesian Stool, along with The Canon and Scholarship.) Later, Derleth revised the story, changing Holmes and Watson's names to Pons and Parker for *The Memoirs of Solar Pons* (1951)

The original Holmes version was republished in *The Game is Afoot* (1994), edited by Marvin Kaye. Now it's available here as well, and a comparison with the Pons version contained in *The Memoirs* will allow the reader to decide just how this case should be classified – Is it a Holmes adventure, or a Pons adventure? As a keeper of extensive Chronologies for both of them, I lean toward giving this case to Pons, although Holmes would have been proud to have solved it.

For those meeting him for the first time, Pons is very much like Holmes. He solves crimes by using ratiocination and deduction. He plays the violin, smokes pipes, and lounges around his rooms in dressing gowns, as well as occasionally conducting chemical experiments there. His brother, Bancroft Pons, is an important fixture in the British Government, rather like Sherlock Holmes's brother, Mycroft. His landlady is Mrs. Johnson, and his closest contact at Scotland Yard is Inspector Jamison. And his friend and biographer, in the mold of Dr. John H. Watson, is Dr. Lyndon Parker.

While most of Holmes's Canonically-recorded adventures stretch from the 1870's until his retirement to Sussex in 1903, Pons operates in the post-World War I-era, with his cases extending from when he and Dr. Parker meet in 1919, after Parker has returned to England following his war service, to 1939, just before the beginning of World War II. Pons had also served in the War, in cryptography, and when the two meet, Parker is disillusioned at the England to which he has returned. However, this is quickly subsumed as the doctor's interest in his new flatmate and friend grows when he joins Pons on a series of cases that he later records.

For too long, the Solar Pons adventures have been too difficult to obtain. Fortunately, these new editions will change that. Here's how that came about.

In the late 1970's, I had been a Sherlockian for just a few years, having found Mr. Holmes in 1975. Those were the early days of the Sherlockian Golden Age that began with the publication of Nicholas Meyer's *The Seven-Per-Cent Solution* in 1974, and has continued to the present. Meyer reminded people that there were *other* manuscripts by Dr. Watson out there, still waiting to be found – hidden in attics, filed away in libraries, or suppressed by paranoid individuals for a plethora of reasons. These began to be discovered, one by one. Meyer himself subsequently published the amazing *The West End Horror* (1976), along with an explanation as to how the appearance of the first book had led to the second. Other Sherlockian adventures continued to surface – *Hellbirds* by Austin Mitchelson and Nicholas Utechin (1976), *Sherlock Holmes and the Golden Bird* by Frank Thomas (1979), and *Enter the Lion* by Sean Wright and Michael Hodel (1979), to name just a very few. The Great Sherlockian Tapestry, after consisting of mainly just sixty main fibers for so long, was about to get much heavier.

And around that time, someone with great wisdom realized that Solar Pons should be a part of that.

Pinnacle Books began reprinting the Pons adventures in late 1974, just months after the July publication date of *The Seven-Per-Cent Solution*. In the world of book publication, at least in those days when things took forever, Pinnacle certainly didn't jump on the bandwagon at the last minute to get the books immediately into print, after seeing how popular both *The Seven-Per-Cent Solution* and Sherlock Holmes were. Rather, the re-publication of the Pons books must have been planned for quite a while, and it was just their great good luck that their Pons editions appeared right around the same time as Meyer's *The Seven-Per-Cent Solution*. Planning and setup would have required a great deal of planning and effort, as would designing the distinctive "Solar Pons" logo that they would use on both their Pons books, and later on Sherlock Holmes books by Frank Thomas. And most of all, they would have needed time to solicit the wonderful cover paintings of Solar Pons and Dr. Parker.

It was these paintings that drew me into the world of Solar Pons.

Living in a small town in eastern Tennessee, finding things related to Sherlock Holmes in the latter 1970's was difficult. My hometown had both a new and used bookstore, and I regularly scoured them looking for new titles. Strangely, several of my most treasured Sherlockian books from these years were found – not in the bookstores – but on rotating paperback racks at a local drugstore. However, it was at the new bookstore, a few weeks before my fourteenth birthday, that I happened to notice seven books lined up in a row, all featuring a man wearing an Inverness and a deerstalker.

I grabbed them, thinking I'd found a Holmesian motherlode. Instead, I saw that they were about... *Solar Pons?*

I had a limited amount of Sherlockian research material then, and I don't recall if I found anything about Mr. Pons to explain why he dressed like Sherlock Holmes. (I had quite forgotten then, although it came back to me later, that I'd first read a Pons story back in 1973 – before I'd ever truly encountered Sherlock Holmes. That story, "The Grice-Paterson Curse", was contained in an Alfred Hitchcock children's mystery anthology, and I credit how much I enjoyed it then with shaping my brain to be so appreciative when I first read about Holmes a couple of years later, in 1975. That one is still my favorite Pons story to this day.)

Those seven books haunted me, and I somehow managed to hint strongly enough to my parents about it that they ended up being birthday gifts a few weeks later – along with some other cool Holmes books. And so I started reading the Pontine Canon, as it's called – the first of countless times that I've been through it. (It's strange what the brain records. I vividly remember reading and re-reading those books frequently in an algebra class throughout that year – particularly one story on one certain day, "The Man With the Broken Face". I was lost and behind for a lot of that year in that class, and instead of trying to catch up, I'd pull out a Pons book, which felt much more comfortable. The teacher, who later went on to be beloved and award-winning for some reason that escapes me, knew what I was doing and did nothing to pull me back. Pfui on her! But I did like reading about Pons.)

As time went on, I discovered additional Pinnacle paperbacks, featuring new Pons stories by British horror author Basil Copper. It was great to have more Pons adventures, but his weren't quite the same. Around the time I started college, I discovered that Copper had edited a complete *Omnibus* of the original Pons stories, and it was the first grown-up purchase that I made with my first real paycheck. (Many thanks to Otto Penzler and The Mysterious Bookshop!) I was thrilled to see that the stories had been arranged in chronological order, which appealed to me. (That kind of thing still does.) Little did I realize then that Copper's editing had been so controversial within the Pons community.

For it turned out that Copper had taken it upon himself to make a number of unjustified changes. For instance, he altered a lot of Derleth's spellings in the *Omnibus* edition from American to British, causing some people to become rather upset. I wasn't too vexed by that, however, as I was there for the stories.

Copper continued to write new Pons stories of his own, published in various editions. I snapped those up, too, very happy to have new visits to 7B Praed Street. Over the years, I noted with some curiosity that Copper's books came to take on a certain implied and vague aspect – just a whiff, just a tinge – that Pons was *his* and not Derleth's.

Meanwhile, the Battered Silicon Dispatch Box published several "lost" Pons items, and also a new and massive set of the complete stories, *The Original Text Solar Pons* (2000), restoring Derleth's original intentions. It was in this book that I read Peter Ruber's extensive essay explaining Copper's changes in greater depth, and the reaction to them within the Ponsian community. However, Ruber didn't mention what I found to be Copper's even more egregious sin. But first a little background...

Over the years, there have been various editions of the Pons books – the originals published by Derleth's Mycroft & Moran imprint, the Pinnacle paperbacks, the Copper *Omnibus*, and the Battered Silicon Dispatch Box *Original Text Omnibus*. (There has also been an incomplete set of a few titles from British publisher Robson Books, Ltd.) Only a few thousand of the original Mycroft & Moran books were ever printed, and for decades, Pons was only known to a loyal group of Sherlockian enthusiasts by way of these very limited volumes. The Pinnacle books made Pons available to a whole generation of 1970's Sherlockians – such as me – that would have never had a chance to meet him otherwise if he'd only remained in the hard-to-find original editions.

As time has passed, however, even these Pinnacle books have become rare and quite expensive. For modern readers who have heard of Pons and are interested in learning more about him, or for those of us who are Pons enthusiasts who wish to introduce him to the larger world, it's been quite difficult, as all editions of his adventures are now quite rare and expensive, unless one is stumbled upon by accident. The Mycroft & Moran books can be purchased online, usually for a substantial investment of money, and the Copper and Battered Silicon Dispatch Box *Omnibi* were always expensive and hard to come by, and now it's only worse. Finally, with these new publications, the Solar Pons books will be available for everyone in easily found and affordable editions. With this, it's hoped that a new wave of Pons interest will spread, particularly within the Sherlockian community which will so appreciate him.

In 2014, my friend and Pons Scholar Bob Byrne floated the idea of having an issue of his online journal, *The Solar Pons Gazette*, contain new Pons stories. Having already written some Sherlock Holmes adventures, I was intrigued, and sat down and wrote a Pons tale – possibly almost as fast as Derleth had written his first Pons story in 1928. It was so much fun that I quickly wrote two more. After that, I pestered Bob for a while, saying that he should explore having the stories published in a real book. (I choose real books every time – none of those ephemeral e-blip books that can disappear in a blink for me!) When that didn't happen, I became more ambitious. Bob put me in touch with Tracy Heron of The August Derleth Society, and he in turn told me how to reach Danielle Hackett, August Derleth's granddaughter. I made my case to be allowed to write a new collection of Pons stories, as authorized by the Estate, and amazingly, I received permission. I introduced Danielle (in this modern email way of meeting people) to Derick Belanger of Belanger Books, and then set about writing some more stories, enough to make a whole book. Amazingly, the first new authorized Pons book in decades, *The Papers of Solar Pons*, was published in 2017.

But that started me thinking...

Realizing that this new books had the possibility to reawaken interest in Pons, or spread the word to those who didn't know about him, I wondered if the original volumes could be reprinted. After all, interest in Sherlock Holmes around the world is at an all-time high, getting the word out by way of the internet has never been easier, and shifts in the publishing paradigm mean that the old ways of grinding through the process for several years before a book appears no longer apply.

The Derleth Estate was very happy with the plan. Now came the hard part.

Being fully aware of the controversy surrounding Copper's *Omnibus* edition, it was evident that that new editions had to be from Derleth's original Mycroft & Moran volumes – for after all, he had edited and approved of those himself. Thankfully, modern technology allows for these books to be converted to modern electronic files with only a moderate amount of pain and toil.

I had several friends, upon hearing of this project, who very graciously offered to help me to "re-type" the original books. I can assure you that, if these books had needed to be re-typed from scratch, there would have been no new editions – at least not as provided by me. Instead, I took a copy of each of the original Mycroft & Moran Pons books, of which I am a very happy and proud owner, and scanned them, converting them all into electronic files. So far so good – that only took several hours of standing at a copy machine, flipping the pages of the books one at a time, and hitting the green button. (And sometimes re-doing it if a scanned page had a gremlin or two.)

After that, I used a text conversion software to turn the scans into a Word document. That raw text then had to be converted into another, more easily fixed, Word document. Then came the actual fixing. Early on, it was decided to try and make the new editions look as much like the originals as possible. Therefore, many inconsistent things that niggled me as an editor-type remain in the finished product, because they were that way in the originals. For instance, Derleth's punctuation improved quite a bit from his early books to the latter – but it was very tempting to start fixing his punctuation in the earlier books. If you see something that looks not-quite-right, chances are it was that way in the original books.

There were times that a letter or a note, as quoted in a story, would be indented, while on other occasions it would simply be a part of the paragraph. I wanted to set up all of those letters and notes in a unified way throughout the various books, but instead I kept them as they had appeared in the original editions, no matter how much the style varied from story to story. Finally, some of the racial stereotyping from those stories would not be written that way today. However, these are historical documents of sorts, and as such, they are presented as written, with the understanding that times have changed, and hopefully we have a greater awareness now than before.

Since the early 1980's, whenever I've re-read the Pons stories – and I've done so many times – it's been by way of the Copper *Omnibus* editions. I enjoyed having them all in one place in two matching handsome and heavy books, and I was very pleased that they were rearranged for reading in chronological order. The fixing of British-versus-American spelling didn't bother me a bit. This time, as part of the process to fix up the converted-to-text files, I was reading the stories as they had originally appeared, in the order that they had been published in the original volumes. I hadn't done it that way for years. The conversion process captures everything, and that means some items do have to be corrected. For instance, when setting up for printing, original books from the old days often *split* words at the end of a line with hyphens, whereas modern computer programs *wrap* the text, allowing for hyphens to be ignored. When converting the text of the original books, the program picked up every one of those end-of-line hyphens and split words, and they all had to be found and removed. Likewise, the text-conversion program ignores words that are italicized in the original, and these each have to be relocated and re-italicized. (However, in some cases, Derleth himself was inconsistent, italicizing a word, such as a book title or the name of a ship, at one point in a story, and not at a later point. That had to be verified too.)

I have long been a chronologicist, organizing all of the thousands of traditional Sherlock Holmes stories that I've collected and read into a massive Holmes Chronology, breaking various adventures (book, story, chapter, and paragraph) down into year, month, day, and even hour to form a *complete* life of Holmes, from birth to death, covering both the Holmes Canon and traditional pastiches. It was inevitable that I would do the same with Pons. For several decades, I've had a satisfying Pons Chronology as well, based on research by various individuals, and largely on Copper's arrangement of the stories within his *Omnibus* – with a few disagreements. By re-reading the original stories in their original form, for the first time in years, I realized that, in addition to changing spelling, Copper had committed – as referred to earlier – a far bigger sin.

I discovered as I re-read the original stories for this project that a number of them weren't matching up with my long-established Pons Chronology, based a great deal upon Copper's arrangement in his *Omnibus*. Some of the stories from the originals would give a specific date that would be a whole decade different from where I had placed the story in my own chronology. A quick check against Copper's *Omnibus* revealed that he had actually changed these dates in his revisions, sometimes shifting from the 1920's to the 1930's, a whole decade, in order to place the story where he thought that it ought to go. Worse, he sometimes eliminated a whole sentence from an original story if it contradicted his placement of that story within his *Omnibus*.

As a chronologist, I was horrified and sickened. This affront wasn't mentioned in Ruber's 2000 essay explaining why Ponsians were irritated with Copper. I can't believe that this wasn't noticed before.

There has always been ample material for the chronologist with the Pons books, even without these changes. Granted, the original versions, as written, open up a lot of problems and contradictions about when various stories occur that Copper smoothed out – apparently without anyone noticing. For this reason, and many others, I'm very glad and proud that the original Solar Pons adventures, as originally published by Derleth, are being presented here in these new volumes for a new generation.

David Marcum
"The Obrisset Snuffbox", PSI
(excerpted from the Belanger edition reissues)

WHAT COUNTS AS CANON?
BY DERRICK BELANGER

Imagine if you will that a previously unpublished Sherlock Holmes story written by Sir Arthur Conan Doyle is found tucked away in a tin dispatch box at his estate known as Undershaw. The story, "The Adventure of the Two Coptic Patriarchs", is a classic Sherlock Holmes story written in the author's hand at the same time as he was writing the stories included in *The Adventures of Sherlock Holmes*. It is an excellent mystery that includes an aggrieved client, the bumbling Inspector Lestrade, and Holmes using ratiocination to solve the case. The literary world is thrilled at this discovery, and the story is published in *The Strand* magazine in what becomes the magazine's best-selling issue.

If this story were truly discovered (sorry to say that it has not), it would set off a lively debate in the Sherlock Holmes community. It is almost universally accepted that The Canon of Sherlock Holmes stands at sixty stories (*i.e.* four novels and fifty-six short stories). Would the Canon expand to sixty-one stories? One side would argue that "Yes, indeed, this story is Canon. It is a Sherlock Holmes story written by the Master." They would argue that this story was even mentioned in another Sherlock Holmes story, "The Adventure of the Retired Colourman", which shows that the story is already a part of The Canon and therefore, this story, originally believed untold, should be allowed to be a part of the accepted Canon.

But wait! The other side counters that this story, while very good, was never published by Sir Arthur. Why did The Master hide the story away? Clearly, if he wrote it at a time when he was publishing many of his adventures, he must have intended for the story to remain unread. Further, the timing of the story is definitely not at the same time as "The Adventure of the Retired Colourman", and therefore, this must be a different adventure than that mentioned in the published story, albeit one involving two different Coptic patriarchs. So, they will conclude, that this story should be read and enjoyed, but it should not be added to the Canon.

Who would win this argument? Most likely no one. The arguing would go one for years with neither side yielding.

That's the trouble with reaching a definitive conclusion on The Canon. There is currently no Sherlock Holmes story like the one imagined above. Even so, the debate over what constitutes an "official" Sherlock Holmes story is ongoing and includes a number of non-Canonical candidates. There are currently several books compiled of such works by Doyle which *may* include the great detective and *may* be considered "official" Sherlock Holmes stories. Books such as Peter Haining's *The Final Adventures of Sherlock Holmes*, Jack Tracy's *Sherlock Holmes: The Published Apocrypha*, and Leslie Klinger's *The Apocrypha of Sherlock Holmes* include works that some have argued could (or even should) be added to The Canon. The problem with these works is none of them really fit as traditional Sherlock Holmes stories. We get stories with hints of the great detective (*i.e.* "The Lost Special" and "The Man With the Watches"), but the mysterious detective in these cases doesn't much act like Holmes and makes egregious errors in putting forth incorrect theories to solve these cases. There's the stories that do include Holmes and Watson ("The Field Bazaar" and "How Watson Learned the Trick"), but these are not mysteries. They are short, comic interludes. Then there are the plays, but these are either different versions of stories that already exist ("The Stonor Case"), or have a character from The Canon not really acting like they do in The Canon (see Dr. Watson in "The Angels of Darkness"). All of the works included in these volumes are quite different than those contained within The Canon, which is why it is generally agreed that they should remain left out.

That leads to our own difficulty in creating *The Apocrypha of Solar Pons*. Some of the work contained within these pages is definitely fringe material. We have essays written by August Derleth about Solar Pons. These are excellent insights into the mind of the author. However, they are not Pons stories. There is also the fragmentary story "The Adventure of the Green Stars" which is incomplete and therefore should remain excluded from the official Canon.

The decision on official stories begins to get less clear with the Solar Pons stories from *Fantasy and Science Fiction Magazine*. These short stories are excellent, even some of the best Pons stories written by Derleth. But are they Canon? This would be a great debate. Derleth did include Fu Manchu references (Si-Fan) in the story collections. He also hinted at other pulp fiction characters in "The Adventure of the Orient Express" a novelette contained in *The Chronicles of Solar Pons*. The mystical detective Carnacki is mentioned in the story "The Adventure of the Haunted Library", where Pons tells Parker that the ghost-finder is legitimate. And the Sherlock Holmes of Praed Street wrote of Cthulhu in his own *An Examination of the Cthulhu Cult and Others*. So, if The Great Old Ones can exist in the world of Solar Pons, why not accept vampires and psychics as well?

Even more difficult to determine are the previously uncollected traditional Solar Pons stories contained in this volume. These stories could fit nicely into any of the six Solar Pons story collections. The only reason one might consider them to be outside The Pons Canon is simply because they were excluded from an official Mycroft and Moran publication. The same could be said for "From the Notebooks of Dr. Lyndon Parker", as well as the short novel *Terror Over London.* (*Please note that even though* Terror Over London *was moved to our book* The Novels of Solar *Pons, it is considered to be part of* The Apocrypha. *It was not published in Derleth's lifetime*). If one were to insert these stories into the official Canon, it would be nearly impossible to argue why they should be removed.

This brings us to the big questions: Does the exclusion of these works from the "official" books make them non-Canonical? Should we include the traditional stories in this collection as Canon, but exclude the more fringe works of science fiction? Should we keep them all in or keep them all out? These are questions better left open to debate, and I will not pretend to be the expert who will provide the final answers to them. I look to the armchair Pons experts and Pontian societies to continue this lively, never ending debate.

Derrick Belanger
October 2018

The Apocrypha of Solar Pons

Praed Street Papers
and
A Praed Street Dossier

For Luther Norris
Lord Warden of the Pontine Marshes,
Godfather to the Praed Street Irregulars...

The Original Front-piece for
A Praed Street Dossier

Two views of the real No. 7B Praed Street, London, taken by Ian M. Law. On the left – the front of the building from across the street; on the right, a close-up of entrance.

EDITOR'S NOTE

In 1965, August Derleth published Praed Street Papers, *a slim chapbook that contained several essays regarding Pons's beginnings, as well as Derleth's favorite pastiches, an early version of Robert Pattrick's incomplete Pons Chronology (that was later published in* The Reminiscences of Solar Pons), *and some – but not all – of a series of entries from Dr. Parker's* Notebooks.

Also included were two Pons adventures rendered as very awkward comic strips by Derleth's friend Frank Utpatel. (These are not reproduced here due to their poor quality.)

In 1968, Derleth published A Praed Street Dossier, *which contained all of the same essays found in* Praed Street Papers, *the same entries from Parker's* Notebooks, *four new Utpatel illustrations, and two of the four "Off-Trail" Pons stories that were co-written with science-fiction author Mack Reynolds. (The Utpatel comic strips were not reprinted in* A Praed Street Dossier.*)*

COMMENTARY
BY RONALD A. KNOX
(From Praed Street Papers*)*

When you take to writing detective stories, the measure of your success depends on the amount of personality you can build up round your favorite detective. Why this should be so, is not immediately obvious; it might have been supposed that this kind of fiction had a merely mathematical appeal. But, whether because Sherlock Holmes had set the standard for all time, or because the public does not like to see plots unraveled by a mere thinking machine, it is personality that counts. You are not bound to make your public *like* the Great Detective; many readers have found Lord Peter Wimsey too much of a good thing, and I have even heard of people who were unable to appreciate the flavours of Poirot. But he must be real; he must have idiosyncrasies, eccentricities; even if he is a professional policeman, like Hanaud, he must smoke those appalling cigarettes, and get his English idioms wrong... But how seldom does an author manage to spin out a formula indefinitely; how signally Conan Doyle failed to do it!

A WEEKEND WITH AUGUST DERLETH

(From Praed Street Papers)

(An Introduction)

BY PETER RUBER

I can't think of August Derleth without enjoying a quiet chuckle or two and calling to mind old Chris Morley's words in *Pandora Lifts the Lid* – *"You can't understand great writers unless you understand the human conditions and inspirations out of which their music sprang."* In August's case the conditions have been money, the inspirations a determination to write as he pleased, and he has been successful at both by nurturing a healthy contempt for everything that would interfere with his ambitions. No garret lodger living on yesterday's failures and tomorrow's dreams, August is an incurably practical man, but no less an artist at the typewriter. His sensitive awareness of the human spirit and of life around him has created a landscape of characters that he looks upon with worldly pride. I refer, of course, to his Wisconsin and Sac Prairie Sagas – a more ambitious undertaking Balzac never dreamed of – in which he has chronicled the life of his community and state since 1800 in an unending parade of novels, verse, nonfiction, prose, and what else. But that's not all he does – there is Solar Pons, a flattering pastiche on the Sherlock Holmes tales in a Twentieth Century British setting who, by no more than a stroke of fate, has become larger than August's own expectations. To make matters worse, a society was recently formed to extoll the virtues of Mr. Detective Pons, and in a sense this book makes a timely appearance.

Given the opportunity to write this introduction, I have elected not to write about Solar Pons – one can add little to the admirable introductions by Vincent Starrett, Ellery Queen, Anthony Boucher, and Edgar W. Smith to previous Pontine books, and to this book itself – but, instead, to write about the author. Actually there is a correlation, as we became friends over Solar Pons.

The time is a few years ago, and I was a not too bright editor of a not too good literary magazine, and August Derleth was one of the sympathetic subscribers. When he read in the third issue that I planned to suspend the magazine with the fourth – a spectacular illustrated affair I hoped would obscure my previously juvenile efforts – August wrote and asked if I would like a short article called "The Beginnings of Solar Pons". I accepted immediately, feeling that if people enjoyed reading detective stories, why shouldn't they enjoy reading about the detectives themselves. We entered into a prolific correspondence, and in May of 1962 I set out to visit him at Sauk City, Wisconsin, the Baghdad of the dairy belt. It was the season of the morel mushroom and I became a victim of outdoor hazards, from which I emerged strongly resolved never to visit him that time of year again.

It was a stockily-built man of medium stature with an almost leathery face that greeted me at a Madison club we arranged to meet in soon after my train arrived from Chicago. I looked upon him with no lack of surprise: He was dressed in a green corduroy pullover shirt with a turtle-neck collar, gray corduroy slacks, very gay socks and sandals. He said I looked ghastly and that a mushroom hunt would fix me up, I was amused by the placemats on the table and I commented on the illustrated

Wisconsin shrines: The Governor's mansion, the home of the circus, and Sauk City, "Home of Author August Derleth".

"One of the ill-omens of fame," he said. "But it allows me the privilege of acting as I damned please – and I usually do – because some people in this part of the country still regard writers with suspicion. If the Wisconsin reversed its flow tomorrow, they'd convince you I was responsible."

Flying would be a more appropriate term than driving toward Sauk City – it seemed as if August had tied a brick to the accelerator and merely guided the steering wheel. On the way he pointed to a section of marshland where at dusk can be seen an eerie glow of light. It had once suggested to him the plot of his favorite tale of horror. Every sight, sound and fragrance of nature, for that matter, suggests a plot to him, and the ideas are filed away until the plots fully reveal themselves. I suppose if he banged his toe he'd have material enough for a novel. That evening we drove halfway across Wisconsin to a place that featured seafood dishes. August is almost to the point of being a fanatic about food: He forewarns his coming whenever possible and instructs the chef on the preparation of his meal.

At six o clock the next morning a tree crashed against the door to my motel room and I crawled over to investigate. By the time I reached the door I saw August had given up: he had returned to his car and began to toot the horn totally unconcerned with the other sleeping occupants. He shouted a friendly greeting and tooted twice more to make sure I was fully awake. We breakfasted in town and I looked at more "Home of Author August Derleth" placemats. I wondered secretly if he had a financial interest in the printing concession. The drugstore we breakfasted in had an assortment of picture postcards, among which I found one of his home, "Place of Hawks". I bought a handful.

August had been awake and working since three o'clock – as he is every day – and had written some book reviews, part of his weekly column, and a chapter in his new novel. With that behind him he planned to tour the village with me as it was still too misty to begin the mushroom hunt. I delighted in seeing the landmarks and somber old houses that had become familiar to me through his books. He recalled for my benefit capsule histories of the events tragic, comic and mysterious. At that moment I thought of him as a kind of paradox. To one segment of his reading public he is known exclusively as a writer of horror and detective tales, which contradicts the elegant simplicity and passionate understanding he reveals in his Sac Prairie books. But both segments of his literary output draw you inevitably to one conclusion – his loathing of violence, though physically powerful in person. He carefully avoids the violence usually associated with this field, and his tales contain a violence nothing more than a psychological manifestation of horror like that of the Gothic writers Sheridan Le Fanu and H. P. Lovecraft. Even in his sweeping historical novels, a Revolutionary or Indian battle gets no more than a one paragraph by-the-way treatment, and he would break off to describe the flight of a hawk. This annoyed Sinclair Lewis, who went to great pains to say so in a portrait of August he wrote for *Esquire* in 1945.

At his home August set himself to the task of answering the daily flood of mail, while I chatted with Donald Wandrei, a writer from Minnesota who visits August every year during the mushroom season. In a room down the hail his children, April and Walden, squealed with happiness, and I received my first glimpse of this Sleepy Hollow village coming to life.

By late morning the dew had sufficiently evaporated for the hunt. Armed with baskets and a notebook in which August has recorded every square foot of morel-producing ground in his county for some thirty years, we stormed the mountainside. Hour after hour he led us at military pace through snake-like vines and pitchfork-pointed thorns, stopping now and again to consult his notebook and scattering us in all directions in search of tree markings, trees the base of which had previously borne this mushroom of connoisseurs. The more, I suffered the more he appeared to be enjoying the hunt. Our baskets filled we returned to where we had parked the car. It was a long and circuitous route through an excavated gravel pit, down mud slides, and over rotting stream crossings, and, lastly, through a pasture of excited bulls. We ran like hell.

Back home again, the sprawling affair called "Place of Hawks", Don Wandrei and I began to string the mushrooms for drying and moaned at one another. August, without so much of a rest, resumed his writing, joining us in conversation at the same time. His power of concentration reminded me of Dickens, who used to write his monthly serials in the same room where his wife might be entertaining a party. Behind August's desk is a framed letter in which he received the Apostolic Blessings of Pope John XXIII for his part in the creation of the Vision Books series on the lives of the Saints for children. When it arrived, in 1959, he conspired with the editor of the local newspaper and that week the banner blazed 'Derleth Blessed by Pope". For a time the stunned town folk argued the merits of the blessings bestowed on their most notorious citizen.

August is fond of children and his door is always open to them in whatever number they wish to come, for a party or to talk about their ambitions. In earlier days it wasn't unusual that he had a roomful of teenagers kicking up their heels to the latest dance records, while he labored away on a new book, observing their entitle out of the corner of his eye, after which he would read ghost stories to them. To be liked by August was a social symbol among the teenagers, contrary to their parents' wishes that they find more suitable Pied Pipers such as the mayor, sheriff, or minister. Vigilante groups of enraged parents were not unknown to descend on him with accusations the day after an affair. To compound their suspicions he would plant rumors about himself, and the results would creep thinly disguised into his stories. The town council, in order to lessen the blow of an unpopular ruling, would debate him at the weekly meetings, and the local association of businessmen forced his resignation because, they argued, writers and publishers don't sell things across the counter. After a bad season they tried to lure him back, but he demanded such exasperating terms that they stormed out angrier than ever. His last foothold in the community was his chair on the Board of Education and that didn't last long. He persisted in tightening the curriculum and innovating new teaching methods. But the rock candy and *Little Women* citizens saw what education had done for him – made him all-fangled modern and a man who made his living writing words! Yet when the town library burned to the ground, it was August who headed the movement to have it rebuilt, and then donated a few thousand books from his personal collection.

My last day in Sauk City was a Sunday, and August charitably permitted my dreams an extra two hours. With his parents and April and Walden safely delivered at church, I tagged August as be conducted some business in the shops. At one end of town some of the local inhabitants had set up their own version of a flea market and busied themselves in trading their junk with one another. August stopped to exchange a word or two with the bargainers. I was out of earshot, but when we moved on his eyes told me he had picked up a useful item of information. He dropped me off at his oar and then disappeared into a house down the street.

He looked quite pleased with himself when he returned. "There's mischief in the wind," he said, taking me into his confidence. It seemed The League of Church Women were to have as their speaker that afternoon an old boyhood friend of his who had made a good thing out of being an evangelist writer and lecturer. August, believing in the spiritual God, saw no purpose gained in shouting the fear of Satan, and he had stopped off to inform one of the channels of gossip that he planned to visit the meeting hall after the trembling was over.

At dusk we were driving to Madison for my farewell dinner before boarding the train for Chicago. August was entertaining the three of us – Don Wandrei, his assistant Rikki who had been with us on the mushroom hunts, and myself – with the aftermath at the meeting hall, where he had debated the speaker while the women looked on in mortified silence. He concluded that they "don't always get a double feature for the price of one. If they weren't so narrow-minded, they could read the word of God in their bibles, and no one would pass the hat or charge admission like when God's messengers performed."

We had reservations at the most elegant supper club in Madison, and August, in the same unconventional attire be had greeted my arrival – except for an even gayer pair of socks – led his troops inside. The *maître d'* with her primrose air went to pieces. "Please, Mr. Derleth!" she pleaded. "Not again!" With the smirk of a cheshire cat my host said: "Tut, tut, good woman! You know how fond your clientele is of a celebrity. I give this place life." And as we were ushered to the best table in the club: "Packed to the rafters as if they were expecting me!" I felt my tie drawing tighter around my neck. We had no less than the head chef come out to discuss the preparation of our banquet, and he delighted in August's epicurian palate. The affair was one to remember.

I returned to Chicago that evening dizzy and enraptured. When I called on Vincent Starrett, who has known August since the days he first broke into print, he was anxious to hear about my adventures. He listened in silence and puffed on his black cigar, and when I had finished he nodded but briefly and said, "That's Augie. Things are never dull in Sauk City." He said these words with restrained laughter, and I suspected he knew much more than he would ever tell me. If someone doesn't beat me to it, I shall write a book about August, but I wonder if this man who has become to many of us a legend larger than life isn't just a little beyond the reach of my talents.

Peter Ruber
New York City
May, 1965

THE PICTURED PONS

(From Praed Street Papers*)*

Solar Pons came into bud in "comic strip" form but – happily – he never blossomed, for , of course, Pons could hardly be fitted into anything that might pass for one of the adventure tales pictured for comic strip addicts. My longtime associate, and the illustrator of some of my stories and books, Frank Utpatel, tried his hand at a picture strip of one of the early Pontine tales, "The Adventure of the Missing Tenants" (published originally in *The Dragnet*, but not yet revised sufficiently to warrant book publication) and followed this strip with a version of "The Adventure of the Limping Man".

The Utpatel Pons – and Parker, for that matter – looked like adventure strip stereotypes, but the essential flaw in the strip was its extreme wordiness and lack of action. Utpatel took it to market in the early 1930's, but after two rejections, it was quietly interred at Mycroft & Moran.

Editor's Note: It was impossible to include the complete versions of the Utpatel comic strips, due to the fact that the quality of their appearance in Praed Street Papers *did not lend itself to additional reproduction. The effect would have been like a Xerox copy of a copy of a copy. However, the following page gives a sample of one of the panes from "The Missing Tenants"...*

62 ACACIA ROAD
THIS STATEMENT LEFT ME WONDERING IF
WE WERE TO BECOME ENTANGLED WITH
THAT HUGE ORGANIZATION, THE BLACK HAND

ILLUSTRATIONS FROM
A Praed Street Dossier
BY FRANK UTPATEL

Editor's Note: Derleth's friend, artist Frank Utpatel, provided four original illustrations for A Praed Street Dossier, *reproduced here. Additionally, he produced a number of later Pons drawings that were included in* The Solar Pons Omnibus *(1981), edited by Basil Copper.*

Solar Pons

Inspector Jamison

Alfred Peake

Dr. Parker and Solar Pons

Dr. Parker and Solar Pons

Solar Pons: Marginalia

THE BEGINNINGS OF SOLAR PONS

> Pons, Solar, born ca. 1880, in Prague. Son of Asenath Pons, consular official at Prague, and Roberta McIvor Pons; younger brother of Bancroft Stoneham, in His Majesty's Service. Public school education; Oxford *summa cum laude*, 1899. Unmarried. Member: Savile, Diogenes, Athanaeum, Cliff Dwellers, Lambs. Est. private inquiry practice at 7B Praed Street, 1907. British Intelligence, World War I, II. Monographs: *An Inquiry into the Nan-Matal Ruins of Ponape* (1905); *A Logical Approach to the Science of Ratiocination* (1917); *The Chess Problem and the State of the Mind* (1919); *The Inductive Process* (1921); *On the Value of Circumstantial Evidence* (1925); *An Examination of the Cthulhu Cult and Others* (1931). Widely traveled. Residences: New York, Chicago, Paris, Vienna, Prague, Rome, 7B Praed Street, London, W.2. Telephone: Ambassador 10000.

This is what one reads of him today, but it was not always thus. As a matter of fact, even this much information was not known about Solar Pons until close to two decades ago [*from when Derleth wrote this in 1968 – Editor*] when Anthony Boucher pressed me for it, and I had to examine the chronicles to discover these facts.

Solar Pons came into being out of Sherlock Holmes, just as Holmes came out of C. Auguste Dupin, all chronicled data about Dr. Joseph Bell of Edinburgh University to the contrary. In a sense, Sherlock Holmes *is* C. Auguste Dupin. In the same sense, Solar Pons is Sherlock Holmes. But while Sir Arthur Conan Doyle considerably updated Sherlock Holmes, I made little attempt to do so with Solar Pons, save only for a couple of decades or so. He remains for Pons a retired contemporary to whom Pons always refers as "the Master".

At the outset, I wrote to Sir Arthur to ask whether he intended to write more adventures of Sherlock Holmes. I waited for at least a year after publication of *The Casebook of Sherlock Holmes*. Early in autumn of 1928, when I was in my junior year at the University of Wisconsin, and holed up in a solitary back room at 823 West Johnson Street, Madison, Wisconsin (now the site of a rather impressive new dormitory), he replied – by means of a terse message scrawled upon my own letter – that he did not. He seemed, as I recall it now, unnecessarily emphatic about it, as if this decision, made once previously and set aside, were now irrevocable, and no amount of persuasion would this time cause him to change his mind. I wrote him that if he were not going to write further adventures, I would try my hand at it – but of course, this was impossible, for who was I to put upon paper new adventures of the illustrious Sherlock Holmes, of whom my maternal grandmother had always spoken as "the greatest detective who ever lived", since she, like so many other readers of The Canon, was firmly convinced that Sherlock Holmes lived, not in that sense of the continuing life given him by the Baker Street Irregulars, but as an actual man of flesh and blood, who might be appealed to in cases of dire necessity.

The form the stories must take was patent. Not that ridiculing imitation designed for laughter, the parody, but that fond and admiring one less widely-known as the pastiche. I needed first a name, syllabically similar to that of Sherlock Holmes. So Solar Pons was born because I thought of Solar in its suggestion of light, and Pons as the bridge – "bridge of light" seemed to the adolescent mind singularly brilliant, which, of course, it was not.

Any other setting but England seemed out of the question. But in point of fact I knew very little about England, and even less about London. The England I knew and loved – having been all my life a pronounced Anglophile, despite an ancestry originally French, now largely Bavarian – was the England of Thomas Hardy, George Eliot, John Galsworthy, Jane Austen, Richard Jefferies, Gilbert White, Joseph Conrad, Mary Webb, W. H. Hudson – and the London that was the highly romantic and colorful city of Charles Dickens, Sir Arthur, Sax Rohmer, R. Austin Freeman, and some other writers of detective and mystery fiction. This was admittedly neither much nor very accurate, insofar as even a tenuous reality for the Pontine tales was concerned.

Not long before beginning the first adventure of Solar Pons, I had read and enjoyed a novel by Cecil John Charles Street, under his pen-name of John Rhode, entitled *The Murders in Praed Street*, published in 1928, and when I cast around for the setting of the Pontine quarters, it was Praed Street that came instantly to mind. Perhaps my memory of the Dr. Priestley novel included some impressions of the milieu – that is, the naming of streets familiar to the Canonical works, but of this I can no longer be certain. When I consulted *Baedeker's London and Its Environs* – which I had found necessary to buy, the first book on an expanding shelf that must now number close to two-hundred books, ranging from street and provincial guides, to such comparatively recent works as A. J. P. Taylor's *English History: 1914-1945*, Eilert Ekwall's *The Concise Oxford Dictionary of English Place-Names*, Paul Ashbee's *The Bronze*

Age Round Barrow in Britain, the Allen-Maxwell *The British Isles in Color*, and John Betjeman's *An American's Guide to English Parish Churches* – and learned that Praed Street was, for a hardy walker, actually within walking distance of 221b Baker Street, the Praed Street address seemed providential.

Thus Praed Street became the headquarters of Solar Pons, and specifically number 7 – for no reason but that this number came to mind and was set down, and number 7B, because Holmes was at 221b, though I then supposed that *B* indicated the second floor, when in fact, in London *B* designates the third floor – or what to American readers would be the third floor, since the first floor in London is that floor above the ground floor, which is the American first. I had no idea whatsoever about the actual and real Number 7, Praed Street, until late 1961, when Mr. Ian M. Law, who had visited Place of Hawks that summer, returned to England and considerately provided me with photographs of 7 Praed Street, which turned out to be next door to a cinema, and did have three floors, and could very readily have housed a private investigator and his amanuensis in their third floor quarters.

With the background fixed, however vaguely, in mind, I sat down and in one afternoon and evening wrote "The Adventure of the Black Narcissus" – my Baedeker's *London* at my elbow – which is precisely the kind of tale an amateur of nineteen would be likely to conjure up. Thereafter, this feat accomplished, the career of Solar Pons might have flatted and come to an unnoticed end, had it not been for a small circumstance. Harold Hersey, an indefatigable publisher, was at that time beginning a new string of pulp magazines in New York, and on impulse I sent the first Solar Pons story to him. Within a week came a check for $40.00, and – even more important, a letter saying that he would buy as many more Solar Pons stories as I cared to write for his magazine, *The Dragnet*.

With this promise of monetary reward added to what had already developed into a powerful compulsion, I went to work and in rapid succession, by dint of cutting classes here and there, I wrote "The Adventure of the Missing Tenants", "The Adventure of the Broken Chessman", and "The Adventure of the Late Mr. Faversham". Harold Hersey bought them at once. In "The Adventure of the Black Narcissus" Solar Pons made his initial public appearance in the February, 1929 issue of *The Dragnet*. He appeared for the second time in the September issue of that year with "The Adventure of the Broken Chessman".

I was now committed. In one day I turned out three pastiches – "The Adventure of the Viennese Musician", "The Adventure of the Limping Man", "The Adventure of Gresham Old Place" – and before the week was out, I had added "The Adventure of the Muttering Man", "The Adventure of the Black Cardinal", and "The Adventure of the Sotheby Salesman". Two were immediately scheduled for publication, and the others accepted. And, counting my dollars to come in on publication, I went out to satisfy the most ardent of my desires – the acquisition of a library to supplement my shelves of Conan Doyle, Sax Rohmer, J. S. Fletcher, H. C. Bailey, Ernest Bramah, Lewis Carroll, Mark Twain, and half a dozen other favorite authors. In one heady afternoon of buying, I acquired – on a charge account – $400 worth of books – by Proust, Dostoievsky, Tolstoi, Thomas Hardy, Turgenev, Robert Frost, Edgar Lee Masters, Sherwood Anderson, Sinclair Lewis, Andre Gide, Oscar Wilde – everything, in fact, I had wanted most badly – $400 worth, which I counted on Solar Pons to pay for. But alas! – the month was October, 1929 – the market crash separated Harold Hersey and Solar Pons from *The Dragnet*, and, though Pons made three more appearances – in *Detective Trails* and *Gangster Stories*, in addition to *The Dragnet* in December, with "The Adventure of the Late Mr. Faversham" – his career had been effectively arrested.

I was left with $400 in debts and several returned manuscripts, as well as one new story of which I thought a trifle more favorably than I did its predecessors – "The Adventure of the Norcross Riddle". Though I had learned so early in my career a valuable lesson every writer must learn sooner or later – not to count my chickens before the eggs were hatched! – Solar Pons was put on the shelf, while I went to work to complete studying for my B.A. in 1930, and then after graduation took an editorial post with Fawcett's, at that time in Minneapolis – the result of Donald Wandrei's recommendation after his rejection of the offer of that post. It was not congenial work, for all that my associates were pleasant and co-operative; I could not stick it much longer than four months and came home to do or die at writing, having managed in my short time as associate editor of *Mystic Magazine* – a short-lived Fawcett venture, to pay off my indebtedness, not alone at my editorial salary, but with the addition of payments for fiction and non-fiction turned out in my spare time.

I settled in at home and began to chronicle the saga of Sac Prairie, turning my inclinations toward detection into a series of book-length stories featuring Judge Ephraim Peabody Peck, who appeared in ten books and no more – *Murder Stalks the Wakely Family, The Man on All Fours, Three Who Died, Sign of Fear, Sentence Deferred, The Narracong Riddle, The Seven Who Waited, Mischief in the Lane, No Future for Luana,* and *Fell Purpose*. My regional fiction and poetry began to find berths in a gratifying variety of magazines ranging from little reviews like *This Quarter, The Midland, and Pagany*, to established magazines like *The Atlantic Monthly, The New Republic, Scribner's, Household, The Commonweal*, and many others; mystery novels were being followed into print by serious works like *Place of Hawks, Still Is the Summer Night, Wind Over Wisconsin, et al.*, and I had been awarded a Guggenheim Fellowship to carry on the Sac Prairie Saga. As the years went by, Solar Pons was all but forgotten, but, truth to tell, Solar Pons had always had more reality in my thoughts than Judge Peck, for all that the estimable Judge operated in a milieu I knew very well indeed.

Yet Solar Pons might have been forgotten, had it not been for another fortuitous circumstance. Over a decade after the last – and I thought final appearance of Solar Pons (in *Gangster Stories* for March, 1930, in "The Adventure of the Black Cardinal") – Ellery Queen began to assemble stories for his anthology, *The Misadventures of Sherlock Holmes* (1944). I remembered "The Adventure of the Norcross Riddle" and wrote to Fred Dannay, asking whether he would like to see the pastiche. He welcomed it. So I undertook a retouching and retyping and sent it in. He accepted and published it; Irregulars read it with pleasure. Both Dannay and Vincent Starrett inquired about Solar Pons and, learning that there were enough tales for a group, urged that they be put out in book form.

Even so, I was far from convinced. I looked them all over; they seemed to me very amateurish indeed. None ranked with the single story published in the *Misadventures*, and I quietly resolved to let the idea of a Solar Pons collection die. Quite by chance, however, while discussing with Ray Palmer, then with Ziff-Davis in Chicago, the idea of a horror story anthology (later successfully published by Rinehart as *Sleep No More!*), I mentioned the possibility of a Solar Pons collection. Palmer urged me to put it together and, without committing Ziff-Davis to it, asked to see such a book with a view to publication.

With that added incentive and the promise from Vincent Starrett to write an introduction to the book, I went home and got to work to assemble a collection to be titled *"In Re: Sherlock Holmes": The Adventures of Solar Pons* – because, on the day I had decided to write a Holmesian pastiche, I had opened my desk calendar at 823 West Johnson at random and written "In re: Sherlock Holmes" to remind myself to write the story on that day, which I did. But when I re-examined those early stories – published and unpublished – there were then an even dozen – I found most of them simply too inept to be published. So I got to work and wrote new stories, while revising the old.

I kept "The Adventure of the Black Narcissus", "The Adventure of the Norcross Riddle", "The Adventure of the Sotheby Salesman", "The Adventure of the Limping Man", and "The Adventure of the Late Mr. Faversham". The new tales were "The Adventure of the Man with the Broken Face", "The Adventure of the Frightened Baronet", "The Adventure of the Purloined Periapt", "The Adventure of the Lost Holiday", "The Adventure of the Three Red Dwarfs", "The Adventure of the Retired Novelist", and "The Adventure of the Seven Passengers". These stories made up the first collection, which was duly submitted to Ziff-Davis, and presently rejected.

By this time, however, I was infected with the virus. I was no longer so willing to trust any publisher with Solar Pons and, since I already had a publishing venture of my own in Arkham House – begun in 1939, six years earlier – I took especial pleasure in establishing a new imprint – Mycroft & Moran, the directors of which were, of course, Mycroft Holmes and Colonel Sebastian Moran ("the second most dangerous man in London") – in fixing upon Baskerville type for the Pontine tales, and commissioning a deerstalker as a colophon from Ronald Clyne, who had lent his artistry to the improvement of jackets for Arkham House books – and in 1945 Solar Pons made his bow in book form in the first collection, a full-length pastiche of *The Adventures of Sherlock Holmes*.

THE SOURCES OF THE TALES

Without exception, the Solar Pons stories have been written around titles. None of the stories was ever conceived without the prior challenge of the title. Curiously enough, no plot ever challenged me as much as a title. Sometimes the title comes straight out of the canon – *The Adventure of the Remarkable Worm*, *The Adventure of the Late Mr. Faversham*, *The Adventure of Ricoletti of the Club Foot*, *The Adventure of the Grice-Paterson Curse*, *The Adventure of the Trained Cormorant*, *The Adventure of the Red Leech*. This last-named title had challenged me for some years, and it was not until I looked up leeches in the *Encyclopaedia Britannica* and discovered that there was actually, like the remarkable worm, no such thing as a red leech, that the story worked itself out.

Sometimes – perhaps in the majority of cases – a title is purely imaginary, a title occurring to me because I liked the sound or the promise of it, and teasing me until I have brought into existence a story to fit it, though, alas! I am forced to conclude far too often that the story does not measure up to the promise of the title. On occasion, a title is chanced upon in something seen or read, like *The Adventure of the Whispering Knights* and *The Adventure of the Mosaic Cylinders*, both of which grew out of letters published in *Country Life*, one of several British magazines to which I subscribe.

Under the heading of *Midland Stonehenge*, one "M. W." of Hereford wrote concerning the Rollright Stones on the boundary of Oxfordshire and Warwickshire. His letter was accompanied by a photograph of this Bronze Age stone circle, which instantly appealed to my imagination. In the final paragraph of the letter occurred this line: "About 100 yards east of the circle is a large Megalithic burial chamber, called the Whispering Knights..." Then and there the title was born, and it went into its gestation period for a shorter time – only a month – than usual. It took precedence over another title, The Adventure of the Ritual Survival, tucked away in mind after reading of a presumably ritual murder set forth in E. Spencer Shew's *Second Companion to Murder*. I combined the two, discarded the earlier title, and wrote *The Adventure of the Whispering Knights*.

Lest it be thought that this writing came wholly out of my imagination, I should point out that, in addition to the letter in *Country Life* and Shew's admirable *Companion*, I had to draw upon these books for the story's background – *The ABC Railway Guide*, Baedeker's *Great Britain* (1927 edition), George Long's *The Folklore Calendar*, Lewis Spence's *The History and Origins of Druidism*, Violet Alford's *Introduction to English Folklore*, Sydney R. Jones's *England West*, Robert Munro's *Prehistoric Britain*, and the *Britannica*. Every story in the Pontine canon has required more or less books for what I hope is the authenticity of its background. The writing of the first Pontine novel, *Mr. Fairlie's Final Journey*, for instance, required descriptive guides – some of the *Little Red Guides*, supplied by G. Ken Chapman – of areas around Frome, Somerset, Scotland, and Wales – and application to Chapman and Michael Harrison for specific details of idiom.

The Adventure of the Mosaic Cylinders was suggested by another letter in *Country Life*, in the issue for June 26, 1958, accompanied by an illustration of a sovereign box, designed as a puzzle box, locked by a cipher – very much as that described in that story. *The Adventure of the China Cottage* took rise virtually over night from a lavishly-illustrated article in *Country Life* for December 5, 1963 – *Cottages to Scent a Room*, by G. Bernard Hughes. I have in my files at least a dozen letters or random paragraphs clipped from this fine magazine from any or all of which future pastiches may grow.

Now and then, too, real life has afforded me an adventure for the series. Any reader interested enough to look into *Bernard Spilsbury: His Life and Cases*, by Douglas G. Browne and E. V. Tullett (George G. Harrap & Company, Ltd., 1951) will discover the source of *The Adventure of the Cloverdale Kennels* in the account of the unsolved Coverdale Kennels shootings, on pages 351-355, and the source of *The Adventure of the "Triple Kent"* in an account of the murder of Mrs. Dorothy Fisher, her daughter, and Miss Charlotte Saunders in the village of Matfield, Kent, in 1940, on pages 349-351. The former story in the series is wholly imaginary, for all that it has its source in the Spilsbury biography, while the latter incorporated some of the facts of the tragedy in the fiction. It is not a coincidence that the name "Spilsbury" occurs now and then in the pastiches.

The challenge of an unsolved mystery is always provocative – the Coverdale Kennels crime is one such, and the almost legendary account of strange footprints in the snow discovered February 1, 1855 in Devonshire – footprints that resembled some very large hoofed creature, all in a line that led through seventeen towns for a distance of approximately a hundred miles, leading along roads, through woods, fields, and gardens, across streams and farmhouse roofs alike, and made without any sound to alert the natives, is another. The mystery of the footprints was never solved, but the tale gave rise to *The Adventure of the Devil's Footprints*, just as the account of the famous Lost Dutchman mine in the American Southwest – a tale integral to the legendry and lore of the Southwest – brought into being *The Adventure of the Lost Dutchman*.

Just as I go about constantly in the microcosm of Sac Prairie alert for aspects of life to chronicle, I am always alert for an idea or a plot that will lend itself to a Pontine pastiche. It may be an incident – a newspaper account of an unsolved murder – *The Adventure of the Sotheby Salesman*, for example, took rise from a brief account of the discovery of a murdered man thought to be a tramp in an empty house – a chance remark, an historical trifle – *The Adventure of the Rydberg Numbers* had its inception in the scientific inquiries into the possibilities of atomic fission that went on in the 1920s both in England and on the Continent – an event in the news – *The Adventure of the Stone of Scone* roughly follows the events of the actual theft of the stone from Westminster some years ago.

On occasion, nothing more than a whim gives motivation for a story. *The Adventure of the Penny Magenta* was written simply because I wanted to write a pastiche with a philatelic background; *The Adventure of the Mazarine Blue* because I took a fancy to the name of that butterfly (ironically, the editor of the magazine that published it, retitled it *The Thirteenth Coffin*). Sometimes, too, I am taken up by what someone has written. While convalescing in the hospital some years ago I read Ivor Brown's *A Word in Your Ear* and *Just Another Word*, and I was so enchanted by the lost words in the language that I evolved *The Adventure of the Amateur Philologist*. Similarly, that magnificent book, *Tutankhamen*, by Christiane Desroches-Noblecourt, suggested *The Adventure of the Crouching Dog* in its reproduction of the seal on the tomb of the Pharaoh.

On the other hand, at least one story grew out of a dream. I dreamed one night that I was secreted somewhere in a copse or grove in the dusk, and from this hiding-place saw a man, surrounded by six mastiffs, running through the twilight without a sound other than that made by their steps; within hours of waking from that dream, I had evolved *The Adventure of the Sussex Archers*, into which I incorporated the events of the dream.

An announcement from the Folio Society of London about the Society's forthcoming publication of *Dickens' London* was the inception for *The Adventure of the Unique Dickensians*. The Society's book was a collection of the essays Dickens had written about the city, to illustrate which the announcement reprinted not only some of the old Cruikshank illustrations but also some of the London street cries of the period – for example, *Cherries*:

> *Round and sound*
> *Twopence a pound*
> *Cherries, rare ripe cherries!*
> *Cherries a ha'penny a stick*
> *Come and pick! Come and pick!*
> *Cherries big as plums!*
> *Who comes, who comes?*

These caught my fancy, and, given a natural predilection for Dickens, the sort of double pastiche that became *The Adventure of the Unique Dickensians* was born, and set down in the space of seven hours (over a period of four days) immediately after completion of *Mr. Fairlie's Final Journey* early in 1968.

There are in my Pontine files newspaper clippings without number which have caught my eye suggestively; at any time a pastiche may grow from one of them. Their headings range widely – as I hope for the pastiches to range – *Timber Scribing*. (another letter in *Country Life*) – *A Memory of Exmoor* – *Britain's Great Train Robbery* – *Last Days of a Gothic Masterpiece* – *Christmas at Caldermoor* – *Grouse Hawking in Caithness* – *Rothern Bridge Doomed* – *Is Clophill Magic as Black as It's Been Painted?* – *The Haunted Hills of Wales* – *The Great Portuguese Banknote Swindle* – *Letters of Guilt* – *Patterns of Murder – Brown Windsor for Dr. Johnson – Stock Exchange Under Fire – Nightjars on a Southern Common – The Varied Fortunes of a Derbyshire Spa – Witches and Wizards of the Fens.*

Some titles persistently resist explication. *The Adventure of Cagliostro Second*, for example. Perhaps a new biography of Cagliostro, on my desk as I write, may provide me with a lead. Or *The Adventure of the Pope's Guardsman* – I am reluctant to move Pons to Rome, and what would a member of the Swiss Guard be about in London? – certainly not his business. Or *The Adventure of the Lost Metternich* and *The Adventure of the Italian Letters* – perhaps these resist me because there are other tales pressing more urgently to be written – like *The Adventure of Mr. Peppercorn's Folly* or *The Adventure of the Aluminum Crutch* or the tantalizing *Adventure of the Sussex Beekeeper*.

I suspect there are always more suggested plots and themes – and more titles for new stories – than I will be able to write before the basic repetitiousness of the pattern intervenes to end the series – or I myself shuffle off this mortal coil.

CONCERNING DR. PARKER'S BACKGROUND

Mr. Charles H. Wareing of Birmingham, England, a solicitor by profession and a Pons enthusiast by inclination, was appalled on reading *The Adventure of the Black Narcissus*, to discover how very un-English Dr. Parker was, and subsequently Michael Harrison, the distinguished author of many books – among them several pertinent to the London of Sherlock Holmes and associated subjects – pointed out, after beginning an acquaintance with Solar Pons, that Dr. Parker wrote prose that could best be described as "semi-American".

I was not unduly surprised to learn of their reactions, for, truth to tell, that fellow Parker has had some dark antecedents, and seems to have come upon the scene by fortuitous happenstance. "I had been sitting for some time in a pub not far from Paddington Station, ruefully reflecting that the London to which I had returned after the first World War was not the city I had left," he writes of himself, "when a tall, thin gentleman wearing an Inverness cape and a rakish cap with a visor on it, strode casually into the place." This is certainly ambiguous, to say the least.

There is nothing about his antecedents; he mentions the London to which he "returned" after the war, and we are told that he "left" London, but nothing is said as to when he left it, and Michael Harrison has suggested that there must be "a good reason for" Parker's writing "in a style full of Americanisms."

Dark hints, these. There is evidently some chapter in Parker's life that will bear examination and revelation, and perhaps in it we shall find an explanation for his peculiar prose, which is neither really British nor fully American, and is adequate proof that, as Harrison puts it, it is hardly "possible for a writer trained in one idiom to write, even as a careful exercise, in another," a premise I cannot dispute.

Harrison has suggested bluntly that Parker must have spent some of the years before the war – perhaps as a youth – in the United States and, indefatigable explorer of past times that he is, has promised to investigate those earlier years. A pity I had not done so myself. Of course, it is now too late. Being a writer trained in the American idiom myself and hence peculiarly blind to the flaws in Dr. Parker's prose, I am at this point far too apprehensive about what I might turn up to dig back a little into his antecedents. It should have been done before this.

It is all very well to say, as Harrison does, "you can now say anything you like about him," but can I? I doubt it. Here he is now, as I conceived him, a stolid, middle-class, rather unimaginative Englishman, not without a certain wit and loyal attachment – to Pons particularly, and to England generally – and it is altogether too unsettling to think that this may be simply a front – a protective covering, as it were, intended to deceive me, of all people, and, of course, through me, an ever-growing host of others who are, like me, prepared to take him at face value.

Perhaps there is indeed a good reason for Parker's rather consistent self-effacement in the little chronicles about his friend, Solar Pons. I had not noticed this, either, until the persistence of Michael Harrison brought it to my attention. Parker does not bring himself into the adventures any more than need be. And when he does so in his own Notebooks it is only because Pons draws information out of him, as in the entry for 28 September 1919; even here he chronicles his replies to Pons's queries "reluctantly", and "somewhat stiffly". I had thought this only proper for him in the role he played – as an observer, in most cases, of his companion's skill at deduction and detection, but his motive may have been quite otherwise. There are certain disquieting references in Dr. Parker's Notebooks, not all of which have seen the light of day.

I think it best, after all, to leave this entire subject to other, more impartial hands.

THE FAVORITE PASTICHES

It is no secret that Sir Arthur Conan Doyle looked upon the Sherlock Holmes tales with a highly critical – and sometimes a jaundiced eye, a point-of-view which readers have always found difficult to understand, but which any other writer of series stories understands only too well. The repetition of devices, gambits, situations tells considerably more on the patience of the author than on that of the reader, and helps to accentuate the shortcomings of the individual stories in any series.

It should therefore be not surprising to learn that only two of the pastiches satisfy their author – The *Adventure of the Purloined Periapt* and *The Adventure of the Six Silver Spiders* – and that only perhaps a dozen others seem to me of merit. It is also the fixed conviction of the author that Solar Pons is at his best in the shorter form, and that the deductive detective of this stamp functions at somewhat of a disadvantage in the form of the novel.

Editorial and reader perspectives sometimes differ, however, and I have found it interesting to take note of these differences. Frederic Dannay manifestly prefers *The Adventure of the Six Silver Spiders* over all the other Pontine tales; it alone saw publication in *Ellery Queen's Mystery Magazine;* Anthony Boucher shares the author's preference for *The Adventure of the Purloined Periapt;* and Vincent Starrett has always preferred *The Adventure of the Late Mr. Faversham* – perhaps because it takes rise in one of the unwritten tales of Watson – with Dannay's first choice coming in second. "But I have never failed to read a Solar Pons adventure with satisfaction and pleasure," he writes.

Luther Norris, who prepared the *London Map of Solar Pons* and inaugurated the Praed Street Irregulars, sets down as his prime favorite *The Adventure of the Norcross Riddle*, one of the earliest of the tales; "Here is the tradition of deduction at its very best," according to him. Following this one on Norris's list comes Starrett's favorite, *The Adventure of the Late Mr. Faversham*, and then, in order, *The Adventure of the Black Narcissus*, *The Adventure of the Six Silver Spiders*, *The Adventure of the Camberwell Beauty* ("the double pastiche is a pure delight!"), *The Adventure of the Rydberg Numbers*, *The Adventure of the Frightened Baronet*, *The Adventure of the Penny Magenta* ("A nostalgic reminder of London and Baker Street days."), *The Adventure of the Purloined Periapt* and *The Adventure of the Intarsia Box*.

Peter Ruber selects, without placing them in any order, *The Adventure of the Mosaic Cylinders*, *The Adventure of the Purloined Periapt*, *The Adventure of the Circular Room*, *The Adventure of the Six Silver Spiders*, *The Adventure of the Rydberg Numbers*, *The Adventure of the Norcross Riddle*, *The Adventure of the Lost Holiday*, *The Adventure of the Broken Chessman*, *The Adventure of the Swedenborg Signatures*, *The Adventure of the Magazine Blue*, and *The Adventure of the Orient Express*. "I should probably substitute other titles if I were to sit down and reread all the stories," writes Ruber, "but, as in the Holmes series, my favorites number only six or seven: it is the whole series that is important."

Robert Bloch's esteem, too, "extends to the entire canon." He adds, perceptively, "Aside from the personal pleasure I derive from reading any dispatch from Praed Street, there is another dimension that delights me. Specifically, I think of a small boy in a midwestern farm community – a small boy curled in a chair before the glowing coal stove on a bleak winter evening and devouring with wide-eyed wonder the exploits of Sherlock Holmes in the London of far away and long ago. I think of that boy grown to manhood and creating his own colorful criminologist and his own legendary London – and thus adding to the enjoyment of all of us who remember, as he does, the enchantment that commences when the game is afoot. In a word, I cannot dissociate the exploits of Solar Pons from the exploits of his Agent – and I'm grateful for them both."

Poul Anderson finds it as difficult as the majority of readers to select one Solar Pons story as *the* favorite. "They are all such delightful pastiches, and good yarns in their own right. So if *The Adventure of the Ball of Nostradamus* stands out especially in my mind, it is because of another element – the fantasy, the deft use of the paradoxes inherent in prediction. Yet the story is more than a brief entertainment. It raises a moral issue which lies at the very foundations of real-world politics and much other human action. Think about it."

Joseph Payne Brennan, himself the author of a sleuthing series, chooses as his three favorites *The Adventure of the Grice-Paterson Curse, The Adventure of the Late Mr. Faversham*, and *The Adventure of the Crouching Dog*. He points out that "stories quite often appeal for quite personal, rather than literary, reasons. I like the atmosphere of brooding horror hanging over that mysterious island of Uffa in *The Adventure of the Grice-Paterson Curse*... Mr. Faversham came close to committing the really classic crime! He might have been a really great criminal – cut from the same cloth as the great Moriarty! (By what mischance we miss enduring fame!) And I suppose *The Adventure of the Crouching Dog* appeals to me strongly because I am carried back in reminiscence to the great days of the immortal *Hound*. The brooding moor, the great paw prints, the curse – all are there, all the lovely lethal ingredients! Apart from the supernatural, what can rival a mysterious canine killer bounding across a darkened moor toward its terrified victim?"

A personal inclination decided A. E. Van Vogt's choice of favorite story – *The Adventure of the Mazarine Blue*. "Over the years I have occasionally read a story in which an insect is utilized as a major factor. The very first time I was impressed by the astuteness of the author in conceiving such a plot, and it seemed to me that, surely, it could be done only once or twice with effectiveness in the whole of literature. When Derleth did it – again – in *The Adventure of the Mazarine Blue*, I felt an admiration not diminished by any other of the pastiches."

A wide variety of selections come from many sources, but it is nevertheless evident that the author's two prime favorites are mentioned frequently enough to suggest that the principal criterion of judgment would appear to be similarity to the Holmesian canon, and by this standard, *The Adventure of the Purloined Periapt* and *The Adventure of the Six Silver Spiders* are the most Holmesian of the pastiches thus far written.

Yet the odds-on favorite deductive passage does not appear in either of these stories. An overwhelming majority of Pontine devotees have chosen as their best-liked deductive passage the opening paragraphs of *The Adventure of the Norcross Riddle*, following upon Pons's invitation to Parker to address his "intuition" to a calling card. The passage follows –

> The card bore an embossed legend: "Mr. Benjamin Harrison Manton," and in one corner, in smaller print, "Norcross Towers." I turned it over. The caller had written on its back, Will call at three.
>
> "My observation tells me that the gentleman used a broad-point pen; the character of the writing indicates that he is firm and steady. I see he uses the Roman e consistently; my intuition tells me he is an intelligent man."
>
> Pons's smile widened, and he chuckled again.
>
> "What do you make of it?" I asked, somewhat nettled.

"Oh, little more," replied Pons matter-of-factly, "except that the gentleman is an American by birth, but has resided in England for some length of time; he is a man of independent means, and is between thirty-five and thirty-nine years of age. Furthermore, his ancestry is very probably Southern United States, but his parents were undoubtedly members of the American Republican political party."

"You have seen the man!"

"Nonsense!" Pons picked up the card. "Observe: – the name Manton is more common to the southern part of the United States than to any other region; undoubtedly it is English in ancestry. In that part of the States, political sentiment is very largely Democratic, but it is not amiss to suggest that Manton's parents were Republican in sentiment, since they named him after a Republican president."

"Well, that is simple," I admitted.

"Precisely, Parker. But there is no intuition about it. It is mere observation. Now test yourself – tell me how I know he is of independent means."

"He calls at three." I ventured. "Certainly if he were not of independent means he could not break into an afternoon like that.

"He might well get away from his work to visit us," objected Pons. "Examine the card more closely."

"Well, it is embossed; that is a more expensive process than simple printing."

"Good, Parker. Come, you are getting there!"

"And the card itself is of very fine quality, though not pretentious." I held it up against the window. "Imported paper, I see. Italian."

"Excellent!"

"But how do you know he has lived in England for some time?"

"That is the most elementary of all. The gentleman has purchased or rented a country place, possibly an abandoned English home, for 'Norcross Towers' is certainly the name of a country house."

"But his age!" I protested. "How can you know the man's age merely by glancing at his calling card?"

"That is really absurdly simple, Parker. In the States it is considered fashionable even today to name children after the president in office at the time of the child's birth; doubtless the American tendency to hero-worship plays its part in that, too. Harrison was president from 1889 to 1893; hence it follows that our man was born in one of the four years of Harrison's term. The age is more likely to be thirty-nine years, because the tendency to name children in such fashion is strongest during the inaugural period."

I threw up my hands. "The contest is yours!"

A *propos* favorites, my daughter April Rose, at ten years of age settled that matter decisively. I put out for her one day two stories to read – *The Adventure of the Speckled Band* from the Master Canon, and *The Adventure of the Lost Locomotive* from the Pontine pastiches. She read them both with interest and declared that she liked them equally well. I observed, however, that it was to Sherlock Holmes that she returned, and not to Solar Pons.

From the Notebooks of Dr. Lyndon Parker

Within a few months of my joining Solar Pons in his quarters at 7B, Praed Street, and before I turned to chronicling his cases at full-length, I began to keep a notebook – not one of daily accounting, but only of random jottings, having become interested enough in his methods to seek to preserve some of his feats. For, in addition to adventures I later set down, there were many instructive moments in his company, and many lesser problems that came and went, that I wished to set down in some fashion for my own edification, and, later, to refresh my memory, since the memory of man is fallible, and time diminishes it or distorts what is locked in it. The entries that follow all date back to my first year at 7B.

17 August 1919

After a brief lecture on the art of observation and deduction in a pub in Camden Town today, Pons singled out a disgruntled-looking young man of not over thirty sitting by himself and put me to the test.

"What do you make of him, Parker?"

"A laborer," I said.

"Too general," retorted Pons.

"He is upset and brooding about something. His face is morose, he hardly touches his ale."

"Capital!" cried Pons. "Go on."

"He seems to be engaged in some sort of manual labor. His hands are rough."

Pons looked at me keenly, his eyes twinkling. "Nothing more?"

"Except that he seems to have come away hastily. He is in his working clothes."

"Well, that is a good beginning," said Pons. "You have really missed only a few little details. Come, let us just go over and talk with him."

So saying, he rose and led the way to the corner where the object of our attention glowered into his ale. The fellow did not look up when we came to pause before him.

"Forgive me for interrupting your black mood," said Pons, "but perhaps your wife will come around and you can patch up your quarrel."

The fellow looked up, amazement spreading across his face. After a brief hesitation, he growled, "I'm done with that."

"Things are never as black as they seem," pursued Pons. "Perhaps by this time she has contemplated your wedding ring long enough to reflect on her position."

"It's the first time I took it off," he answered.

"You are by trade a mason?"

"Aye."

"Specifically, a bricklayer."

He nodded.

"Left-handed, I see."

The fellow now gazed at Pons with increasing bewilderment.

"Childless, too."

"Look here, I don't know your game..." The fellow pushed back his chair and would have got up, had not Pons dropped a coin to the table in front of him.

"Have another pint, young man," he said, and walked away.

Once outside, Pons explained the simplicity of it. "The fellow's dark mood coupled with the fact that the band of relatively clean skin on his ring finger betrayed the recent removal of what could only have been a wedding ring suggested that he and his wife had quarrelled. He would not be likely to take himself off so violently if there were children to consider.

"As for his calling – the fingertips of his right hand show the worn, shiny stigma of the bricklayer. Since the mason habitually lays bricks with his left hand while his right is busy with the trowel, it follows that our man is left-handed. Always, in scrutinizing anyone, look for the stigmata of his calling – if there be such. Observe, for instance, this slender young man approaching us. What do you make of the mark on his neck not far below his left ear?"

I looked as closely as I could at the area Pons designated, and identified it as an *acneform dermatergosis*.

"But what does it tell us?" asked Pons. "That is an area too high to be irritated by his collar."

I could not guess.

"Why, it is plain as a pikestaff that he plays either the violin or the viola, and I submit that it is the violin. The mark is characteristic of an irritation caused by holding that instrument alongside the chin and against the neck."

28 September 1919

In our quarters today Pons surprised me by saying, "I have often reflected upon the fact that you have been somewhat less than comprehensive in your account of yourself to me, Parker."

"Why do you say so?" I asked.

"You have impressed me with the Order of Osmanieh bestowed upon you by the Khedivial Government as well as with His Majesty's Government's commission to continue the work at Mansura, Egypt. You have spoken of your education at Dover College, University College, and Heidelberg, and I have been privileged to read your series of articles on opthalmia in *The Lancet*. But you are curiously reticent about your years in America. Yet they must have been of some duration."

"Ten years," I said reluctantly.

"You have fallen rather pronouncedly into the American idiom and I observe that you speak what can best be described as semi-American."

"I am not aware of it," I replied, I fear, somewhat stiffly.

"Oh, it is unmistakable," persisted Pons. "Let me illustrate. Only this morning you spoke of a shop's being 'on' Edgware Road, whereas we customarily say that it is 'in' this or that street. The American, however, usually says 'on'. You referred yesterday, in speaking of that unfortunate matter of the Curate's Mistake, to a 'stoop' when any Englishman would have said 'porch'. I cite but these two examples, of what I should say is an Englishman's speaking semi-American. You seem to have been spared some of the curious accents affected by Americans, however."

"Ah, that entire period is a painful one for me," I said.

"You did not enjoy your sojourn in the States?"

"No, it was not that. I was graduated from Columbia and then for two years, to 1903, I served as principal medical officer for the Allegheny Sheet & Tube Corporation. Those years were pleasant enough."

"Ah, it was your marriage."

"Say, rather, its unfortunate ending. Louisa's death in the *Titanic* disaster ended not only an entire period in my life, but a kind of life. The war followed hard upon it, and our world has changed since then. I have closed that door – Praed Street is as far from those American years as from my Egyptian sojourn."

With this he appeared to be satisfied, or, out of delicacy, said no more.

11 October 1919

Pons on Calluses, &c. – "Certain calluses are almost invariable. The stonecutter, for instance, is likely to have a broad callus at the base of the little finger of his left hand, on the back, of course, where the chisel rests on the finger. A trumpet player – or a tuba player, for that matter – is likely to show a callus on the right little finger, whereas that of the French horn player will show on the left little finger. The jeweler or engraver may show calluses in several specific places, including the palm of the hand, the tips of thumb and index finger, particularly of the left hand.

"Men who work with coal tar and petroleum derivatives may show melanosis of exposed parts of their bodies, and anyone working with tetryl in any form is apt to show the red and yellow stains on skin and hair, whereas silversmiths tend to absorb enough silver to give a characteristic slate gray color to their skin.

"You will yourself be familiar with the stigmata of disease."

12 October 1919

I had been reading Pons' *The Varieties of the Criminal Method*. When I put the book down, I asked him whether there was such a thing as "the criminal type."

"I fear that is a fallacy," said Pons. "The fault for its existence is probably traceable to Lombroso, who held that there was such a thing."

"But you will admit that certain people look like criminals."

"Nonsense. They may perhaps fit the viewer's concept of what a criminal ought to look like, no more."

He got up and took down his files. From them he abstracted four photographs and laid them before me.

"Which of these is the criminal?" he asked.

"I suspect they are all criminals or you wouldn't have them in your files."

"On the contrary. Logical as your deduction is, your conclusion is false."

I examined the photographs carefully and finally selected one.

"Why?" asked Pons.

"You have only to look at him – the beetling brow, the shifty eyes, the thick-lipped sensuous mouth, the cauliflower ear. The fellow looks evil."

"And the others do not?"

"No."

"Why do you say so?"

"Well, look at the first one. There is an ascetic face, if ever I saw one," I said. "The fellow looks like a minister."

"He was. The Reverend Athelny Foster."

I fear I chuckled in triumph.

"Of Chipping Fulham. The name means nothing to you?"

"It is surely enough that I identified his calling."

"He poisoned his wife in favor of a barmaid," said Pons dryly. "Next?"

"This one is as dignified as a Sunday School Superintendent."

"You name him so?"

"No. A judge or a lawyer. And so is the other."

Pons laughed in that way of his I should describe as "heartless." "The one is a swindler of some renown – Patrick Donovan. The other is indeed a lawyer – Charles Conyers. He suffocated a client in order to conceal his peculations from his estate."

"And what did the 'criminal type' do?"

"He caught them. He was the late Commissioner John Flinders of New Scotland Yard. I trust that will curb your romanticism."

17 October 1919

A lady called to see Pons today. She gave her name as Mrs. Rose Murray. She was simply dressed and wore a little straw hat with straw flowers decorating it, together with a bit of black cloth.

"A seamstress, I see," said Pons.

"Yes, sir," she said. "I didn't think it so plain to tell I made my own clothing."

"The mark of the thimble is easy to see on your finger," said Pons. "Not long widowed?"

"My husband was killed last March in an accident on the Great Western," she replied. "I have quite got over it, though."

"Not quite enough to remove that bit of crepe on your hat, and yet enough to call yourself by your own Christian name rather than his."

"Yes, that is true."

"And what can I do for you, Mrs. Murray?"

"Why, Mr. Pons, I am an acquaintance of your landlady, and since you and Dr. Parker are bachelors, I took it you might have some sewing for me to do."

19 October 1919

Pons' persisting habits –

He toys with his ear, pulls at the lobe – usually his left, when in deep thought. (Freud would have something to say about this!) He also closes his eyes frequently to concentrate the better.

He is an attentive listener. Sitting, he tends to tent his fingers. Standing, he leans against the mantel most frequently. On occasion he paces back and forth, hands clasped behind him.

His eyes seem alternately grey or grey-green. They seem to be extraordinarily keen and alive. He seems to miss nothing. His glance is quick – "darting" would be the word, and he seems to look into one.

He smokes the most abominable shag ever prepared by the hand of man. I could believe it to be a mixture of cabbage leaves, string, and the Chinese tea smoked from the burning of yak dung. He keeps it wherever the fancy suits him – the coal scuttle, the toe of a slipper, the pen cup, etc.

He delights to display his deductive powers, but at the same time he vastly appreciates it when the joke is on him.

His is devoted to his Inverness and deerstalker, but I wonder sometimes if he does not wear them for effect only. (If that is blasphemy – *mea culpa.*) He has dressing-gowns in several colors, all dark – and all well worn. He shows no inclination to get himself a new robe.

He is much given to disguising himself. He fancies, because he has deceived me so readily several times, that he is very good at disguise, forgetting that, as he has pointed out on even more occasions, I am not as observant as I ought to be.

7 November 1919

Inspector Jamison called today to lay a problem before Pons. He was apologetic about its trivial nature – repeated housebreaking in Park Lane – but it was evident that he was vexed about it, nevertheless. He gave an account of seven break-ins all within two blocks, and ended finally with, "The crux of the matter, Pons, is its senselessness."

"I daresay its meaning has not yet become evident," said Pons dryly.

"Everyone a clumsy break-in, and nothing of value taken."

"An amateur's work, clearly?"

"No doubt of it."

"Or made to seem so. Let me see, now," Pons went on, leaning back in his chair at the fireplace, his eyes closed, his fingers tented before him. "A Chinese piece stolen at the Forrer home?"

"Value about one pound," said Jamison.

"Nothing more?"

"Nothing. One item from each house."

"A gold-plated pen from the Beston house."

Jamison shrugged. "Ten shillings – if that. It wasn't the loss Beston reported so much as the breakage – a pane of the back door broken in while they were gone."

"In all cases the householders were absent," mused Pons. "So the burglar seemed to have some knowledge of their movements."

"Yes, yes, Pons – all that is elementary," said Jamison impatiently. "What good did it do him to watch these houses if all he meant to take was some trifling article? That's the work of an imbecile."

"I would not say so," said Pons. "The most expensive item taken appears to have been a cheap brooch from the Kendall home," he went on.

"Under two pounds value," said Jamison.

"And entry, if I understood you, seems to have been made in every case before midnight."

"In two cases before ten-thirty o'clock. The householders got home by ten-thirty."

Pons smiled. "This suggests nothing to you, Jamison?"

"The man's a fool. Or he means to be a nuisance. Perhaps he wants to put the wind up somebody in that neighborhood."

"I submit it is more than that," said Pons with an annoying habit, which I had observed before, of saying too little.

"I suppose next you will be telling me to look for a short fat man with a limp, who smokes nothing but imported cigars and is supporting his mother-in-law," said Jamison with heavy sarcasm.

Pons laughed heartily. "I regret I cannot oblige you this time, Jamison. I think the honor of catching him must be yours. But then," he added, his eyes dancing, "it always has been, has it not?"

"You *can* describe him then?" asked Jamison, incredulous.

"I do not know whether he is short or tall, fat or lean," said Pons, "and at this point, I am sorry to say, the case does not seem to me interesting enough to challenge me. And, if I may say so, it is too elementary."

Jamison got to his feet as abruptly as his bulk permitted. "I shall have to look elsewhere."

"I suggest you sit tight and let him betray himself."

"Ah, and how many times will he have to do a burglarious entry before then?"

"I rather think he has done almost as many as he needs to do," continued Pons. "At any time now he will make a mistake."

Jamison's interest quickened. "What sort of mistake?"

"He will steal something of value. Perhaps of great value. And something certain to be heavily insured. You will then, of course, investigate thoroughly the financial situation of the gentleman who reports the theft. I submit you will find that all the other burglaries were performed only to make his own loss credible. I can foresee the headlines: *Inspector Jamison Scores Again!*"

"And if nothing of the sort happens?" asked Jamison skeptically.

"Then by all means call on me again and I will be happy to look into the matter."

18 November 1919

At my place at breakfast this morning, Pons, who had gone out, had left the morning paper with a small item circled in red crayon. "Inspector Jamison Scores," I read. "Mr. Geoffrey Thompson was taken into custody this morning and charged with a series of burglaries in Park Lane. Mr. Thompson had only two days ago reported himself as the victim of such a burglary, having lost a valuable pearl necklace belonging to his wife..." No mention of Pons, of course; but that is how he prefers it.

21 November 1919

A short man, introducing himself as Mr. Howard Robinson, retired, came to see Pons this morning. He was not over five feet in height, and thin almost to cadaverousness. His bearing was military. A moustache he wore would on almost anyone else have looked fierce, but on him had the appearance of something attached for effect. He had rough hands.

"I have, Mr. Pons, a rather delicate problem." I observed that he pronounced "rather" in two distinct and separate syllables. "Late yesterday I received a sealed envelope in which my solicitor forwarded to me a certain legacy in banknotes. While the covering letter was enclosed, the banknotes were not. Yet the seal was unbroken. My solicitor is a man of the utmost honesty, so that one of the three persons through whose hands this envelope passed from him to me must have taken the banknotes. But how? I looked in on Thornydke, but he was in Scotland. I took the liberty of coming to you without an appointment.

All prim and proper, and very businesslike.

"You have the envelope, Mr. Robinson?" asked Pons.

"Yes, sir."

Robinson produced it, carefully wrapped in gauze, from a pocket case of hard leather. He handed it to Pons.

"I see by its shape that it certainly did at one time contain something of bulk," said Pons at once.

"I thought so. I opened it with an opener. The letter, you see, has plainly been wrapped around something – certainly the banknotes."

"Let us just see." So saying, Pons carried the envelope over to the corner of our quarters where he amused himself with chemicals. He sat down there, took up his magnifying glass, and studied the seal. I heard him chuckle. "Pray step over here, Mr. Robinson."

Robinson did so. I was at his heels.

"See there, sir," said Pons, pointing to a mere speck of grey on the maroon wax of the seal. "This is plaster of Paris. Someone took off the seal and replaced it."

"But how, sir?"

Pons leaned back. "Why, by a common method indeed. Someone oiled the seal and poured on to it some freshly burned plaster of Paris. As soon as it was set, the seal was raised. After the money was taken out of the envelope, the seal was renewed from the oiled mould. It is almost inevitable that flakes or grains of the plaster will stick to the seal. There is evidence here that some grains were removed."

"It will hold up in court?"

"Any competent witness can testify to it successfully."

"Would you be willing to do so?"

"If I am called upon, Mr. Robinson. If I am called upon," said Pons. He stood up so suddenly that Mr. Robinson fell back. "That will be two pounds, sir."

"Two – two pounds?" stuttered Robinson.

"Two pounds," said Pons with such finality that Robinson paid him forthwith.

He bowed himself out.

Pons threw the notes to the table and walked over to the window to watch our late client emerge from 7B.

"Nature provides an infinite variety in mankind," he reflected. "What did you make of him, Parker?"

"An ex-military man," I said at once.

"Capital!" said Pons. "But obvious. It has been a long time since he was in military service."

"And a man accustomed to clerical work."

"Ah, you make progress. You saw the typical middle-finger callus of a man who has used a pen for a long time. Nothing more?"

"I did think his clothes a trifle old."

"Excellent. And worn. The fellow is a miser. You saw how taken aback he was when I asked a fee."

"I did indeed."

"I submit, moreover, that he is very probably also a potential thief. There was plaster of Paris also under one of his fingernails. He came here to test his plan. Greed has made a bungler of him. He ought never to have opened the envelope save in the presence of witnesses. We shall hear no more from him."

26 November 1919

Our landlady, Mrs. Johnson, tapped rather timidly at our door today. When I had opened to her, she excused herself, apologized for her temerity, and addressed herself to Pons.

"Mr. Pons, sir, I wonder it it would be too much if I asked Lillie Morris up to talk to you. What with the new will they found, she's that upset and all."

"What is her trouble, Mrs. Johnson?"

"Why, it's the new will," she said, as if he might have known. "The old will gave everything to her – and the new one nothing. And after she took care of the old man, too!"

"Pray ask her up, Mrs. Johnson," said Pons, his eyes twinkling.

I could not help saying, after our landlady had gone down to her quarters, "More than once, I've had that particular failing called to mind – some woman who gives a decade or more of her life to taking care of an aged father or mother or other relative is done out of her rightful due by another member of the family who shows up from time to time and who sends around little gifts now and then. Old people exaggerate the little differences that invariably develop between them and those who care for them, and fail to realize that it is quite the easiest thing to do them an occasional kindness without the day to day exchange arising to sully the impression so easily created."

Pons nodded. "That is only another trifle of evidence in support of human frailty."

"Do you know Mrs. Johnson's friend?"

"I have never heard of her before."

Mrs. Johnson presently appeared with Lillie Morris in tow. She was a woman in her early thirties not ill-favored in looks, with brown eyes at present a bit clouded with trouble. She was neatly but not expensively dressed, and wore her ash-blonde hair attractively piled on to her head. Since she wore no wedding band, I concluded that she was unmarried.

"Pray sit down, Miss Morris, and tell me your trouble," invited Pons.

Miss Morris had brought up her reticule, and this she now put beside the chair on which she sat. Mrs. Johnson took a seat between her friend and the door, and sat leaning forward expectantly, as if at any moment a miracle might be produced by my companion to ease her friend's mind.

"Thank you, Mr. Pons." And what a pleasant, well-modulated voice she had! "Mrs. Johnson said you would be kind enough to listen to me, though I'm sure I am imposing upon you. For the past eleven years I have had my living with my grandfather who needed someone to take care of him, and when he died, he left a will leaving his house and what he owned to me."

"A considerable sum or a modest one?" interposed Pons.

"I believe it is considerable, Mr. Pons. But it seems I am not to get it after all. A later will has turned up, and he has left it all to my cousin Percy, with whom he was on friendly terms."

"Percy lived with him?"

"Oh, no, Mr. Pons. Percy lives in Soho. But he came around now and then and took grandfather out for a day. Mrs. Johnson says I ought to contest the will, and so do some of my other friends."

"You have seen the will, Miss Morris?"

"I was sent a photographic copy of it."

"Ah. Pray let me see it."

Miss Morris took a fat envelope from her reticule and from this took the document in question and passed it to Pons.

He unfolded it and glanced at it. His eyes narrowed. "Why, it is dated less than a half a year ago," he said.

"My grandfather died two months past," said Miss Morris.

Pons read rapidly through the will. "Each page separately signed, I see."

"Yes, Mr. Pons. I am afraid there is no doubt it is my grandfather's signature. No doubt at all. Even I would have to testify to it."

Pons' eyes, I saw, grew intent as he looked at first one page and then another, until he had finished the fourth page. He lowered the will but continued to hold on to it while he gazed thoughtfully at Miss Morris.

"How old was your grandfather when he died?" he asked.

"He was eighty-seven, Mr. Pons."

"I have no doubt there were differences between you."

"I suppose there were bound to be. Old people are occasionally unreasonable. But nothing very serious, Mr. Pons. Certainly nothing serious enough to bring him to make such a change in his will."

"Your grandfather was in good health?"

"He had been failing for some years, Mr. Pons. No, I shouldn't say he was in good health – or had been in the past three years. He was – well, uncertain on his legs, as one would say."

"Shaky, Miss Morris?"

"Yes, sir, He still got around, but only with difficulty."

"You are mentioned here, Miss Morris – for five hundred pounds."

"I know, Mr. Pons. That was the exact sum my grandfather once mentioned he would leave Percy."

"Indeed. Excuse me, Miss Morris."

Pons got up and went over to that corner of our quarters in which he kept his chemical paraphernalia. He sat down there and carefully scrutinized one page after another of the will Miss Morris had given him, using a magnifying glass, and putting the pages over light, one atop the other. Mrs. Johnson assured Miss Morris *sotto voce*, while they waited, that Pons was a great detective who could unravel any problem at all, but Miss Morris did not seem entirely convinced.

Presently Pons returned to his chair at the fireplace. "There are two courses open to you, Miss Morris. You can contest this will, or you can lay a claim to wages covering the years you took care of your grandfather – unless, of course, he paid you a salary."

"Oh, no, Mr. Pons – short of providing my living, he paid me nothing. Then, uncertainly, she added, "Which would you do, Mr. Pons?"

"Contest, by all means!"

"But how can I do so, Mr. Pons? I know that is my grandfather's signature."

"Very well. Let us accept that it is indeed Mr. Lemuel Morris's signature. But this will, Miss Morris, is a forgery."

"How can you say so!" cried Miss Morris.

"Each of four pages has been signed in precisely the same way. There is not the slightest deviation among the signatures. One is a precise copy of the other. I submit, Miss Morris, that no man of eighty-seven – and certainly not a man who was shaky – could possibly perform such a feat. I am far from that age myself, and I never to my knowledge indite my name in exactly the same way twice in succession. Nor does Dr. Parker.

No, Miss Morris – I rather suspect that your cousin Percy is at the bottom of it. You need only apply to a competent solicitor and lay these facts before him. There are plenty of capable experts who will present the court with all the proof necessary."

Mrs. Johnson beamed, as if her faith in Pons's infallibility had been proved.

3 December 1919

Pons on Probability. "Though there are always several possible or probable solutions to every problem, there is only one that will exactly fit all the facts. One proceeds initially to apply the facts to the solution that seems most likely in the circumstances, and then, if they do not fit, to one after another until the correct solution is found.

"If, however, all the probable solutions are eliminated – if none fits all the facts – then whatever remains, no matter how improbable, must be the correct solution. This was the course invariable followed by the Master. In my opinion, no other course is proper for an investigator.

"Occasionally the police, before they fall back upon this method, seize upon the most likely solution as the correct one, and then attempt to make the facts fit the solution. This has had the happy result of bringing to my attention problems I might not otherwise have encountered."

11 December 1919

When Pons came to the breakfast table this morning I had the satisfaction of reading a lead in the morning paper to him. "'Morris Will Case: Percy Morris Charged.'"

"Ah, that young woman took the most sensible course," observed Pons. "I was inclined to think her a little soft –

perhaps ready to accept some compromise from her cousin. I am delighted that it is not so."

"Why?" I asked.

"It is a simple matter of seeing justice done, my dear fellow," he replied. "There is a great deal being said today about rehabilitation rather than punishment. I have dealt with the criminal element long enough to know that this idealistic humanitarianism takes rise out of ignorance rather than any well-founded knowledge. Rehabilitation is fine theory, but let us have punishment first."

I could not help observing that my companion sounded like a character from *Alice in Wonderland*.

He ignored me, as he often does. "There is, too, an abundance of prattle about guilt. 'Crime and the criminal are the fault of society,' and it follows to these people who talk in this manner, that 'the criminal is not responsible, society is.' Now, it would be idle to deny that poverty and filth are fertile soil for crime, but it is nothing short of lunacy to suggest that it follows upon this admission that *all* crime rises from such a background, and that all criminals are therefore free of social responsibility. But this ridiculous claim is being made by ever noisier elements of our society. The denial of personal responsibility is fatuous. I do not know a single jurist of my considerable acquaintance who will subscribe to such nonsense."

"You cannot very well rehabilitate a man who has been hanged," I said.

"Ah, well, if he deserved hanging in the first place, there is very little that can be said in favor of trying to rehabilitate him. We are coming dangerously close to a world in which everything is done in behalf of the law-breaker – and at the expense of the law-abiding citizen. That is the road to anarchic chaos. It is the end result of indulgence in idealistic sentimentality, not of rational thought. We have always had the conflict between the individual and society, and the ultimate goal is to protect society by legal means at the least possible loss to the rights of the individual. But as the earth's population increases, it becomes inevitable that the rights of the individual must give way increasingly to the well-being of the social structure as a whole. Yet here we see the beginnings of a movement that goes counter to this inescapable fact – the outcry is for the protection of the rights of precisely those elements of society who have forfeited their right to demand such protection by anti-social acts. We are reversing Darwin – by insisting that the unfit survive."

I thought him unduly harsh and said as much.

He brushed this aside impatiently. "It is not a matter of harshness or softness. It is simply a failure to see the forest for the trees. Miss Morris's counsel has certainly taken the correct course. Contesting the forged will meant charging the forger. He should get what is coming to him, though, in view of what happens in our courts all too often, it may be thought infantile to expect adequate justice."

14 December 1919

Pons was speaking of the commonplaceness of the average crime this morning when Inspector Jamison paid us a visit.

"I put it to you, Jamison," said Pons, "is it not true that the majority of capital crimes committed in England are utterly without imagination?"

Jamison nodded. "Dull, if I may say so. Very dull. Of course, it's not every crime that has one of these private inquiry agents hanging about to colour it up a bit."

"*Touche*!" cried Pons.

"It's little more most of the time than some bloke breaking in and killing a man in the course of a robbery – or a man killing his wife out of jealousy or something of that kind – open and shut cases. The only trouble we have is in the courts – we know we've got our man, but counsel confuses everybody."

Pons smiled. "What problem troubles you today, Jamison?"

"This is just a friendly call," said the Inspector, faintly indignant.

"Not a mystery to be solved in all London?" pressed Pons with a note of disappointment in his voice.

Jamison shook his head. "We've had three murders and one accidental death in the past week."

"All solved, I take it," said Pons dryly.

Jamison hedged a little. "We've got one murderer – and we're onto the other two."

"Capital!" exclaimed Pons. "And the accidental death?"

"Ah, that's a miserable business," said Jamison. "Young woman fell off a train on the London, Brighton and South Coast Railway on Sunday night."

"I don't recall reading about it in the papers."

"I believe it would make nothing more than a small paragraph on the inside pages," said Jamison.

"I see by your preoccupied air and the way you finger your vest button, Jamison, you're not happy about it."

"She was badly injured, Pons – fractured skull, one leg cut off."

"How old was she?"

"Just twenty-three. I'd have called her a good-looking woman. Angela Morell. A clerk in a dairy in Lavender Hill."

"Go on," urged Pons.

"The body was found in Merstham tunnel. There seems to be no question but that a fall from the train was the cause of her death. None. She couldn't have fallen from any train but the 9:13 p.m. from London Bridge to Brighton, or the 9:33 p.m. from Charing Cross to Reading. But both these trains came out of the tunnel with all carriage doors shut. I don't know what kind of feat it would be to fall from a carriage and shut the door behind you. It may not be impossible."

"But it is certainly improbable," conceded Pons.

"Then, too, she had a bit of veil in her mouth."

"Her hat had a veil attached?"

"None."

"Ah," said Pons, his interest quickening.

"Caught on a tooth, in fact."

"A gag."

"Perhaps. But let us say somebody pushed her. Then we come up to the question of why? – and who?"

"I take it she was unmarried."

Jamison nodded.

"You've traced her movements?"

"That's routine, as you know. She left her lodgings at seven that night, saying she was going for only a short walk, and would be back within the hour. But one of her friends said that in the afternoon she had looked through a railway timetable."

"She had an assignation then," suggested Pons. "Was she accustomed to walking out?"

"The landlady said she had two gentlemen friends. But there were nights when she went out alone. She was always back by eleven on such nights. She didn't speak of them to anyone."

"Assuming that she permitted two gentlemen to call for her openly, there must then have been a strong reason why she should be clandestine with a third – *if* her assignation was with a man."

"Why do you intimate it may not have been?"

"I wonder what manner of man carries a veil about with him. But I am out of touch with the world of fashion."

"No, no, it's true – a woman would be more likely to carry a veil."

"A woman perhaps who had followed her husband to a clandestine meeting with another woman."

"You are certainly colouring it up, Pons," said Jamison.

"Ah, well, if you are content with a verdict of accidental death, there is surely no need to pursue the matter further. I submit, however, that you are anything but satisfied with that verdict. Let us be as objective as we can about the matter. We are given a young woman – not ill-favored in looks – who is attractive enough to appeal to members of the opposite sex. She goes off to what must certainly be an assignation and is found dead. Very well, then. Eliminating accidental death, we are left with suicide or murder. Had she any patent reason for suicide?"

"We are aware of none."

"Then we come back to murder. Certain limited possibilities are open to us. Though the young woman had been careful to maintain a reputation for good character, we do not have in hand any proof that she was indeed a woman of good character. She could have been conducting a liaison with a married man – and fallen victim either to him or his wife. She could have been a prostitute engaged in blackmailing selected victims, one of whom took this method of disposing of her. She could as easily have been followed by someone violently jealous of her liaison and murdered by him in a rage. Within the boundaries of the known facts we can hardly speculate farther without entering the realm of pure imagination. I submit, however, that the fragment of veil found in her mouth suggests a certain premeditation."

"A contrived accident is what you make it, Pons."

"I think it unlikely that it was accidental death," replied Pons. "The fragment of veil caught on her tooth and the closed carriage doors both suggest the presence of some other person in the compartment from which she was thrust. You saw the body?"

"A horrible sight."

"Were there any marks suggesting that her hands and feet had been tied?"

"None."

"Very well, then – she might have been stunned to keep her quiet, and gagged to prevent her crying out if she came to her senses before the tunnel was reached. I take it there was nothing to suggest robbery?"

"She was carrying five pounds and wore two rings – one a diamond, one a ruby."

"On the wages of a dairy clerk?"

Inspector Jamison was disconcerted.

"I put it to you, Jamison, it might be interesting to pursue the inquiry with the conviction that Miss Morell was murdered. Try to ascertain where she got on to the train, whether she was accompanied by anyone, and what her destination was. I rather suspect that the place of the assignation was in a specific compartment on the train, not on the platform, so that her murderer need take no chance of being seen with her."

After Inspector Jamison had gone, Pons said, "I take a dim view of the Yard's finding her murderer. That young woman, if indeed she had been engaged in some criminal activity or a course that would not meet with social approval, seems to have covered herself very well – so well, in fact, that she may defeat all attempts to discover the identity of her murderer. The kind of clandestine affair in which she may have been engaged is commonly extremely difficult to uncover."

21 December 1919

I touched Pons on a sensitive point today when I observed that the evidence offered to convict the Moat Farm murderer was almost entirely circumstantial.

"I seem to detect a note of disapproval, Parker," he said with some asperity. "Yet circumstantial evidence is the strongest of all possible evidence."

"As strong as the testimony of eyewitnesses?"

He chuckled dryly. "Stronger! Circumstances cannot lie. They may be misinterpreted, but they cannot lie. Eyewitnesses can, and do – sometimes by design, but usually because they are simply mistaken. I put it to you that no half dozen eyewitnesses will tell precisely the same story; their accounts are certain to vary. All things being relative, some will see a short man, some a tall one, some a fat one, some a thin man, some brown, some hazel, some blue, some green. But that is not so of circumstances."

"The outcry against circumstantial evidence cannot be that ill-founded," I protested.

"It can and it is. I suspect it was begun by criminals who were fairly caught by circumstances. Wills in *On Principles of Circumstantial Evidence* puts the case well when he says, 'The distinct and specific proving power of circumstantial evidence depends upon its incompatibility with any reasonable hypothesis other than that of the truth of the principal fact in proof of which it is adduced; so that, after the exhaustion of every other mode of solution, we must either conclude that the accused has been guilty of the act imputed, or renounce as illusory the results of consciousness and experience, and such knowledge as we possess of the workings of the human mind.' And Lord Coleridge, summing up in the trial of Dickman, the railway murderer, in 1910, said: 'If we find a variety of circumstances all pointing in the same direction, convincing in proportion to the number and variety of those circumstances and their independence one of another, although each separate piece of evidence, standing by itself, may admit of an innocent interpretation, yet the cumulative effect of such evidence may be overwhelming evidence of guilt.' I recognize no intelligent argument that runs counter to these statements."

"Why, we read interminably of the police trying to convict on evidence that is demolished readily enough by counsel," I said.

"I fear that is only too true. I submit, nevertheless, that you are taking issue with a police action, or the flawed decision of the prosecution. That is a matter of attempting to make of circumstances what they are not. I have no sympathy with it – but it does not bear any relation to the proper interpretation and use of circumstantial evidence."

"But surely you cannot deny that circumstantial evidence takes strength from inference, and that is a matter of opinion."

"It is opinion supported by facts. Indeed, it is opinion rising out of the available facts. I think, if you care to examine the records, you will find that far more wrong convictions have resulted from false and mistaken direct and positive testimony than from the wrong inferences drawn from circumstantial evidence. No one fact is employed alone in the building of a case on circumstantial evidence; no, it is the accumulation of facts that, taken together, related together, are so strong as to establish a clear indication of guilt. Compared to the fallibility of human beings, circumstances invariably present the stronger case.

23 December 1919

Pons' wholehearted respect for time was clearly demonstrated today. Having no problem to engage him, he spent the entire day adding to his store of knowledge, which far exceeds my own. He reads reference books, once he had done with the papers – the current issue of *Whitaker's Almanack* – Skeat's *Concise Etymological Dictionary of the English Language* – *A Dictionary of Dates* – Isaac Taylor's *Words and Places* – *Whitaker's Peerage* – a guide to the cathedrals of France – certainly a hodgepodge of books on a singular variety of subjects.

Seeing me observing him, he smiled and said, "Nothing is as unique as a fact, my dear fellow, and nothing as fascinating. You and I – indeed, the entire universe, depends on facts."

"It is even more fascinating to realize what some people make of facts," I said.

"Is it not!" he agreed, his eyes twinkling.

27 December 1919

A note today from Jamison.

"'In regard to that Merstham tunnel murder,'" Pons read, interjecting, "Aha! He now clearly calls it 'murder'! – 'the woman Morell appears to have been involved with a number of men from her past. New evidence suggests that she has been blackmailing them. A search of her room turned up a small notebook with seventeen names – two of them women. No addresses, but we'll find them. Curious notations under each name indicating payments. Apparently none ever came to her address – she met them by appointment. It will take time, but we'll find him (or her!) eventually. Other than these occasional appointments, her life in Lavender Hill would seem to have been straightforward enough.'" Pons's eyes twinkled as he dropped the note into the coal scuttle at the fireplace. "I daresay Jamison will have it, in time to come, we coloured it up a bit."

7 January 1920

Mrs. Johnson this morning showed up to our quarters a clergyman who had sent ahead his card announcing himself as the Reverend Howard Foster. He proved to be a lean shank of a man, with a face like a closed rat trap, very dour and grim. His jaws were clamped together, and his bushy sideburns, now greying, were wiry and stiff. He wore clerical garb, withal a trifle shiny from wear, and carried an umbrella rolled up under his arm, though the day was fair and rather cold.

He addressed himself forthrightly to Pons. "I am taking the liberty, sir, of bringing to you a small problem which I believe is not one for the police. I understand you have some little knowledge in these matters."

"There are those who say so," admitted Pons.

The Reverend Foster drew from the inner pocket of his long black coat an envelope which he handed to Pons.

"Addressed to a lady," ventured Pons. "And in type."

"My niece."

Pons opened the envelope and took out the paper inside. From where I sat, it appeared to be a half page of proof or print. It was ragged along one edge, as if it had been torn from a book.

Pons narrowed his eyes. A kind of gleam came into them. He gazed provocatively at our visitor.

"My niece received this yesterday by post. I was in the study when she opened it. She gazed at it, and I presume she read it. Her face went pale. Then she moaned softly and ran – no, let me amend that, Mr. Pons – she tottered from the room. I ran to her aid, but she thrust me aside. I begged her to tell me what the matter was, but all she did was shake her head and say, 'It's no use. I must go away – far away!' Since then she has hardly come from her room and I have not had a word from her. She walks about like a dead woman. Can you make anything of that? I picked it up when she dropped it, but I cannot make head or tail of it save that it appears to be from a book – not the kind of text that I with my limited time would be likely to read."

"I will need a little time to examine it," said Pons. "I take it your niece has not always lived with you?"

"Only since the death of my wife short of two years ago. She came back unexpectedly from America. She had gone there in 1910 intending to return in a few years, but the war caught her there, and she stayed until it was no longer dangerous to come back. Her father – her last surviving parent, my brother – had died in the meantime; so she naturally came to live with me."

"Ah, she is then no longer a very young woman."

"She is thirty-four."

Pons glanced again at the envelope. "Posted in London. And not far away." He looked up. "I see that you have come up from the country, since the address on the envelope is obviously your home. Presumably you have other errands in London. If you will stop around in an hour or two, I believe I may have some explanation of this mysterious communication."

The clergyman moved as if dismissed by his bishop.

He had hardly left our quarters – indeed, his footsteps could still be heard on the stairs – before Pons subjected me to one of those little games he enjoys playing so much. He thrust the page from the envelope at me.

"What do you make of that, Parker?" he asked.

I had only to glance at it to say, "It is clearly a page torn from a book."

"No, no," cried Pons vigorously. "It is clearly a torn page – but not necessarily from a book. Have a closer look at it."

I read it with care –

> "Faithless Dick," said Silver. "I've a gauge on the keg of rum, mind, wretch. There's the key; fill a pannikin and bring it up."
>
> Terrified as I was, I could not help thinking to myself that this way Mr. Arrow will have got the strong waters that destroyed him.
>
> Dick was not to come for a while, and during his lengthy absence Israel spoke straight and soft for the cook to hear. I caught but a word or two – "I" and "you", yet I gathered some very important news, that it was certain that not all the crew could be made to join in a mutiny against the captain or yet in any crew of John Silver's, no matter what the circumstances. It made me

feel good to hear, and I knew that whatever happened there was still time to stand with valor against Silver.

End of Chapter XI:
What I Heard in the Apple Barrel.

When I looked up, Pons's eyes were keen upon me, and dancing with delight. "Now, then, what do you make of it?"

"It is surely no mystery," I said, sure of myself. "I know the book from which it comes very well – and it *is* a book."

"Is it, indeed?"

His sharpness ought to have given me pause. "Yes – and you ought to be able to name it as well as I. Wherever else would you find 'Mr. Arrow' and 'John Silver' but in *Treasure Island*?"

"Where else, indeed! Where else but in that miserable revision of the concluding paragraphs of chapter eleven!"

"What do you mean?" I cried. "I remember the scene well. Jim has fallen asleep in the apple barrel, and when he wakes learns for the first time what a scoundrel Long John Silver is – planning the mutiny and the murder of Squire Trelawney. It is one of my favorite books. That is the way the chapter ends."

"On the contrary," said Pons, with that air I had found so annoying, of being inevitably right. "It ends with the voice of the lookout shouting 'Land-ho!'"

Even as he said it, I knew that it was with these words that the chapter did indeed end.

"Whatever Stevenson was not, he was not a careless stylist, was he, Parker?"

"I should not say so."

"Indeed not. Fancy his having written – I commend the fourth line to your attention – the 'way Mr. Arrow will have got the strong waters that destroyed him.' Will have got' indeed! Stevenson would never have been guilty of such a construction."

I conceded the point. "But it is clearly in print," I said, a trifle bewildered now.

"Ah, Parker, I fear you share the common man's reverence for print. He will tell you, 'I saw it in the paper!' as if this were the final bit of proof needed to support whatever contention he may have uttered. 'I saw it in print' – sometimes it is 'cold print', though all print is by its very nature cold; if it has any warmth it is the author's artistry, not the printer's."

I looked at the page again. "Then," I said, venturing boldly into Pons's domain, "then clearly, that construction was necessary to the printer!"

"Capital! Capital!" cried Pons, clasping his hands together and raising them aloft as in tribute to heaven or to himself – certainly not to me. "You have begun to learn the elements of ratiocination. The printer is not an illiterate, yet he prints such a construction as this. Why?"

Thus emboldened, I ventured again. "The lines contain some message which the woman – Miss Foster – could read."

"That is a trifle elementary, Parker," said Pons, a little more subdued. "I should have thought that anyone so familiar with and fond of Treasure Island could have read the message at once. At first glance."

"You flatter me," I said, with an edge of sarcasm I could not withhold.

"Not in the slightest," he said, adding generously, "You do certainly possess the intelligence, you are just not applying it. This is a simple hidden message – I should not call it a cipher, it is too elementary."

"I fail to see it."

"Let us just have a look at a copy of *Treasure Island*." So saying, he got up and found the book among the jumble on his shelves. He was turning to chapter eleven as he came back to his chair. "Ah, here is the first line. '"Dick," said Silver, "I trust you."' – but this hapless specimen has '"Faithless Dick"' – why?"

"Because 'faithless' was necessary to him," I said firmly.

"Then if that absurd construction in the fourth line was also necessary, and if, obviously, 'faithless' must then be the first word of any message this page conveys, the whole should be plain as a pikestaff."

He got up and put the Stevenson novel away again. Then he came to stand before me, lighting a pipe of the shag he smoked, and watching me struggle with the hidden message the page contained.

"A certain order must necessarily be imposed upon even the crudest concealed message," said Pons. "In this one it is precisely as mathematical – if not as intricate – as in one of His Majesty's secret codes. Have a go at it, Parker."

"I am studying it," I said.

"Let me point out again that we have two words – 'faithless' and 'will' – begin with them."

"Why must it be 'will'?" I asked. Why can it not be 'will have'?"

"One word at a time, Parker," said Pons with infinite patience. "'Faithless' is the first word, is it not?"

"You have said it must be, and it stands to reason that it is," I agreed.

"And it is in the first line."

"Elementary," I said.

"And 'will' is in the fourth line."

"And it is the fourth word," I said.

And there for a few moments – long enough to permit Pons to sigh and wonder with evident pity if all my teachers had so difficult a time with me – I stuck, and then, of course, it came to me. I had been searching for something more complex, but the simplicity of it deceived me. With "faithless" as the first word in the first line, and "will" the fourth word in the fourth line, I tried the second word in the second line and the third in the third and had "Faithless wretch I will" and from there went rapidly down the lines and read it aloud with a shout of triumph.

"*Faithless wretch, I will come for you all in good time*!"

"I congratulate you, Parker," said Pons. "A trifle slow, but you came through. Now then, who wrote it?"

"You have me there, Pons."

"Do not say so. A printer wrote it."

"I concede that a printer set it, but how do you know he wrote it?"

"Why, because he is an American."

"An American!" I cried. "Pons, you are making sport of me. That is a *non sequitur* if I ever heard one."

"My dear fellow, I try manfully to avoid *non sequiturs*. Would any Englishman have set 'valour' in that American fashion? – 'valor'? Not on your life. Even if an American had handed the copy in so, he would have spelled it 'valour'. So it follows that the American set it himself."

"With every day that passes, you amaze me more," I said, knowing how it would please him.

He bowed. "With so well grounded a beginning, you will do as well in no time at all."

"To say nothing of so good an instructor," I added.

But at this moment our little game was interrupted by the return of our client, too impatient to remain away for even an hour. I opened the door to his knock.

"Come in, come in, my dear Reverend Foster," cried Pons. "Pray be seated."

"I trust you have some information for me, Mr. Pons," said the clergyman, seating himself in the chair Pons thrust forward.

"I fear I may have some unpleasant news, sir," said Pons, taking his stand with one arm on the mantel. "It depends upon some intelligence you may be able to convey to me."

"If I can," said our client.

"It is about Miss Cordelia. Pray tell me, was she married?"

Our client's face expressed some dismay. "If so, I do not know of it."

"How was she occupied during her years in the United States?"

"She was employed in a printer's and stationer's shop in New York.

"And if not married, engaged in a liaison," said Pons.

The Reverend Foster's face flushed angrily.

Pons gave him no opportunity to speak. "One or the other, and she feared to tell you, knowing your restrictive views. She left the man—husband or lover—and returned to England. We do not know why. She may have had just cause. Now he has followed and found her and he has sent her this message."

"What message?"

"'Faithless wretch, I will come for you all in good time.' It has an ominous sound, sir. By its very nature, it suggests that some sort of bond exists between the sender and your niece. I submit that they were or are married. He means to frighten her and uses a simple code she must have known and apprehended instantly. See there – " He took the page from my hands as he spoke, and pointed out the words of the message " – how it is framed. For some reason, they used this code to communicate in earlier years. It may well have been a legitimate reason. I am not prepared to say."

Anger, bewilderment, disbelief – plainly our client was unwilling to entertain the thought that his niece had been involved with a man in any disreputable matter.

"This is, indeed, a matter for the police, Reverend Foster," said Pons quietly. "I suggest you repair to them without delay and ask them to find an American printer not long employed in London, in the area from which this message was posted. He will be a man very likely not over forty, one who cannot resist gloating, vain and perhaps ill-tempered, for only such a one would so taunt and frighten a woman."

Our client folded the page and thrust it back into its envelope, and this in turn he put into his pocket. He got up. "I will need to think of this for a while, Mr. Pons. I had better put it to my niece."

"Do not delay," warned Pons.

"Not such a man as would inspire confidence in a young woman," said Pons reflectively after he had gone. "One confined by a narrow view of the world. That poor woman must carry her burden alone."

9 January 1920

I watched Pons today as he read the paper. The process never varies.

He turns first to the political news, scans it briefly, then to news of the international scene. He reads this too, only cursorily.

But any account of a crime enlists his undivided attention.

He will sit tugging at the lobe of his left ear, long after he has read the account, his eyes staring right through the paper. Manifestly, he is turning the problem of the crime over in his mind.

Now and then he makes some comment at random about the "blindness" or the "stupidity" of the police.

More rarely, he commends them, with, "The police are not all fools, thank heaven!"

Having read the paper, he gets the scissors and cuts out any account of a crime that interests him and adds it to his voluminous scrapbook.

The paper is then discarded. He assumes invariably that I have already read it, whether or not it is so.

11 January 1920

A grim-faced Pons greeted me when I came in from my morning round today.

"Have you seen the paper?" he asked.

"I had an early confinement," I answered, shaking my head.

Without a word he passed the paper to me, folded so as to emphasize a few paragraphs under the heading, *Tragedy in Herts*.

"Westmill, Herts," I read. "Miss Cordelia Foster, niece of the Rev. Howard Foster, was seriously wounded last night by a mysterious gunshot, as she walked across the lawn toward the rectory. Her assailant was concealed behind a hedge that separated the lawn from a small formal garden.

"An American printer, Clarence Farwell, employed by Messrs. Godwin of London, W. 2, is being held. The American claims that Miss Foster is his wife, and that she deserted him. Miss Foster has denied his claim, stating that Mr. Farwell was previously married.

"Inquiries are under way."

"I was afraid that fellow Foster would do nothing," said Pons. "If he put it to her, she very probably denied it, and he accepted her denial at face value because he wished to do so, out of some desire to avoid a challenge to his concept of morality. A foolish man, whose pride has led to this."

14 January 1920

The Adventure of the Bookseller's Clerk. Pons called me over to the windows looking down into Praed Street this morning. "What do you make of that fellow?" he asked.

Below, on the kerb, stood an elderly man, clad in a foreign-looking fur cap, and a long coat, with a thick scarf wound around his neck and hanging out over his coat. Even through the light snow falling, I could see that his shoes were very definitely British. Moreover, they were wet.

"He has been walking for some distance," I said.

"Or some time," amended Pons. "In so light a snowfall it would of necessity be one or the other."

"At the moment he is studying 7B. I suppose he may be a client."

"I should think that likely."

"He looks like a countryman," I ventured.

"I think not," said Pons. "That is not a countryman's garb."

"He seems to be in no hurry."

"True. But at the same time he appears not to have shaved this morning; it is possible that he left home in some agitation."

"But it is almost noon. He couldn't have come directly here," I protested.

"He may be a shopkeeper who had to wait upon his assistant to arrive. Or he may have closed early for the noon hour. But see, he has decided to come in. We shall hear what he has to say."

In a few moments we heard his heavy tread on the stair, preceded by the lighter footfalls of Mrs. Johnson. And presently he stood on the threshold introducing himself.

"Mr. Pons? My name is Jason Brompton."

"A dealer in second-hand books," said Pons.

"I am, indeed. Perhaps you have been in my shop in Edgware Road."

"No, Mr. Brompton. The mustiness of old books is unmistakable. Pray sit down and tell me how I can be of assistance to you."

Mr. Brompton came forward and sat down somewhat stiffly near the fireplace where Pons stood with his back to the mantel, his hands in the pockets of his dressing-gown.

"Well, sir, it's an old man's fancies, I'm sure, but the fact is I'm troubled about my assistant, Dennis Golders. I very much fear he lives beyond his means – and I don't understand how he can do so. I knew him to be in poor circumstances when he applied for the position, and while I cannot pay him very much – times are difficult, Mr. Pons; one need not buy books, as I am sure you know – he has begun to spend far more on clothes than he earns. They are made for him, Mr. Pons, in Bond Street!"

He said this as if he were speaking of some personage far above his station.

"He may have come into a legacy."

"No, sir. I would certainly know it if he had."

"How long has he been with you?"

"Two years."

"His work is evidently satisfactory."

"Indeed, it is. I have no complaint."

"His accounts are in order?"

"Perfectly. My concern, I assure you, is for his welfare. I cannot rest until I learn how he comes by such means as to make it possible for him to live far beyond the scale even I can afford."

"How did he come to you?"

"He applied with the best references."

"From other booksellers?"

"Oh, no, sir. He had held various other positions – if I may say so – considerably better than the one for which he made application; but he professed to a love for books – and that is not uncommon in our trade, Mr. Pons, and, since my shop has a good clientele, and has been there for many years – you may have heard of Brompton's – he came with the intention of learning the business."

"Who referred him, Mr. Brompton?" pressed Pons.

"Lord Arthur Savile, for one."

Pons' eyebrows shot up; his eyes began to twinkle. "Indeed!" he said. "Who else?"

"Sir William Joynson-Hicks, H. G. Wells, and Lord Northcliffe."

Pons preserved an almost mask-like face. "I should very much like to see his references, Mr. Brompton."

Mr. Brompton's grizzled face broke into a broad smile. "I rather thought you would, Mr. Pons. I have them here."

He produced four letters from a letter-case in his pocket. Pons unfolded one after the other and read them. His face remained inscrutable. Presently he looked up.

"Mr. Golders is now at work?"

"Yes, Mr. Pons."

"How many other clerks do you employ, Mr. Brompton?"

"One who comes in evenings, when I have open hours. And a part-time clerk, when one or the other of us must be away."

"If you can arrange to remain away from the shop for an hour longer this noon, Dr. Parker and I will walk around to Brompton's."

"Oh, that is easily done, Mr. Pons. Mr. Golders – with uncommon thrift – always brings his own lunch, thus giving me a considerable latitude insofar as time is concerned. I have appreciated it."

"And if I may, I will retain these references for the time being."

Mr. Brompton looked a little dubious, but he assented readily enough.

"If you will step around this afternoon, I may possibly be able to satisfy your concern about Mr. Golders," said Pons. Once Mr. Brompton had taken his leave, Pons began to chuckle. His eyes now positively danced.

"Have you ever before encountered such bedfellows as those gentlemen who gave Mr. Dennis Golders references, Parker?" he asked.

"Well, they are impressive. I don't, though, know Sir William Joynson-Hicks."

Pons' laughter burst forth. "Your indifference to politics causes you to miss some considerable entertainment. That fellow Joynson-Hicks is quite possibly the most jingoistic, egotistic ass who ever brayed in the halls of any government in the world."

"But the others, of course, I know. Indeed, I have a signed *Tono-Bungay*."

Pons sobered once more. "By all means produce it."

"I have it in my trunk," I said, and got up to get it.

It was not without some pride of possession that I laid the book before Pons, open to Well's signature.

Pons unfolded Wells' letter of reference and laid it beside the autograph in *Tono-Bungay*.

"Identical," I said.

"Let us compare Northcliffe's signature," said Pons. "Any copy of the *Daily Mail* will do."

He found the paper and presently discovered the newspaper magnate's signature – the bold *Northcliffe* on the editorial page. "They are certainly the same," I admitted.

"And we may assume that Sir William Joynson-Hicks's signature is as genuine," said Pons. "But Lord Arthur Savile's is another matter entirely."

"You are more familiar with the peerage than I," I said. "The name means nothing to me."

"Lord Arthur Savile," said Pons, "is a character in a mediocre short story by Oscar Wilde. I daresay Mr. Dennis Golders is not entirely lacking a sense of humor."

"And Mr. Brompton is not as familiar with his stock in trade as he ought to be."

"Oh, I would not say so. It is just such a name as Mr. Brompton must certainly have heard, but, since it appears in a relatively trivial work of fiction, it is not such a one as he might readily relate to its source, and, coming upon it as the signature to a letter, might quite conceivably conclude that the writer was a peer of the realm."

"What cheek that fellow Golders must have!"

"If you can forego lunch, Parker, let us just walk around to Brompton's and have a few words with Mr. Golders."

"By all means!" I said.

But Pons was not quite ready. He fancied a disguise. He laboriously affixed sideboards, changed his clothes to rather severe garb, and clapped a pince-nez on a black ribbon to his nose and a bowler to his head.

"You look," I said, "like a private enquiry agent dressed up to resemble a businessman."

"That is close enough," said Pons. "Let us be off."

Mr. Dennis Golders was of rather shorter than average height. He was a blonde, well-built young man, alert and bright-eyed. When we entered Brompton's, he did not thrust himself upon us, but permitted us to browse among the shelves and bins of books. There were two other customers in the shop, but these presently bought books and departed.

Only then, seeing that we had not evidently found anything to our liking, did the clerk approach us.

"May I help you, sir?" he asked Pons, since it was plainly Pons who seemed to be in search of something.

"Thank you, I think not," answered Pons crisply.

"You are obviously a bibliophile," said Golders.

"Ah, is it so patent?"

"If I may say so. You must, then, have favorite authors."

"Hardy, Keats, Byron, Shelley, Dickens, Meredith." Pons rattled these names off with a professional air.

"I may have something for you, sir," pursued Golders. "But it will come rather dear."

Pons's eyes narrowed. "Price is no object," he said, though his attitude belied it.

"Let me show it to you."

Golders plunged into the rear of the shop where, reaching behind shelves of books which were separated from the wall of the shop by a counter, he drew forth a book which he handed to Pons.

I saw that it was Dickens's *Nicholas Nickleby* in fair condition.

Pons glanced at Golders rather than at the book. "A first edition?" he hazarded.

"No, sir. But it will cost four pounds just the same."

"Four pounds!" cried Pons.

"Please open it to the flyleaf, sir."

Pons did so.

Disclosed on the flyleaf was the autograph of Charles Dickens, with a line of greeting and the date.

"Aha!" murmured Pons. "Indeed, I do want this. Four pounds is a trifle clear, as you say – but a signed Dickens!"

He handed the book back to Golders to be wrapped, while he himself took four pound notes from his pocket and laid them on the counter.

"Do you by any chance have anything more like this?" asked Pons.

There was the barest hesitation in Golders's businesslike wrapping of *Nicholas Nickleby*. Then he resumed, as he said, "These items are not commonly come upon, sir. Once in a great while we buy a library with such a treasure among the books, but it is not a frequent occurrence. You might look in again. Of course, some modern authors like Hardy and Conrad are more readily found in signed copies, but Dickens is less readily discovered."

"But this is surely not the only signed book on the premises," persisted Pons.

"Well, no, it isn't," admitted Golders.

"Then, if you have another, let me see it," demanded Pons impatiently.

Having completed his parcel, the clerk reached behind the same shelf of books and came out with another.

This time it was H. G. Wells's *The First Men in the Moon*, the Newnes edition of 1901. It bore but a simple, undated signature.

"How much?" asked Pons.

Golders seemed visibly to take Pons's measure. "I realize Wells may not be one of your favorites, sir, but there are those who collect him. Two pounds six."

Pons paid it with no more than a grimace.

"If you are interested in stopping in from time to time – preferably at this hour, sir," said Golders, as we went out, "I may have other such treasures for you to examine."

"Extraordinary luck!" I said, as we walked along Edgware Road toward Praed Street. "That you should be able to acquire two such signed books!"

"You did not think it unusual?"

"No. Many such treasures are in fact lost in private libraries. Only the owner knows they are there. Once the owner dies, however, it is another matter, for in many cases his heirs are not aware of everything on the shelves. That is particularly true if the library is a large one. Thus, it is eminently possible for a dealer like Brompton – who buys up entire libraries to keep stock on his shelves – to get hold of such books at a very reasonable price and make a fair profit. Though these did seem to me more dear than the average."

"Well, let us just have a closer look at them when we have them home," said Pons, and would say no more.

Once back in our quarters, Pons compared the signature in the Wells he had bought with that in my *Tono-Bungay*. He scrutinized them under a magnifying glass. I did the same. There was no significant difference between them, save that the one in the book he had just bought seemed to be an older signature in that the letters were slightly larger than the signature in my book, and they had clearly been written with different pens.

"Would you say they were written by the same man?" asked Pons.

"I would indeed."

Pons turned next to the Dickens. He examined it thoroughly, from the front matter to the rear of the book. Then he handed it to me with the adjuration, "Pray examine the inside of the front cover, Parker."

"It is blank," I said.

"Say not so. Look again."

I studied it with care. It was somewhat stained, as by age and exposure, and the edges were rubbed.

"Does it not seem to you that an erasure has been made in the upper left corner?" asked Pons.

"The original price seems to have been removed," I said at last, detecting the area of the erasure.

"And what does it seem to you that price was?"

"Two and six."

"Two shillings sixpence," repeated Pons. "For a book signed by Dickens?"

"Obviously the book was so priced before the signature was discovered," I said.

"It may be so. We shall just wait upon Mr. Brompton to tell us."

So saying, he retired behind the morning newspaper.

Our client returned at two o'clock. He had had his lunch and he was now eager to return to his shop.

"I have been away far too long, Mr. Pons," he said, a little breathless from the exertion of climbing the stairs to our quarters.

"I fancy young Mr. Golders will not take it amiss," said Pons.

"He is a model of propriety," said Brompton. "But I hope you may have something to tell me of his means."

Without a word Pons put before him the signed copy of *Nicholas Nickleby*.

Brompton picked it up and turned it round in his hands. "Ah, you bought this in my shop. Two and six. But surely you don't want it. You must let me reimburse you."

"Four pounds," said Pons.

Our client dropped the book as if it had turned to hot coal in his hands. "Not in my shop!" he cried.

"But indeed." Pons bent, picked up the book, and thrust it again at Brompton. "Pray look at the flyleaf."

Brompton did so. His eyes bulged. His mouth fell open. He was manifestly astounded.

His hands trembling, he laid the book carefully down on the table. He took a deep, gulping breath before he spoke.

"Mr. Pons, I had no such book in my shop."

Pons bent again, flipped back the cover, and pointed to the spot where the original price had been erased.

"Look there, Mr. Brompton. The indentation is clear enough. Was that in your hand?"

"It seems to be my script," said Brompton. He leaned back in his chair. "But I cannot understand it. It is seldom indeed that a signed book comes into the shop."

"Do you to your knowledge have any signed books?"

"Well, yes, I have a Machen and a de la Mare. I had a Hardy, but Mr. Golders sold it and at a good price."

"Duly entered?"

"Yes, sir. I know my stock, and the entry was proper."

"You have not had a signed Wells?"

"No, Mr. Pons."

"Like this?" Pons produced *The First Men in the Moon*.

"That looks like the book I had in stock. Not signed, of course. One and six."

Once again Pons opened the book, revealing the signature.

Our client grew pale, then flushed redly.

"I submit, Mr. Brompton, that if you now return to your shop you will find these sales entered – *Nicholas Nickleby* at two and six, *The First Men in the Moon* at one and six. The difference between those prices and four pounds for the Dickens, and two pounds six shillings for the Wells has gone into Mr. Golders's pocket. I submit further that it is by just such sales that Mr. Golders has been able to improve his standard of living over quite some time. Mr. Golders seems to have a considerable knowledge of graphology."

"That is forgery, Mr. Pons. I shall discharge him at once," cried Brompton, coming to his feet, swelling with indignation and purpose.

"Do not be too hasty, Mr. Brompton," said Pons. "Mr. Golders is apparently content to live on but a small measure of illegal gain, and out of some considerable talent and ingenuity."

"I shall give him in charge," said Mr. Brompton angrily. "But first – let me reimburse you." He reached for his pocket.

Pons stayed his hand. "Let me persuade Mr. Golders to reimburse me instead," he said. "When you return to the shop, wrap up a book – any book – and ask Mr. Golders to step around here after work to deliver it."

"If you say so, Mr. Pons. But I cannot continue to employ him."

"Let me just talk to him first."

Mr. Brompton assented, but unwillingly. "I have been taken in – and I cannot undertake to estimate how many of my customers may have been swindled."

He was still muttering angrily when he departed.

"I rather think Mr. Brompton is more angry at having been deceived than at discovering that some of his customers may have been mulcted of small sums," observed Pons.

Late that afternoon, Mr. Dennis Golders knocked.

Pons threw open the door and invited him in. Golders did not immediately see me, and, since Pons had removed his disguise, he did not recognize him.

"I am delivering a book from Brompton's," said he.

"Come in, Mr. Golders, come in," said Pons.

As soon as Golders had taken a few steps into our quarters, Pons closed the door and stood with his back against it.

At the same moment Golders caught sight of me. He started guiltily, but quickly composed himself.

"Those books on the table are yours, are they not, Mr. Golders?" asked Pons.

Golder's eyes dropped to the signed books Pons had left lying out.

"No, sir. They are yours," said Golders, his equanimity restored. "You bought them this noon. I recognize your voice now even without sideboards, bowler and eyeglasses."

Pons chuckled. "Pray sit down, Mr. Golders."

Golders did so, alert but unafraid.

Pons came away from the door. "You have a considerable talent in forgery, Mr. Golders."

"Can you prove it, sir?" asked Golders.

"Yes, yes – if need be, easily," said Pons. "But I am not interested in proving it."

"The return of your money then," said Golders. "And, of course, I will take along the books again."

"I think not," said Pons. "Tell me, Mr. Golders, have you ever thought of turning that remarkable talent of yours to honest accounting?"

Golders looked at Pons calculatingly. "You are sure you have something 'honest' in mind?"

Pons shook his head disapprovingly. "Ah, you are already challenging the honesty of everyone else on the basis of your temporary lack – I say 'temporary' hopefully."

"Is there an honest way?"

"I believe there is –and there may even be occasion in it for such flights of your fancy as the forging of Lord Arthur Savile's signature."

Golders grinned. "And at a decent salary?"

"Quite sufficient for the style to which you have become accustomed, Mr. Golders. Are you willing to try it?"

"I am, sir."

"I have written a note to my brother who is in the Foreign Office. There is a constant need for the services of someone with your uncommon skill in the cryptology department. Take it around there tomorrow, for your place at Brompton's has clearly become untenable."

"There is an alternative?"

"Indeed, yes. Mr. Brompton is ready to give you in charge. And I have these books against that contingency. I trust it will never be necessary to use them. Such skill ought to be put to good use."

Golders began to laugh. "Forging letters and signatures of diplomats, couriers, intelligence agents, eh?" he said. "I never thought of it. It is still forgery, though, however you look at it. I suppose it all depends upon one's point-of-view, Mr. Pons."

"As does all life, Mr. Golders," said Pons. "Good luck!"

Golders took his leave as jauntily as if he had not a care in the world.

23 January, 1920

Pons announced today that his brother Bancroft had secured a provisional place in the Intelligence Division of the Admiralty for Dennis Golders, the bookseller's clerk who proved so adept at forging the names of an astonishing variety of gentlemen.

I could not keep from chaffing him a bit, for I had had some reservations about his course of action in regard to Golders.

"Surely that is a kind of rehabilitation," I said.

"I daresay it may be so looked upon," answered Pons.

"Do I not detect a certain inconsistency here?" I asked.

He shot a sharp glance in my direction. "'A foolish consistency,'" he began to quote Emerson, but I interrupted him.

"... is the hobgoblin of little minds.' Yes, I know. But let me quote another eminent authority – 'Rehabilitation is fine in theory, but let us have punishment first.' By courtesy of Mr. Solar Pons."

Pons laughed heartily. "I fear you have me there. But does not that depend upon the nature of the crime?"

"You have not said so," I said. "As I recall it, you did not discriminate at all."

"The nature of the crime in the previous instance was a considerable fraud," said Pons. "I am sure that Golders can be prevailed upon to reimburse his victims. But there is a fine point here I rather think you have not taken into consideration."

"In other words," I put in caustically, "when it comes to punishment, there is all the difference in the world between a large fraud and a little one?"

"There is not the slightest difference in fact, but only in degree, and the difference in degree affects only the degree of punishment."

"But Golders is not being punished, as far as I can see."

Pons chuckled. "I had no idea you felt even more strongly than I about this matter," he said. "If it will ease your mind – or your conscience, whichever it is – Bancroft has had some long conversations with Golders. Golders is perfectly willing to reimburse the purchasers of his forgeries out of his salary. But, quite apart from the fact that he cannot remember all of them, there is that fine point you have not considered."

"Pray enlighten me," I said.

"Why, it is simply the attitude of the purchasers. I submit that not one in ten would appreciate being told he did not own, in fact, a signed copy of a book he treasures. Far rather ignorance than repayment! Collectors are a curious lot – and book collectors are in many ways the most curious of them all."

"But what if one of them discovers the fraud and demands his money back from Brompton?"

"Why, then, Brompton will reimburse him – and Golders will reimburse Brompton."

"And as for the others?"

"They have simply paid for the happiness of possessing a forged signature they do not recognize as a forgery. Their lack of knowledge does not in any way affect their happiness in its possession. I know, Parker, in the interests of propriety, you would disillusion them. But to what end? It would not satisfy them, it would in fact leave them, I submit, far more unhappy than they are in their possession of their elaborate forgeries, which, actually, are so well done, as to make each of these books an 'item' in itself in the world of collectors."

"Nevertheless," I said, but subsided into silence, not quite convinced, and feeling obscurely certain that Pons had not given an inch.

"I understand, Parker," said Pons with unaccustomed gentleness. "We would all like our world composed of black and white or right and wrong, but unfortunately matters are not as simple as all that. Would that they were! But if they were, how infernally dull life would be!"

27 January, 1920

Coming in from attendance on a patient this evening, I found Pons absorbed in his crime files. Clippings from the newspapers, tearsheets from magazines and books, and photographs of criminals lay upon and all around the table – a veritable encyclopedia of crime.

As I entered, he glanced at me through the smoke wreathing about him from his pipe. "Ah, I see by your almost fatuous expression that Mr. Simpkins is making a satisfactory recovery," he said.

I acknowledged that my patient was indeed improving and, having divested myself of my greatcoat – for the wind howled outside, and snow was in the air – I went around to look at what engaged his interest at the moment. He held in his hand an account of the death of Edwin Bartlett in Pimlico in 1886, for which his wife Adelaide had been charged with murder – and acquitted.

"Did she do it?" I asked.

"I think it likely. She was enamoured of the Reverend George Dyson, a young minister who was foolish enough to write poems to her – if one could call them poems. Listen to this bit of doggerel – " He quoted from the account of the trial at the Old Bailey.

> "'Who is it that hath burst the door
> Unclosed the heart that shut before
> And set her queenlike on its throne
> And made its homage all her own – My Birdie.'

"'My Birdie,' indeed! There are manifestly some unhappy human beings for whom the simulation of love is a disease."

"You are being cynical, Pons," I said.

"The follies committed for the sake of what some people call 'love' are positively incredible," reflected Pons, not without a certain relish. "And the domain of crime offers innumerable examples."

"Well, it is certain that Bartlett could hardly have swallowed a bottle of chloroform without extreme agony – it would have seared its way to his stomach."

"Yet somehow it got there," said Pons. "As one learned medical man remarked after the trial – 'Now she's acquitted, she should tell us, in the interests of science, how she did it.'"

He put down the Bartlett account and took up another.

"And no area of human activity so aptly demonstrates the mawkish gullibility and stupidity of the innocent," Pons went on. "As an example, consider the case of Bruneau, the priest, who led a career of crime from the age of thirteen onward and, though caught stealing even in the seminary, was nevertheless ordained in the same year that Edwin Bartlett came to his end, and continued in his career of theft, robbery, fraud, arson, and lechery until it culminated in the murder of his superior, the Abbé Fricot, whom he battered about the head before pushing him into the rectory garden well to die. He was duly executed at Laval in 1894 – but after his burial some pious fools fostered a legend that Fricot had been murdered by a woman caught in theft, who had subsequently confessed her crime to Bruneau and so sealed his lips – a tale so ridiculous and so utterly without foundation that one would have to be somewhat less than a moron to credit it; yet hundreds of people were gullible enough to believe it – people have a positive horror of the obvious – and Bruneau was held to be a saint and a martyr. Indeed, some imbeciles actually brought sick children to Bruneau's grave in the hope that the 'sacred' earth above the body of this murderer, who was without a single redeeming feature, might heal them!"

"Does it give you pleasure to read about these crimes?" I asked. "I have seen you at these files quite often."

Pons raised his eyebrows. "That has the sound of a clinical question, Parker."

"No, no, I am only curious," I protested.

"Let us just say then that I find these accounts instructive."

"In what way?"

"Why, in reaffirming my low opinion of the rationality of the average individual, criminal or otherwise – or my alternatively dim view or high regard for the blundering or, on the other hand, the efficiency of the police – or my admiration for a crime well conceived and well investigated. Will that satisfy your curiosity, clinical or otherwise?"

I assured him that it adequately answered my inquiry.

"Though it is true that the average crime is without imagination," Pons continued, "there are those that offer some interesting points. Consider the infinite trouble to which the pathetic Dr. Hawley Crippen went in order to indulge his passion for Ethel Le Neve! This was, incidentally, one of the earliest cases in which Spilsbury shone as medical examiner."

"Was it not also the first case of a British murderer's having been apprehended in America by dint of the police taking a faster boat?"

"No, no, that is a common misconception. It seems to have been the first time the wireless was used to apprehend a murderer. But Franz Muller, the first known train murderer – he killed Thomas Briggs in a train between Bow and Hackney Wick in the summer of 1864 and threw the body out on to the line – was apprehended as he stepped from the *Victoria* in New York, Tanner, the detective, having taken the faster ship, *City of Manchester*."

He dropped the clipping and picked up a magazine account. "Now here is a classic American case – a miscarriage of justice – that of Lizzie Borden, who was acquitted of murdering her father and stepmother in Fall River, Massachusetts, on a hot day in August, 1892."

"I know the case," I said.

"I find the doggerel written about Lizzie much more to my fancy than set down by the Reverend Dyson for Adelaide Bartlett –

'Lizzie Borden took an axe,
And gave her mother forty whacks.
When she saw what she had done,
She gave her father forty-one.'

– And much more appropriate, too."

"You have no doubt of her guilt?"

"None. She alone had motive and opportunity. All other theories are the most elaborate fabrications, a testimony rather to the lubricity and wilful imagination of their authors, than to the inescapable facts of the matter. It is another incidence of people refusing to accept the obvious; for some reason they are infected by chronic doubt of what seems to them too simple, too straightforward; they prefer something more devious, more romantically sinister. The lunatic antics of the irrational skeptics in such cases are not without amusement. – But enough. I have had my fill of this entertainment for this evening."

As he gathered up the clippings and cuttings, he added reflectively, "Still and all, I suppose there is no domain of human behavior that so well illustrates the complex nature of man as that borderland in which he is impelled toward murder."

1 February 1920

"I am always inclined to be dubious about the testimony of 'experts'," said Solar Pons today, looking up from a sheaf of clippings in one of his files. "The Small wife-killing is a case in point."

"Small?" I said. "I don't recall it."

"I should have thought you might. It took place, I believe, when you were in the States – at Lake Ossipee, Massachusetts, in 1916. Frederick Small went to some trouble to murder his wife, Arlene – he chloroformed and battered her, then strangled her and, to make very sure of her death, shot her. After that he put together an ingenious machine involving a kerosene tin with cog-wheels, springs, and an alarm-clock attachment to set fire to their home on the shore of the lake while he was in Boston watching a film, with witnesses thinking to destroy the evidence of murder. The prosecution produced the "arson machine" which enabled him to set a timed fire."

"And the experts?"

"Defense called in a college professor who made light of the machine and ridiculed the idea," said Pons.

"Would that not have been the logical defense?" I asked.

Pons chuckled. "Except for the fact that the prosecution answered by bringing into court a mechanic who made such an "arson machine" on the spot and demonstrated it. Small was convicted and sentenced to death. I do not recall reading in any of these accounts pertinent to the case any record of the 'expert's' chagrin."

3 February 1920

When I came in from a patient's bedside this afternoon, I found Pons at his microscope. He was examining a trio of hairs.

"Human?" I asked.

"That is elementary." he replied. "Jamison brought them in an hour ago. I find it instructive to reflect upon the countless clues afforded by even the most apparently insignificant detail. What do you make of these?"

He moved to give his place to me.

I peered for some moments at the hairs on the slide. "They came from a man who is beginning to grey," I said finally.

"Capital!" cried Pons. "Young, middle aged, or old?"

"I don't see how that can be told," I said, I fear, somewhat testily.

"Let us just say early middle age," retorted Pons confidently. "Observe in the medullary substances numbers of jet black pigmentary cells. We can conclude therefore that these hairs came from a man who is very probably just moving into his middle years. What else?"

"I see nothing more."

"Come, come, Parker. It is plain as a pikestaff that he has recently had his hair cut. Observe the sharp ends. More, he is balding – you can see that the roots of the hairs are wasted. Further, the hairs carry mamillary prominences in the epithelial parts, undoubtedly because of perspiration, so that we may venture to say he is rather heavier than his height and age warrant."

"You *know* the subject," I accused him.

"Not at all. I have no more than these hairs to use as evidence. Hair is likely to be extremely informative – it will disclose the approximate age of a decomposing corpse, the constitution of a dead man, whether he has been poisoned and by what substance if it is deposited in the hair. In this case further tests are hardly necessary; I could subject the hairs to a solution of caustic potash to fix the age of the subject a trifle more firmly, but it is hardly necessary. The hair of children dissolves at once in such a solution; that of older subjects resists the action of the solution sometimes for hours in direct proportion to the subject's age. However, the primary importance of hair in cases of capital crime lies in the fact that it does not decompose for a long time, and thus retains what may be important information for the investigator. But that is Spilsbury's department, not mine – and I fancy Jamison is only having a little sport with me during Spilsbury's absence on holiday."

5 February 1920

As we walked in Edgware Road this morning, Pons called my attention to a man of middle age obviously waiting for a bus. He was stockily built, beginning to gray, and wore a short, cropped beard.

"Occupation?" asked Pons.

"Certainly not professional," I ventured.

"What then?"

"Clearly some kind of day-laborer. He is on his way to work."

"Ah," said Pons, "but what kind of work?"

"His hands are rough. There are knuckle calluses on his left hand, thickest on the carpometacarpal knuckles of the middle and ring fingers."

"Capital!" said Pons. "You are learning to observe. Now I fancy you can tell me why there are no such calluses on his right hand."

I threw up my hands. "You're asking too much!"

"I think not. It is easy to see that the fellow is engaged in some sort of work that involves leaning on his fisted left hand while he works with his right. What manner of work might that be if not landscape gardening? He is a landscape gardener."

6 February 1920

Inspector Jamison came by late today.

"You've had time to look at those hairs I left with you?" he asked, settling himself and lighting his pipe. "We've made an arrest in the case."

"A man in early middle-age, balding, overweight; he has had his hair cut within the past week."

Jamison smiled. "You've come a cropper this time, Pons. Our man is underweight, if anything, lean, not more than thirty, and with a good head of hair. How do you explain the discrepancy?"

"We are talking about two different men," said Pons curtly. "You didn't say – was it a capital crime?"

"Murder."

"Did the hairs come from the victim or the suspect?"

"The suspect. They were found in the murdered man's hand."

"Ah, then the explanation is simple. You've arrested the wrong man."

9 February 1920

A police car drew up at the kerb where Pons and I walked this morning. Inspector Jamison looked out.

"Care to come along on a little matter?" he asked. "Theft."

"One can never tell what the day may bring," said Pons dryly.

We got into the car with Jamison and rode to the house of Mrs. Marcy Folwell in St. John's Wood.

An attractive young blonde woman met us at the door and, immediately on Jamison's introducing himself, began talking.

"Nobody could have got in," she said. "Nobody. I was in and out of the room all the time. The jewels were in a small soft leather case. I'd taken it out of the wall safe to select jewelry for a party last night. I didn't put the case back, but I thought I'd done so – so I didn't miss it until this morning."

"When did you last see it?" asked Jamison.

"At about nine o'clock last night."

"And when did you miss it?"

"As I went out. I was in a hurry. I looked over there –" she had now led us into her boudoir and was pointing to the edge of the dressing-table – "and saw that the case was gone. I thought I'd put it back – it's the kind of thing you do without thinking about it."

"Its contents were valuable?"

"Inspector, the jewels are worth at least four thousand pounds," she said impatiently.

"No sign of entry, I take it," said Jamison.

"None. I did have the window open briefly but, as you see, the dressing-table is beyond the reach of anyone outside. I shut it perhaps half an hour after I opened it."

"And when was that?"

"Twenty minutes past nine."

"Did you see the jewel case at that time?"

"I can't honestly say. I don't recall looking that way."

Pons, meanwhile, was gazing around in his customary manner. He dropped to his knees at the window and looked intently at the sill. A fine film of dust lay there. If he hoped to find prints of any kind, he could clearly abandon that hope. There was nothing to be seen in the dust except a rough line, as if a string or wire had been laid across it, and its outlines blurred.

Pons raised the window and climbed out.

"Who is that man, Inspector?" asked Mrs. Folwell, a trifle indignantly.

"One of our assistants," said Jamison blandly.

I leaned out the window and watched Pons.

He was busy measuring what I assumed was a footprint. As I watched, he ventured farther out, into the street, where he walked carefully up and down on both sides of the road, pausing in one spot to look back toward the house he had quitted. Presently he retraced his steps and climbed back into the room, shutting the window behind him.

"What it looks like," Jamison was saying, "is somebody catching sight of that jewel box and taking it when you were out of the room. He could have got in through the window."

"No evidence, no evidence," said Pons crisply. He turned to Mrs. Folwell. "You live alone?"

"I have a maid by day," she answered. "She doesn't live in.

"I observe you wear a wedding band."

She tossed her head back scornfully. "I divorced that little runt four months ago. It cost him a good deal, too. Always running after gypsies the way he did! Fancying himself writing a book about them."

"Ah, he was a writer?"

"A journalist."

"Albert Folwell," said Pons. "I've seen his byline. Tell me, Mrs. Folwell, during the interval between your taking out the jewel box and your discovery that it was missing, did you hear any uncommon noise?"

"I can't say that I did."

"Like something falling, for example? A ball bouncing? Anything of that sort?"

"No."

She seemed to resent Pons's questions. I put her down as something of a termagant. Her ex-husband very likely was well rid of her.

"Well, Madam, we'll look into it," promised Jamison.

Back in the car, Pons asked Jamison, somewhat laconically, "Do you want to recover the jewels?"

"Ah," answered Jamison, not without sarcasm, "you know where they are!"

"'Know' isn't the word," said Pons, with unaccustomed modesty. "But I fancy you could turn them up if you liked."

"It's my job," said Jamison sententiously.

"Someone's spent quite some time watching the house," said Pons. "There are cigarette butts across the street from the boudoir side. A light man, small of foot. His prints outside the window are clear. Short of stature too, I daresay. He's been standing there for more than one night, for the butts are varied in age. Last night he had the opportunity to take the jewel case."

"So he came over, opened the door, and walked in while Mrs. Folwell was taking a shower or something of that kind," said Jamison heavily.

"A lady hardly selects the jewelry she means to wear before taking her bath," said Pons. "No, he put to good use something he learned from his associates. He flung through the open window a leaden ball into which four fishhooks had been set, hooked the case, and pulled it out of the room – to where he could reach it handily through the window. It was done in a matter of seconds, and the heavy carpet prevented any but the softest sound. The mark of the cord is on the sill."

"Hooks in a lead ball!" exclaimed Jamison. "That's as farfetched a theory as I've ever heard from you, Pons."

Pons smiled. "It's a gypsy throwing weapon often used for grappling loot capable of being hooked."

"Gypsies? Wasn't her ex-husband studying gypsies?"

"A 'little runt', she called him," said Pons reflectively. "And divorcing her, she boasted, cost him 'a good deal.' I daresay in taking the jewels – most of which he had probably given her – he was getting back some of his own. It may be incapable of proof if you don't turn up the jewels. I hope it is. Women like Mrs. Folwell are consciously predatory. Pray forgive me if I fail to wish you luck."

11 February 1920

Pons tossed in my direction today a marked copy of the *News of the World*.

"Inspector Jamison's Deductions Score Again," I read. "After releasing a suspect in the case of Richard Wexler, found to have been murdered, Inspector Seymour Jamison arrested another yesterday. The arrest followed upon some astute deductions made after a close, microscopic examination of what were believed to be hairs from the head of the murderer found on the scene..."

"Such are the fruits of perseverance," observed Pons dryly, his eyes dancing.

15 February 1920

In Paddington Station this morning Pons drew my attention to a laborer, both of whose hands were badly callused – and not alone callused. The worst dermatoses appeared along the forefinger, but were present on all the fingers, along the palm down from the forefinger and on the thumb.

"What do you make of that fellow?" he asked.

"Why, he is obviously engaged in some occupation that calluses his hands."

"Nothing more? Are not some of those calluses raised and the area around them inflamed?"

"Yes, that's so," I agreed.

"This suggests nothing about the nature of his occupation?"

"Well, his calluses some of them appear to rise above blisters. So he works with something hot. Perhaps iron."

"Capital! Capital!" exclaimed Pons, as our subject moved to board a train. "Now carry on."

"His occupation could thus be one of a number," I said defensively.

"I think not. I submit he is a glass-gatherer in a glass factory. His calluses are typical of those made by the heat of the gathering iron. The blisters beneath the calluses are distinctive."

17 February 1920

Inspector Jamison came in this afternoon, his face aglow with satisfaction. He carried a well-wrapped parcel which he laid before Pons.

"Take a look at that, Pons," he said triumphantly. "We've been looking for it a long time."

Pons carefully unwrapped the parcel, revealing an old book. "*Wiener Kinderlieder*," he murmured. "Printed in 1437."

"Stolen from Baron Edouard Larbeau's collection six months ago. It turned up at Sotheby's."

Pons was examining the rare volume with sober attention, his keen eyes narrowed. "You took the thief?" he asked, looking up.

"Unfortunately, no. We turned up the book in a lot bought by Sotheby's for auction. It was only one of Larbeau's books to be stolen and it came in without being detected at first. Of course, they'd had word from us to be on the watch for it. So we were called – traced the seller but our bird had flown. Two others of the missing books were in his quarters. This book, though, was the most valuable and the one Larbeau wanted above all."

"A pity," said Pons crisply. "I fancy Baron Larbeau will not be entirely pleased."

"Oh, as to that," said Jamison, "it's the book he wants – not the thief. Though we'd sooner have had the thief."

"I rather think that the book is not quite in the same condition it was when it was stolen," said Pons dryly.

Apprehension flickered in Jamison's eyes. "What do you mean?"

"Why, it has been taken apart and rebound," said Pons. "Quite skilfully, too. Clearly not the work of an amateur."

"What would anyone want to do that for?" demanded Jamison with the kind of truculence that hid his disbelief.

"Many of the forms of these old volumes were enclosed in parchment, which frequently bore inscriptions of more value to today's collector than the books themselves. The bands of this book have been recently removed and the book rebound. A highly professional piece of work. Small wonder it was turned in."

Crestfallen, Jamison muttered, "Larbeau may not notice it."

"I daresay he could not help doing so," said Pons. "Depend on it. Collectors are immediately aware of such details, however trivial they may seem to you or to me."

18 February 1920

Pons on the Stupidities of Forgers. "Some forgers are incredibly skillful, yet often overlook some inconsequential detail inconsequential, that is, to them. Latouche, a forger in the early decades of the last century, once prepared a fraudulent document dated to the fourth century. He used parchment which had been gnawed by mice, leaving a patently identifiable hole. On the initial page of the document, Latouche broke a word at the left edge of the mousehole, and carried on with it on the right, suggesting that the parchment had been so damaged when the document had been prepared; but on the second page he stupidly omitted a portion of the word between the edges of the mousehole, as had the recreant mouse gnawed it away. Manifestly, then, if there had been a hole in the parchment when the first page of the document had been prepared, but none when the second was done, the fraudulence of the document was clearly established.

"In many cases a simple lack of knowledge betrays the forger – the use of ink or paper not yet invented at the time the work was purportedly dated – the making of erasures, which can always be detected either by chemical analysis or the use of ultraviolet light, the so-called 'black light' the misspelling of words by one presumably too educated to have been guilty of such errors the use of documentary stamps not yet in use at the dating of the document in question, most commonly here in England the use of a King's head stamp on documents executed during the reign of our late Queen – such stamps, of course, being not then in existence. You will find many similar stupidities set down in Gross, Lucas and other authorities in the domain of criminal investigation."

21 February 1920

In the course of a visit to 7B today Inspector Jamison remarked that the police had at last captured a member of a "smash and grab" gang that had operated successfully for several months. The captive was a girl of seventeen.

A flicker of interest shone in Pons's eyes. "Does it not seem unlikely that so young a girl would be a member of a professional gang of criminals?" he asked.

"Oh, the criminal classes make no differentiation among the ages or sexes," Jamison answered ponderously. "She claims she was hired to do it – a likely story! She sticks to it though, and she's belligerent about it."

"Let us just have a brief resume of the case," suggested Pons.

"It happened at Carville's Jewelers two days ago. An ordinarily clever operation. The thieves came in – three young men, two together, the other separate. The girl, Cicely Evans, was there when they came in, just looking around. Of a sudden she fell to the floor in a faint or some sort of spell, and when Carville and one of his lady clerks came around the counters, the thieves acted. They'd had time to locate the gems they wanted, broke the cases, scooped them up, ran to a car outside and got away. They had a Daimler with a chauffeur waiting. It went so fast no one got the number. Carville was suspicious of the girl, and detained her until the police came. They had a doctor examine her. Nothing could be found wrong – though of course fainting doesn't show much in the way of physical symptoms. They put her through it until she finally confessed with the story."

"How was she 'hired,' as you put it? Did she explain that?"

"Oh, yes she had a ready explanation. She was sent out the evening before to get something, a package of cigars at a shop a few blocks from her home," said Jamison. "When she got near to the house on her way back, a woman got out of a car that stood across the street, crossed over, and offered her ten pounds to be at the store at that hour of the morning, and when the three young men were in it, to give them a little time to look around, and then to faint. She did it."

"Telling no one?"

"Oh, she said she talked it over with her uncle and aunt. She lives with them. Her parents live in Surrey. They didn't get along. Her uncle and aunt are a ruddy couple. They didn't seem to think there was any harm in making ten pounds that easily. But they claim the girl's always been a problem – stubborn, fiery of temper, hard to get along with."

Pons sat for a few moments in thoughtful silence.

"There's no reason to accept her story," said Jamison defensively.

"Let us just examine it," said Pons. "She was sent out for cigars. When she returned, the woman in the car was waiting for her?"

"So she says. Highly unlikely."

"I submit that in matters of this kind one is faced with one of two alternatives only either the story is true, or it is not true. You have subscribed to the latter alternative. Let us suppose, however, that the Evans girl is telling the truth. Has she given any description of the woman?"

"Only such a one as would fit roughly two hundred thousand women in London," said Jamison grudgingly. "She had answers for us when she made up her mind to give them."

"It does not occur to you that if the woman and the car were there, someone must have known that the girl was coming along?"

"If the woman and the car existed, yes."

"You've asked her to name her accomplices?"

"We've been all through that," said Jamison impatiently. "She claims she doesn't know them. Or to put it plainly she won't talk about them."

"Let us accept for the nonce the statements she has made." Jamison shifted uneasily in his chair. "How could that alter the fact that she did fake that spell to distract Carville and his clerks?"

"It doesn't. She hasn't denied that. In any case, there were witnesses."

"She made no attempt to escape?"

"Oh, yes. She panicked. But she was restrained by Carville." Jamison got up abruptly. "There's no use in this fiddling, Pons. She's in it, no denying it. And we'll get her accomplices."

"I fancy she has none," said Pons. He sat now with his eyes closed, his fingers tented. "I put it to you, Jamison, you are looking in the wrong quarter. If the girl was being waited for, then someone in that car must have known that she was going to the shop and returning at that hour, someone who was acquainted perhaps in league with the gang." Pons's eyes opened; they were dancing. "Change your tactics and put her uncle through it, Jamison. I think it extremely likely that he will be able to give you the names of the accomplices, if he will."

23 February 1920

Pons put down the *News of the World* this evening with a melancholy chuckle. "A pharmacist has been hospitalized suffering from accidental arsenical poisoning," he said. "A pharmacist of almost thirty years" experience. Does that sound logical to you, Parker?"

"Hardly. A pharmacist of little experience might somehow contrive to give himself enough arsenic to make himself ill, but one of as much experience as this fellow would never be able to do it unless he were bent on suicide – and if that, he would have at his fingertips many more lethal and quick-acting poisons. He would hardly resort to arsenic, when a little cyanide would do the job rapidly."

"His story does not seem to have been questioned by the examining physician," continued Pons. "Yet it is plain as a pikestaff that his sister was poisoning him for the sake of such small inheritance as might come her way."

"How can you say so?"

"The facts are only too clear. This fellow lived with his sister. He went nowhere, and ate all his meals at home. During the noon hour his sister took his place in the pharmacy, so that he could come home to eat the meal she had prepared for him. It is a simple matter of having both adequate motive and opportunity – opportunity to get at the arsenic while she tended the pharmacy, and of putting it into the meals she prepared for him."

"Will you enter the matter?"

He shook his head. "The dosage was not fatal. Unless he is an idiot, he will have come to the correct explanation of his poisoning, and will make sure that he is not again put into jeopardy."

24 February 1920

Pons left beside my breakfast plate this morning a marked paragraph in the morning *Telegraph*. Under a heading, "Jewel Thieves Caught," I read: "Two members of the gang that made a smash raid at Carville's Jewelers on Tite Street last week were apprehended today; a third and fourth are being sought. Information was lodged with the police on enquiry by

Theodore Evans, an associate of the thieves, and uncle of a girl thought to be implicated in the robbery. Credit for astute detection must go to Inspector Seymour Jamison of Scotland Yard..."

The Rediscovered Cases

THE ADVENTURE OF GRESHAM OLD PLACE

It was in the middle of a particularly stifling June in 1923 that the diabolical affair of Gresham Old Place came to Solar Pons' attention. Pons was moving restlessly to and fro in our lodging, irritated in a measure that he had no problem to set his mind on, and sullenly annoyed because he could not get his latest experiment to work out. I looked up from my book occasionally and watched him, for when his tall figure stooped over his test tubes and retorts, and his face took on that look of intense concentration, he looked indeed the "Sherlock Holmes of Praed Street," as he had often been described in the papers.

My attention was immediately drawn to a great pounding on the outer door, followed by a tremendous clatter on the stairs. My book slipped from my knee to floor, and I looked across at Pons, whose eager eyes were fixed upon the door in the keenest anticipation. Then the door seemed to bend inward under some terrific impact before it was flung open, precipitating into the room a huge, burly man, whose very aspect caused me to spring up in alarm and reach backward for any weapon of defense I could find within my reach.

The intruder's face was marked by hard lines, and was heavily scarred. His small pig eyes fixed themselves on Pons with anything but a friendly expression. His clothes were awry, as if he had struggled into them in darkness, and his long hair straggled out from beneath his cap. His thick, sensual lips were working convulsively as he shut the door and fell back against it, bracing himself against the wood. It was no idle motion of mine, this reaching for a weapon of defense, for I thought that at last that Limehouse had sent someone to even scores with Solar Pons.

"Pons!" exclaimed our visitor in a hoarse voice.

I looked over at Pons. There was in his face a mixture of surprise and delight, and I saw at once that he anticipated no danger from this strange individual, now looking suspiciously over at me. I dropped my cricket bat with a loud clatter.

"Bart Powers," said Pons, coming forward. "What brings you to me, man?"

I started at the name and I looked with new interest at our visitor, for he was one of the most notorious bank robbers of the decade.

He made no move away from the door. "You've read the papers lately, Pons?"

Pons nodded. "What is it?"

"That Gresham Old Place affair! If I've been followed here – God help me!"

Pons raised his eyebrows and watched him make his way to a chair, in surprise. "Dear me!" he murmured, "you sound serious, man. What's up?"

Powers gestured toward the paper Pons was taking from the stack at his side. "Read it."

Pons scanned the account hastily; then, for my benefit, he read slowly aloud:

"'MYSTERIOUS ACCIDENT AT
GRESHAM MARSHES
Lured Into Bog by Call for Help,
Jason Hamilton Vanishes'

"'From Gresham Marshes comes a curious report of an accident which took place recently. On Thursday night last, Mr. Jason Hamilton, who lived at Gresham Old Place on the edge of the fens, was startled by a cry for help which seemed to come from the bogland, at a spot along the winding footpath where dangerous mire bordered both sides of the path. Despite the admonitions of his cousins, Mr. Samuel Compson and Mr. Lee Barson, who occupied the house with him, Mr. Hamilton took off into the marshes to investigate the sound. He did not return.

"'The following morning, when Mr. Hamilton had not returned, his cousins set out into the low country to look for him, but no trace of him could be found. It is assumed that both the mysterious person who called for help and the unfortunate Mr. Hamilton, his would-be rescuer, are victims of the mire.

"'Later and garbled reports have it that the cousins were shot at as they investigated the footpath leading through the marshes. There has, however, been no confirmation of these reports.'"

Pons looked up from this account and fixed his eyes on our visitor. "Which one of the three are you, Powers?" he asked.

"Barson," replied Powers unhesitatingly.

Pons chuckled. "A respectable name for you, Powers. And who are these other two?"

"Hamilton, rest his soul was Jimmy Cams," said Powers, "and Compson is 'Fixer' Sims."

"A fine lot," observed Pons. "How comes it that three former bank robbers of such deserved notoriety are lost in Gresham Marshes? A more lonely district is hard to imagine. You are in hiding, then. From whom? Surely not the authorities!"

Powers shook his head. "I only wish it were the authorities! They're easy to get away from, all due respect to you, Pons. But the man who called for help – he'll call until we come, and if we don't come – he'll come to us."

The man's almost primitive face was the picture of abject terror. Little beads of perspiration stood out on his forehead. He looked at Pons in utter helplessness.

"Surely it's not as bad as all that!" exclaimed Pons. He shook his head sadly. "Powers, you were once a criminal worthy of the Yard's best."

"That's past," said Powers. "Pons, I want you to save us from him."

"Why not move?" asked Pons.

"It's no good. He'll follow us, and it had better come to an end now. I couldn't stand running from one place to another, and waiting until he caught up."

"You have an idea, then, which one it is?" asked Pons.

Powers shook his head. "None. It may be either Hicks, Hemmerby, or Brade – or all three."

Pons bit his lip reflectively. "King's evidence has its compensations, Powers – but, alas, it also has its pitfalls. Where did you go after Brade's trial?"

I now began to understand the conversation that had passed between our visitor and Pons. It became evident to me that these three men on Gresham Marshes were undergoing persecution, evidently for turning King's evidence in a trial against the three greatest bank robbers in recent history – Hicks, Hemmerby, and Brade: and it was certain that whoever the persecutors were, they would not stop until the remaining two men had paid the thieves' debt they had incurred when they turned against their fellow robbers. The crime must have been committed some years before, for I remembered only the names involved.

"We dodged here and there," said Powers wearily, "until we felt we had given them the slip. We've been down at Gresham Old Place for seven years now. It's lonely, as you say, and that's what we wanted. No one can approach without being seen; but that works for him now, too, for no one can get away from the house by day. I tried it once, and almost got shot for my pains – and I saw no one. I've looked over the marshes as far as I could see with glasses, long distance glasses – not a soul! Yes, we were shot at the other day; we never got the chance to look for Jimmy's body – we'd been finished off right there if we'd gone out on that marsh.

"I did get out in the darkness tonight – we'll have to get back to that house in the darkness. Will you come tomorrow night, Pons? I'll find some place to stay tomorrow – I've still a few friends in London."

Pons considered for a moment. "Well," he said at last, "your trouble interests me. Of course, there isn't much of a problem – I take it you want some plan to outwit the fellow on the marsh?"

"Exactly Mr. Pons. If it were anyone but you, I tell you frankly, I'd ask to have the fellow killed."

Pons nodded thoughtfully. "I daresay it would be best for you, Powers."

"Will you come, then?" asked Powers, leaning forward eagerly.

"I think we can make it. What do you say, Parker?"

"By all means let us go," I answered hastily. "It's been a long time since I've been in a position to be shot at, and this is as good a chance as any. There'll be some excitement to compensate for the monotony of the past few days."

Pons smiled "Very well, Powers. We'll expect you to call tomorrow night then; as soon, I suppose, as darkness falls."

"I'll be here," said Powers.

The door had hardly closed behind our visitor before Pons had popped into his bedroom, from which he emerged in the space of a tern minutes attired as a lounger of the lowest type.

"To Limehouse?" I asked, looking up.

He nodded. "I'm off to see Frick. What danger threatens the men at Gresham Old Place emanates from one the trio sent to

Dartmoor ten years ago on the evidence of Powers, Cams, and Sims."

"Yet I'm certain that those three men are still behind bars at Dartmoor. Then they can't be down at Gresham Old Place."

"Logical enough," agreed Pons moving towards the door, "but, the movements of men often fail to follow the course of logic, Parker."

I sat for a moment in silence after he had gone. I had forgotten my book, and only remembered it now to pick it from the floor. Then I considered what I could do to satisfy myself regarding the whereabouts of the three men suspected by Pons of beginning an attack upon the occupants of Gresham Old Place. Though it was already late in the evening, I decided at last to call upon Inspector Jamison for the information I desired.

I had little trouble getting him on the wire. "I say, Jamison," I began, "Pons has become interested in the bank robbers, Hicks, Hemmerby, and Brade. Can you tell me where those three are at the present time?"

Jamison laughed good-naturedly "You never can tell about Pons, eh, Doctor? Whatever he's on to, tell him to forget those three; they're still down at Dartmoor, and they'll be there a good time yet. What's up, by the way?"

"The Gresham Marshes affair."

"Well, if that matter has caught his eye, there may be something in it. I'll look at it again. Can't see, though, what connection those fellows in Dartmoor have. That affair looks to me like pure accident."

"I think that's the most likely assumption," I put in, for I had no authority to tell Jamison of our visitor. "You're sure, then, that those fellows are still in Dartmoor."

"Positive," said Jamison emphatically. "I talked with Brade myself only two days ago. I remember it, because I remember that the fellow had a cold. So that lets those three out."

Not long after midnight Pons briskly entered the room.

"Well, what have you found?" I asked.

"Brade is our man," said Pons confidently divesting himself of the shabby coat he wore. "The fellow is out; how, I don't know."

"That's impossible," I said, with a poor attempt to conceal the triumph I felt.

But Pons was not in the least disconcerted. "Indeed," he said. "It strikes me you're taking liberties with the impossible and possible."

"Not so!" I retorted. "I called Jamison not so long ago, and he assured me that all three men were still secure in Dartmoor. Why, he spoke to Brade himself only two days ago."

Pons' eyes narrowed thoughtfully. "How could Jamison be sure?"

"He ought to know Pons. He remembers because it struck him that Brade had a cold at the time – it was the way he talked."

For a moment Pons said nothing. Then abruptly a startled expression grew on his features. He looked at me excitedly. "Had a cold, did he?" Then he reached for the coat and vest he had just discarded and made for the door. "Of course he had a cold – he had to have!"

And with that cryptic sentence he left the room, ran rapidly down the stairs, and out into the street, from where his voice calling a cab drifted back to me. For a few moments I sat in bewilderment, and not a little irritation because Pons had dropped no hint of what was passing in his mind. Though I had determined to go to bed, I now promised myself that I would sit up until his return even if he took the entire night to come back.

But it was not until we were seated at table for a late luncheon next day that Pons condescended to speak about the matter that was uppermost in my mind.

"I daresay my sudden departure last night rather disconcerted you, eh, Parker?"

"First time I've seen a mere cold upset you so."

"Quite so, but the fact that Brade had a cold explained quite satisfactorily why the man could be in two places at once."

"Indeed!" I exclaimed, astonished. "If Brade can be in two places at once, then tell me about it immediately. I, for one, am content to take Jamison's word."

An expression of mock humility crept across Pons' face. He shook his head. "Your attitude is very well for one who doesn't know the facts. Grant me the liberty to speak literally – Brade is in two places at once. He is in Gresham Marshes – of that Bart Powers and I are assured. But he is also in Dartmoor, and of that the rest of the world is assured."

"You can explain that paradox, I hope."

Pons nodded in some amusement. "As a matter of fact," he went on, his voice losing its edge, "Brade is a twin. His brother, who bears the name Lester, has for some time lived at a sailors' dive in Wapping. The two men, quite naturally, bear a remarkable resemblance to each other. It would take an acute observer to tell the difference between the two, provided Lester does not talk, for Lester has a peculiarly harsh voice – a very low bass voice, which might well give the impression of a cold."

"A substitution!" I exclaimed.

"Precisely," said Pons. "A substitution has been made. Lester is in Dartmoor, and is to all appearances his brother Adam; while Adam is in reality somewhere in Gresham Marshes. Thus far, the matter is simple. Frick led me to Lester Brade's room; of course, no one was there. I found a few things of interest, however."

Pons reached into his pocket and took out a folded paper, which he tossed on the table. I took it up and saw at first glance that it was a letter. I opened it, and read:

"Dear Les,

"As usual, there is no news. We're getting fine treatment here – lots better than you might expect from what we've been used to hearing about this place. I suppose you will come to visit me again next week. I hope so. I hope you will have all your affairs straightened out by that time. At least, it would be best all around if you had.

– Adam"

I looked up. "Code?" I asked.

Pons shook his head. "No," he replied. "It is just the letter telling Lester Brade that all is ready now for the attempt. You will note that it is dated somewhat over two weeks ago. I assume then, that the substitution took place last week, and that Adam Brade went immediately to Gresham Old Place – for someone must have learned the thereabouts of the three men and through Lester must have informed him. Adam was excited about the break – he writes of his treatment in Dartmoor as if he had just been there – after ten years. Odd that the officials didn't get suspicious at that. But this note," he continued, "is in code."

The letter Pons now drew from his pocket and threw to me was but a short note of a few lines.

"Dear Les,

"When will you be ready to have me help you? If you want to take any of my things, you may. It is not my place, of course, to talk of helping you. I will help, when you want me to. Do let me hear from you. As always,

– Adam, your brother"

"What do you make of it?" asked Pons, watching me closely, with an amused twinkle in his eyes.

"I don't see the code, of course," I said slowly. "On the surface, it would strike me that the note is just a repetition of an offer of help made by Adam Brade to his brother, who is evidently facing some problem."

"Exactly," said Pons. "And yet, there's a carefully worded message there. If you'll take the fourth and fifth words of every sentence, it will become apparent. The real message will then read: 'Be ready to take my place when you hear from your brother.' It is, as you may have seen from the written date, an earlier message than the first one I showed you."

I nodded. "Yes, it's clear now. I suppose, then, that Adam had a severe cold for some days before his brother's last visit."

"Precisely, Parker," agreed Pons. "Certainly a daring scheme, but the likeness of the brothers is remarkable enough to enable them to carry it out. The most difficult part of the matter was the changing in the cell; it's quite possible that a guard was taken into their confidence, though it's not usual for Adam Brade to work in that manner."

"What do you intend to do?"

"I daresay that we can only wait for Bart Powers to come. The problem is rather unusual, insofar as it is by no means the typical armchair problem, but demands, on the other hand, almost too much action for my liking."

Pons shrugged his shoulders and turned to a sheaf of papers on the table. He had hardly begun sorting them when we were again interrupted by a succession of noises almost exactly similar to those of the night before. It was, therefore, no great surprise to us when Bart Powers burst into the room.

Though he had looked dangerous and evil the night before, Powers now looked positively wild. His hair was dishevelled, and his flashing eyes roved wildly around the room. He lay back against the door, breathing heavily.

"Great Heavens, Powers!" exclaimed Pons. "You shouldn't have ventured out in the daytime. What's up? I see you carry a paper – today's. I daresay."

"You haven't seen it, then," said Powers, still breathing heavily. He tossed the paper to Pons. "Gresham Old Place was almost burned to the ground last night." Pons was startled. "And Fixer..." Powers made a despairing gesture with his hands "they got him... he's dead."

"What!" exclaimed Pons.

Powers nodded. "I'm afraid it isn't much use, Pons – your coming out there now." He made a wry face.

Pons glanced hurriedly over the report, reading occasional sentences aloud for my benefit. "'SHOCKING TRAGEDY AT GRESHAM MARSHES... Gresham Old Place burned almost to the ground... The charred body of a man, identified as one of the inhabitants, was discovered in the ruins. Search is being made for the missing tenant... It is understood that the dead man was shot through the head!'" Pons looked up. "Good God!" he murmured. "We shouldn't have waited, Powers."

Powers shrugged his shoulders hopelessly and sank into a chair. "What can be done now? Have you found out which one it is?"

Pons nodded curtly. "Brade. There's been a substitution in the prison. Lester is taking Adam's place."

Powers looked the picture of abject misery. "It couldn't be worse. Of the three, I'd rather have had both of the other two than Brade."

"There's now but one man against three, Powers," said Pons.

Powers smiled wryly. "It was one man to three once before, Pons. And two are gone..."

Pons said nothing. He was sunk in deep meditation, and both Powers and I could see that he was gravely considering some move to make in this perplexing problem. He sat in silence for some time; then suddenly he raised his head and looked speculatively at Powers.

"Are you certain that you weren't followed here, Powers?" he asked.

"Absolutely, Pons," replied Powers. "I came over from the north side – from a little place in Upper Hampstead where I know I'm among friends. I wasn't followed."

Pons stepped over to the windows looking out upon Praed Street, pulled the curtains carefully aside, and looked down. After a moment he dropped the curtains, nodding in a satisfied way, and said, "Good. Then for the next day or so – I think it would be best if you stayed right here in these rooms."

"In the meantime, Doctor Parker and I will spend some time in Limehouse and Wapping. When we return, I hope I'll be able to say that it will once more be quite safe for you to venture out, Powers."

"I'll do whatever you say," said Powers.

"That's agreed, then." With that, Pons passed into his bedroom, where he spent some minutes rummaging about his old clothing. He emerged at last in the same guise he had once before put on.

"There's a suit of clothing laid out on the bed in there, Parker," he said as he came out. "You'd better put it on. It wouldn't be healthy for us to be seen in our ordinary clothes where we're going, especially if I should be recognized."

I slipped into the bedroom and found there a nondescript array of old clothes, none too clean, which Pons expected me to assume. I put them on without hesitation, and, having seen that Pons had somewhat altered his face, I ventured to change my own as far as it was within my power to do so.

I finished at last and came out of the room to find Pons waiting impatiently. Together we descended to the street, called a taxicab, and were soon speeding down Edgware Road toward Wapping. Pons was sunk in the deepest thought on all the long ride, and roused himself only at its termination by leaning forward suddenly to tap the driver on the shoulder as a signal for him to stop. I looked from the cab and found to my surprise that we had gone considerably beyond Wapping and were in Limehouse district, for the street that greeted my eye was Limehouse Causeway. It was for the most part taken up with single and grouped Orientals, with here and there shabby-looking loungers like ourselves. We descended from the taxicab and made our may slowly along the street, paying no attention to the shifty glances of the loungers – for the Orientals did not condescend to notice us in any way.

We had gone for a few streets when Pons drew up before a shabby three-storey building abutting on the walk. The entrance to the lower floor was gained through a pair of swinging doors; I saw that the place was a pub of some kind, and I was immediately struck with its squalor and dirtiness. Looking up, I saw an awkwardly painted sign which read, *Shen Han's*, and realized that this was indeed Pons' objective. Pons looked carefully around him; seeing no one watching, he pushed open the door, and we entered.

We stepped directly into a low dark room, the atmosphere of which was heavy with smoke; in which I caught the distinct odour of opium – certainly not being smoked in the room, but probably behind some of the thin partitions to the rear or below the floor. The dusk of the room was broken here and there by odd green lanterns, exotic in their appearance in the smoke. We strolled casually across the room, passed close to the bar, where I saw a wrinkled Oriental sitting on a high stool behind the bar, and came finally in a meandering way to a stop before a sequestered table against the wall, where a thin, shifty-eyed individual sat. To all appearances this fellow was somewhat the worse for drink, but I knew this to be illusory, for a quick, almost imperceptible sign passed between him and Pons.

We sat down at this table, and Pons and I entered into conversation, which we continued for some while in low tones. The fellow opposite us stared at us disinterestedly, and presently lowered his head to his arms. He sprawled forward somewhat over the table, and at once Pons' voice changed.

Though apparently still addressing me, he spoke now in a still lower voice to the fellow across from us.

"Start a rumor that you've seen Bart Powers in Limehouse. Lay it well, where Brade will hear of it soon. Is Brade here?"

Our table companion shook his head awkwardly.

"Good," Pons went on. "Remember, you've seen Bart. Looking sharp. Scared. Lying low for a while. Get that? Brade will soon be here; quick as he finds his last bird flown."

Very casually Pons and I now rose and shuffled from one table to another, seldom attracting even a passing glance, and presently we found ourselves once more on the street, walking up Limehouse Causeway in the same direction as we had come just before. It was a considerable distance until we left Limehouse Causeway, but it was not until we were well on the West India Dock Road that I questioned Pons.

"Frick?" I asked in a guarded voice, for I had learned in long association with Pons that the most extreme care should constantly be taken in situations of this nature.

Pons nodded.

"Now what?" I asked.

"We go to Lester Brade's room, and we'll stay there until something happens. I depend upon Frick to do his work well; though there may be no necessity for having him go to this trouble, it's best. Brade may not want to come to London at all unless he's sure that Powers is here. If Brade is not already in the city, and apparently is he not, then such a rumor will certainly bring him in short order. And when he comes, I think it best for an adequate reception committee to see him first. I consider us that committee."

Pons now hailed a cab that was driving slowly down the street, and we scrambled into it. We were driven leisurely along, and pulled up at last before a disreputable *cul-de-sac*, which bore no name that I could see, and ended in a high brick wall. Down this *cul-de-sac*, Pons and I went. The entire length of the short street seemed to be made up of nothing but low boarding houses and dives. It was into one of these dives that Pons finally found his way.

He went rapidly through a small bar-room, and despite glances from its inmates went on up a flight of rickety stairs; I trailed closely and reluctantly in his wake. Without hesitation, however, he went down the hall of the second floor, paused before a low door, and opened it with a key that he produced from one of his pockets. We slipped into the room, and Pons locked the door after us.

"Good heavens," I murmured. "Where are we?" I stepped over to a small window and looked out at the drab buildings about us. "Is that Wapping Wall over there?"

"Yes," answered Pons. "This is Brade's room."

"What if we should be discovered?"

Pons chuckled. He made a suggestive motion and nodded in the direction of the Thames. "Nothing is accomplished without risk. Discovered as we are, we're safe; if I were known..." He shrugged.

"My word!" I exclaimed. "This sort of thing is bad for the heart."

"Stimulating," returned Pons matter-of-factly. "But come, let's look around a bit." He went over to a rough table near an unmade bed, just opposite the window where I stood. "I've already gone over some of this," he said. "This ragged blotter, for instance. Study it before a mirror, and you'll see a scrawl suggesting the word '17th' – in figures, followed by the 'th', taken off a letter, apparently. Evidently the date of the exchange – it checks up."

"How long are we to stay here?" I put in.

"A day – possibly two. Not more, and most likely less. You've a revolver in your right coat pocket, unless someone has relieved you of it."

I reached down and felt the weapon; I had not noticed it before, though the coat had seemed curiously heavy.

"I put it there before we left. I, too, have one. I also have some interesting paraphernalia – a pair of manacles, for instance, which I hope will become extremely useful before our vigil here is over. And some fine silk rope – really more like Inspector Jamison's usual baggage." He broke off and stepped over to the window. "Four-thirty," he murmured. "What do you say to getting a little sleep? It would be best to take the watch alternately, I suppose."

"Not in that bed!" I protested.

"Certainly not," said Pons. "Doze off in that chair – it looks comfortable enough; at least, it's the best one can do here."

Half-consciously, I had heard a clock somewhere strike midnight, then suddenly I felt my shoulder roughly grasped, and at the same instant Pons' voice hissed at my ear.

"Arm yourself. There's someone on the stairs."

I was awake on the instant, and at Pons' bidding, I crouched down behind the chair in which I had been sleeping, while he himself took up a position nearer the door through which our visitor – if indeed the noise on the stairs presaged a visitor – must enter.

Wary footsteps approached along the hall, and presently there came a fumbling at the door. Suddenly the door swung open, but in the inky blackness it was impossible to see anything. Softly it closed again, and I trembled, for I felt rather than saw the presence of a third person in the room. Now there came a scratching noise, and abruptly a tiny match flame sprang into existence; in the feeble glow of the flame I saw, apparently hung in the air, a brutal, beetling-browed face, bending over cupped hands. The fellow went carefully over to the table, lifted the glass off a lamp, and applied the dying flame to the wick; immediately the room came to life, and I saw

Pons standing grimly beside the closed door, his revolver in his hands, eyeing the fellow in saturnine amusement.

This midnight visitor still bent over the lamp, as if to assure himself that the flame would continue to burn. He flung his hands up at last, and made as if to remove his great-coat, when suddenly Pons spoke.

"Leave it on, Brade!" he said sharply.

Brade whirled about with an oath; then, as he saw the weapon, his hands shot into the air. I rose from my crouching position behind the chair. Brade looked from one to the other of us in some amazement.

"Well," he snarled, "What's the game?"

"Dear me," murmured Pons. "So soon forgotten? Don't you remember me, Adam Brade?" Pons stepped forward, so that the light from the lamp struck him more fully.

"You've got me wrong," said Brade. "I'm Lester – not Adam."

"Indeed?" said Pons. "You forgot Lester's bass – your cold, Adam."

"By God! It's Solar Pons!"

"Guilty," said Pons.

"Well, by God!" said Brade in disgust.

"No fault of yours, Brade," said Pons. "If Powers hadn't come to me, I daresay no one would have suspected, and you'd have been able to even up scores with the three at Gresham Old Place and get back to Dartmoor without the slightest suspicion."

"Bart Powers came to you!" exclaimed Brade.

"Rather unexpected, what? I'm afraid, Brade, that I must ask you to hold out your hands – Parker, keep him covered."

Pons stepped forward and manacled Brade, who was too much astonished to offer resistance.

"And it's necessary for you to be tied down for an hour or so. If you'll sit down in the chair before Dr. Parker, I can manage you, I think. The most comfortable chair in the room, too," he added.

Pons completed his work, ending up with firmly gagging Brade. "Done," he said. "I elect you to stand guard, Parker. I'm going out to call Jamison. I look forward with relish to the estimable Inspector's astonishment when I present him to Adam Brade and he discovers that Adam has lost his erstwhile cold."

THE ADVENTURE OF THE BURLSTONE HORROR

(The Sinister House)

For many years Solar Pons advised me not to chronicle the singular affair of the Burlstone murders, for he believed that the public would forever remain incredulous about the facts of the case. "The matter will only reflect upon your earlier chronicles" he would say. There will be some who will still retain doubts about the reality of our findings in the sinister house at Burlstone, and for their benefit, I would recommend the recently published monograph of Dr. Heinrich Metz, *The Brain of Man as an Organism,* which uncovers now for the first time some astounding facts about the workings of the human brain, facts which are peculiarly pertinent to this narrative.

The case of the Burlstone murders came to our attention just after Pons had closed the affair of the Sotheby Salesman. We had come into London shortly after dawn and had taken a taxicab from Victoria Station to our rooms in Praed Street. As we ascended the steps of Number Seven, Pons looked curiously up at our windows.

"Either we have visitors already, or we forgot the lights last night, Parker," he said.

Pons threw open the door to our rooms, and we found ourselves facing a thin man of medium height, whose bright eyes flashed expectantly as we entered.

"Well, Pons," he said in a gruff voice not quite compatible with his appearance, "you certainly keep late hours."

"Danforth" exclaimed Pons. "What brings you here?"

Albert Danforth, I remembered, was one of the Commissioners of the C.I.D. I looked at him with new interest. Certainly he was much older than he looked. His black moustache seemed no more a part of him than his gruff voice. Yet his face was smooth and bland as a child's and his cheeks were pink and healthy, though his hair was greying at the temples. I had never personally met the commissioner, though I had heard much of him.

"It's a curious affair, most curious," said Danforth. He paused and looked rather dubiously at me.

Pons introduced us shortly.

"Do you two always spend your nights out?" Danforth asked, smiling.

"We've been down at Sotheby," replied Pons, "looking into a little affair for Hudson."

The commissioner dropped his smile. "Had I known," he said, "I could have wired you to go right over to Burlstone – that's where Jamison is now."

"Well, what's the problem?" asked Pons, facing the commissioner. He brought himself up against the mantel before the fireplace, and clasped his hands behind his hands behind his back.

The commissioner reached into his inner coat pocket and brought forth a small packet of clippings.

Pons made a wry face. "That means the matter has been going for some time," he said, indicating the clippings.

Danforth nodded. "But there are plenty of new developments. Have you read anything at all of the Burlstone Horror, as the papers are beginning to call it?"

"Finding of a headless body in the River Medway?"

"That's it," said the commissioner. "Here," he continued, extracting a clipping from the packet and reading from it, "*Gruesome Discovery at Burlstone* – that's the first one." He handed the clipping to Pons, and immediately proceeded to read the next one aloud. "*Arrest of Dr. Hanford* – that's next."

"Are there more?" asked Pons.

"Four clippings," said Danforth without looking up, "and two more bodies."

"Two more bodies!" exclaimed Pons. "After Hanford's arrest?"

Danforth nodded glumly. "After, yes. Jamison thought..."

Pons struck his hands together and chuckled. "I can well imagine how and what Jamison thought, Danforth. Most estimable Jamison! A good man, Danforth, but too prone to jump at conclusions."

"We can't condemn Jamison right off like that, Pons," protested the commissioner. "He had a good case; you'll have to grant that."

"What was it?" asked Pons while rapidly conning the clippings.

"This man Hanford was a rival of the dead man, a business rival of a sort," began Danforth.

"Body identified then?"

"No difficulty about that," said Danforth. "The fellow had a tattoo mark on the left breast. Man by the name of Graves – a physician, like Hanford, Hanford had repeatedly threatened to kill Graves, in the presence of witnesses, too. He was the last person to see Graves alive; he admits it. He's a hot-tempered fellow, too; immediately threatened to do Jamison in when he was taken."

Pons chuckled. "Weak link already. Does he admit threatening Graves?"

"Why, yes. Said he had nothing to conceal."

"Hm! Straightforward, at any rate," observed Pons. "Anything else?"

"Most important," continued Danforth "is the fact that Hanford had got some considerable reputation as a surgeon, and it's been shown that the man who severed Graves' head must have been a surgeon. The cut was made between the second and third cervical vertebrae, and the job is perfect. Of course, it's an elaborate way to conceal the identity of the dead man, but no chances were taken, apparently."

"Surely that's not all?" asked Pons, obviously astonished.

The commissioner nodded.

"Well, Jamison has certainly bungled matters very badly," said Pons then. "Very badly, indeed."

"On the contrary, the case is fairly good. I admit having doubts about the arrest of Hanford."

"Certainly arrest was not justified," assented Pons. "Had Jamison stopped to consider, he would have found that Hanford's honesty in admitting everything except the actual crime is a point definitely in his favor. The clipping I have here states that Hanford came forward voluntarily and deposed having seen deceased near midnight of the night of his disappearance; I take it no one witnessed the meeting?"

"Apparently not."

"Then, too, his threatening Jamison clearly indicates the man's temperament; I personally very much doubt that he would ever kill anyone after a threat like that."

"It's easy enough to say so," said Danforth, somewhat nettled, "but there are a number of facts which can't be disposed of so glibly. For instance, Hanford was the only physician in Graves' acquaintance – that is, as far as we've been able to ascertain. The severing of the head to prevent identification is surely the idea of a physician and surgeon."

"Oh, but, my dear Danforth," objected Pons, "surely it is obvious that the severing of the head was not done to prevent identification!"

For a moment Danforth looked at Pons in amazement. "Then for what reason was it done?"

"That we must determine," said Pons suavely. "When you take into consideration that a man supposedly removes the head and clothes to prevent identification, and pays no attention to such an obvious mark of identification as a tattoo design, there's but one logical conclusion to come to – that the man's head was removed for some reason of which we are as yet completely ignorant."

"That's certainly logical," admitted Danforth.

"It strikes me as the only possible view to take. Circumstances have conspired against Dr. Hanford, and I have no doubt that Jamison can be brought around to seeing his error before it's too late. Even now the man may take action against Jamison, in which he would be justified."

"What must be done? Must Hanford be freed?"

"Not necessarily," said Pons dryly. "It has occurred to me that some arrangement might be gone into whereby his further detention might give the actual criminal an added feeling of security."

Danforth hesitated before saying, "Yes, that might be best."

"Let us look first into the other two tragedies," continued Pons, taking the clippings up from the table. "*Second Tragedy at Burlstone*," he read. "'Body thought to be that of a young engineer staying at *Hound & Horn* Inn... Found near Maidstone, the body is believed to have been carried with the current of the River Medway to the reeds among which it was lodged. As in the former case, it was stripped of clothing, and the head had been very carefully severed." Pons lowered the clipping and began to read from the second. "*Another Victim of Burlstone Horror*... 'Kentish village tragedies now number three... The body was found early this morning by a fisherman; it was discovered against a sand bank in the river just beyond the village of Burlstone. The condition of the body is precisely similar to that of the two preceding victims.'... No identification," concluded Pons, looking up at last.

"Not yet," said Danforth, shaking his head moodily.

"The date of the first discovery is nine days ago; four days ago Dr. Hanford was arrested, and in the morning of the following day the second body was found at Maidstone. And this morning the third body was discovered at Burlstone."

"That's right," said the commissioner.

"We are thus left at the outset with a group of peculiar facts and an army of questions. It would be useless to go into them all, but doesn't it strike you as peculiar that the victims, as far as examination seems to bear out, are all young men?"

Danforth nodded. "Spotted that, yes," he said. "At first we thought of sadism, then of an amazing series of coincidences."

Pons shrugged his shoulders. "Coincidence is at best a poor straw to grasp. We have an apparent motive for the death of the first victim, but thus far none whatever for the second and third, unless as you suggest Dr. Hanford turns out to be a sadist, which is most unlikely. The first and third bodies were discovered at Burlstone; the second at Maidstone; therefore it follows that the murders were committed at or somewhere beyond Burlstone. In what relation do the deaths in their actual occurrence coincide with the movements of Dr. Hanford?"

Danforth smiled wryly. "It's been shown that, excepting for the moment the question of motive, Hanford could well have killed the second victim, but the third is extremely questionable. In fact, Jamison wired this morning to say that he contemplated Hanford's release sometime today. Of course, I instructed him to do nothing until I had seen you."

Pons nodded abstractedly. "Hanford's out, I fear, and we shall have to start all over again." He stood for a moment with his arms folded across his chest, staring down at the rug in an attitude of concentration. "No," he said at last, shaking his head, "I'll have to run down there and look into the affair at first hand. Further speculation is both idle and futile."

"Good!" exclaimed Danforth. "When can you go?"

"Not until early evening," replied Pons. "Neither Parker nor I has had any sleep for a good many hours, and there's nothing like sleep to freshen one up. You had best wire Jamison that Parker and I are coming, else he might go off and do something rash."

The afternoon passed in uninterrupted sleep, for Pons had wisely disconnected both the outer bell and the telephone, and at five o'clock we were comfortably seated in a train bearing us away from Victoria Station down to Burlstone, where Inspector Jamison would be waiting for us.

We traveled for some considerable distance in silence before Pons spoke suddenly. "I wonder what he did with the heads?"

"That's curious," I agreed. "Did the papers state, by the way, whether all three heads were amputated the same way?"

"Yes," said Pons, drawing the clippings from his pocket. "All three were severed between the second and third cervical vertebrae, and from all reports, the amputations were perfect in each case."

"Certainly a surgeon's work."

"No doubt of it," agreed Pons, "and I'm very much inclined to think that the purpose of these murders will prove to be more obscure than Jamison, at least, thinks it to be. Undoubtedly committed by the same person, the motive in each murder must prove similar."

"On the face of the matter, the motive for these atrocious crimes seems difficult to suggest."

"Precisely," said Pons. "That's exactly the point. Let's assume that Hanford had a motive in getting rid of Graves; then we are confronted with the problem of two other motives in the case of the engineer and the as yet unidentified victim – unconnected, in all probability. The papers mention no connection between young Dr. Graves and the engineer, and we can for the present assume that such a connection would not have been overlooked. Indeed," added Pons, after consulting the clippings, "it appears that the engineer came to Burlstone the day after Graves' disappearance. I'm afraid that Dr. Hanford is definitely out as a suspect."

But a surprise awaited us at Maidstone. Jamison had evidently wired the latest developments, and startling ones they were, to Danforth, who had rewired them to us, together with prefatory comment of his own. The entire telegram was in code, but Pons knows the Yard's code at sight, and was able to read the wire as it stood:

> YOUR THEORY HIT JAMISON'S LATEST REPORT FOLLOWS STOP – BLOODSTAINED INSTRUMENTS FOUND IN HANFORD'S HOUSE SCALPEL ETCETERA HAVE PREPARED FORMAL CHARGE AGAINST HANFORD WILL WAIT FOR PONS HERE STOP AUTOPSIES ON THREE BODIES REVEAL DEFINITE TRACES MORPHINE STOP MEN EVIDENTLY HEAVILY DRUGGED BEFORE DEATH STOP THIRD VICTIM IDENTIFIED GARDENER ON ESTATE RETIRED DR CONSTANCE NEAR BURLSTONE STOP MAN HAD DISAPPEARED FOUR DAYS AGO STOP IDENTIFICATION BY ONE OF DOCTORS ATTENDANTS – DANFORTH

"Well!" exclaimed Pons. "Either Jamison has uncovered something, or the whole thing is a prime piece of asininity; and I'm afraid I look very favorably toward the latter possibility. At any rate, the doctor will have to explain the presence of bloodstained instruments; surely it is unusual and unethical for physicians to leave bloodstained instruments lying about!

I'm sure you haven't that bad habit, Parker." Pons chuckled. But the telegram had upset him.

"I wonder whether this Dr. Constance is the old fellow who retired some time last year," I put in. "I used to know him quite well during the short time I spent in active medical practise."

"I daresay it's he," said Pons. "I seem to recollect that he went somewhere into Kent. We may be able to make use of him, for he must be pretty well acquainted with the inhabitants of Burlstone and the country roundabout by this time."

"A good idea," I put in. "If there's anyone thereabouts who is acquainted in any way with surgery or medicine, Constance will know him. It's quite likely that there may be someone who has been overlooked by Jamison."

Pons took up the wire again and looked at it. "Danforth, at least, looks favorably on Jamison's report. To prepare a formal charge is a pretty serious thing, and of course I shall not let it go through if it's in my power to prevent it. 'Jamison will wait for Pons.' Rather good, that touch, isn't it, Parker?"

I nodded.

The smile on Pons' face vanished as quickly as it had come, and he was serious again. "But morphine – that could be easily traced. Of course, in the case of a physician, morphine would be in his possession already. In all probability, he would get his morphine from a distributing house rather than from the local chemist's. Nevertheless, I'll make it a point to inquire at Burlstone."

The train began to slow down. "This must be the place," I ventured, peering out into the night.

Pons took up his portmanteau and stick, and I opened the compartment door as the cars ground to a stop beside a long platform. We stepped from the train, and immediately a plump figure detached itself from a group standing under a station light some distance away, and came toward us.

"Jamison's at hand, at any rate," said Pons, "and, judging from the way he's coming at us, something now has happened."

Jamison came up to us, nodded curtly at me, and seized Pons' arm. "Thank God, you're here, Pons," he said in an agitated voice. "There's a madman loose on the village – a fourth body was found only an hour ago!"

"Good heavens!" exclaimed Pons, "this is getting interesting. Has it been identified?"

Jamison nodded. "Brother of the third man found. Also employed on the Constance place. The identification was made by the same man – Dr. Constance's assistant. Both of the dead men had been missing four days."

"Well, we'd better waste no time," said Pons shortly. "Let's go somewhere where you can give us those details you have uncovered and disclosed."

"I've engaged rooms for you at the *Hound & Horn*, where I'm staying," said Jamison, "and we can go right over. I've ordered dinner for you there."

We passed the group of men among which Jamison had been standing, and the Inspector made a sign to a young constable, whom I recognized as Mecker, a man who had on more than one occasion been of service to Pons. Greetings were exchanged. I dropped back and walked at Mecker's side, leaving Pons and Jamison to go ahead. Pons evidently had no desire to talk of the Burlstone murders, for he walked in silence, looking about him at the rambling streets with considerable interest.

It was only after we were seated before the hot dinner that Jamison had had made ready for us that the matter of the headless bodies was opened once more.

"Now, Jamison," said Pons, "I should like a brief outline of the facts just as you have discovered them."

"Very well." Jamison drew from his pocket a notebook, in which he quickly found a group of closely written pages.

"I'll read you first what notes I've taken in summary thus far. Then Mecker, who has some additional findings, will detail those."

Jamison bent over his notebook and began to read from an outline evidently prepared for Pons' scrutiny. His account was merely the summary of the murders which we had already got from Commissioner Danforth. However, a few new facts emerged. Examination had disclosed that on all four bodies occurred a small scar near the left arm pit; this suggested a hypodermic injection of some sort. Subsequent autopsies had shown that morphine had been used. Dr. Hanford, when questioned, admitted that he could sever a head, but denied that he could do such perfect jobs. Hanford, in explaining the enmity between the physicians, said that when Graves and he had parted after their clinical work, Graves accused him of taking from Graves the majority of Graves' practice; this was the basis of the quarrel between them. Hanford had last seen Graves on a road south of Burlstone shortly after eleven o'clock on the night of 3rd August. Graves was not seen alive after that date.

The second victim had been definitely identified by means of an injured foot as Robert Henderson, the young engineer staying at the *Hound & Horn*. He had last been seen walking away from the Inn early in the evening of 4th August.

Neither Graves nor Henderson had relatives with whom the police could get in touch.

At this point Pons cut in. "What about the last two victims?"

"Well, they had an employer, at least."

"But no relatives?"

"No near relatives, no."

The remainder of Jamison's account was taken up with the last two victims, who had been identified as Justin and Laurence Massey, brothers in the employment of Dr. Constance. The bodies had been identified by Dr. Henry Staunton, assistant to

Dr. Constance. One of the dead brothers had a crippled thumb which made identification easy.

"As to Hanford," Jamison concluded, "I had doubts, but not anymore. The Massey brothers were missing since the 12th of August. Hanford was taken on the night of the 13th – just after he hid the bloodstained instruments we found. He had just been on a mysterious call somewhere in the country. He has so far refused to explain for what these instruments were used."

Pons nodded absently. He made as if to speak, but thinking better of it, nodded to Meeker, who stepped forward and began to read in short clipped sentences those facts regarded as important.

"In each case, the following facts appear: a) Heavy morphine injection; suggestive of drugged state at death; b) Neither family connections nor close friendships, suggesting careful premeditation; c) Comparative youth of victims, ages vary from 28 to 34; d) Bodies those of strong, vigorous men; e) Uniformity in hypodermic injection scars, and the condition of bodies precluding the possibility of any kind of struggle, indicate some relationship between the murderer and his victim, perhaps for some length of time before the crime. In this connection we looked up Robert Henderson, and found that he was known to Dr. Hanford, Dr. Constance, Dr. Staunton, and to Dr. Mark Dillingham of Maidstone; all these men were members of an undergraduate club while at college some years ago, a club presided over by Dr. Constance.

"Since the work was certainly done by an accomplished surgeon, we looked into the ability of surgeons roundabout. Dr. Hanford, Dr. Constance, and Dr. Dillingham of Maidstone could have performed the amputations. Dr. Constance, assisted by Dr. Staunton, performs experiments upon animals in his house south of Burlstone; he has occasionally received large quantities of morphine through the local chemist, and perhaps also orders from the distributing house direct.

Of Dr. Dillingham, little is known, save that he has a large and influential practice in Maidstone. We have learned that between the date of Graves' disappearance and Hanford's arrest, the latter spent considerable time each night away on an important case. He admitted this, but refused to say where he had been.

"Finally, the first theory that the heads had been removed to prevent identification, has been weakened by the presence on the bodies of such obvious marks as the tattoo design, the injured foot, and the crippled thumb."

Mecker looked up, closing his notebook, and Jamison glanced expectantly at Pons. Pons, however, sat in silence for a few moments longer.

"Well, what do you make of it, Pons?" asked Jamison.

"Some preliminary bungling," said Pons bluntly, "but you get down to hard facts at the last. Before I can venture anything on the matter, I want to see the prisoner, Dr. Hanford, and arrange to keep him detained until the real culprit is caught."

Jamison made a wry face; behind him, Meeker's thin lips suggested the ghost of a smile.

"Then I'll want to examine the bodies and look about a bit for myself. And, of course, I'll want a look at the bloodstained instruments found in Hanford's house."

"We have them here," said Jamison, and turned to signal to Mecker, who promptly brought forward a meticulously wrapped parcel.

Jamison carefully undid the string that bound the parcel, and in a moment the suggestive instruments lay before us, just as they had been found. Pons and I bent over the array. Then, with one accord, Pons and I turned and looked at each other. The quizzical smile on his lips reflected my own.

"What do you say, Parker?" he asked. "Caesarian?"

"Without a doubt," I replied unhesitatingly.

Jamison's smile of triumph gave way to dismay.

"These instruments were used in a Caesarian operation, Jamison," said Pons. "I'm afraid they could never have performed the heavy task you hint they did."

"Then why didn't Hanford tell us?" asked Jamison.

"It would have been unethical for him to tell you," said Pons. "Most likely circumstances on this case were such as to cause severe scandal, were Hanford to have told you where to go to verify his night calls."

Jamison's face reflected his disgust.

Pons chuckled. "Come, we all make mistakes, Jamison. But the faster we get on with this matter, the better. I hope it's not too late to see Hanford."

"Not at all," replied Jamison. "I can have him brought here, or we can go directly to the village gaol, where he is being kept."

"Let's go to the gaol, then," suggested Pons, adding, "I'll want to stop in at the chemist's on the way."

The local chemist's was an antiquated little shop standing in the feeble glow of an ancient street lamp not far removed from the gaol. Into this the three of us sauntered; it was still open, though the hour was already late. A curiously beat old fellow looked up from behind a counter as we entered; he stared at each of us in turn, and finally allowed his eyes to rest on Jamison, whom he undoubtedly recognized as the Scotland Yard man in charge of the investigation now disturbing the peace of his little town.

"Evening, sir," he said.

"Good evening, Mr. Bromley," said Pons, who had seen the old man's name on the swinging sign outside.

The old chemist looked dubiously at Pons, and then at Jamison, who nodded curtly. "What can I do for you?" he asked.

"As you know, Mr. Bromley, Inspector Jamison here is in charge of the investigation, and I've come down from London to help a bit. I'd like to know whether you sell much morphine here."

"Lord bless you, sir," said the old fellow with some enthusiasm. "Seems like I ain't selling anything else of late. Between Dr. Hanford, and Dr. Constance, and until just lately, Dr. Graves, I do manage to get rid of quite a bit. Strange, too, because the doctors could get it from the house direct."

"Did Dr. Graves get much from you?" asked Pons.

"Not so very much, compared to what Dr. Constance got."

"I understand that Dr. Constance is quite an old man, and does not go out very much," ventured Pons.

"Oh, it's not Dr. Constance as comes to get it. It's his young assistant, Dr. Staunton, and sometimes they sends Woofy – that's Jim Laird; he's a bit gone – to get it with a note from the doctor himself, and sometimes one of the Masseys came."

"I see," said Pons.

"They use quite a bit at that house, what with their goings-on there. I tell you, sir, I ain't one for saying anything, but between us, I've heard said that Dr. Constance is a fine surgeon – one of the best there's been in practice."

Pons nodded abstractedly, and turned to leave the shop. I felt as if someone had struck me a sudden blow in the face, for the chemist's hint was too broad to mistake. My old friend, Dr. Constance, was suspected of having a hand in the Burlstone murders. I wanted to dismiss the thought, but I could not do so. It was true that I could well remember how often the doctor had wished to be able to perform experiments on animals as he was now apparently doing. What if he had extended his experiments – to human beings!

At the gaol we found the prisoner, a thin pale young man, who, at first glance, did not look very much like the cold-blooded murderer Jamison had pictured him to be.

"Well," said Dr. Hanford, as we came up, "what is it this time? Have you found the missing heads in my house now?"

Jamison coughed in some embarrassment. "Mr. Solar Pons has come down from London to look into this matter, Dr. Hanford, and he would like you to answer some questions."

Dr. Hanford's face brightened perceptibly. "I've heard of Solar Pons, and I'll be glad to answer any of his questions."

"Very good of you, indeed," said Pons shortly. He seated himself before the prisoner, adding, "Of course, you realize you needn't answer my questions, Dr. Hanford. But I have very little to ask. There's one important matter that must come first: I want to know whether you would be willing to further the official investigation by consenting to remain here as a suspected murderer until we've caught the real criminal, at which time we can give it out that you've actually been assisting the investigation all along."

Hanford cane to his feet with a joyous cry. "Then you believe me innocent, Mr. Pons. And Inspector Jamison – ?"

"I'm afraid I have no alternative," said Jamison.

"I'm sure I have you to thank for this, Mr. Pons," said Hanford, "and if my consent will help you, you have it here and now."

"Excellent," said Pons. "And now, one more question. My colleague, Dr. Parker, has assured me that the incriminating instruments found in your house were used to perform a Caesarian operation, and I assume that to mention the name of the young lady involved would not be quite politic in the circumstances."

"Exactly, Mr. Pons," said Dr. Hanford, and looked from one to the other of us in delight. "I couldn't possibly bring my patient into this matter, for circumstances are such that it would be disastrous for her. I can say, however, that she lived a good distance out in the country, and I was forced to visit her at night."

"As I thought. Very well, then. I think I can promise you release and full compensation within forty-eight hours."

Dr. Hanford was shown from the small room with something very much like deference. Inspector Jamison watched him leave with distinct uneasiness, and finally turned a very cold eye on Pons. "Well, now that we've got this far, what comes next?"

"I think I should like to look at the last body found."

"Good enough," Jamison replied. "We've got the last two laid out in a room just off this one."

The inspector crossed the room and threw open a door which led into a small, dimly illuminated room, which had evidently been hastily made into something resembling a morgue. The bodies lay on improvised slabs in its center.

Pons bent to examine them with keen interest. Together we noted the extreme precision with which the heads had been severed, and the obvious exactness with which the hypodermic injections had been made. There was, however, nothing left to discover here, and Pons cut short his examinations.

"Anything else?" asked Jamison, when we stood once more in the street before the gaol.

"Not tonight," said Pons.

"Tomorrow then."

"Come to my rooms at the Inn at four tomorrow afternoon," said Pons. "If I want you before, I can let you know easily enough."

"Very well," said Jamison, and here the matter ended, for the three of us trudged back to the *Hound & Horn* in unbroken silence.

From all evidence, Pons had left the inn long before I awoke the following morning. Nor did he appear again until shortly after three o'clock that afternoon. He came into the room with a preoccupied expression on his face, and I knew that his mind was busy with the Burlstone murders.

"Learn anything?" I asked.

"Oh, I managed to gather a few scraps here and there. It appears that Dr. Constance's house has a rather sinister reputation, due largely, I suspect, to the villagers' attitude toward experimentation. Many of these people have heard inhuman screams coming from the place, and not one of them will go near the estate, with the single exception of this fellow Jim Laird, known as Woofy, who is little more than an idiot. I saw him at a distance and made for him, but he ran off toward the estate."

"You saw Constance's place, then?"

"Indeed, yes. I went up that way. It's perched on an eminence, and seems to be walled in – takes up the entire plateau-like top of the rocky knoll. The road which leads to it is pretty well surrounded by dense bushes and overhanging trees; a rather pleasant drive, I should say."

"I'll have to call on Constance one of these days."

"You sound as if we were likely to spend some considerable time here, Parker," remarked Pons dryly. "As a matter of fact, I hope to leave tonight. As for Dr. Constance, I think that Jamison and Mecker will accompany us to his place when Jamison appears."

I sat for a moment in silence. "I think," I said at last, "that I know what you're suggesting, Pons, but I can't believe it."

Pons raised his eyebrows and chuckled. "Indeed, Parker," he murmured. "You're apparently falling back upon your old habit of jumping to conclusions."

"I've known Dr. Constance for many years, and I know he's absolutely incapable of crimes like this," I protested.

Pons shrugged. "You seem to forget that the human mind is extremely complex. More than once a scientist, eager to exploit his theories, has been found guilty of murder simply because he had arrived at that stage in which he regarded a human life as just another means of gratifying his desire for knowledge."

I would have gone on in spirited defense of my old friend, had not Jamison and Mecker entered the room at this moment. Jamison looked unusually glum.

"Don't take off your things," said Pons. "The four of us are just about to walk up to the Constance estate."

Jamison looked somewhat dubious, but he nodded. Pons bent to slip a revolver into his pocket, eyeing me sardonically.

The walk through the quiet sunny village streets and out upon the road was refreshing. There was an air of brooding peace upon the village which even the thought of the brutal crimes so recently committed here could not disturb. We walked slowly and in silence for the greater part of the way, with our eyes fixed upon the roof of the house behind the wall reaching up into the sky ahead of us. I reflected that even in this cheery afternoon sunlight the house did look somewhat sinister, but I found it difficult indeed to connect anything sinister with Dr. Constance. We had started the ascent through the shady wood, when suddenly my meditations were interrupted by what sounded like a continuation war-whoop and scream.

The four of us stopped abruptly. Again came that shrill cry, and before either of us could move, a tall thin figure, poorly clad, came shooting out of the bushes on the right side of the road. It was a man, wild and dishevelled, and he stood in the middle of the road, confronting us. In his uplifted hand he waved a large object which looked like a large knot of dirty wood.

"Jim Laird," muttered Jamison, and made as if to go for him.

As he did so, the idiot screamed once more, and launched the object he had been waving straight at us. It fell to the road with a dull thud, and came rolling toward us, stopping almost at Jamison's feet. The inspector looked at it stupidly for a moment. "My God!" he exclaimed, "*it's Dr. Graves' head*!"

Together we crouched down in the road to examine the gruesome object. "It's been buried," said Mecker.

Pons nodded. He reached out to pick up the head, and without a word, he handed it to me. I took it, trying to conceal my distaste as best I could. "Why!" I exclaimed involuntarily, "how light it is!"

"Precisely," said Pons dryly. "I think you'll find that the brain has been removed."

It was true. Without a doubt the skull had been opened, the brain removed, and the scalp again skilfully sewn up. Jamison was suddenly in a fever of excitement. He took the head and handed it to Meeker.

"Round up some of the villagers and the local police down there and beat the woods," he directed. "And if you can get him, take the idiot. We'll find out from him where he got this."

Pons smiled. "I wouldn't beat the woods, if I were you," he objected. "Quite a bit of woods, you know," he added, looking about him.

"But..." demurred Jamison.

"Wait a little," suggested Pons. "You can always beat the woods as a last resort."

"Very well," assented Jamison grudgingly.

"Then let's be on our way," said Pons quietly.

I felt certain from his attitude that Pons either knew or suspected with some definite assurance more about the affair in hand than he cared to admit at the moment. I think Jamison, too, felt this, for he said nothing, and we completed the walk in silence.

The heavy gates to the estate were wide open, and we found Dr. Constance in his garden. He had been an old man when last I knew him, and since then he had changed very little. His beard had grown longer perhaps, and his shoulders somewhat more bent. His ruddy face lit up as his eye fell on me.

"Dr. Parker," he said. "I'm glad to see you again. It's been a good many years now, hasn't it!"

I took his outstretched hand with some emotion, and rapidly introduced him to Pons and Jamison.

"Looking into that awful affair in the village, are you, gentlemen?" asked the doctor, as we strolled toward the house with him.

Pons nodded.

"A horrible affair, horrible," murmured the doctor. "Of course, since I don't go out much, hardly at all, in fact, I know very little of what has happened. I understand about the bodies, certainly, and was horrified to learn that Dr. Hanford had been taken. I would have gone down at once to put in a good word for him, had not my assistant assured me that he would soon be at liberty."

"Your assistant – that's the young man who identified the last two bodies, isn't it?" cut in Pons.

"Yes – Dr. Staunton. One of my very best men. But often unnecessarily cruel with the animals. Here he comes now," added Dr. Constance, as a young man rounded the corner of the house facing us and came forward reluctantly at the sight of us.

He was introduced to us and shook hands in a jerky manner, as if he were preoccupied with some problem, as indeed he was, for he muttered a few commonplaces, and turned to Dr. Constance, saying, "I'm sure the gentlemen will excuse us for a moment, but I must have a word with Dr. Constance."

The old physician nodded and stepped back. "Now what is it?" he asked in a lowered voice which did not conceal his exasperation.

"The morphine, Doctor," said Staunton. "It's gone again – we need it badly."

"What!" exclaimed Dr. Constance, raising his voice. "Gone again! Are you mad, Staunton? Why, I just got a shipment in, not less than a week ago. What happened to it?"

Staunton shrugged and looked coldly at his superior. "I don't know," he snapped.

Dr. Constance's face went suddenly grim. "Very well," he said stiffly, "see me immediately after dinner."

"A very fine place you have here," said Pons, as the old doctor turned again to us.

"I like it, yes," said Dr. Constance. "This little pinnacle, with the river flowing so close at its base – and under, too..."

"The Medway flows under the pinnacle, you say?" asked Pons.

"Yes," replied Dr. Constance. "The house is set quite deeply in the rock, and I discovered that from the lowest cellar there opens down a sort of well, a hollow in the wall, as it were, at the bottom of which one can easily see the water below. Whether it flows or not, I don't know. Very likely it's nothing but a quiet pool – spring water, probably. But I have always entertained the fancy that the Medway flowed beneath my house."

"Interesting," said Pons casually, but he had looked away with an intent concentration in his eyes. "I say, Doctor," he said suddenly, "I wonder whether it would be possible for you to show us through your laboratories?"

"Immediately?" asked Dr. Constance.

"As soon as possible," said Pons, looking significantly at Inspector Jamison.

"I, too, should like to see them," said Jamison.

The doctor laughed, uneasily, I thought. "You embarrass me somewhat, gentlemen, for I'll have to admit that I seldom venture out of my private laboratory into those under Dr. Staunton's control. But then, we shall do it. Let us start with mine."

I confess that I was distinctly uncomfortable as this examination, which I knew to be nothing less than a search, began. But Pons listened politely to all Dr. Constance said as we went through his laboratory, and even struck me as doing his best to hurry my old friend. We came from the laboratory at last, and descended a short flight of stone steps to the laboratories of Dr. Staunton below.

"Down there," said Dr. Constance, pointing along the hall to the darkness at its end, "is the opening I told you about. Through it you can see the water in what appears to be a smooth rock-walled well."

Jamison grunted something, and the doctor turned abruptly to open the first door in the series running the length of the hall. But before he could reach it, it swung open, and immediately young Dr. Staunton stepped out and confronted us, closing the door behind him.

"What do you want, gentlemen?" he snapped.

"We're going to look about your laboratories, Staunton," said Dr. Constance mildly.

For a moment Staunton said nothing. He looked from one to the other of us and muttered something under his breath. "I'm conducting a very delicate experiment in here just now," he said at last, "and I would much rather you went through the other laboratories first."

"What!" exclaimed Dr. Constance, "you're carrying on an experiment in there? Why, the room's dark – I saw it when you came out."

"But I intend to see this room first, Dr. Staunton!" It was Pons who spoke.

"You've no right here," said Staunton, and threw out his arms to bar the way.

"Indeed!" exclaimed Jamison, stepping forward. He looked coldly at Staunton. "Inspector Jamison, my dear sir," he said pompously. "You may consider Scotland Yard in charge. I order that room opened."

For a moment there was complete silence.

Then, suddenly there came a burst of hysterical laughter, and just as the three of us pressed toward Dr. Staunton, he jumped forward with unexpected vigour, burst past Pons and

Jamison, and ran with great speed down the long hall into the darkness at its further end.

"After him, Jamison," shouted Pons, but he himself made no move.

Jamison started down the hall, but at almost the same instant, there came to our ears a muffled splash, and Jamison put on an extra burst of speed. Dr. Constance stood trembling in our midst.

"Gentlemen, gentlemen," he said shrilly, "I don't understand. What is this?"

In answer Pons stepped forward and flung open the door of the laboratory. For a moment we could see nothing in the darkness, but there came to our ears a weird whispering sound, as if someone were lashing long whips in the air about our heads. Dr. Constance pressed forward and turned up the light.

As if by magic, all eyes were rivetted on the ghastly apparition which seemed to appear from the opposite wall. For there were lined up against this wall four large glass containers, and from openings at the tops came long flesh-like appendages, lashing the air in unaccountable fury. For a moment we stared, and then our glances fell toward the contents of the containers.

"Good God!" gasped Dr. Constance.

At the same instant Pons drew his revolver and shot four times in quick succession. For each of the ghastly glass containers held a human brain!

Dr. Constance put one hand up before his eyes, and with his other, turned out the lights. Together, we stumbled out into the hall.

"That's where your morphine disappeared to," said Pons to Dr. Constance. "Into the bodies of Staunton's victims."

Jamison came running toward us. "Who shot?" he demanded, and his glance fell to the revolver in Pons' hand.

"Where's Staunton?" asked Dr. Constance in a quavering voice. "Gone down that hole," said Jamison. "He's done for, I think, – the wall's smooth; he can't get a hold anywhere."

"Can he swim?" asked Pons, turning to Dr. Constance.

"Very well."

"Then Jamison, I should advise you to get as many men together as you can and watch the river bank – especially near the estate and the woods surrounding it. Go at once, for I have no doubt in the world but that the river flows beneath the water in that pool."

Jamison ran quickly up the steps and out of the house, with Pons and I not long after him, though it took us some time to calm Dr. Constance sufficiently to explain briefly to him.

"Well," said Pons, as we were seated in a train bearing us swiftly toward London, "I daresay Jamison will have no trouble in piecing the thing together. He has the primary knowledge and the explanation; the facts will come of themselves."

"You knew that it was Staunton, then, all the time?" I asked.

"On the contrary," said Pons. "I suspected him that's all. But I knew he was the man we wanted when Dr. Constance mentioned him as trying to dissuade him from aiding Hanford in any way. The suspicious absence of the morphine, and the pool beneath the house were all I needed to act. Obviously, Staunton, too, thought this a quiet pool, and sank the bodies in it; unfortunately for him, the river current carried the bodies out into the light. He must soon have known this, but with the arrest of Hanford, he became unnecessarily careless. I daresay he buried the heads somewhere, though he might as well have thrown them into the pool.

"The fellow was probably a little mad. He wanted agile human brains for experimental purposes, and he got them. He took men in their prime. I daresay he had no trouble with Graves, who as a physician, was probably willing enough to work with Staunton, providing no evil consequences came of the experimentation; Staunton probably took him in very easily. And with the gardener and his brother, I assume that they knew very little better —probably thought the doctor was giving them a dose of medicine. Most likely he had the greatest trouble with Henderson, whose acquaintance he had made some time before. He certainly used enough morphine, it seems; using both the shipment from the clearing-house, and sending to the local chemist's in Dr. Constance's name.

"But at the most, this is mere conjecture; we shall not know until Staunton can be induced to confess. Whatever he was trying to prove for himself with the aid of the human brain is also a matter for conjecture. I'll not soon forget that horrible picture of the brains and their flailing tentacles."

But whatever Staunton might have confessed we were destined not to know, for late in the following day came a wire from Jamison. Pons read it meditatively and threw it to the table.

"The body has been found just below Burlstone," he said. "And the heads were uncovered in Constance's garden – where I imagined we might find them. Apparently the idiot led them to the place where he had brought the first to light."

THE ADVENTURE OF THE VIENNESE MUSICIAN

No doubt the astonishing and daringly executed murder of Manfred Menheim, world famous musician, still lingers in thousands of minds connected with the musical world. The affair caused some little excitement at the time, and the press eagerly seized hold of such details as were furnished it by Scotland Yard, then none too careful in withholding the facts of the case. This scattered group of people will remember that the matter was suddenly and inexplicably hushed up; only a few persons outside of His Majesty's Cabinet ever knew that the metropolitan newspapers had been silenced by the pressure of Lord Penryn, at whose home in Park Lane the unfortunate affair had taken place. Fewer persons yet were aware of Solar Pons' connection with the case, and because of the studious secrecy maintained by the official police on this point no one was more pleased than Pons himself, for he had been so angered by the absurd mistake made by Inspector Jamison that he withdrew, leaving that worthy official to take upon himself all credit for the series of remarkable deductions that finished the case for the public eye.

In view of the actual facts that Pons brought together, it was only politic that the matter be kept from print in any form; consequently, for many years the case of the Viennese musician remained locked in Pons' files. The incidents of this story are now some twenty years old, and since the persons connected with it are scattered over the globe, Pons has at last permitted me to dig out the facts from their seclusion.

The case first came to Solar Pons' attention late in the night of the same day that we returned from Northumberland. Both of us had retired early, for the many sleepless nights that we had gone through in the mysterious adventure of the limping man had begun to tell on us. Pons was the first to respond to the insistent knocking on the door, for Mrs. Johnson rarely, if ever, woke up once having gone to sleep. Half consciously I heard Pons ascend the stairs, followed by another, by whose ponderous steps I identified as Inspector Jamison, the best known of the Scotland Yard men. In a moment Pons pulled aside the heavy curtain and poked his head into my bedroom. I rose on one elbow. "What is it?" I asked.

"Murder. Want to come along?"

"I'll be dressed in a moment."

Jamison stood in the middle of the room, legs spread apart, both hands deep in his trousers' pockets, as I entered. His chubby face wore a puzzled look, and he made no effort to hide it.

"Good evening, Parker," he greeted me affably. "Pons routed you, eh?"

"Yes," I answered "What is it all about?"

"A queer business, Parker. Menheim, the musician, fell dead at the piano at about nine this evening. He was reciting at Lord Penryn's in Park Lane."

"Why spare us the details, Jamison?" interrupted Pons.

"What do you want to know?" demanded Jamison, somewhat nettled.

"Exactly what happened immediately preceding his death. For instance, how did he act when he entered the room? His attitude? Did anyone speak to him? And so on."

Jamison drew out a notebook and consulted it for a moment, Pons winked broadly.

"Well, let's see," mumbled Jamison. "He was perfectly natural all evening; Lady Penryn says he seemed in splendid health. He came into the room at almost nine, together with his wife, who followed him to the piano. On the way to the instrument he stopped and talked to his host and hostess and to Lord Brangwyn, who sat near them. At the piano he turned to Arthur Penryn, Lord Penryn's eldest son, who was to assist him in the recital, and whispered something into his ear."

"Did anyone catch it?" asked Pons quickly.

"No one. But Lady Penryn says that Madame Menheim frowned ever so slightly and spoke to her husband in an undertone. Arthur Penryn immediately stepped back, followed by Madame Menheim, and the musician seated himself. Lord Penryn reports that he noticed a certain paling and reddening of Menheim's features as he sat down, but he cannot be sure because the light in the room was somewhat dimmed."

"Where was Lord Penryn sitting?" asked Pons.

"Somewhat to the side; he would have seen Menheim's face very well."

"Hmm! Go on."

"There's not much more. Menheim struck the first note, and fell forward on the piano."

"He struck only the first note, eh?" Pons hesitated a moment. "That would be C-sharp in the third octave of the minor scale."

Jamison stared at Pons. "How could you know that?"

"Because Menheim always opens with *Au Comte Ladislas Telekey*, the second of Liszt's fifteen *Rhapsodies Hongroises*."

"Of course," said Jamison, obviously disconcerted.

"That was a little after nine, you say. When were you called?"

"Not until almost eleven – ten minutes to when we got there."

"Why the delay?" asked Pons.

"The fellow had a weak heart; subject to attacks. It was thought that he'd had a heart attack. It wasn't until after the doctor had made his examination that poison was discovered."

"Indeed?" exclaimed Pons. "Where was it found?"

"The prick of a needle was discovered in Menheim's wrist; the flesh about the puncture had started to discolour. Dr. Bardsley, the Penryn's family physician, suggested that the needle had been dipped in a syrupy solution of prussic acid. It is our theory that Menheim was poisoned just before he sat down to the piano."

Pons looked sharply at Jamison. "Of course, you questioned everyone present at once?"

"Yes. That is, all but Madame Menheim, who was too overcome to answer our questions."

Pons nodded. "And you suspect... ?"

"No one!" declared Jamison with emphasis. "Not one of those present had a motive as far as we can see."

"My dear Jamison! Don't you think you had better find a suspect first and look for the motive afterwards? In the light of your theory, there are five persons you must logically suspect."

"And they are?" asked Jamison dubiously.

"Lord and Lady Penryn, Lord Brangwyn, Arthur Penryn, and Madame Menheim. By your own admission those five persons are the only people Menheim came in contact with from the time he entered the room to the time he fell dead."

Jamison said nothing.

"Did you by any chance mention your theory to Dr. Bardsley?" Pons asked.

"No, I did not – I saw no need to."

"Ah! No? Of course, there was no need. – I suppose. But are you quite sure of yourself, Jamison?"

"What are you driving at, Pons?" Jamison regarded Pons half angrily.

"How much time elapsed between Menheim's conversation with the elder Penryns and Lord Brangwyn, and the moment of his death?"

Jamison hesitated a moment. "I should say about... well, not under four minutes."

"And how long did it take him to settle himself for the recital after his words with young Penryn and Madame Menheim?"

"Almost two minutes; it usually took him that long to make himself ready."

"Dear me! Are you quite sure, Jamison?"

"Certain, Pons."

"Singular! I'm afraid you'll have to give up that theory of yours, Jamison!"

"And why?"

"If you had proposed it to Dr. Bardsley, he would have told you that prussic acid acts within a minute after its injection."

"But it did act," expostulated Jamison. "Lord Penryn mentioned that Menheim flushed and paled when he seated himself."

"Yes. I believe you said something about that. I do not recall that a sudden paling and flushing of the features is a symptom of prussic acid poisoning. I suppose the body is now quite cold – and perhaps moist and livid, Jamison?"

"Of course, the body is cold. And I think it is somewhat reddish in colour, but as to its being moist... well, I don't know. I didn't examine the body closely; left that to Bardsley and my own man, Dr. Brennan."

Pons nodded. "No matter. I suppose we are at liberty to go there at any time?"

"Quite," said Jamison. "The sooner you appear, Pons, the better it will be for all of us. Penryn is very influential."

Pons chuckled. "And you want someone just as influential with you, eh?" He rose. "You've a cab downstairs, I suppose?"

"Of course."

The night was extraordinarily clear and warm, and the cab that Jamison had waiting for us was nothing less than an open police motor, into which Pons climbed with obvious pleasure. Though the distance from Praed Street to Lord Penryn's home was short, we were soon making our way with all speed down Edgware Road toward Park Lane.

A constable stood on guard at the gate to the grounds in Park Lane. He saluted stiffly as we passed; Jamison gave him a curt nod. Pons, however, stopped a moment to light his pipe. He gave the constable a searching look.

"Mecker, aren't you?"

"Yes, sir."

"Did anybody leave?" Pons asked.

"No one, sir. That is, since we've come."

"And before?"

"The guests departed before we were called."

"And no one since, eh?"

"No one! Arthur Penryn – he is the eldest son – came to the gate and had a few words with me, but that's all."

"What did he say?"

"Remarked on the weather, sir, and hoped this matter would be cleared up soon."

Pons remained silent; then, with an abrupt nod, he came after Jamison, who had paused some little distance up the flagstone walk. We entered the house, passing another constable at the door. Jamison led us directly to the drawing room, where the musician's body lay on a davenport near the piano. No one was in the room except two constables placed there at Jamison's order, and Dr. Bardsley, who had just entered the room from the second storey, where he had been attending to Madame Menheim.

Pons went at once to the body, and, lifting the scarf that covered it, threw it to one side. He examined the body rapidly, paying special attention to the punctured wrist which was obviously livid. He rose at last, with a satisfied expression on his face, and stood for some moments looking down at the body.

"I should advise you, Jamison, to send out a number of men to all the nearest drug shops for a list of those who have purchased any form of prussic acid within the last three days – especially in the last twenty-four hours."

"Very well, Mr. Pons," said Jamison. He left the room. No sooner had he gone than Pons turned to Bardsley.

"What do you make of it, Doctor Bardsley?"

"Quite amazing, Mr. Pons. The fellow had a heart attack; someone who came to help him as he fell upon the keyboard tried to poison him by pressing the point of a needle dipped in a syrupy solution of diluted hydrocyanic acid into his wrist – a ticklish procedure, done, I infer, by someone who was desperately anxious to get the man out of the way. Quite ironic, too. Menheim would unquestionably have died from the heart attack, but someone wasn't taking any chances."

"You regard the prussic acid as a contributory factor, then?" asked Pons.

"Undoubtedly, Mr. Pons, though I'm taking quite a bit on myself in making that statement. You have already seen that Menheim shows neither the moistness nor the lividity of body characteristic of prussic acid poisoning. However, the wrist is quite livid, and his blood is very dark. I'm distinctly in a quandary; since the man would have died from the attack, did die from it, one might easily say, you see how difficult it is for me to pronounce his death murder. Yet Brennan, a man well qualified, insists on murder." The doctor shrugged his shoulders.

"I sympathize with you, Doctor," said Pons.

At that moment Jamison bustled into the room. "Well, Pons, what have you discovered?"

"Nothing of importance as yet, Jamison," Pons answered. "There are a few more things I should like to know. For instance, how long were Menheim and his wife in London?"

"Eight days; they spent them as house guests of the Penryns."

Pons meditated a moment. "Did they by any chance bring their own domestics with them?"

"No! Domestics were furnished them by the Penryns."

"Capital!" exclaimed Pons. "I want to speak to the young lady who attended Madame Menheim the last eight days."

Jamison turned to a constable and murmured an order. The constable immediately left the room.

"You might bring Menheim's man along," Jamison called after him. "I suppose you'll want to speak to him," he continued, turning to Pons.

"Yes, of course, Jamison." Pons was silent for a moment. "Did you by any chance take the trouble to ascertain who was first to reach Menheim when he collapsed?"

"Why, yes, I did. It appears that Arthur Penryn and Madame Menheim reached the musician simultaneously. You remember they were sitting together after they left her husband."

Pons nodded. "Have you received Brennan's report?"

Jamison shook his head, "Not yet."

"Hmm! Well, he'll tell you that prussic acid was administered after Menheim fell forward."

"After? But, Pons..." Jamison turned to Dr. Bardsley. "Is that true, doctor?"

"Quite, Mr. Jamison." Dr. Bardsley nodded.

"Then one of the two..." Jamison began.

"Perhaps," said Pons. "Or just as probably one of the others who immediately crowded around the man." Jamison grimaced. "How many guests were there, Jamison?"

"Eleven," said Jamison, "I have a list of them all!"

"Together with the Penryns and Madame Menheim that makes sixteen, doesn't it?"

"Fifteen – the younger Penryn was not present."

"Fifteen then; fifteen persons who must come under suspicion."

Jamison smirked, "Picture me suspecting Sir Gordon Cruesbury, His Majesty's Secretary," said Jamison sarcastically, "Or perhaps old Lord Vrennersley, already so infirm that I'll wager he was the last to reach Menheim."

Pons chuckled, "Do as you please, Jamison. But here, if I am not mistaken, are the Menheim's domestics."

Jamison's constable had returned, ushering into the room a comely young woman of not more than twenty-five and a man of about forty. Pons nodded to them, and they came forward. Both were, of course, fully dressed, for the murder had roused the household.

Pons first gave his attention to the man, who sat on the edge of the chair that Pons indicated. Pons said nothing for a few moments; Jamison, meanwhile, could not understand Pons' motive in questioning people who were not even present at the scene of the crime.

"What were your impressions of Mr. Menheim?" asked Pons suddenly.

The man was taken aback. He looked vacantly at Pons and shifted about in his chair, though not nervously. "What do you mean?" he asked at last.

"What about his conduct? – his habits, for instance?"

"Well... He was very irregular in his habits, sir. He seemed to have no respect for anyone but himself."

"Ah! So? What was his attitude toward his wife?"

"He treated her like a servant, sir."

"She resented this, I suppose?" ventured Pons.

"Oh! Not so much, sir. There were other things they had trouble about."

"Ah! indeed? What, for instance?"

The man flushed and hesitated. "Well, sir, it is pretty common knowledge here that his affairs with women caused a good many quarrels with his wife. But none of them were ever serious, though; she was very jealous, however, and often threatened him."

At this Jamison sat up a little straighter, as if afraid of missing something. Pons, however, seemed to regard the information as of no importance, for he stood a moment in perplexity.

"They had high words just before they came downstairs last evening, sir."

At this Pons leaned forward. "And did you, by any chance, overhear any of their conversation?"

"Only one word, sir. Madame Menheim was talking and said something about 'letters'."

"Now, what would you say she was referring to?"

"It was my idea that she referred to packets of letters he'd stored away in his travelling bag; I suppose they were from young women."

"Ah!" exclaimed Pons, and hesitated. "Now one more question: was Menheim in the habit of clothing himself in an air of secrecy?"

The domestic started obviously. "Why, yes, he was. Indeed, he was most secretive, sir. I often caught him watching me out of the corner of his eye, almost like a – a madman, sir! Often I've heard him talking to himself, or to someone else he'd got into the room somehow. Often, too, I would find packets of letters hidden all over his rooms."

Pons smiled. "That will do," he said, and waved the man away. He turned now to the young lady, who had several times shown signs of wishing to corroborate some of the testimony given by her fellow domestic.

"Can you corroborate what little this man has said of Madame Menheim?" asked Pons.

The young lady nodded, "Yes, sir, except that I don't think Madame Menheim meant it when she threatened her husband. No, sir, she isn't the kind of a woman who'd ever do anything serious, not she!"

"You don't think so, eh?"

"No, sir. It's never the one who talks most about murder who commits it, sir."

"Dear me!" exclaimed Pons. There was a touch of admiration in his voice. "But you must remember, young lady, that there is no rule to that effect."

The girl nodded and smiled. "I know that, sir."

"Did you also get the impression that Menheim's affairs with other women were bothering his wife?"

"In a way, yes sir! But it always seemed to me that she was more concerned about those letters. Why I felt that way, I don't know – intuition, maybe, sir. Once I caught her crying in her room; she said she didn't feel well, but I knew that she had had harsh words with her husband over some of those letters. There seemed to be one particular packet she was anxious to get hold of; from what I heard, he always carried this packet about with him."

"Did you at any time hear any names mentioned between them?"

"Oh! yes, sir. They often talked about the Penryns, especially young Mr. Arthur, sir. Then there was someone by the name of Worthing, and a young lady they called Irene. That's all."

"That will be quite enough," said Pons. "It will be better, I think, if you say nothing to Madame Menheim about this interrogation... at least for the present."

"Very well, sir."

Jamison now came up, and Pons turned to him at once.

"That will be all I can do now, Jamison," said Pons. "But I shall see you tomorrow, I hope. I'll want to borrow Mecker for a time also – let us say, until tomorrow at one?"

Jamison nodded.

"I'll not need him tonight, however. Tomorrow morning I want you to send him to me with complete reports on what your men find at the drug shops. Any telephone message to or from the house is to be taken verbatim – send that with Mecker also. If anyone attempts to leave the house, allow him to do so, but keep him under surveillance. I shall want those points accurately reported."

"Certainly, Mr. Pons," said Jamison, nodding again, "as long as we are working together, I shall certainly see to that."

Pons favoured Jamison with a dry smile, to which Jamison responded in kind. At the threshold Pons turned.

"Might I suggest that you get a list of ships leaving Liverpool for America tomorrow?"

Jamison's jaw dropped, and he stared after Pons in amazement. Pons chuckled. "If the man is shrewd enough, that will tell him what he wants to know. Unfortunately however, Jamison likes to add two and two and get five." Pons stopped on the path. "I'll wager that before morning Jamison will have charged Madame Menheim with the murder of her husband – as if the poor woman hadn't gone through enough already."

"Then Madame Menheim didn't – ?" I began, for I confess I had fixed on her as the murderer.

"No, no. Dear me, no, Parker! Where are your wits, man? That was obvious from the start, I should say."

At the gate Pons borrowed Mecker's flash and started back along the path, examining it as well as he could with the light. Often he went to his knees, and in spite of the dampness of the ground, crept along for some distance. He spent some time midway up the path, but his search proved fruitless, as the annoyed frown on his face when he returned gave evidence. He stood for some time in silence, paying no attention to the conversation that Mecker and I were carrying on. Suddenly his eye lighted on a broken twig on the ground, somewhat off the walk. With a smothered exclamation he picked it up, looked at it closely, and ran quickly back along the path, flashing his light into the trees. Both of us followed him with our eyes, and saw him stop and examine the branches of a tree. It was not long before he was back again, but he had nothing to say of his strange conduct, and I knew better than to press him.

"I say, Mecker," he said, "Jamison will send you to me with an official report sometime tomorrow. Get it to me as fast as you can – say, about noon, eh?"

Mecker nodded. "Yes, sir."

"I'm afraid Jamison didn't take the last of my instructions seriously. I repeat, then, that I shall want to know what ships leave Liverpool for America tomorrow."

"Very well, sir," answered Mecker. Then, seeing us about to leave he continued, "Shall I call a cab, sir?"

"No," said Pons. "We'll walk; it's not far, and the night is excellent."

We walked rapidly up Park Lane, crossed to Bayswater Road, and turned up Edgware Road, where Pons set a slower pace, for the night was indeed remarkably clear, and the traffic along Edgware Road was very light, though an hour later would see a continual row of cabs, cars, and omnibuses rushing up and down in the dawn. We had passed two streets before Pons broke from his meditations.

"By the way, Parker, what did you think I examined the path for?"

"I don't know," I replied, "unless it was to look for the needle."

"Yes, that was it. I thought at first that it might have been pressed into the ground, but a man or woman pressing anything into the ground would be pretty suspicious – especially with Mecker standing there at the gate, and his fellow constable at the door. I found it, of course, but not in the ground. It isn't at all suspicious to see a man break a twig off a tree – even if he does use two hands and more than necessary effort to do it, is it?"

"No," I replied.

Pons stopped in the glow of an arc light and drew out his pocketbook, from which he took an ordinary needle. He held this up in the light. I could see a whitish discolouration coating half the needle.

"It was pressed into the branch where the twig had been broken off. Rather a clever idea; done by someone pretty sure of himself." Pons hesitated. "You know the kind of man who must virtually force himself to go astray, but once gone, he is as immovable as steel. Such was our murderer – he wanted to poison Menheim before the recital, but lost his nerve. The moment Menheim has a heart attack, he sees his chance, and in the melee, pricks him in the wrist with the needle. All the time he was in the room – even after the police came – he kept the needle on him; it was only when comparative quiet had been restored that he dared rid himself of it.

Pons restored the needle to the pocketbook, and returned the latter to his pocket. We were already opposite Marylebone Road, and we completed the remainder of the walk in silence. Before ascending the steps of Number Seven Praed Street, Pons stood for a moment listening to the subdued roar of trains and trams from the great terminus at Paddington. I have noticed many such odd inconsistencies in Pons' character. Just as the roar of incoming and outgoing trains now fascinated him, so did the whir of night cars attract his attention on our recent vacation in Northumberland. It was not for long that he stood there, however, and soon we were comfortably established in our rooms. Now enveloped in the folds of his dressing gown, Pons again took up the subject uppermost in my mind, approaching it from an entirely different angle.

"There is a certain form of criminal abnormality – or, perhaps I should better say insanity – that amounts to monomania. Dr. Krafft-Ebing handles the subject most adequately in those two German volumes you have on your shelves, Parker. (The two books Pons referred to here were Richard von Krafft-Ebing' *Grundzüge der Criminal-Psychologie auf Grundlage der Deutschen and Osterreichischen Strafgesetzgebung für Juristen*, Stuttgart, 1882, and *Lehrbuch der Psychoatrie auf Klinischer Grundlage fur Praktische umgearbeitete Auflage*, Stuttgart, 1890.) There are several minor monographs on the subject which you also possess; I assume, then, that you are quite familiar with the type I mean."

"The affliction I have reference to might come under the classification of *idiots savants*, but I do not feel fully justified in putting Menheim in that class."

"But you don't mean that Menheim was in any way abnormal?" I cried.

"Menheim was one of the most peculiarly constructed individuals I have ever known. A great musical genius, but unquestionably abnormal. The man was, before all, noticeably mediocre in anything but the field of music. This, in itself, is no sign of abnormality, but Menheim was afflicted with a certain mania – which he might have called anything from a pastime to a business. Since the remuneration was usually handsome, I presume he called it a business."

Pons rose and went quickly to his shelves, where he scanned the books. He returned with a ponderous notebook volume in his hands; this was his "encyclopedia" as he called it, and contained compact notes on all criminal cases of major and minor significance on the Continent and in England. It had in compact form all that the archives of Scotland Yard held, and much more. This book he leafed through, stopping at last, to read:

"'Menheim, Manfred Thomas: Born, August, 1877, of poor parents in Vienna. Was caught stealing at ages of nine and fourteen; environment largely blamed. At fifteen mixed up in petty blackmail plot. Early showed special aptitude for music. Wealthy burgher-patron made possible his musical education. Speedily advanced. First concert in Vienna on 17 March, 1899, two months after he married Lady Caroline Hahn-Hahn in Berlin. Paris recital, 1900; London, 1901. Two tours of the United States and Canada, 1903 and 1905. Connected with the concert stage since.

"'In 1902 Menheim was proven a party to a blackmail plot in Vienna; he was with difficulty extricated. In 1904 he was party to the notorious Desmoreaux plot at Lyons; in 1906, to the von Meimertz plot in Vienna. Supposed to have professional agents in London and the Continental cities. His work shows no noticeable deviation from standard blackmail plots.'

"What do you make of that, Parker?" finished Pons, closing the book, and rising to replace it.

"Then the letters Madame Menheim referred to were blackmail letters, eh?" I ventured.

"Precisely, Parker."

"But whose letters were they?"

Pons chuckled, "You haven't guessed, eh?" I shook my head negatively. "Well, we can leave that until later this morning, then. For the present, I suggest that we go to bed. Mecker will rout us out when he comes; before that I will want to do nothing."

But with Mecker's coming a surprise awaited us. The young constable came shortly after ten o'clock. Without more than a short greeting, he threw a paper down before us. It was the Mirror; on the top of the front page was the mystery of the night before, already solved! This headline greeted us:

WIFE KILLS MENHEIM SUICIDES!
MUSICAL WORLD SHOCKED
AND GRIEVED
AT DOUBLE TRAGEDY

> An unfortunate occurrence last evening deprived the musical world of two of its greatest figures, Mr. and Mrs. Manfred Menheim. One of the most widely known concert pianists, Menheim was scheduled to recite privately at number 23 Park Lane, where he and Madame Menheim had been over the week guests of Lord and Lady Penryn.
>
> Mr. Menheim fell dead at the piano just as he was opening his recital. It was first supposed that Mr.

Menheim was the victim of a heart attack, for he was subject to seizures. Further examination showed that the unfortunate musician had been poisoned by prussic acid administered through the skin of his wrist. No clew to the situation was found, and it was only when Inspector Seymour R. Jamison of Scotland Yard examined the Menheim domestics that he discovered Madame Menheim's intense jealousy of her husband. Inspector Jamison immediately suspected Madame Menheim, but when he went to question her, he found that she had committed suicide by drinking prussic acid. Near her body was found a note pencilled in her hand, as follows:

"I killed my husband by pricking him in the wrist with a needle dipped in diluted prussic acid just before we went downstairs. I cannot live without him."

Inspector Jamison's subsequent investigations disclosed that Madame Menheim had purchased prussic acid nearby. The motive was obviously jealousy, as the Scotland Yard man very ably demonstrated by pointing out that ashes in the fireplace of her room were certainly those of old *billets doux*, about which Madame Menheim had been known to quarrel with her husband.

All credit for this remarkable work goes again to Inspector Jamison, who has already so often proved his mettle. Scotland Yard is again to be commended.

Pons burst into a hearty laugh – to which he did not often give way. "Most remarkable work, indeed!" He sank into his chair. "Parker, that man will be the death of me yet. Such untoward laughter wears on me! Wise Jamison; the commendable, most worthy Inspector." He took up the paper and stared at it; then suddenly he was intent.

"But, at that, perhaps the estimable Jamison has unconsciously done us a good turn. I'm not sure that the entire matter shouldn't be left like this."

He sat back in his chair and appeared to muse for a moment. Then, he turned abruptly to Meeker. "Well, Meeker, what have you found?"

For a brief moment Meeker consulted his notebook. "You asked me specially to look up ships leaving Liverpool for America; *H.M.S. George IV* leaves at five o'clock this afternoon."

"Very good, Meeker; go on."

"Very well. Now as to the drug shop investigations. Three people were found to have purchased prussic acid; a nearby physician, Dr. Inders Bardsley, the Penryn family physician, by way of mention, who is treating a patient with it in 2% solution in doses of two to six minims; Madame Menheim, who had got the necessary permit from this doctor; and an old woman, unidentified, with a permit also from Doctor Bardsley."

"I hope that you took the trouble to identify this person, Meeker," Pons broke in.

"I considered that essential to my report. The woman is Mrs. Adelaid Marks, the Penryns' housekeeper."

"Capital!" exclaimed Pons. "Nothing could be better."

"In regard to telephone calls, only one went out that was not official – none came in except a call from Scotland Yard. The call that went out was made by Arthur Penryn to a Miss Helen Worthing, a young lady with whom he had been on friendly terms for some time. I took the trouble to look her up and found that she comes from a very high family – their position quite equals that of the Penryns. The call that Penryn made was to the effect that he would call for the young lady at three this afternoon."

Pons made no comment; for a short time he sat in deep thought. Then, finally, he rose, moved over to the table and sat down to write out a note. This he finished in a moment. He re-read it, folded it, and handed it to Mecker.

"Get this to Mr. Arthur Penryn as soon as you can, Mecker; then report back here and join us at lunch."

"Very well, sir." Mecker nodded and withdrew.

"It shouldn't take him long," said Pons, looking at the clock on the mantel.

"Is Arthur Penryn our man then?" I asked.

"Of course. Penryn is the real murderer in this case. You should have seen that, Parker."

"But what connection has the *George IV*?" I ventured.

"If you had watched the society columns of our papers recently you would have seen a notice to the effect that Mr. Arthur Penryn was rumoured to be planning on leaving for America this week. As this is Saturday, I took it for granted that he would leave today if at all. This morning, before you were up, I called Liverpool and got the booking offices; Penryn had booked passage for two."

"Two?"

"One for his wife."

"To the best of my knowledge, Penryn isn't married," I objected.

"No." answered Pons, looking at his watch. "Not yet."

"What was the note you sent him?"

"Merely a request for him to see me at one o'clock." He rose and went into his chemical laboratory. He returned shortly, holding up a small glass phial containing a dark brownish liquid.

"Recognize it?" he asked. I nodded. "Exhibit A; one phial of *the* most rapid poison known!"

Half an hour after our return from lunch, the doorbell rang sharply. We could hear Mrs. Johnson going to answer the door. Pons turned to Mecker.

"You'd better go into the back room, Mecker," he said. "It might disconcert the boy to see an official man here." Mecker rose. "And remember that anything you hear is a secret between the three of us."

"Very well, sir." Mecker vanished into the adjoining room.

Pons and I looked up expectantly as our landlady showed a young man of about twenty-eight into the room. He was tall and well-built, and his firm mouth showed determination in every line. He resembled Lord Penryn, his father, very much. He stood regarding us in silence for a moment.

"Mr. Arthur Penryn, I take it," said Pons. He waved his hand toward a chair. "Will you sit down?"

Penryn made a tentative movement toward the chair.

"You sent for me, Mr. Pons. – Why?"

"Have you seen this morning's paper, Mr. Penryn?"

"I have, though I cannot see of what assistance I can be to you. If you have read the paper you will see that the unfortunate affair has been satisfactorily cleared up."

"Dear me! Mr. Penryn. Don't you think you are insulting my intelligence? Every intelligent man will see through that newspaper account immediately."

For a moment Penryn said nothing. "What do you mean?" he said in a low voice.

"I sent for you," said Pons slowly, "to ask you why you did it."

"Sir!" Penryn advanced on Pons, but faltered before Pons' steady gaze. "It would be best, I think, to explain fully."

"I have nothing to say," said Penryn. "You may hold me if you wish, but I warn you against doing so, for my father will be most unsparing in his efforts to punish you for the outrage. You are not, I believe, an official man."

"Quite so; you are informed correctly, Mr. Penryn. I take the liberty of informing you also that people do not speak to me in that manner. Be so good as to sit down. Since you do not intend to give me the information I desire, perhaps you will permit me to repeat it to you – for your verification, if nothing else."

Penryn seated himself, glaring defiantly at Pons. He glanced suggestively at the clock on the mantel.

"It is unfortunate, is it not, Mr. Penryn, that young men in love will permit themselves to write indiscreet letters. This is especially true if the letters are addressed to young ladies of none too circumspect character – if we may thus classify your Irene."

At this, the colour in young Penryn's face gave place to a sudden paleness, accentuated by the stare of fear that he now directed at Pons.

"It was, of course, not to be surmised that those letters would reappear at some future date in your life. Certainly you had no suspicion that they should by any chance fall into the hands of Miss Helen Worthing, your fiancée, with whom you are planning an elopement to America this afternoon."

Penryn gripped the arms of his chair; he was making a noticeable effort to control himself. Pons went on imperturbably.

"You realized, of course, that Miss Worthing, owing to her position, would be forced to summarily dismiss you, should the letters be made public. Thus you were placed in somewhat of a predicament when early this week you received from the man Menheim a demand for – how much was it, Mr. Penryn?"

"Ten thousand pounds," answered Penryn almost inaudibly.

"The alternative was the publication of the letters in some salacious news-sheet; your former friend, Irene, was possibly in need of money and disposed of the letters to Menheim's agent in the city, or quite possibly to Menheim himself. Since your plan to leave for America today had already been formulated, as the rumour reported in the social notes indicated, you found the demand very excessive indeed. Ten thousand pounds is a huge sum; it was impossible for you to supply this money and still make your journey; yet Menheim calmly kept pressure on you all week, giving you until Friday night, to perhaps midnight. He frequently met you in his rooms, within hearing of his wife, who was naturally aware of former trouble his peculiar mania had got him into. Your constant reiteration of your inability to raise the sum demanded, and her fear of another disgrace, caused Madame Menheim to approach her husband against his plan. This double fire of arguments continued for perhaps two or three days before Menheim's recital, attracting the attention of the domestics your parents furnished.

"Knowledge of the recital finally suggested a way out. You managed to obtain prussic acid, by sending your housekeeper out with a permit signed by Dr. Bardsley. Just before the recital, you, who have had excellent training in chemistry as I have ascertained, you mixed a syrupy solution of prussic acid which adhered to a needle. At the same time that you made up your mind to make away with Menheim, his wife, who had suffered constant disgrace, and who was cursed with that peculiar temperament that bound her to her husband, determined to kill both him and herself if he insisted on collecting the sum demanded.

"Now, let us rehearse last evening's occurrence. When the Menheims descended the stairs, you came hurriedly from your rooms with the needle held carefully concealed in your palm. You intended to poison him before he began his recital, but, knowing the action of prussic acid, you hesitated, and lost your opportunity. Then he sat down to the piano, and you had by this time practically given up the idea of going through with your plan. When he fell forward because of a sudden heart attack, you jumped forward with others, pressed the needle home in the disturbance, and made certain of his death thereby.

"Madame Menheim had determined to kill both of them when she heard her husband turn to you a moment before he began and whisper – what did he say, Penryn. 'Til midnight'?"

Penryn nodded.

"When she saw her husband fall forward, she immediately assumed that he had another seizure and was immensely relieved, collapsing from the lifting of the strain she was under and the descent of her grief at his death. The first thing she did was to go up to her husband's rooms, and destroy all questionable letters in his possession, by burning. Whether she got your letters, which Menheim carried with him, or not, I can't say; I leave that to you."

"I got them from his inner pocket during the disturbance, Mr. Pons." Penryn's voice was calmer now.

"Ah! So? And disposed of them as quickly as you could, eh?"

Penryn nodded.

"Quite so. The needle, however, you found not so easy to get rid of; indeed, you had to wait until after the police arrived, and then daringly press it into a broken branch. The moment that Madame Menheim was given to understand that her husband had been poisoned, she realized what had happened. Immediately she takes the only step open to her – that is, sign a spurious confession and kill herself. This she did, but unfortunately the lady was ignorant of the immediate action of prussic acid, for she says that she poisoned him before they descended the stairs. In that case, fully ten minutes elapsed between the poisoning and his death. Unfortunately, however, Scotland Yard accepts the missive, and the case is solved."

Pons ceased speaking. For a moment Penryn said nothing; then he rose and held out his hands. "Here," he said, "I don't suppose there's any use in fighting you. I surrender."

"You need not, Mr. Penryn. Since I am not official, I will take no official action. The case is obvious; if the official police discover their mistake, well and good – I've no doubt a capable barrister could extricate you from a charge of murder. I have only to warn you against taking the law into your own hands in the future; there is, you know, a great possibility of its getting you into trouble."

Penryn bowed. Pons nodded curtly and looked at the clock on the mantel. "You'd better hurry if you want to keep your appointment with Miss Helen Worthing."

Only after Penryn had gone did Mecker appear, and then with protest on his lips.

"Mr. Pons, how can you allow that man his freedom?"

"Dear me! Mecker, how disappointing. You sound almost like Jamison." He turned seriously to the young constable. "I have your word, have I not, that you will repeat nothing?"

"You have, Mr. Pons."

"Very well. Then let us see what Jamison has to say about that note." He reached for the telephone and called a number. Immediately Jamison's voice came over the wire. "Are you there, Jamison?... Ah! yes, my congratulations... I wondered, though, about that note. The action of prussic acid, you know... Ah! so. Dear me!... Yes, quite so!... Yes, drop in some time and tell us how you did it, eh, Jamison?" Pons laughed as he replaced the receiver. "I might have suspected it – Jamison says the woman obviously made a mistake, since she was overwrought."

"But do you think you are fully justified in allowing Penryn to escape?" I put in.

Pons rose and took down volume twenty-two of the *Encyclopedia Britannica*. He leafed quickly through its pages.

"Here we find under the heading – '*Prussic Acid*: the diluted form... will cause symptoms usually within a few seconds. The patient is quite unconscious, the eyes are motionless, the pupils dilated, the skin cold and moist, the limbs relaxed, the pulse slow and barely perceptible, the respirations very slow and convulsive. *Post mortem* the body is livid and the blood very dark.'"

He closed the book with a laugh. "'Within a few seconds!' Death usually occurs within two minutes; in pure form, prussic acid is instantaneous death." He slid farther down in his chair and reached for his pipe. "So you see, I'm not even convinced that there was a murder; the chances are even, and in my mind, Penryn has the better of the two."

THE ADVENTURE OF THE MUTTERING MAN

Among the great mass of cases that engaged Pons' attention in the year 1929, none emerged and seized upon my fancy with such singular succession, as does the remarkable and utterly astounding affair of the muttering man. The matter came upon us in the night, out of the great fog that gripped London in May of that year, and it came to us in a most curious fashion.

In the spring of 1929 it had become Pons' habit when not otherwise engaged to go prowling about Stepney, Limehouse, and Soho. Sometimes I accompanied him on these wild rambles; as often I did not, for the dangerous streets of Limehouse district held no appeal for me. On the night in question, Pons and I had walked through the thickest of fogs along Commercial Road East where it intersects for almost two miles the poor district of Stepney, and had found our way somehow to Salmon Lane where it crosses Regent's Canal. As we walked slowly ahead, Pons talked in a low voice about the scene of a pitched battle between two anarchists wanted for a notorious Houndsditch murder, and the police and military establishment in 1911 at Number 11, Sidney Street, which we passed in crossing down to walk along Commercial Road East. He had almost reached the end of his account, when he suddenly stopped and reached out to grasp my arm.

At the same moment there came to my ears a low sound from somewhere ahead in the fog. We stood there listening,

Pons and I, and as the sound approached it resolved itself into the unmistakable sound of muttering. It was certainly not continuous, but on the contrary, very broken, and the voice was that of a man – if I were any judge, a sick man. We stood silently, until suddenly there loomed up in the fog very close ahead, the reeling, unsteady figure of a man.

"A drunkard!" I thought, and was about to step aside in disgust, when the fellow stumbled and fell against me, gave vent to a sobbing moan, and collapsed on the street.

At once Pons bent forward to take the man's arm, and I reached to take his other. Together, we managed to raise him to a standing position, whereupon he began to mutter with ever increasing rapidity.

"Not back! Not back! Not back! Not back! Not back!"

These words came with such fierce intensity, that Pons reached over and touched me as I supported the stranger.

"Not drunk, certainly," ventured Pons.

"I don't think so, no," I replied. "Strikes me it's delirium."

"You shall not go back," said Pons sharply at the man's right ear.

At this the fellow stopped muttering for an instant; then, to our utter astonishment, he began again, this time with a different set of words: "I shall die. I shall die. I shall die."

"Singular," murmured Pons. "most singular, indeed. Come," he said, in the same sharp voice with which he had before addressed the mysterious stranger, "you shall not die!"

At once our strange captive was silent, and Pons was encouraged to try again. "What is your name?" he asked.

The stranger raised his head and regarded Pons for a moment out of his curious dark eyes. Then, still regarding Pons, his lips began to move, and from them, the words tripping over one another, came this: "No name. No name. No name. No name. No name."

"Dear me!" exclaimed Pons. "There is certainly something seriously wrong with him. We must take him with us." He turned to the stranger, who was still muttering the same pair of words in an almost unintelligible voice, and commanded, "Stop!"

At once there was silence.

"My word!" exclaimed Pons. "You are going with us!"

Again the stranger started his curious muttering, this time repeating the words he had first used in our presence. "Not back! Not back!"

"Stop!" commanded Pons, and as before, there was silence immediately.

Whatever else Pons was about to say was cut short by the sudden sound of swift running feet. In an instant Pons had divined their meaning, and turned to me.

"Quick!" he said in a low voice, "let us get him into a doorway somewhere. There's someone after him."

Without a further sound, we hurried our strange captive from the street into the protecting niche of a fortunate doorway close by. The fellow came readily enough; though his obvious weakness necessarily made our progress slower. We had hardly got to this cover when the runners, two of them, ran by. Only two doors down the street they came together and paused; a muffled conversation now took place, no word of which escaped us. Delirious though he was, our strange captive kept curiously silent during this interval.

"Christ!" came a voice out of the fog. "If he got away I'd as soon be at the bottom of the canal!"

"Don't suggest it," came a second voice, obviously that of a more cultured person. In both voices there was a wealth of fear.

"He must have come this way!" said the first voice again.

"In this fog it's hard to say."

"Say, you don't think, maybe... that he..."

The voices were lowered, and I looked toward Pons, but in some manner Pons had slipped away. The stranger was huddled up against me, and some nameless fear held his burning eyes. Suddenly the voices came again.

"Hullo, there, you!"

There was a grunt and a cough, and a second after, Pons' voice, disguised almost beyond my recognition.

"'Tis a col' night, maties; a col' night."

"You see anyone on this street, matey?" came the wheedling voice of the first speaker.

"Not as I know of," came Pons' voice in a lumbering dialect. "Sum 'un on the bridge, maties."

"On the bridge, you say?" came the voice of the second pursuer. "How long ago?"

"Not s'long. An' drunk, he was. Oh! 'ow drunk he was. He'd more in 'im 'n I got in a week."

"Which way did he go? Quick. Which way?"

There was a sudden silence. "'E went down, maties. You'd likely find 'im at the bottom of the canal by now."

A sudden simultaneous exclamation of relief came from the pursuers, and without a further sound that I could hear, they turned and ran back along the way they had come. In a moment Pons was at my side, and together we took our captive back upon the street, and began to walk along Salmon Lane toward Oxford Street. With our support, the stranger, still muttering at short intervals, was more steady on his legs.

In Oxford Street we were fortunate enough to get a taxi, though the fog had kept most of them from the streets, and now made driving almost as slow as walking. At Whitechapel Road intersection of Commercial Road East, we were held up in the fog for a good quarter hour, owing to a traffic tie-up because of a crash that had occurred some moments before. But Holborn and Oxford Street proper were for the most part devoid of anything resembling heavy traffic. After a few moments of more careful driving on Edgware Road, to combat the heavier traffic from London's north end, we turned at last into Praed street, and drew up before Number 7.

In our rooms at last, we were free to scrutinize our strange captive, whose eyes were searching the room wall after wall. He was a tall, dark man, not unlike Pons in his figure, but he was considerably older; I would have placed him at forty, or thereabouts, with a strong suggestion of premature ageing. His face was deathly white, in strange contrast to his black eyes. His hair was black and long, and his thin, pale lips worked convulsively while he watched us.

"Suppose you get him a whisky and soda, first of all, Doctor?" suggested Pons, and was about to go on, when a sudden outburst from our captive interrupted him.

He looked at me in terror, and in his fright he strove to speak, but the poor wretch's tongue clung to the roof of his mouth. He shuddered in his chair, and twisted his hands wildly. Pons bent to soothe him, but as I came forward, he shrank in the utmost terror.

"Certainly there is a physician to fit in this puzzle somewhere. Get the whisky and soda; we'll see what we can do with him."

When I re-entered the room with the stimulant, the muttering man calmed, though he still regarded me with fear in his eyes. Pons took from me the whisky and soda, and bade the fellow drink it. This he did, but with some little hesitation, and to our extreme gratification it had a noticeably good effect.

"Now," said Pons, again in the sharp voice he had used to address the stranger before, "tell us your name."

The man looked from one to the other of us in mute appeal; then he slowly shook his head.

Pons tried again. "Have you forgotten your name? For-gotten?"

Again the man hesitated before answering; at last he began to nod, slowly, and almost at once began again the low muttering with which we had become so familiar: "No name. No name. No name."

"Stop!" commanded Pons; the effect was magical. "Hm!" continued Pons, turning to me, "The man has evidently been under hypnotic influence at some time or other."

"That would certainly account for his condition," I agreed.

"He is greatly run down, and has certainly had a good scare at some time or other. Nor is he altogether without intelligence even now, for I can catch understanding in his eyes every now and then."

"I think he should be allowed to sleep," I put in. "I'm sure that would help him."

"Of course," said Pons.

He turned and helped the fellow to his feet, and led him to a couch set against the wall opposite the bed in the adjoining room. There our strange captive stretched himself full length, and looked at Pons expectantly.

"You are certainly right, Pons," I said, "it looks very much as if he were awaiting a command."

Pons nodded, and bent closer to the stranger. "We would like to have you sleep!" said Pons sharply. "Sleep!" he repeated, and again. "Sleep!"

In a few moments our strange captive was sleeping easily, and Pons and I returned to our lounging room.

"I daresay you have noticed his eyes, Parker," said Pons.

I nodded. "Quite watery and weak. It seems evident that some narcotic has been frequently administered."

"Quite so," assented Pons. He lit his pipe slowly and looked away into the distance. "He was once a sailor, I should say," he continued, "but he has now either retired or risen to commanding rank on his ship; there is a tattoo mark upon his wrist, the common sailor anchor design, but his clothes, obviously his own, even while having been roughly used, are certainly of a better grade than those an ordinary sailor would buy. He is surely not native to Stepney, though he may be familiar to the district."

"Why not examine his pockets?" I put in suddenly, certain that such a method would yield something of interest.

"I have already done so," returned Pons, to my surprise. "I saw to that while we were getting our man into the doorway in Salmon Lane."

"And you found nothing?" I asked.

"Nothing... but this." Pons reached into his pocket and drew forth a crumpled piece of rough paper, which he spread carefully on the table. "Obviously someone has written something in ink, but the ink is so smudged and blurred that it is almost impossible to decipher anything. However, there are five letters distinct enough to give me a suggestion of a word." With his index finger, Pons now indicated the letters. "Here we have a capital '*H*', followed by an indistinct loop, which I take for an '*e*'; the next few letters are too blurred for even suggestion; then follows a '*g*', and after another bad blur, the combination '*ay*'... that is '*He... g... ay.*' I take the first group of blurred letters for an equal letter combination, the '*g*' following, suggests '*ing*', and the next blur I can only guess at: I daresay the word is '*Hemingway.*'"

"Well, that is certainly not much help," I ventured.

Pons shrugged his shoulders. "Why not? I daresay that with this one word I shall be able to uncover something concerning this man."

"Perhaps his name is Hemingway?" I suggested.

"No, certainly not," said Pons at once. "You can see that easily if you will note that the name Hemingway appears at the bottom of the paper; I take this paper to be some message addressed to our muttering man, and the name Hemingway as the signature."

"Yes," I agreed, "that is surely the situation. But then," I protested, "what can you do with the name? There must be hundreds of Hemingways in London!"

"Quite so," assented Pons imperturbably. "But our man—if we assume that this note has any connection with the state of the muttering man —resides in Stepney, or possibly Limehouse."

"Well, that limits the search, certainly," I said, "But you cannot, after all, go after a man without sufficient ground. What do you intend to do — when once you find him?"

"First we must find him. And for that," said Pons, "I have chosen the one man who can find him and at the same time tell me what I want to know about him. That man is Frick... whatever is brewing in Limehouse or Stepney, he will know it."

"Yes," I agreed. "That is the best plan."

"Frick has failed me only once... that in a matter he could not know very easily. The underworld is open to him, as it is to no other man."

"When shall you see him?" I asked.

"It is now almost midnight; say about twelve-thirty I shall leave for Limehouse. Before that, there is work to be done. For one thing, it would be good to check up on recent disappearances in the city."

Pons reached now for a file of clippings concerning all of the last month's unsolved crimes. Through these he leafed with great rapidity, reading here and there as he went. At length he withdrew one from the packet, and read it.

"Ah! I fancy this is what we want, Parker. 'Lost: three days ago, Mr. Guy Chillingham, second mate on the *Greyhound*. Mr. Chillingham was last seen at Regent's Canal Dock, Limehouse, on the night of 21 April. Mr. Chillingham is described as a tall, dark man; black eyes; smooth face. His age is given as 37. There is a tattoo design on his left wrist; that of an anchor. Anyone bearing news of him will please notify Captain Reynolds of the *Greyhound*.' That one is almost two weeks old; here is a clipping dated two days ago. 'There has been no news regarding Mr. Guy Chillingham to date. Efforts have been made to locate the man's relatives, but these efforts have been so far unsuccessful; any friends or relatives unknown to the police are asked to come forward. The matter is now under the supervision of Inspector Jamison of Scotland Yard. Since the *Greyhound* has now sailed, all communications are to be addressed to him.' Here follows the usual description of our muttering man."

"Well, our captive is certainly Mr. Chillingham – that is one point settled."

"Quite so!" exclaimed Pons. "But I notice in this account a peculiarly disturbing sentence; 'efforts have been made to locate the man's relatives, but these efforts have been so far unsuccessful.'"

"There is nothing peculiar about that, surely?" I protested.

"Not alone, no," assented Pons, "but when you consider the fact that within the last six months, those same words have appeared in four distinct accounts of mysterious disappearances, a disturbing element emerges. It can mean one thing; someone in London has carefully ascertained the social relations of certain people; when such people have proved literally unconnected, they disappear."

"But how can you say that?" I protested.

"Almost five months ago the words I quoted appeared in the account of the disappearance of a Mr. Hilary Maddison, last seen in Wapping somewhere. A month later they came up again in a notice concerning the vanishing of one Herman Jenkins, an American sailor. Again, two months after that, the words were seen in the account of the finding of the body of Mr. James Featherwell, who had disappeared two weeks before; the body was found, if I recall rightly, at the juncture of Limehouse Cut with the River, not far from Regent's Canal Dock, where Mr. Chillingham was last seen. Now, certainly the similarity of this point in all accounts tends to support my theory."

Pons rose now and retired to his bedroom, from which he emerged some ten minutes later in the guise of a typical Limehouse lounger of the most extreme type. His face was ravaged with liquor and narcotics; had I not seen him emerge from his room thus, I should myself never have recognized him. It was not often that Pons thought it necessary to use disguises in his work; and the few times he did resort to them, it was done largely for the sake of Frick, and the others of that underworld group who found it convenient to look upon Pons as a friend. For to the members of this group, Pons had more than once appeared in the guise of a saviour, drawing them time and again from the clutches of the law, and placing them where they could serve rather than break the law.

"I daresay you may as well go to bed, Parker," said Pons. "I can't say when I shall return, of course; in all probability you will find me in bed when you get up tomorrow morning. However, I shall certainly be here before tomorrow noon. If I am not here at seven, look for me at eleven."

"And our patient?" I put in.

"Do what you can for him," answered Pons. "I daresay he will sleep for some hours... longer than you, certainly. When he wakes, if he does wake before I return, find what you can from him."

"Very well," said I. "No doubt, the first thing he will want when he wakes is food; certainly, with that I can supply him."

"You are the doctor, Parker."

"I shall look for you at eleven, then."

"If not before," returned Pons. The door closed softly behind him. Shortly after ten o'clock the following morning, Pons returned; at that time Mr. Chillingham had not yet come out of his sleep.

"Well?" I asked, as Pons was removing his disguise, "What have you discovered? You found Frick, I suppose?"

"I had no difficulty," answered Pons. "I found him in Shen Han's place, where he usually spends his time."

"You asked about Hemingway?"

"I did. It appears that Hemingway is a doctor of some kind. He has an establishment on Rhodeswell Road, just off Salmon Lane. Frick says something goes on there, for certain, but he has no knowledge of what it is. Men have gone into the house, but they have not come out. The doctor himself is a rather mysterious individual, seldom seen. Once, near midnight, he saw a man arrive in an expensive motor; since this man opened the front door with a key, Frick took him for the doctor.

"It is the common belief at Shen Han's that the doctor's place is a blind for an opium den; there is a possibility of it, but that surmise fails to account for the muttering of Mr. Chillingham."

"Well," I put in, "it is quite certain that Mr. Chillingham has been drugged frequently. I examined him in the night, and found a great number of hypodermic scars on his arms."

Pons nodded. "Administered to further some purpose, I daresay," he replied. "Though the house from the street carries out the impression of an opium den, I do not take favourably to the theory."

"You have seen the house, then?" I asked.

"Yes, I examined it at my leisure this morning. From the street it looks very much like a deserted house. Some of the windows are boarded up, and there are general signs of non-usage – a typical blind, I should say. I have set Frick to watch the place more closely. If our man Hemingway is in reality a physician – and Mr. Chillingham's condition seems to indicate that he is – then I am convinced there is some sort of illegal experimentation going on in that house, and the sooner a stop is put to it, the better."

"I daresay it would be a good thing to find who owns the house?" I suggested.

"Precisely," agreed Pons. "That I have done also. The house belongs to Sir James Harwell, the famous landowner, whose agent tells me that it was rented from him seven months ago by a young man representing Dr. Hemingway. The young man gave excellent references – among them the names of Dr. Alonzo Cantor, the famous psychologist and nerve specialist, and Lord Merivale, head of The East End Hospital, to say nothing of two prominent Members of Parliament. The situation is rather perplexing, I confess. I called Dr. Cantor and asked about the young man; he tells me that the name is Harry Stone; says he had him under his instruction for some months, a most promising student; he has not heard from him for some time now."

"Perhaps he was one of the two pursuers of last night?" I suggested.

"So I thought," continued Pons; "beyond that, we learned nothing."

"Well, what is to be done?" I asked.

"There are two things which must be effected as soon as possible. First, we must awaken Mr. Guy Chillingham and question him; let us hope that sleep has done him some good. Second, we must call in the estimable Jamison, for, the moment that Frick calls to tell me that Dr. Hemingway is in the house, the place must be raided. For that, Jamison and his men are needed."

I nodded in agreement.

We had no difficulty in awakening Mr. Guy Chillingham, whose immediate query for food was intensely gratifying. Mrs. Johnson responded with a copious allotment of eggs and toast; there was no coffee, for I had forbidden it, but there was more milk that he would drink. It was only after he had thoroughly completed his meal that Pons saw fit to question him about Dr. Hemingway.

"Do you now remember your name?" asked Pons first.

"It is very curious," responded Chillingham, "but I seem to have lost all memory of myself previous to my stay with Dr. Hemingway."

"Quite so," said Pons. "Your name is Guy Chillingham. Do you remember that?"

"Now that you mention it, I do. But I associate very little with it. I seem to have some suggestion of a ship, and there is a vague recollection of some kind of dog."

"Ah! that is better!" I exclaimed. "It is certainly coming back!"

"Yes, that memory is good; before your incarceration by Dr. Hemingway, you were second mate on the ship *Greyhound*."

"Of course!" exclaimed Chillingham, springing up. "And that reminds me... I must get back to my ship before it sails."

"You may sit down, Mr. Chillingham," said Pons. "Your ship sailed some days ago."

A look of astonishment came into the man's face as he reseated himself. "But surely..." he protested. "It cannot have gone ahead of schedule!"

"No, Mr. Chillingham," answered Pons. "But you were unwittingly detained beyond your leave."

"The *Greyhound* was to have been docked for seven days!"

"Quite so," assented Pons. "And you have been kept prisoner in Dr. Hemingway's house for two weeks."

Pons reached for his clippings regarding the man before us and handed them to him to read. The look of comprehension in our man's eyes deepened as he read the two short notices by means of which Pons had identified him.

"This is indeed strange," he said, handing back the clippings, "but I seem to have no recollection of how I spent the time."

"Precisely," said Pons, "and that is what we are going to determine. It will be necessary for you to recall your actions from the time you left Regent's Canal Dock, where you were last seen."

"I remember walking along Commercial Road," began Mr. Chillingham, "and turning up a side street... It had an odd name... I think it was Dalgleish Street."

"Yes," said Pons. "it branches from Commercial Road."

"On Dalgleish Street I was accosted by a young man, a rather striking young man, who presented a very favourable appearance. I happened to run into him just as he was leaving a little shop abutting on the walk – a tobacconist's shop, I recall. I excused myself and would have gone on, but he stopped me and asked me for a match. It was this that held me. My curiosity got the best of me – the young man asked for a match; yet his cigarette was glowing in the darkness, and he had besides just come from a tobacconist's. I gave him the match without comment and watched to see what he would do; he deliberately and gravely relit the cigarette. My interest in him was aroused, and when he proposed walking with me the length of the street, I acceded with celerity."

"Ah so?" said Pons. "Let me anticipate you. The young man entered into a conversation with you; in the course of this conversation, he discovered that you had few friends in London, and no relatives. He said he was interested, and asked you to stay with him."

"Yes, that was just it, Mr. Pons. Exactly!" exclaimed Mr. Chillingham. "He said we could have great sport together, since he was also alone in the world, so it appeared."

"Did he give you his name?" asked Pons.

"Yes, his first name. But he gave me no other."

"His first name was Harry, I daresay?" ventured Pons.

"Why, yes, it was. But how you know that, Mr. Pons, is beyond me."

"How I know that is of no importance to you, Mr. Chillingham. The young man's last name was Stone, had he cared to tell you; however, I daresay, he would have given you a false surname. Go on with your tale."

"We walked around quite a bit, and I pretty well lost my direction. We'd gone into a few pubs, and had a little ale – not much, but I was never one for ale, and I was beginning to feel somewhat groggy, when we came to Harry's home."

"Did you notice anything about this place?" asked Pons.

"I think I said something about its being deserted, but Harry only laughed, and we went on in."

"The house on Rhodeswell Road," I put in.

"Quite so," agreed Pons. "Go on, Mr. Chillingham."

"From then on I remember little, I am sorry to say," answered Mr. Chillingham. "First thing I saw when I got into the house was a tall, striking man – I noticed that even though I was somewhat under the weather – who took one glance at me and turned to Harry and said, 'Fine. Fine. A fine one, my boy! He is like the others? Alone?' Harry said something, and the tall man stepped forward. He looked into my eyes and said, 'You will sleep!' He repeated these words some few times, and that is the last I remember.

"Once after that, I have a hazy recollection of waking up on a slab. I think I was naked, but I'm not sure. I remember hearing voices saying something about 'marvellous mind... nerves... like others...' Then they must have discovered that I was listening, and I heard a sharp voice say, 'The needle; quick!' I was conscious of intense pain, and a jab in the arm – that's all I know. I think I ate occasionally; I'm not sure of that either! I can remember that I was horribly afraid – I thought I should die.

"Then, last night... it was last night, wasn't it?" he broke off.

Pons nodded.

"Last night, I woke up, and at once I felt that I was alone in the house. I was in a small room, on a cot; my clothes were on a chair next to me. I don't know how I ever managed to get into them, but I did. I had only one thought, to get away... and when I did get out of a window, and had started down the street, I felt that if I were to go back, it meant death. Then, I met you... my mind was clearing even then."

"Now one more question, Mr. Chillingham?" said Pons. "The tall man who struck you, and who, incidentally, hypnotized you, is known to us as a certain Dr. Hemingway. Little is known of this Dr. Hemingway, for he seems to have no active practice. Do you think you could identify the man again, if we brought him before you?"

Mr. Chillingham nodded. "I could. I know I could. But I can't for the life of me give you a description of him now!"

"That is quite all right, Mr. Chillingham," said Pons. "It is necessary that someone identify the man, and you will serve this purpose. For the present, I consider it advisable for you to stay here with us... we can easily accommodate you."

"That is certainly very kind of you, Mr. Pons," said Mr. Chillingham. "Had you thought to notify Captain Reynolds of the *Greyhound*?"

"I had thought of it, certainly; but I considered that this may as well be deferred, for last night I gave your pursuers the impression that you had fallen into Regent's Canal. It would not do now to let anyone know that you had been found; for this would make it certain that Dr. Hemingway would temporarily cease his activities.

"And now," said Pons, "for Jamison." He reached for the telephone and gave a number; almost at once Jamison's voice came over the wire. "Ah! Are you there, Jamison?... How are you getting on in the matter of the disappearance of Mr. Guy Chillingham?... Indeed? That is certainly depressing news. You think it just another case of a drunken sailor falling into the Thames, eh?" Pons chuckled: Mr. Chillingham smiled. "And how about the case of Mr. Hilary Maddison?... And that of Herman Jenkins, the sailor?... Ah! Indeed?... Yes, if you have a bit of time, run around. I think it highly probable that I can throw a little light on these mysterious vanishings... I shall look for you then shortly after luncheon."

"He is coming, then?" I asked.

"At about one o'clock," said Pons. "As usual, he is 'frightfully busy' – to quote him; I daresay he is. But if I know Jamison, he'll not let any chance of my lightening his burden slip by."

Shortly after one o'clock, Jamison appeared. The three of us were waiting for him.

"Well, Mr. Pons," asked Jamison, "you've got something for me?"

He regarded Mr. Chillingham curiously, but there was not the least sign of recognition, or even of suspicion: for, as it later turned out, Jamison was so certain of finding Mr. Chillingham a dead body somewhere in the Thames, that it never entered his head that Chillingham might suddenly appear before him.

"Rather," said Pons. "First of all, I should like you to know an acquaintance of mine – Mr. Chillingham. Mr. Guy Chillingham Inspector Jamison of Scotland Yard."

Jamison's jaw dropped. "Say..." he sputtered, "If this is your idea of a joke, Mr. Pons..."

"Dear me, no!" returned Pons, chuckling. "This is the missing Mr. Chillingham, right enough."

"I haven't had so much pleasure in meeting someone for months, Mr. Chillingham!" exclaimed Jamison, taking the other's outstretched hand. "And how did you find him?" Jamison continued, turning to Pons.

"Why, we met him on the street one night," said Pons. "He blundered into us in the fog, and we had quite a time with him."

"Indeed!" exclaimed Jamison. "On the street – and where has he been all this time, may I ask?"

Pons now went on to relate the story of Mr. Chillingham, together with the information he had got from Frick, and then began to suggest his plan for the capture of Dr. Hemingway.

"You think, then, that this Dr. Hemingway, as he calls himself, is behind all these mysterious disappearances?" asked Jamison.

"I am certain of it," replied Pons. "And we must bag him to prevent any further cases cropping up. That is to be done this way: When Frick learns that the Doctor... who evidently does not live in the house on Rhodeswell Road, has returned there, he will call me at once. I will then call you, and you must go there immediately with selected men and raid the house. Take everybody prisoner, confiscate all the paraphernalia in the house, but do not injure any mechanisms you may find. The Doctor is a tall, striking man; that is all we know of him, but it is enough in the circumstances. This man I want brought up here as soon as you take him. Mr. Chillingham, here, will identify him; and you will have a strong case for the prosecution."

"I am to get my men ready, then?" asked Jamison.

"That would be the best way, I believe," answered Pons. "The call from Frick may come any night. As a matter of fact, I expect it tonight, for it is reasonable to suppose that when the doctor hears of the escape of Mr. Chillingham, as he must have heard by now, he will come to the house. I suspect, of course, that Dr. Hemingway is an alias, and that our man will not find it expedient to visit in Rhodeswell during the day; hence, he will come at night."

"Very well," said Jamison, rising. "It is now three o'clock. At the most, it will take me two hours to select the men and make them ready. I daresay, they will not be called before darkness comes on."

"No, certainly not," said Pons. "But select enough of them, for the fog tonight will be little less intense than it was last night. Mistakes are easily made in such a fog; tonight there must be *no* mistakes. The house must be surrounded with a cordon of men, so close that they can touch each other. Nothing living must break through this cordon. I daresay you will clear up a number of disappearance cases when you take that house."

"Let us hope so," said Jamison at the door.

"Expect to hear from me tonight, then, Jamison," instructed Pons. "I think the most likely time will be about nine o'clock."

"I will be waiting at the telephone. Good afternoon, and good afternoon to you, Mr. Chillingham."

But we had not to wait as long as Pons had thought. Pons had gone out shortly after Jamison left, spending his time until six o'clock, as he later said, searching through the files of the *Times* and the *Mirror*, looking up details bearing on the case in hand.

It was seven o'clock when the call from Frick came, and Pons relayed the message to Jamison at once, instructing Frick at the same time to leave the scene in order not to be collared together with the residents of the house and grounds on Rhodeswell Road. We sat back now to await Jamison's coming with the report on the raid.

"It has occurred to me, Mr. Chillingham," said Pons, "that if anything goes wrong in the raid tonight – if it should happen that the doctor escapes Jamison in this fog – it would be best to do what we can to stimulate your memory. I daresay you have heard of Dr. Alonzo Cantor?"

"Mind specialist, isn't he?" asked Chillingham.

"Yes," answered Pons. "Today, while going through the files for the last months I saw in the newspapers several rather striking articles written by him. One was entitled, 'The Mind of Man Under Hypnotism' and the other, 'Narcotics, the Nerves, and the Human Mind' – both exceedingly interesting documents. It has occurred to me that Dr. Cantor should be called in to do what he can for you; it is just possible that through his intervention you will be able to recall the features of Dr. Hemingway, sufficiently, at least, to add enough to our knowledge of him to broadcast more detailed information. What do you say, Parker?"

"Yes," I replied, "that strikes me as a very good plan. We should have thought of that before."

"It is not too late now," returned Pons. "And we shall do it, if Jamison is left empty-handed."

At nine o'clock Jamison came – alone. From the story as he told it, two men had been taken, one of whom he had no doubt was the man Stone; and the other, a common character, used as a sort of caretaker. This latter fellow was dumb with terror, and was ready to tell all; but he knew little, save that illegal experiments on the human body were certainly carried on in the house. He himself had never seen the doctor, but lived in unholy terror for his life, though he was paid well.

From the house had been recovered the body of Herman Jenkins, and three patients, not yet seriously injured, one of whom had been identified as Mr. Hilary Maddison. But the doctor himself had flown.

Pons was not so taken aback as I might have thought. He commended Jamison on his good work, and revealed to him the plan for calling in Dr. Cantor, asking Jamison to stay until Dr. Cantor had made his diagnosis. To this Jamison assented readily enough.

"Very well," said Pons. "Then I think we may as well call Dr. Cantor. Dr. Parker, will you get him on the wire? I think it will add strength to our case if a fellow physician is to call him."

"Certainly," I answered, and reached for the telephone directory, where I found his number easily. A gruff voice answered my call. "This is Dr. Parker speaking," I explained. "Dr. Parker of 7B Praed Street. I have a patient here who is most curiously affected by a mental-nervous strain; his memory has been seriously impaired. He has been given to frequent muttering – very incoherent for the most part."

An exclamation came over the wire. "Muttering, you say? Well, that is most peculiar, Doctor. I am interested. Can you tell me more?"

"I would rather have you come at once, Doctor Cantor," I replied. "You will find my patient most interesting from the point-of-view of mental disturbance."

"I will come at once," answered the doctor.

I turned from the instrument.

"What does he say?" asked Jamison.

"He will come," I said. "He seemed surprised that the man was given to muttering."

"Indeed?" exclaimed Pons. "That does not surprise me... in a case of this kind, I daresay muttering is the most common element – since a chaotic mind dictates chaotic thoughts which emerge in repetition."

"I'm afraid Dr. Parker put it somewhat hard," put in Chillingham. "I'm sure I'm not that bad!"

"I'm equally sure, Mr. Chillingham," answered Pons. "But Dr. Cantor is not easily got as consulting physician." He turned now to Jamison. "By the way, Jamison, have you a pair of manacles with you?"

"Yes," said Jamison ruefully. "They were meant for Dr. Hemingway."

"Do not despair, Jamison," said Pons, chuckling. "They may yet fit Dr. Hemingway. I venture to predict that Dr. Cantor will so surely restore Mr. Chillingham's mind that we shall be able to bag Hemingway this very night."

"You have your eye on him, then?" asked Jamison eagerly.

Pons nodded. "My finger, Jamison. I am moving my finger and summoning Dr. Alonzo Cantor to my assistance. Mr. Chillingham will be given a chance to identify Dr. Hemingway through Dr. Cantor; when this identification is made, you will have your man, Jamison!"

In a surprisingly short time, considering the heavy fog outside, Dr. Cantor arrived. There were two imperative rings of the doorbell, and Pons arose at once to usher into the room the Doctor we so eagerly awaited.

But a startling surprise awaited us. No sooner had Dr. Cantor stepped into the room, than Mr. Chillingham sprang to his feet with a great cry, "It is he!" At the same instant Dr. Cantor lunged forward, his face convulsed with fury, and would have struck Chillingham had not Jamison stepped forward and received the full impact of the blow. Pons leaped away from the door and swung his long arms about the doctor from behind, imprisoning his arms to his side, so that Jamison was able to manacle the doctor before further damage could be done.

"*An outrage*!" shouted the doctor in a hoarse voice. "This is an outrage!" He fixed a baleful eye on Jamison. "You seem to forget, sir, that a man of my position... has *influence*!"

"Ah! my dear Doctor," put in Pons. "Perhaps that is true... but not enough influence to combat the Yard and the evidence it has against you."

"Evidence, indeed!" sneered the doctor. "What jury would take the word of that rat," he indicated Chillingham with a contemptuous gesture of his manacled hands, "against mine?"

"Your house on Rhodeswell Road was raided this evening, as you no doubt know by this time. There are three other men to give evidence against you; there is also one of your employees. I daresay, a promise of immunity and a subtle picture of a ruined future could induce Mr. Harry Stone to speak."

"You are a fool, Mr. Solar Pons!" said the doctor in a rasping voice.

"Such an accusation I never deny, my dear Doctor," said Pons in some amusement. "But as a fool, I have had the good foresight to picture the reaction of an intelligent jury to a comparison between the experiences of your patients, as related by them, and the remarkable conclusions you have arrived at in your recent syndicated articles, especially the two, *The Mind of Man Under Hypnotism* and *Narcotics, the Nerves, and the Human Mind*."

Pons turned from the suddenly fear-stricken face before him to Jamison. "I daresay you can take him away now. And, as usual, Jamison, my name must not appear in connection with the matter."

A Fragmentary Adventure

THE ADVENTURE OF THE GREEN STARS

[From the Editor's Note in *The Pontine Dossier*, 1977, Vol.3, No.2]

During the period of his residency at Park Lane in London, Baron Ennesfred von Kroll was unquestionably one of the most formidable adversaries ever to confront Solar Pons. Dr. Parker invariably accords the Baron a measure of deference and awe reserved only for an archenemy whose genius matched Pons's own, and even in his native Germany Kroll was considered to be a supreme master among espionage agents. He remains today an altogether legendary figure in the anals of crime; in the 1963 edition of Keliber/Furt-wangler Real-Encyclopaedie der Schrecklicher *(Kohler Verlag, Berlin), the irredeemably evil and ruthless character of this man is succinctly described on page 238:* "Ennesfred Kroll konnte sich damit begnügen, den Menschen nur fusserlich zu quälen, indem er die Angriffe und Bedrangungen vervielfachte, oder auch innerlich peinigen...." [Editor's Note: This translates as "*Ennesfred Kroll could be satisfied with tormenting the human only by multiplying the attacks and constraints, or torturing them internally." No wonder Pons once alluded to the Baron as "the most dangerous man in London!"*

Pontine scholars will recall that Dr. Parker records only two adventures in which Ennesfred Kroll plays an appreciable role, "Seven Passengers" and "Lost Holiday", although the Baron is mentioned peripherally in two additionally cases, "Trained Cormorant" and "Praed Street Irregulars". Not generally known is the existence of a story fragment involving Baron Kroll, begun by young August Derleth during the early 1930's, but apparently never completed. The extant of the manuscript is presented here in its entirety:

The curious affair of the green stars, as Pons has labeled it, was the second of my companion's actual encounters with that criminal genius, the Baron Ennesfred Kroll. The affair took place approximately two months after the events related in "The Adventure of the Seven Passengers," and it came to our attention in a manner fully as dramatic as any of Pons' cases.

Pons and I were sauntering slowly up the Edgware Road one morning about one o'clock, when we noticed in the distance, a car careening around the corner from Praed Street to the Road, and coming rapidly down upon us. As it approached, we could identify it easily as a police motor, for it bore the familiar green lights. The vehicle flashed rapidly past us, and Pons turned slightly to glance after it, when abruptly it screeched to a stop and almost immediately began to reverse. A figure appeared in the space of the opened window and waved wild arms in our direction.

"Extraordinary," muttered Pons. "But undoubtedly Jamison. What can he be wanting at this hour? Something is brewing, that is certain."

The car came up to the kerb opposite us, and the door swung open. With surprising agility for his embonpoint, Jamison jumped out.

"Been looking for you, Pons. Just came from Number Seven, as a matter of fact."

"What has happened?" asked Pons.

"Murder," said Jamison, breathlessly.

"That is nothing unusual," Pons replied.

"You haven't seen the body, Pons. I guarantee you a shock when you do."

Pons shrugged his shoulders. "Well, I suggest that we get started, Jamison. What do you say?"

"Come on," said Jamison, and entered the car once again.

Pons and I followed more slowly.

"Now," said Pons, settling back in the seat, "let us have the details."

"A constable discovered the body," began Jamison. "Only about an hour ago, that was."

"Where?" interrupted Pons.

"It's the best district, Pons; down the road a bit. Culross Street – do you know where that is?"

"Leads off Park Street, if I am not mistaken," returned Pons.

"Exactly, that's the place. My constable found the body stretched out under an arc lamp. Reported him as a man, about fifty years old. Had on a masquerade suit – yellow clown, black stripes. I went down, and took a look at the fellow." Jamison paused.

"Go on," urged Pons.

"It was one of my best men. Peter Pendleton. I had sent him out to cover the Baron Ennesfred Kroll."

"What!" exclaimed Pons, sitting bolt upright in his seat.

"That is not all," Jamison continued. "Pendleton was found clutching in his hand two green stars..."

The editor of The Pontine Dossier *continues...*

"The Adventure of the Green Stars" tantalizingly breaks off at this point, and we very probably shall never know how August Derleth might have completed the fragment. There is no reason, however, why the Praed Street Irregulars cannot exercise their powers of ratiocination by attempting a logical explanation for the events detailed thus far. In the advancement of Pontine scholarship, the Dossier will award a $50.00 first prize for the most ingenious reconstruction of this story, in five hundred words or less, specifically explaining why one of Inspector Jamison's agents was found in costume clutching two green stars, and how this singular occurrence might conceivably involve the Baron Kroll. All entries should be received by this journal during calendar year 1977, and a report on the results of the competition will appear in the next Pontine Dossier.

As our old friend would say, "The game is afoot!"

Solar Pons Off-Trail

AUGUST DERLETH EXPLAINS...

One January day in 1953 Mack Reynolds submitted to The Magazine of Fantasy and Science Fiction *a Holmesian pastiche entitled* The Case of the Snitch in Time. *Editors Anthony Boucher and J. Francis McComas read the tale, and, in describing it in a letter to The Agent, McComas pronounced it "a story with a brilliant idea – that Sherlock Holmes is visited, via time machine, by a visitor from an alternate time-space continuum and solves a problem for said visitor. This is a honey of a plot; it combines beautifully the possibilities of a wondrous Holmes pastiche and a perfect science fiction story." But, on the distaff side, Mack Reynolds "did not in any sense of the word recreate Holmes, Watson, or Baker Street."*

In his letter of January 19 of that year McComas set forth the proposal made to Mack Reynolds. "We wrote to him, suggesting in general a collaboration with some staunch Irregular; in particular, we urged his OK on approaching you with the thought of working it out as a Solar Pons story. Mack sent along an enthusiastic affirmative. I quote: 'I'd appreciate it if you'd give Augie Derleth first chance at it. It was after reading his Solar Pons stories that I got the idea for Snitch. Besides that, I'm an admirer of the old Seigneur of Sauk City and it would be a privilege to have a story appear under a collaborative byline.' It would also be a privilege," added McComas, "for this magazine to be able to publish one more Solar Pons story – one with a strong science fiction theme."

Both Mack Reynolds and the editors were pleased with the Pontine tale that came from Reynolds's "brilliant idea". Anthony Boucher suggested a few small alterations which could be made in the office, and The Adventure of the Snitch in Time *made its bow in the July, 1953 issue of* The Magazine of Fantasy and Science Fiction, *with, in part, this introduction:*

"In a foreword to Three Problems for Solar Pons, *Mr. Derleth sadly announced that Dr. Parker had, for personal reasons, decided to terminate his literary career. However, a kindly Fate has intervened to upset these plans of agent and author. A Mr. Mack Reynolds, while browsing in the archives of certain space-time continua, stumbled on a cryptic reference (in a most unlikely era) to Mr. Solar Pons. Careful research elicited the broad outlines of what is possibly the greatest triumph of the Pontine powers. Mr. Reynolds consulted Mr. Derleth; Mr. Derleth conferred with Dr. Parker; so persuasive was the agent (as agents should be) that the good Doctor was prevailed upon to give us one more adventure, the complete story of the one truly science fictional problem ever faced by the great detective."*

By this time, Reynolds had come up with a second off-trail Pontine story titled The Adventure of the Mad Dogs of Tomorrow *– another challenge to The Agent. This became* The Adventure of the Ball of Nostradamus, *and it, too, passed muster with the editors of* The Magazine of Fantasy and Science Fiction. *But its appearance was delayed – too much material lay in the files of the magazine for publication – and the story did not appear until the issue for June, 1955. In a sense this delay was fatal, for at least half a dozen off-trail stories had been projected between us – a third had actually been submitted to the magazine, but the editors took a dim view of it, and so did the agent. A fourth – titled* The Adventure of the Extra-Terrestrial *– had also come in, and languished in the files waiting on publication of the second pastiche.*

When that publication came, our ardor had cooled – at one story every two years in the magazine, it would take a dozen years to accomplish publication of half-a-dozen stories. The project, interesting and challenging as it was, was not so much forthrightly abandoned as left to wither away.

August Derleth

THE ADVENTURE OF THE SNITCH IN TIME

On an autumn afternoon of a year that, for manifest reasons, must remain nameless, there came to the attention of my friend, Mr. Solar Pons, a matter which was surely either the most extraordinary adventure ever to befall a private enquiry agent in or before our time, or an equally extraordinary misadventure, the *raison d'etre* of which remains obscure even now, though it might have been born in the circumstances of the moment, for it was one of those days on which London was literally swallowed in a yellow fog, and we had both been confined to our quarters for two days, with no more incident than the arrival of an occasional paper and the unfailing complaint of our long-suffering landlady about Pons' spare appetite.

Even our warm and comfortable quarters, for all that a fire burned at the hearth, had begun to pall on us. Pons had exhausted the microscope; he had abandoned his chemistry set; he had ceased his abominable pistol practise; and for once there was not a single item of correspondence transfixed to the center of the mantelpiece by his knife. He had hardly stopped his restless wandering among the disorderly order of our quarters, and seated himself in his velvet-lined chair, holding forth on the points of difference between Stradivarius and Amati violins, when he rose once more with his empty pipe in his hands.

He was at the fireplace, about to take the shag from the toe of his slipper, tacked below the mantelpiece, when suddenly, he paused. He stood so for a moment, in utter silence, his hawklike face keen with interest, his body seeming actually to lean forward as if to catch the sound that smote upon his ears. "If I am not mistaken, Parker," he said with unaccustomed gravity, "we are about to have a most unusual visitor."

I had been standing at the window looking out, and had just turned. "Nothing has disturbed this fog for the past half hour," I protested.

"My dear Parker, you are looking in the wrong direction. The footsteps are approaching from out there, and a little above."

So saying, he turned to face the door with alert expectation in his gray eyes.

I had for some time been conscious of a curious sound, almost as of water sliding at regular intervals against the roof. Apparently this was what Pons had mistaken for the sound of footsteps. Almost at the same moment of this realization, a most peculiar assault was made on the door to our quarters. I had not heard the outer door; in truth, I had heard no step upon the stair. But now a kind of brushing sound broke in upon us; it began at the top of the door, and did not become a recognizable knock until it had descended to midpanel.

Being nearest the door, I moved to open it.

"Pray be cautious, Parker," said Pons. "And spare me your alarm. Unless I am in egregious error, our visitor is from another world."

I gazed at him, mouth agape. I had heard and marveled at his extraordinary deductions before, but this came from his lips with such calm assurance that I could not doubt his sincerity even while I could not accept his words.

"Come, Parker, let us not keep him waiting."

I threw open the door. There, confronting us, was a strong, healthy man, bronzed by the sun, clad in a fantastic attire of such brilliant hues as to dazzle the eye. His footgear – a strange combination of sandal and slipper – must have made the curious slapping sounds I had at first mistaken for the dripping of water, but which Pons had correctly identified as footsteps, however alien to our previous experience.

Our visitor looked briefly at me and said, "Ah, the famous literary doctor, I presume?" and smiled, as if in jest.

My astonishment at this manner of address, accompanied as it was with an almost insolent amusement, left me momentarily speechless.

"Come in, come in, my dear fellow," said Pons behind me. "Pray overlook Dr. Parker's rudeness. I perceive you have come a long way; your fatigue is manifest. Sit here and relieve yourself of the problem which brings you to these quarters."

Our visitor walked into the room, inclining his head to acknowledge Pons' invitation.

"I hope you will forgive my coming without an appointment," he said, in a somewhat stilted voice, accompanied by florid and Victorian gestures. "I fear I had no alternative. Let me introduce myself – I am Agent Tobias Athelney of the Terra Bureau of Investigation, Planet Terra, of the Solar System League."

Pons' eyes twinkled merrily.

"My dear sir," I could not help interrupting, "levity is all very well, but this is neither the time nor the place for it. Just where are you from?"

Our visitor had taken the seat to which Pons had waved him. At my words, he stopped short, took a small, violet-covered notebook from an inner fold of his robelike costume, and thumbed through it until he found the place he sought.

"Pray forgive me," he murmured. "If we were still using your somewhat fantastic calendar system, it would be the year 2565 A. D."

Pons, who had been scrutinizing him closely, now leaned back, closed his eyes, and touched his fingertips together. "So you represent yourself as a governmental agent of almost 700 years in the future, Mr. Athelney?" he said. "A traveler in time?"

Our visitor grimaced. "Not exactly, Mr. Pons. To my knowledge, there is no such thing as time travel, nor can such travel ever be developed. No, the explanation for my presence here is more elementary. We have recently discovered that the universe is not, indeed, one, but of an infinite number. We have learned that everything that possibly could happen has happened, will happen, and is happening. Given an infinite number of alternative universes, you can easily understand how this would be so. To illustrate, Mr. Pons, there are alternate space-time continua in which Napoleon won at Waterloo; there are still others in which Waterloo was a draw; and there are yet others in which the battle was never fought at all – indeed, in which Napoleon was never born!"

I flashed a glance of mounting indignation at Pons, but my companion's face had taken on that dream expression I had learned to associate with intense concentration. Surely it could not be that he was being deceived by this patent mountebank! "Infinite other universes than this," murmured Pons, "containing other persons identical to myself, and to Dr. Parker, here, who carry on their little lives in much the same manner as we do?"

Our visitor nodded. "That is correct, Mr. Pons. There are still other space-time continua, in which there are no such persons as yourselves, never have been, and never will be." He coughed almost apologetically. "In fact, in this multitude of alternate universes, Mr. Pons, there are some in which you two are fictitious characters, the product of a popular writer's art!"

"Amazing!" exclaimed Pons, adding, with a glance at my dour face, "and yet, not entirely incredible, would you say, Parker?"

"Preposterous!" I answered. "How can you sit there and calmly accept this – this nonsense?"

"Dear me," murmured Pons, "let us not be too hasty, Parker."

"I am sorry to have upset Dr. Parker," said our visitor soberly, "but it is from just such a universe that I have traveled to this. Approximately 700 years before my birth, in my space-time continuum, a series of stories dealing with Mr. Solar Pons and Dr. Lyndon Parker were written, presumably by Dr. Parker, and became the all-time favorites of the literature of deduction."

"Let us assume all this is so," said Pons. "For what purpose have you come?"

"To consult you, Mr. Pons."

"I fancied as much," said my companion with a serene smile. "Though it would seem a long chance indeed to consult a fictitious character."

"*Touche*!" answered our client. "But a fictitious character in my universe and 700 years before my time. But in this universe you are very real indeed, and the greatest detective of all time!" He sighed. "You cannot imagine, Mr. Pons, the difficulty of first finding a continuum in which you were real, and then, on top of that, one in which you were contemporary."

Pons sat for a moment in silence, stroking the lobe of his left ear. "I submit," he said at last, "since patterns of crime and its detection continually evolve, you are haunting the wrong continuum, Mr. Athelney."

"I think not, Mr. Pons, if you will hear me out."

"Proceed."

"One of our most scientifically advanced bands of criminals is named the Club Cerise, after the favorite color of its leader, Moriarty. They – "

"Moriarty!" exclaimed Pons.

"Yes, Mr. Pons. Moriarty. The name is familiar to you perhaps?"

"Indeed it is!" Pons was silent for a moment, his eyes closed. "You know, Parker," he said after a moment, "I have always felt that one death at the Reichenbach was as false as the other."

He sat up in his chair, his gaze now intent on our visitor. "Pray continue, Mr. Athelney! Where my illustrious predecessor could achieve but a stalemate, it seems that you offer me the opportunity for complete victory!"

"Well, then, Mr. Pons," our visitor resumed, "you will not be surprised to learn that Moriarty and his band have managed to escape retribution for some time, and it is in regard to their apprehension that I seek your assistance. The criminal method they have developed is based on the same discovery that allows my presence here. Moriarty and his Club Cerise have been making a practice of invading space-time continua in less developed eras than our own, and, utilizing our most advanced weapons and devices to assure their escape, have been despoiling these universes of their art treasures. Not long ago, for example, they went into a Twentieth Century universe and obtained a Da Vinci, a half dozen Rembrandts, and a priceless collection of Kellys."

Pons' eyes widened a trifle. "You are suggesting that the Irish have developed an artist of the stature of Da Vinci, Mr. Athelney?"

"Indeed, yes. A fellow named Kelly created a work of genius called *Pogo*, which appeared in hundreds of newspapers of his day. These were *Pogo* originals, including some of the very rare pre-strip drawings. With his fabulously valuable treasure, Moriarty and his band managed to return to our own space-time continuum. Obviously, we cannot punish them in our universe, since they have committed no crime there. Under ordinary circumstances, it would be possible to extradite them to the universe they plundered – but there are almost insurmountable complications."

Pons smiled, still giving no evidence of being in the slightest troubled by the mad, ingenious, account of our prospective client. "I daresay 'insurmountable' is the word to describe the problems attendant upon extradition of a group of criminals from a country which doesn't exist in the universe where the crime was committed. I submit that a Twentieth Century nation might be compelled to adopt extraordinary protective measures – if indeed these would be adequate – to deal with criminals seven centuries in advance of the police of that period." But now he shook his head, with a gentle smile on his thin lips. "But we must stop considering these ramifications, or we shall soon find ourselves involved in the higher mathematics of space and time."

"The importance of the problem is greater than might at first be evident," continued our visitor. "Given continued success on the part of Moriarty and his Club Cerise, there can be no doubt that other such bands will soon emulate them, and that eventually endless numbers of space-time pirates will give up other pursuits to devote themselves to the plundering of weaker continua with this type of snitch."

"Snitch?" I repeated.

"Elementary, Parker," murmured Pons impatiently. "Obviously idiomatic for 'theft'."

"The ultimate possibility will not have escaped you, Mr. Pons," continued our client. "Sooner or later, the increasing numbers of criminals would arrive in this space-time continuum and in this era."

I could not be sure, but it seemed to me that at this suggestion a little color drained from Pons' cheeks. And, if a shudder went through that lean frame, he was again under perfect control within moments. He sat then in silence, his eyes closed, his head sunk to his chest with his fingertips gently tapping together.

Our visitor waited in silence.

Pons opened his eyes presently and asked, "Pray tell me, Mr. Athelney – do you have income taxes in your world?"

Athelney groaned. "My dear fellow, last year my taxes were unbelievably high. Bureaucracy runs rampant!"

"Capital, capital!" exclaimed Pons. "Why not prosecute Moriarty for tax evasion?"

Our visitor shook his head dolefully. "The criminals of our days are advanced, Mr. Pons. They pay their taxes."

Once again Pons retreated into silence, taking time now to light up his calabash. But this time his silence was broken more quickly.

"I have some modest knowledge of British law, Mr. Athelney," said Pons, "but your laws may well differ. What type of social system prevails in your world and time?"

"It is usually referred to as Industrial Feudalism."

"I am not familiar with the term, though I can guess its meaning. Pray elucidate."

"In the same manner that Feudalism evolved from Chattel Slavery, and Capitalism from Feudalism, so Industrial Feudalism has evolved in our continuum from Capitalism. Ownership has contracted until a few princes of finance, a few industrial barons and lords of transportation completely control the government and practically all the wealth."

"Do national boundaries still prevail,"

"Terra is united, but we have loose ties with the other planets of the Solar System."

"Then doubtless you have tariff laws between the various planets."

"Very rigid ones. Last month we apprehended some Martians smuggling duppl berries; they were given ten years."

"I submit you have an obvious trap in which to take Moriarty and his Club Cerise, Mr. Athelney. They must pay import taxes on those art objects. Failure to do so puts them afoul of the law."

Our client smiled broadly. "I do. believe, Mr. Pons, you have arrived at a solution of our problem."

He came to his feet.

"I suggest your government pass such tariff restrictions as to make imports from other space-time continua prohibitive. Such a move, in view of the fact that the criminals of your time are so advanced as to pay their taxes, would in all likelihood prevent further depredations."

Though our client was manifestly anxious to be off, he hesitated. "I wish there were some way in which I could remunerate you, Mr. Pons. Unfortunately, we do not use the same system of exchange. All I can do is offer profound thanks in the name of my continuum."

"There is surely remuneration enough implied in the promise that we will not be victimized here in our time and world by such as Moriarty," said Pons. "But, stay, Mr. Athelney – I perceive you are still troubled by some aspect of the matter."

Our client turned from the threshold, to which he had walked. He smiled wryly. "I fear, Mr. Pons, that this is but the initial step in our problem. Moriarty, when he learned I was to travel hither in search of the greatest detective of all time, took certain protective measures. He sent one of his own men to another space-time continuum to acquire the services of a most astute lawyer named Randolph Mason."

"Pray be reassured," responded Pons instantly. "I can refer you to a rising young contemporary, who promises to be even greater, and is gaining a challenging reputation in the legal circles of his world. By an odd coincidence, not uncommon to fiction, he bears a similar family name. His given name, I believe, is Perry. My correspondents on the west coast of the United States have given me flattering reports of his talents. You will find him in Los Angeles, I believe. I commend him to your government. Good afternoon, Mr. Athelney."

As soon as the door had closed behind our visitor, I turned to Pons. "Should not one of us slip after him and notify the authorities of his escape?"

Pons walked to the window and looked out into the fog. Without turning, he asked, "You thought him a lunatic, Parker?"

"Surely that was obvious!"

"Was it, indeed!" Pons shook his head. "I sometimes think, Parker, that that happy faculty for observation which seems to come so readily to me encounters obstacles of demoralizing stubbornness in you."

"Pons!" I exclaimed hotly, "you cannot have been taken in by this – this mountebank and his hoax?"

"Was he both lunatic and mountebank, then?" asked Pons, smiling in that superior manner which always galled me.

"What does it matter which he was? He was certainly one or the other."

"If a mountebank, what was his motive? If a lunatic, how did he find his way here in this fog, which is surely as thick as any we have ever had? I fear some of us have an unhappy tendency to dismiss the incredible solely because it is incredible to us. Tell me, Parker, have you ever contemplated setting forth in the form of fiction these little adventures of mine in the field of ratiocination?"

I hesitated to answer.

"Come, come, Parker, it is evident that you have."

"I confess, I have thought of it."

"You have not yet done so?"

"No, Pons, I swear it."

"You have spoken of your plans to no one?"

"No."

"Our late client spoke of you as a literary doctor. 'The famous literary doctor' were his exact words, I believe. If he were but a lunatic or mountebank, as you will have him, how came he then to know of your innermost hope and ambition in this regard? Or is there some secret communion between lunatics and mountebanks? I perceive, thanks to our Mr. Athelney that, without regard to my wishes, you are destined to become a literary man at the expense of my modest powers."

"Pons, I swear I have never put pen to paper," I cried.

"But you will, Parker, you will. May I remind you of my distinguished predecessor's credo, that when all probable explanations have been shown false, the improbable, no matter how incredible, alone remains? This, I fancy, is one little adventure you will not be able to chronicle without a furtive blush or two.'

In this, at least, my companion was correct.

THE ADVENTURE OF THE BALL OF NOSTRADAMUS

My friend, Solar Pons, the private enquiry agent, has a tendency to be highly dubious of all coincidence – but was it only coincidence that he should refer to the singular adventure of the late Abraham Weddigan on the very day that I had determined to set down the facts about this horrible affair which shocked a continent and, on its successful termination, brought Pons the profound gratitude of millions of people as well as the personal felicitations of His Majesty? From the moment of its conclusion, Pons began to entertain some doubt about Abraham Weddigan, that strange, unforgettable monster – a description of my own which Pons will not countenance – and soon his doubts grew, so that often, when I saw him sitting in profound and troubled thought, and knew no problem had come in to enlist his keen mind, I was aware that he was once again pondering the meaning of the motives of Abraham Weddigan.

On that day in the 1920's that Pons entered the case, in the second decade of our sharing his quarters at Number 7B, Praed Street, I had been reading about the murder of a child – the second in the streets of London. Pons was standing at the window, his long thin hands clasped behind his back, his eyes fastened on the street below.

"I observe that you, too, my dear Parker," said Pons suddenly, without turning, "have begun to wonder – not without some indignation – about the child-murderer in our midst."

"How could you know which account I was reading?" I asked in surprise.

He turned, his ascetic face briefly alight with a smile. "My dear fellow, surely it is elementary. You are agitated, you rustle your paper indignantly, you squirm your disapproval of the police methods in the case, indeed, you all but snort in irritation. What else in the morning paper could stir to such indignation a man who has always been interested in the crime life of London?"

"Ah, you have read of it then!"

"You know my habits, Parker. Little escapes me."

He came over to stuff his pipe with shag from the slipper tacked to the mantelpiece, and sat down in his favorite chair, a frown on his high forehead.

"I fear I neglected to tell you," he went on, "but I am expecting our friend Jamison at any moment. He sent word by messenger this morning before you awoke that he wished to see me on the matter, and it is now some minutes past the hour set for his arrival. Since he is customarily so prompt, I fancy some new facts may have come to light."

"Or another child murder," I put in.

"God forbid! This shocking chain of child murders is far more extensive than Inspector Jamison may know." He listened a moment and added, "But there is the police car now, if I am not mistaken, arriving in Jamison's usual haste."

The outer door opened and closed violently, and Jamison came up the stairs as rapidly as his rotund bulk would permit.

"Dear me," murmured Pons, "I would far rather have Jamison glum than Jamison in such good spirits."

I opened the door to Jamison and saw that he was indeed in good spirits, for a broad smile sprang into being on his chubby face, his eyes twinkled, and his mustache fairly trembled with delight at the sight of us.

"This time, Pons, we have done it without you!"

"My congratulations! But what is it you have done?"

"We have our man for the murder of Terence Allen and Thomas Kanczeny."

"The child murderer!" I cried. "I thought the crimes clueless.

"Ah, so they were," Jamison went on, rubbing his hands together. "We did not set out to arrest Captain Martin Verne for murder – we went only to question him."

"Pray begin at the beginning, Jamison," interrupted Pons patiently.

"Very well. I need not go into detail about the crimes themselves; you are familiar enough with the shocking shooting-down of two defenseless children on the city streets. We have been interested – remotely, it is true – in the activities of Captain Martin Verne – "

"One-time soldier of fortune, gun runner, assassin for hire, last heard of in Morocco, after some years in Nicaragua, in China, and on the Continent," said Pons.

"That's him. Well, Pons, he's our man. When he came to England three months ago, he was living close to the bone. We knew as much, and spread the word that the Yard was interested in Verne. So one day he moved from the hole he lived in out Wapping way, set himself up in Park Lane, no less, new wardrobe, and new night life – all the more expensive restaurants and theaters. A nark passed us the word, and two men went over last night to ask him some questions. Verne must have suspected they were after something else. He tried to put them off, then he tried to shoot his way out. He put a bullet into Police Constable MacEachern's shoulder, but Constable Leeds put him out with his truncheon. Leeds hit him harder than he ought to have done, and Verne died half an hour ago. But not before we got down what he said in delirium; and when we had him conscious for a little while before the end, and put it to him: did he kill the children? – he admitted it. Further, the laboratory tests show that a bullet from his gun killed the Allen boy: no bullet was recovered in the case of Kanczeny. So there we are."

Pons had listened with keen interest. Now, however, his eyes, darkened, his frown returned. "And the motive?"

"He had no time for that. Still, we thought it might be in what he said. You see, the moment they heard him talking, they started taking down what he said. I wasn't called in until after I'd sent word to you. One look at what they'd taken down, and I knew Verne was our man. I brought along a copy of it for you, Pons. You've done me a good many favors in the past."

He took a folded paper from his inner coat pocket as he spoke and handed it to Pons. It was hardly the size of an ordinary sheet of manuscript paper and was, as I saw when I rose and walked over to look from behind Pons, little more than a meaningless jumble of disjointed sentences. Nevertheless, Pons read it with the keenest interest, though for my part I failed to see that Verne's utterances in delirium conveyed anything of signal importance. The typescript was commendably short.

"Terence Allen, aged 9... Escape tutor... the ball knows... savior o' the world... That damned fortune-teller!... two hundred gross of Brens... Look, sir, it's a bit out o' me line... first the smoke, then the picture... Christ! how real it is... Bluddy old Mussolini!... Thomas Kanczeny, Hungarian legation, seven years old... mad dog, mad dog, mad dog... Gentlemen, we aims to quarantine, if you please, to prevent... blast him forever! putting the blood o' kids on me hands!... A pound never looked better to me, and that's the truth, so help me God, but I didn't bargain for that kind of blood money... Guns you ordered and guns you got; I'll look at the color o' your money... Touch the ball, Mister. Fifty quid to have your fortune told. Knows all, sees all, tells the future, tells the past. Fifty quid, Mister... My alibi's perfect. Nobody can touch me but me... And if I wasn't so bad off for money, I'd never take on a dirty job like this... Guns is my line, sir, guns and contraband. I'm the best."

Pons looked up, his eyes fairly dancing.

"Couldn't have made it clearer in a signed confession," said Jamison, smiling happily. "We know the Allen boy was shot when he ran away from his tutor. Now, just to corroborate, we've sent a man out to discover whether there was a dog at or near the scene, plainly enough in evidence, when the Kanczeny boy was killed."

"And how do you plan to establish the connecting link with – let us choose at random – the death of little Ossip Ciciorka in Prague four months ago?" interposed Pons quietly.

Jamison's mouth fell agape. His joviality faded; he grew wary. "Of whom?" he asked finally.

Pons repeated the name and added, "Or, for that matter, of Georges Murat, aged ten, in the Rue d'Auseil, Paris, on May ninth last year; of Giovanni d'Orsini, aged eight, on a holiday in Naples two years ago; of Timor Gushenko, aged six, on the beach of Cannes with his parents three years ago; or even of the abortive attempt on the life of Ana Rabinsohn, a girl of five, in the streets of Bucharest six years ago."

Jamison had recovered his composure. "Pons, you are joking. And an ill-conceived joke it is," said he.

"I daresay you would think so. I regret that it is no jest. I have never been more in earnest. Let us pause for a moment and examine into the matter. There are striking parallels I believe you cannot fail to apprehend. In neither the Allen nor the Kanczeny case was any attempt to kidnap made."

"No."

"Nor to collect blackmail from the parents of these unfortunate victims."

"No."

"Nor was there any molestation of the children themselves."

"No."

"In both these instances murder alone would seem to have been the object of the attack."

"Quite so. It was in all the papers."

"The pattern is precisely similar to their Continental predecessors. All are unsolved crimes. And, of even greater importance, they are seemingly without motive. Or did you discover at the last hour with Verne any trace of one?"

Jamison flushed.

"Ah, you need not answer. I submit, then, that Verne had been hired to commit at least these last two crimes. He may have had a hand in some of the others, but I am inclined to doubt it. Very well then. If not Verne, some other hired assassin. They abound in Europe; each has his price, and most may have been less squeamish than Verne. I put it to you that no one pays a hired assassin to murder a child without some motive, however obscure. No, do not say it Jamison – the psychopath does not hire murder done; he does it himself. We must cast into other waters for our motive, Jamison."

"When word of Verne's death reaches whoever it was who hired him, I'll wager he'll leave London by the fastest means," said Jamison.

"Dear me, I had not thought that Scotland Yard was less intent upon the capture of a murderer than his flight beyond their jurisdiction. I fancy that concept of crime detection will interest the Commissioner."

"Oh, come, Pons, you are taking me too literally. Depend on it, we shall be on the watch for him. But, I confess, we have not the slightest hint of motive."

"I suspected as much," said Pons dryly. "But the picture is not so hopeless as all that, surely. There are several salient facts which are curiously similar in the majority of the murders."

"You believe that those you have mentioned are connected with these in London?"

"Can you doubt it? Consider: the methods in all cases are exactly similar, and so are the circumstances surrounding them. There is a sinister pattern in the very fact that there is no similarity whatsoever – unless we are unable to see it – among the victims of this plague of murder. Those children come from all walks of life. Allen was the son of a poor laborer. Kanczeny belonged to parents in the Hungarian embassy. Cicioka was the son of a Polish librarian. Young d'Orsini, though of an ancient Italian family, was the son of an artist, Murat of a wine merchant, Gushenko of a petty railroad official. And the abortive attempt in Bucharest was made on the daughter of humble Jewish parents.

"Murder of children for vengeance against the parents is not unknown; it was practised at one time by the Mafia. But it is highly unlikely that these murders have a common origin of that nature; they are too widely separated to make it probable that one terror organization could be responsible for these crimes, and to presuppose others is to enter the realm of pure conjecture without relation to facts. None of the parents involved is important enough to have incurred political enmities. Indeed, they are nonentities – even Kanczeny's position at the embassy is that of a minor clerk. In almost every instance, the children were murdered at a supremely felicitous moment for the murderer – when they had strayed or run away, which suggests either a constant watchfulness or an uncanny knowledge. I venture to suggest that all these crimes were the work of one guiding genius."

"A Napoleon of crime," cried Jamison.

"You do Napoleon's memory no service. A modern Herod, perhaps." Pons made an impatient gesture. "But we are wasting time. I beg you to stand by, Jamison. I mean to find the author of these crimes."

When Jamison had gone, Pons turned to me. "If you were to need the services of a fortune-teller – surely one of position, who asks 'fifty quid' a reading – to whom in all London would you apply?"

"Elementary, my dear Pons!" I cried. "There is surely but one such seer: the consultant – so he terms himself – visited by peers, M. P.'s, even persons close to the court – Abraham Weddigan. His fees are exorbitant, and he is never at a loss for patrons."

But Pons was already looking into a London directory. "Let us see. Ah, here we are. His office is in Southampton Row. Let us lose no time. We shall start with him. If we are in error, we shall carry on from there. None knows to what lengths he may be driven now that his hireling is dead."

"Are you not taking the delirium of a dying man too seriously?" I inquired when at last we were in a cab rolling toward Southampton Row.

Pons sat in his accustomed pose, head sunk to his chest, the fingers of one hand toying with the lobe of his right ear, his eyes clouded and dark, fixed on a point not in space but in time.

"No, no," he said impatiently. "I submit that the last words of Verne, however disjointed, nevertheless pointed clearly to some baleful connection with a fortune-teller. 'That damned fortune-teller!' he said. And twice more, he made reference to 'the ball' – which surely is the crystal globe so much an integer in the impedimenta of the seer. We are quite safe in eliminating the references to guns and gun-running; these would be bound to show up in such a scattering of memories as the situation implies. I submit we are on the right track. 'Fifty quid' for a reading. No small sum. No crossing of the palm with mere silver. No indeed. 'Fifty quid' – and for that someone who knows all and sees all will tell the past and the future. Verne had become obsessed by him – and by the magic ball – to such an extent that a rudimentary conscience made him try to flee when, in actuality, none pursued him, and so brought him to his death."

Abraham Weddigan's suite of offices was in one of the most modern buildings on Southampton Row, one given over to business offices representing some of the foremost industries in all England. There, as sedate as any other, Abraham Weddigan was duly listed as a Consultant, and his suite was no secret.

We mounted to his floor, found his number, and were prepared to knock when the door was opened noiselessly from within. There before us stood a Caucasian of dark complexion, a Mauritanian, surely. He wore a turban and complementary clothing. He bowed.

"Mr. Solar Pons and Dr. Lyndon Parker. Step this way, if you please, sirs. The Master is expecting you."

"We made no appointment," I said with asperity.

"The Master knows all save his own fate," said the Mauritanian. "Such is as it was ordained."

He led us down a short corridor to a wide door at its end. There he stood, his head bowed, making no sound.

Nevertheless, a voice from within called out, "Enter."

The Mauritanian threw open the door and stood aside for us to enter a large, almost unfurnished room. In its center was a low divan; opposite it, a conventional but luxurious easy chair. Between chair and divan rose a small round table of Oriental manufacture, supporting a small crystal ball. The occupant of the chair came to his feet and motioned to the divan.

"Mr. Pons, Doctor Parker – pray be seated."

His hands were fine and soft, as delicate as a woman's; his eyes were deep and lustrous; his gray hair was heavy and worn long, the only factor of his appearance that seemed affected, for his dress was conventional – a gray business suit. He was a compelling, extraordinarily handsome man, however old he might have been. As he resumed his seat, Pons and I sat on the divan.

"We came..." began Pons, but Weddigan held up his hand for silence.

"I regret the nature of your call. I regret the circumstances which have brought it about. The children, yes. The crystal told me Verne was not efficient. Now he is dead before my work in London is finished. Shall I go elsewhere to pursue it? I cannot say; the crystal is dark, very dark."

"Do you now confess to having compelled the man Verne to murder two defenseless children?" I demanded.

"Gently, gently, Parker," admonished Pons, laying a restraining hand on my arm. "We shall listen to Mr. Weddigan."

Weddigan inclined his head. "Thank you, Mr. Pons. Fate has implacably determined that we must be opposed to each other. I regret that circumstance. I know you will hinder my plans. How shall I speak of them to you?" An expression of great weariness came into his face, and he shook his head slowly from side to side. "Have I any other course? I think not, gentlemen. I hope and pray that you are not of the race of doubters and the army of the Philistines. I have the gift of true precognition." He laid one hand on the crystal ball before him. "All the myths of mankind, gentlemen, have a root, however remote, in fact – even the dream of seeing man's future in a crystal ball. This is no ordinary crystal, believe me. It is old, very old – it and the strangely wrought base of silver on which it stands. The inscriptions are in Sumerian cuneiform characters. It was ancient before the city of Ur. Of its origin I have no knowledge, but many years ago, in the year 1550, a traveler from Greece, who had found this crystal in the ruins of Delphi, sold it to a Frenchman named Michel de Nostredame."

"The crystal ball of Nostradamus," murmured Pons.

"At least he is not strange to you, Mr. Pons. And was not Nostradamus the most famous seer of all time? Did not his prophecies, one upon another, come true – centuries after he had set them down?"

"The fulfillment of prophecies, like beauty, is too often only in the eye of the beholder," replied Pons. "But I concede that the French physician offers as nearly adequate evidence for prevision as I know."

"This is the original crystal ball and from it stems the information you seek. It was because of what I saw in the future that it became necessary for me to serve my race by destroying the young persons in whom you are interested."

"You wish us to believe that you hired assassins – Verne in London, others elsewhere – to murder harmless children because of what you saw in the ball of Nostradamus?" asked Pons, shaking his head gently. "Sir, I am no seer; I am but an humble practitioner of the art of ratiocination. This is beyond reason."

"Indeed it is," agreed Weddigan. "I repeat it. These children, Ossip Ciciorka, Terence Allen, Timor Gushenko – but I need not name them; you know their names – these children, I say, were destined to become the oppressors, the dictators, the mad dogs of tomorrow, the Mussolinis of their generation, to fire the earth with war and pestilence, to subjugate and degrade mankind to its lowest level. I failed in the case of the girl, Ana Rabinsohn; perhaps I shall have opportunity to try it again. There is but one more in London – Josef Zollern. With your permission, I shall personally execute him."

"I regret our inability to aid your crime, Mr. Weddigan," said Pons.

"Stay a moment, sir. Will you look into the ball? Pray have no fear of chicanery. And you, Dr. Parker. And tell me in a moment or two what you see there."

Pons and I turned to the ball. And in a moment, scarcely more, the crystal had begun to cloud up, as if smoke had somehow entered the glass. I flashed a glance at our monstrous host, and saw him bent above the ball, his hands flat on either side of it, his head bowed, an expression of infinite sadness in his features. Then the ball drew me again, and I saw a scene beginning to take shape, as of a vast concourse of people, before whom stood a fair-haired young man wearing a scarlet tunic, haranguing them passionately and receiving their ovations. The impassioned orator bore a sabre-slash on his right cheek. All about hung the paraphernalia of tyranny. The scene held but briefly; then the clouds swirled up and it was gone.

"I know only too well what you saw, gentlemen," said Weddigan. He rose, clapping his hands.

The Mauritanian appeared almost instantly.

"Forgive me," said Weddigan, bowing once more, his eyes fixed upon some goal far beyond us. "I am an idealist, a perfectionist. I wear a curse upon my soul." And to the servant he said, "Detain Mr. Pons and Dr. Parker for twenty minutes. I leave to protect the future."

The seer stepped behind the servant and vanished into the dark hangings along the wall. The Mauritanian resolutely barred our way, standing with folded arms before us, his sudden menace to make of him a giant. And indeed, his shoulders were as broad as any I have seen, and his girth was in keeping. He weighed well over fifteen stone, and his aspect was formidable.

Neither of us made a move for several moments. Then suddenly Pons reached out, took up the crystal ball of Nostradamus, and at the same time came to his feet and flung the ball with all his might. The surprised Mauritanian fell without a cry, and the ball shattered when it struck the floor beyond the divan.

Pons leaped over the fallen servant and, without turning to see whether I was following, ran out into the hall to the elevators. In the foyer he found what he sought – a telephone directory of London.

"There is but one chance we may save the boy, Parker," he said. "Twenty minutes, Weddigan: said. Let us see... Z... Zollern. Clapham, Loughborough, Norwood – these Zollerns are well over twenty minutes from Southampton Row. Camden Town. Count Helmut von and zu Zollern – he alone is within twenty minutes of these premises. Now, if only we can reach Jamison in time..."

We sped toward Camden Town in a fortuitously discovered cab, and turned into a middle-class residential street just as the tall figure of Abraham Weddigan passed the flats housing the Zollern family we sought.

"Slow down, driver," said Pons.

Weddigan, having reached the end of the street, turned to walk back.

At that moment a small figure emerged from the flats and started across the street. At sight of him, Weddigan changed his pace to swerve toward the boy.

"Now!" cried Pons. "Pray heaven we are not too late! Driver, get down there at once."

Just as the driver started up, a Flying Squad car raced around the further corner and bore down upon Weddigan. The white face of Abraham Weddigan came up, his eyes widening as he saw the two cars coming toward him. His hand darted into his coat and brought out a stub-nosed pistol. He began to run toward the eleven-year-old.

The bulky figure of Inspector Jamison leaned from the window of the police car, heavy Webley in hand. Within the second it spoke sharply, once and again. Weddigan spun around and dropped to the street, his weapon skittering from his hand.

Pons, myself, and Jamison were out of our respective vehicles in a moment. We ran forward, while young Josef Zollern, who had turned at the excitement to look back, began to walk toward Weddigan's body. The four of us reached the scene almost together.

"Done in," said Jamison curtly. "Acting on your information, Pons. We've traced some of Verne's payments to Weddigan. A madman."

"It would seem so," replied Pons, gazing thoughtfully down at the fallen body. "Even if I find it difficult to forget how he spoke of Mussolini. There are more important things in government than making the trains run on time..."

Josef Zollern, a pale, pinch-faced youngster, looked down at the corpse almost with contempt. Momentarily, a fire seemed to flash in the depths in his dark eyes.

"Young man, you were in danger," said Jamison with bluff heartiness.

The boy's lips were touched with disdain.

"I suppose that before my destiny is fulfilled, I shall see a good deal of this," he said shrilly. There was a cutting edge of fanaticism in his voice.

Pons gazed at him as if he seeing him for the first time.

The boy looked back with eyes that were proud and insolent. Then he turned and walked, quite self-possessed, back to the apartment house from which tenants were coming toward the scene.

Happily, that was the end of the inexplicable sequence of child murders which had shocked the Continent. With Weddigan's death, the case was closed, and so it is marked in the police files, despite Pon's annoying, "Only the future will tell, Parker."

THE ADVENTURE OF THE *NOSFERATU*

"My dear fellow," I said somewhat testily to my friend Solar Pons, "I must say that your diversity of interests is amazing."

Solar Pons looked up from the heavy tome he had been perusing so avidly. "Amazing, Parker?"

"How a man of your scientific interests could waste his time on that drivel, is quite beyond me."

His eyebrows went up. "You consider an interest in the occult to be, of necessity, foreign to an intelligent mind, Parker?"

"I would not have put it quite so bluntly," I said, "but, frankly, I do."

"I see." He put down his copy of *The Times* and eyed me thoughtfully while he loaded his heavy briar with shag.

When he had lit up, he relaxed in his chair and touched his fingertips together. "You are familiar with the American Horace Greeley, perhaps?"

"A journalist, I believe. Editor of the abolitionist press during their Civil War period, was he not?" I confess I didn't understand his sudden change in subject.

"Would you judge him an intelligent man, Parker?"

"Manifestly he was a man of considerable education."

"Very well, I shall attempt to quote from memory two paragraphs from his autobiography. *My consciousness of ignorance of the extent of limitations of the natural is so vivid that I never could realize that difficulty in crediting what are termed miracles which many affirm.*

"I know so very little of nature that I cannot determine at a glance what is or is not supernatural; but I know that things do occur which are decidedly superusual, and I rest in the fact without being able, or feeling required, to explain it."

Solar Pons opened his eyes and looked at me quizzically. "And what would you say to Mr. Greeley's opinion, Parker?"

I shrugged in irritation. "I think you are rather stretching a point, using Horace Greeley's words to condone the spending of long hours on such as that." I indicated the large tome he had been perusing.

"Not at all, Parker. As has been said, most, if not all, of our legends, myths and even superstitions have some basis in reality. There is much smoke, perhaps, and little fire, but the fire is there." It was his turn to indicate the book. "Perhaps there is little fire indeed in *The Times*, but it is my amusement and interest to seek it out."

His arguments had not assuaged my irritation. "I have heard expressed before that all myths have a basis in reality, but I have very little evidence to support the thesis."

"Indeed, Parker?" My friend's eyes were sparkling now. "And what myth would you use as an example to indicate that it was not based on an element of truth?"

I chose at random. "Take, for instance, the Greek Centaurs."

A mocking smile twisted his mouth. "You select a poor example I am afraid, Parker."

"To the contrary," I retorted. "Obviously, not only did the Centaur never exist, but not even a reasonable facsimile of one."

Pons smiled back. "There were literally thousands of Centaurs in pre-Homeric Greece. I am afraid your anthropology has been sorely neglected. You should read Lewis Henry Morgan, or at least our British novelist Robert Graves."

That was too much, even to take from Solar Pons. I stared at him. "Do you mean to sit there and contend that in ancient Greece there existed a half-man, half-horse creature? Really Pons! I claim the myth without basis in fact, and you must admit I am correct!"

Solar Pons said, "The Centaurs were an early Greek gens or clan. The horse gens. When its members wished to portray themselves on their pottery, or in other artistic endeavor, they put the shoulders, arms and head of a man on a horse's body. This was perfectly clear to them, and to their contemporaries. They were merely showing that they were members of the horse gens. When man had evolved beyond the point where gens were the basis of society, the Centaurs disappeared. But their art objects remained and the Centaur myth slowly developed. You'll find a parallel, by the way in the fish gens and the mermaid legend."

He looked me in the face. "Come now, Parker, would you still insist the Centaur myth has no base in reality?"

I began to sputter, but events spared me my embarrassment. Solar Pons held up a hand.

"Hark, Parker. Unless I am mistaken, we are about to be visited by a youthful and rather agitated American."

I stared at him. "Confound it, Pons, I..."

But a rapping at the door interrupted me. I came to my feet and threw it open, to confront, as Pons had predicted, a young man attired as no resident of London could ever be on so damp and cold a day as this. I began to suspect that Pons was correct as to nationality.

"Solar Pons?" the newcomer demanded.

"Come in," I said. I motioned to my friend sitting, pipe in mouth, before the fire. "This is Mr. Pons. I am Doctor Lyndon Parker."

Pons came to his feet and accepted the outstretched hand the other offered. "Your name, sir?"

"Bentley. David Bentley."

Pons waved him to a seat. "Pray be seated. I am somewhat puzzled, Mr. Bentley. I detect, if I am not mistaken, that you have recently arrived from the Southern United States, probably from Baltimore, and that you have hastened here – but not to hire my services. To what, then, do we owe the honor of this visit?"

Bentley sank into the proffered chair. "How in the world did you..." He cut himself short and started a new sentence. "Well, you are quite correct, Mr. Pons. I'm not here to offer you a case, at least not in the ordinary sense of the word. I'm here to request that you revenge me if I fail in a job I've set myself."

"Indeed," pons murmured. "Please elucidate."

David Bentley looked up at me. "This ought to be kind of private."

"Almost all of our visitors precede their stories with nearly identical words, Mr. Bentley. Believe me, Doctor Parker's discretion is as great as my own and he is my valued assistant."

Without further preliminaries, our visitor began his story. "I'm in London, Mr. Pons, to kill a monster."

"Indeed?" Pons murmured.

"A monster, Mr. Pons, that has, in its day, been the end of an unknown number of innocent people. Probably an almost countless number."

Solar Pons looked over to me, as he relit his pipe. "Fascinating, eh, Parker," he said.

"Amazing," I returned.

David Bentley went on. "I've been tracing this monster ever since the murder of my close friend James Grunland. Less than two weeks ago I found that Doctor Coty had arrived in London. I took the fastest liner leaving the Chesapeake and docked only this morning."

His eyes went from one of us to the other.

"Pray proceed," Pons murmured.

"Well, I've pledged my life and what little money I have to this job, but if by any chance I don't make it, the world still has to be protected and I want you to carry on my work."

"More details, please," Pons said. "I am afraid that the name Doctor Coty eludes me, although I make a practice of keeping up on activities in the underworld, not only in the United Kingdom but abroad as well."

"Dr. Poula Coty..." David Bentley began.

"Poula Coty!" I injected.

Solar Pons raised his eyebrows at me. "A woman, then," he said. "You know her, Parker?"

"Not personally," I said, "but certainly by reputation. Dr. Coty is possibly the world's outstanding authority on the pineal gland. More than one eminent physician has given her credit for advancing a hundredfold man's knowledge in this field."

Manifestly my words had increased the interest of Pons considerably. He turned to our agitated visitor. "This is the same Dr. Coty, of course?"

"It must be. I don't deny for one minute this eminence of hers in the medical field. I admit I can't explain it, this paradox of a monster and a scientist in the same body. All I say is I know that Dr. Poula Coty was the death of my friend Jim Grunland and how many more only God knows."

Solar Pons rubbed the end of his nose with a thoughtful forefinger. "And why have you not taken your evidence to the authorities, Mr. Bentley?"

"For three good reasons. First of all, I'm convinced she's guilty but my evidence isn't enough to stand up in court. Second, I want the satisfaction of revenging Jim myself."

"And the third reason?" I prompted when he hesitated.

He looked at me, rather defiantly, I thought. "The third reason, Doctor Parker, is that I don't have any desire to be tossed into a nut factory. You see, this monster, Poula Coty, is *nosferatu*."

"Ah," Solar Pons murmured. "I submit that it would be most difficult to prove guilt in the courts. I assume you are armed against your monster, Mr. Bentley?"

Our visitor dipped into a side pocket and produced a small automatic, a .25 or .32 caliber weapon, I would have estimated. "I'm armed, Mr. Pons."

"Indeed, I see you are. And the bullets are of silver?"

"They're silver."

Pons leaned forward and fixed the young man with a severe eye. "Mr. Bentley, ethics prevent me from turning you over to our police authorities, although I am sorely tempted to do so. I consider myself to occupy much the same position as does a doctor, a lawyer, or even a priest. You have come to consult me, I shall not inform against you. However, I demand this pledge. Collect additional evidence against your Dr. Coty, if you will, but before you resort to violence, pledge me that you will consult me further."

David Bentley came to his feet, his face pale. "Okay, Mr. Pons, it's a promise. I'll keep you informed."

He turned and quickly left the room.

Solar Pons sat staring after him, obviously in a high degree of agitation.

"My dear Pons," I said, "how in the world did you know his bullets were made of silver? And why did you deal with his accusations against Dr. Coty so cavalierly? It would seem that at least you should have heard him out at greater length. Dr. Coty is prominent, but prominence is no guarantee that she is not also a murderess."

Solar Pons grunted sourly, but then looked up at me. "Ah, the silver bullets. Are you familiar with the word *nosferatu*, my dear Parker?"

"I admit I am not, but what..."

"*Nosferatu*, Parker, means un-dead."

"Un-dead?"

Solar Pons sighed. "Your study of myth, superstition and the occult is indeed neglected, Parker. *Nosferatu*, un-dead, vampire. Our young friend is of the opinion that his Doctor Coty is a vampire. I am afraid that is why I was not as receptive to his story as ordinarily I might be." His voice was slightly dry. "Nothing is impossible, Parker, but I submit that some things are improbable in the extreme. In my studies of the occult I have found very little fire for all the vampire smoke."

"Vampire," I snorted. "The young man is unbalanced."

"It puts us in an impossible position, Parker. I must admit I hardly know what to do. I sincerely hope the boy will keep his pledge before taking drastic action."

"Good Heavens, Pons! You can't leave it at that. That young man is mad – and dangerous."

"I have no intention of leaving it at that, Parker. But let me think." He sank back into this chair and into one of his characteristic reveries.

For the next three days I saw little of Solar Pons. Up in the mornings before I arose, he was often gone until far into the night. Since this was not overly unusual, and since for a time I was more than ordinarily busy myself handling the practice of a friend on vacation as well as my own, I thought little more of it.

On the third night, however, there was a heavy, definite knock on the door and when I threw it open I was confronted by a nondescript workman, dark of complexion and heavy of moustache. An Ulsterman, I decided, priding myself on the use of the methods of Solar Pons.

"Sure, and could this be after bein' the home of the late Solar Pons?" he said.

To say I was taken aback would manifestly be insufficient, My face must have gone white. "The late Solar Pons!" I blurted.

He took his hat from his head and held it in his hands. "Sure, and you must be his friend, Dr. Parker. A vampire it must have been after bein', sir. Drained of blood, he was."

I staggered back to a chair and slumped into it.

"Oh, come now, Parker," the voice of Solar Pons said. "I was interested in trying my disguise upon you, but surely it is not as superlative as all that. How long must you take to smell a rat?" He chuckled dryly and began shedding his outer clothing.

"Pons!" I blurted, and then, angrily, "Good Heavens, man, you'll be the death of me, Vampires, indeed!"

He chuckled again. "You must forgive me, Parker. I am greatly relieved this evening, after several days of disturbed mind."

I must admit that my interest in his adventures overrode my anger at the practical joke he had played.

"Ah?" I said. "You have been somewhat elusive these days, Pons. Perhaps you would like to tell me how you have spent your time."

He chuckled still again as he removed the last remnants of his irish disguise. "As a bodyguard, Parker. A bodyguard and a dip."

"A dip?" I said, frowning at him.

"A rather Robin Hoodish dip, I would say, Parker. Immediately before our friend was to confront my – unbeknownst to her – ward, I would play the dip and pick his pocket of his weapon. Following his interview, I would replace it. It was rather amusing, Parker."

"Young Bentley," I cried. "The young man who was convinced that Poula Coty is a vampire."

"Capital, Parker!" Pons said. "For the past three days I have been guarding Dr. Coty and observing our young American friend. I am convinced that my worries are about over."

"You have seen this Dr. Coty?" I asked.

"From a distance, Parker. A most attractive young lady, I must say, and I suspect that our young friend is as aware of her charm as am I. But of that we shall soon learn. He is on his way here now."

"David Bentley?"

"Yes, of course. If he comes while I am washing this pigment from my face, pray make him comfortable, Parker." My friend strode to the bath, and soon I could hear him splashing water about most vigorously.

As usual, Solar Pons was correct, for in little more than moments there was another knock at the door and I opened it to find David Bentley, more suitable attired for our climate this time, confronting me.

"Hello, Doctor Parker," he said. "Is Mr. Pons in?"

"Good evening," I said. "Come in and sit down. Pons will be with us shortly." He seemed somewhat more subdued than he had been before, but still I was inclined to be impatient. His superstitious nonsense had been the cause of occupying my friend's time for a full three days without either fee or the satisfaction of contending with an interesting problem.

When he was seated, I said, rather abruptly, perhaps. "And how goes the pursuit of your monster, Mr. Bentley?"

He either ignored, or was unconscious of the deprecating tone of my voice. He said worriedly, "That's why I came over tonight, Doctor. I have to confess that I'm puzzled. Since you two are the only people alive who know about my reason for coming to London, and since I promised Solar Pons that I'd keep him up on developments, I thought I ought to come over and tell you about it."

Solar Pons had entered behind us in time to catch the last words.

"Ah, ha, Mr. Bentley," he called. "I suspect that you are in the process of changing your mind about Dr. Coty. You admit now that it is highly unlikely that she is *nosferatu*." Solar Pons strode to his favorite chair and sat down facing us. His hands went out for a pipe and his tobacco.

"To the contrary, Mr. Pons," young Bentley said. "I'm more convinced of it than ever."

Pons dropped his lighted match, something I had never witnessed before in our many years together.

He stared at the young man for a long moment. Finally he struck another match, lit his pipe and sank back into the fullness of his chair. "Please give us the facts," he said. "I would appreciate them in as complete detail as possible."

David Bentley settled himself in his chair and began. "Well, I spent the first day, almost all of it, in the British Museum, trying to find out as much as possible about the subject. Well, I was disappointed. It's not that there wasn't a lot of material, actually there was so much that it was appalling to see the references. But my lack of language eliminated most of them and I found very little that seemed worth while. The British and American books on the subject all deal with it, well, in one of two manners. Either the author is superstitious, or he's convinced that the legends and myths haven't any basis at all. There isn't any in between. Nobody with a scientific background and an unprejudiced mind has ever investigated the subject. I guess that no scientist has ever realized that this *nosferatu* legend has a real foundation."

"Small wonder," I snorted.

"Please, Parker, let us hear Mr. Bentley out," Pons muttered.

"I suppose I shouldn't complain," the young American said. "I don't mind admitting that I wasn't very quick to be convinced myself. Not until it was too late and Jim was dead. You know, that's one of the most puzzling things about this deal. Knowing Poula Coty for what she was, how could Jim have let down his guard to the point where she was able to get to him?"

Pons opened his eyes and said, "It was your friend James Grunland who informed you that Dr. Coty was a vampire?"

David Bentley nodded, then went on. "I located the apartment hotel in which Poula Coty was staying. It wasn't very hard because she's been getting a lot of publicity as a result of her work in Baltimore and Leyden on the pineal gland. At any rate, I got an idea for getting in contact with her. I presented myself as a newspaper man at her apartment. As a matter of fact, it was, well, kind of a scary proposition. What powers she actually had, I didn't have any way of knowing. I was just hoping that they were less than the legends say the *nosferatu* are supposed to have.

"Well, when I met her it was easy to understand at last how this sinister beauty of hers helped her get so many victims. Did I just say, *sinister beauty*? Well, that's wrong. She's lovely, and her beauty is the kind that you certainly couldn't call evil. I should've suspected that from the first, of course. How is it that when we think of an evil woman we always picture a tall, svelte brunette with dark eyes and a dark complexion? You don't have to look sinister to be evil. This Poula Coty is, well, ethereal. There's a kind of touch of wistful sadness in her face and she's so young that her medical colleagues must wonder how she ever found the years to have reached the prominence she has."

I noted here that Solar Pons had nodded his head as though in agreement with Bentley's description of Dr. Poula Coty.

"And she's smart, too," David Bentley went on, "and pretty difficult to fool. When I introduced myself as Will Ross, a newspaperman, she immediately wanted to know which of the London newspapers I represented. Well, if I'd named one I suppose she could've excused herself and from another room checked by phone. Instead, I told her I was a freelancer who submitted articles under different bylines to a dozen different markets. Well, she was polite enough but she said she had an appointment and told me to come back the next day. She was going to give me material for an article on the pineal gland and the hormone it secretes."

"That takes us up to yesterday," Solar Pons submitted. "And what exactly transpired today?" He relit his pipe, studying our visitor through the clouds of smoke.

"I admit that I'm confused," the other said.

I snorted my acceptance of that obvious fact.

"Well, I'll try to give it word for word. This morning, Poula met me at the door of her apartment. She was dressed in a housecoat, one of these demure things. She looked, well, virginal, saint-like. She said, 'Come in, David.'

"Well, I must have started then, because the day before I had given her a phony name, not knowing whether or not Jim had ever mentioned me to her.

"She smiled, a kind of wan smile, and said, 'Yes, I know who you are, David. Please come in.' When I hesitated, she laughed a sort of bitter and hollow laugh and said, 'Don't be afraid, nine-tenths of what you have read was pure myth.'

"I followed her to her living room and there she offered me a comfortable chair, then cigarettes and a drink. I took the chair and watched her. She sat down opposite me and smiled this wry, wistful smile of hers. 'Let me tell you what you think,' she said, her voice kind of soft and throaty.

"I started to say something but she shook her head. She said, 'No. Permit me, please.' She looked at me very earnestly, and said, 'You think of me as – as a thing which has remained *nosferatu*. You think of me as one who has been the cause of the deaths of many, including your dear friend, Jim Grunland.' She paused and again this wistful sadness came over her face."

David Bentley broke off his story and looked at the two of us. "Maybe I'm stretching this out too much."

"Not at all," Pons told him. "I prefer complete detail. Please continue, sir."

By this time I was thoroughly disgusted and made little attempt to disguise the fact. But young Bentley went on.

"Poula Coty said, 'Probably, David, you have read many books on the subject these last few months, some of them novels, some of them medieval treatises – most of them pure nonsense. In that period have you read even one that attempted to understand us?' My eyes must have widened then because she said, 'Yes, I said us. I do not deny it, David; I am what you think.'"

I bent forward, completely confounded by Bentley's words. "Do you mean to sit there and say that the noted Doctor Poula Coty admitted to you that she was a vampire?" I asked, absolute disbelief in my voice.

Solar Pons was also rather open eyed over this development, but he said to me, "Please, Parker, let the gentleman continue."

Bentley nodded to Pons and continued his fantastic story. "I admit that I became indignant at that point. I said, 'From out of the depths of the Dark Ages. The most evil story of them all...' I was getting madder by the minute. Her eyes showed hurt, but she smiled her wan smile again.

"She said, 'Long and long before the Dark Ages, David, the *nosferatu* have existed throughout recorded history. True, we were more prevalent in earlier centuries and during the Middle Ages the superstitious almost completely destroyed us – almost. There was even less understanding then than there is today, and what the medieval mind could not understand, it attempts to destroy.'

"'You ask for understanding!' I blurted.

"Poula Coty arose from the couch she'd been sitting on and crossed the room to stare down at the street before the hotel. She looked almost childlike standing there, her back to me. I shook my hand sharply and, well, kind of unconscious-like my hand went toward the pocket where I had my gun."

Pons chuckled briefly there, but said nothing.

Bentley went on. "Poula Coty said softly, 'David, what does *nosferatu* mean?'"

"I said, 'It means un-dead. It means vampire,' and I could feel the muscles twitching in my cheek.

"She said, 'It means immortal,' her voice still soft and low. I felt myself staring at her again, wordless for the moment.

"She said, 'In medieval times, David we were so surrounded by superstition – superstition believed by not only the populous as a whole, but by the *nosferatu* themselves – that understanding was impossible.' She returned to the couch, clasped her hands together tightly in her lap and looked into my eyes. She said, 'Man is not an end, David. We know that now. We know that nature is continually striving to produce a more perfect specimen. One important step in this direction is the elimination of death. For the first step we can not only understand this but some of us even take steps to assist her. – As Jim did, David.'

"'Are you crazy?' I snapped. 'What are you trying to say?'

"She didn't answer for quite a while. Finally she said, 'I have already said too much for tonight. I have given you more than you can assimilate. Go now, David; go home and when you have considered all this, come back again.' I came to my feet, as though I was in a daze and kind of stumbled my way toward the door. Just before I left, she put a small hand on my sleeve and said softly, 'And did you bring a pistol with silver bullets, David?'

"I looked at her dumbly. That pain and sorrow was in her eyes again. She nodded and said. 'They would kill me, so would leaden ones. So would a stake through my heart. In fact, so would any other method violent enough to kill a normal person. The next time you come, David, try to leave superstition behind.'"

David Bentley ended his story there and looked expectantly at Solar Pons.

My friend cleared his throat. "So that brings us up to date?"

Bentley nodded. "Less than two hours ago I left her apartment."

Solar Pons leaned back and closed his eyes, his face twisted in exasperation.

I said deliberately, "I have never heard so fantastic a story."

Bentley looked from Solar Pons to me. "It is fantastic, isn't it?" he agreed. "I don't know what to think now. What could she have meant when she said that Jim Grunland had deliberately aided her?"

I snorted, not even bothering to answer him.

Solar Pons sat up suddenly and leaned forward toward our visitor. "Just one thing, if you please. You have attempted to report your experiences with as much care as possible. However, sometimes the most careful reporter misses this point or that. Tell me, Mr. Bentley, is there any chance that our Dr. Coty was jesting? That she was pulling your leg? A facial expression on her part, a twist of phrase?"

David Bentley said, a bit stiffly, "I'm afraid not, Mr. Pons."

Solar Pons sat back in his chair again, drumming his fingers on the armrest. Finally he said, "Mr. Bentley, once again I request that you do nothing violent until consulting with me."

"My promise still stands," David Bentley said, coming to his feet. "As a matter of fact, that's the way I want it. I don't mind admitting I'm all mixed up. I've got to have somebody to talk it over with." He looked from one of us to the other. "Well, good night," he said. "I'll keep you posted."

"Good night, Mr. Bentley," Solar Pons said and watched after him thoughtfully as he closed the door behind him.

I blurted, "Absolute nonsense!"

But Solar Pons didn't answer. He had dropped off into another of his reveries.

In the morning, at breakfast, Pons told me, "Parker, I find it necessary to make a quick run over to the Hague. I shall be gone perhaps three or four days. However, I have various matters on the fire here and hesitate to leave London. I am afraid I shall have to call upon your assistance."

"But of course," I answered him. "Just what is it you require?"

"Merely that you take the phone number of my friends whom I wish to consult in the Netherlands and call me instantly if there are any important developments from this end."

"Simple enough," I assured him.

He had packed his portmanteau and was gone within the half hour, and I was left to my own devices in our rooms.

While Solar Pons was away, I did what I could to remain in our rooms as much as possible. When circumstances called me away, I made sure that our long patient landlady, Mrs. Johnson, knew where to reach me at any hour. But although I received several calls from Pons, it was all quite routine and certainly not of sufficient importance to justify a call to the continent.

It was the first evening after his departure that David Bentley chose to make his third call at Number 7 Praed Street. In many respects it duplicated his first two appearances.

Upon his knock, I met him at the door. "Ah," I said, "Mr. Bentley, our impetuous young American."

"Is Solar Pons at home?" he asked. I noticed that, if anything, he was even more confused than he had been three nights previously.

"I am afraid that he is absent on a trip to the continent," I informed him, somewhat stiffly I must admit.

He seemed oblivious to my attitude, and, although I had not invited him to enter, pushed by me and took a chair by the fireplace.

"Since Pons isn't at home, I suppose I should report to you," he said musingly.

"It isn't really necessary," I told him. "frankly, I think the matter has gone much further than..."

But he wasn't listening to me. "I promised to keep you informed," he said. "I'll try to give as complete a picture as I can, the same as I did the other night."

I sighed in resignation and took my own favorite chair. "Very well," I said. "What is the latest in the case of Doctor Poula Coty, internationally honoured vampire."

He scowled and looked over to me. "I suppose that's kind of a silly word," he said.

I shrugged. "Please recall that it was you who used it first in these apartments."

"Well," he said, settling back in his chair. "That's beside the point, I guess. Suppose I make my report."

"Carry on," I glanced at my watch, suggestively.

"In many ways I've misunderstood Poula. I'm just beginning to realize now how much that pain and sorrow in her eyes really means. She met me at the door of her apartment this morning, dressed in a business suit and looking, well, every inch a modern woman. She took me into the living room again and to the same chair I'd occupied before. She checked the clock and told me, 'I can give you only a few minutes, David. I have a lecture at the Medical Association meeting in only half an hour; a lecture on the hormone secreted by the pineal gland.'

"She waited a minute, as though she was expecting me to say something, but somehow I couldn't get my thoughts together, under the sympathy in her eyes. Finally she said, 'I shall sum this up briefly. Later you will wish to ask questions... many questions.'

"'Some of them I will be unable to answer since my research, although conducted for many years, has been more limited than I could wish. Perhaps you will think me insane for suggesting it now, but one day I hope you will assist me.' I remained silent at that, but I could feel the indignation beginning to swell up inside me.

"She seemed to be gathering her thoughts for a minute, then she said, 'The pineal gland, David, is largely unknown; modern authorities debate the reason for its presence. Actually, in most persons it has no use. In a small fraction of humanity it is quite active and of that fraction those of us who are of the AB-RH Negative blood type have the ability to have it stimulated in a remarkable manner. You see, it is the basis of the vampire legend, and a score of other more obscure myths. A person of this blood type, with an active pineal gland, and given the stimulus of a certain as yet unisolated hormone, becomes... becomes immortal.'

"I started to inject something there, but she silences me with a protesting hand. 'No. don't ask me if all persons within the category I mentioned are... are vampires. They are merely potentially so; given the needed stimulator – which can be received only through another hyper pineal – they can become hyper pineal and achieve immortality. That is, if they continue to secure sufficient supplies of their blood type. You see David, for some reason, another of the problems for which I seek solution, we hyper pineals, once stimulated, are unable to manufacture sufficient quantities of our own blood supplies.'

"I said, 'Then that is the reason for these horrible attacks.'

"She sighed impatiently and said, 'I had hoped you would leave your storybook ideas behind you tonight, David. Can you not see how foolish become the vampire stories in this day of blood transfusions and professional donors? It is true that we need, periodically, supplies of blood, but today it is hardly necessary to creep about by night to secure them. If my experiments are ultimately successful, I shall discover some method of restoring to the bodies of the hyper pineal the ability to produce their own supply and even the transfusions will become unnecessary. Later still, I hope to isolate the pineal hormone. Who knows, David, perhaps it will one day be synthesized in the laboratory and its powers brought to everyone.'

"You can imagine how overwhelming this was. I started to say, 'But Jim..."

"For a minute, Poula buried her delicate face in her hands. When she looked up again, there were tears on her cheeks. She said, 'I loved Jim Grunland, David. His sacrifice shall always mean more to me than I... I...' She broke off.

"While I stared at her, she took a deep breath and went on. 'Jim had originally felt much the same as you do; but when he finally reached understanding and pictured the importance to humanity of my researches, he became as avid as I to explore further. I... I knew that Jim was AB-Rh Negative, but he failed to tell me that the Baltimore donors were no longer able to supply my needs. He drew too strongly on his own body, David, unknown to me, I'll...' She broke down again.

"I came to my feet to go to her, but she suddenly sprang erect and looked through moist eyes at her watch. 'I must leave,' she said. 'I am trying desperately to interest as many others as possible in the study of the pineal hormones. If only I could tell them all I know.' Her little wry smile was there again. 'If I did, I am afraid I should soon find myself in one of the local institutions.' She hurried me out then and went to her lecture."

David Bentley finished and looked over at me. "Well, Doctor Parker?" he said.

I yawned. "You tell a story in vivid detail, Bentley," I told him. "You should write for the cinema."

He flushed. "I wanted to make it all clear."

"Excellent," I told him. "And now that you have reported, in all your detail, I suppose I may bid you good night." I came to my feet.

He stood up too, rather ruefully I thought, and reached his hand into his pocket to bring forth the automatic weapon he had demonstrated the first night of his appearance.

I took a step back, involuntarily. "Now see here..." I began.

He tossed the weapon to the magazine stand which stood beside my chair. "I suppose it was rather silly to carry this," he said. "When Mr. Pons returns, tell him he needn't worry about my resorting to violence."

"If you ask me," I retorted, "the whole affair has been imminently silly. You have been wasting the time of a very busy man. Mr. Pons' services, you know, are continually in demand." I could not forebear adding. "And not for frivolous purposes."

He pursed his lips ruefully. "At any rate, tell him I called again, and let him know that I am leaving my gun here."

"Very well," I said stiffly, "and now, young sir, let me bid you good night, and farewell."

"Goodbye," he said.

In spite of his farewells, I noted the following afternoon that amidst the mail addressed to Solar Pons was a letter from Mr. David Bentley. Assuming that it was a brief note, possibly apologizing to my friend for the manner in which his time had been expended, particularly in view of my harsh words of the night before, I refrained from opening it, and let it await the detective's attention upon his arrival.

Pons returned the next day, his face as anxious as when he had left.

He dropped his portmanteau to the floor and faced me. "Nothing developed in my absence, eh Parker? I was somewhat fearful that it might."

"Nothing important, Pons. Certainly nothing of sufficient importance to break into your short vacation."

He strode to the fireplace and began to stuff shag, from its place in his old slipper, into his pipe.

"Vacation!" he exclaimed. "My dear Parker, for the past two days I have been studying with an intensity I've never surpassed."

"Studying?" I asked him.

"Under Van Lorn, possibly the world's authority on the vampire and werewolf legends. I find him a most interesting scholar, Parker. A man who scorns accepted belief when it conflicts with what he deems the truth. A true scientist in the broad sense of the word, although the scientific world accepts him as a fool or a charlatan."

I was taken aback. "You mean your trip to The Hague was to delve into this ridiculous affair of David Bentley's."

He lit his pipe. "Ridiculous, Parker? At any rate, we have no time for discussion now. I must find our young American as soon as possible."

I stared at him blankly. "He was here but two nights ago."

"Ah!" Pons was tense. "And what did he have to say?"

I shrugged. "Much the same sort of thing. He has evidently given up his foolhardy mission." I strode to the table drawer in which I had placed the weapon Bentley had left, opened it and showed the gun to Pons. "He even left his pistol, complete with silver bullets. I am afraid our young man is rapidly falling in love with the sinister monster he came to destroy."

Solar Pons sank into his chair.

"Quickly now, Parker. Tell me everything he reported to you."

In manifest surprise, I repeated to my friend all that I could remember of young Bentley's story, noting the mounting anxiety that grew in Solar Pons' face.

"And you didn't think this of sufficient importance to phone me?" he cried.

I was amazed at his attitude. "But obviously the matter is now closed. Dr. Coty is no longer in danger." I remembered the letter and added, "A letter from the young man arrived in the post yesterday. It is there on the stand, with the rest of the mail accumulated while you were gone."

Solar Pons sprang to his feet, hurried to the stand I indicated and sorted quickly through the half dozen letters there. He grasped the one from Bentley and tore it quickly open.

I read it over his shoulder.

My Dear Mr. Pons,

This will be in the way of a final report to augment what I told Doctor Parker the other night. I am afraid

> that the good doctor doesn't take me very seriously and I am taking this opportunity to make my final report to you. I feel it necessary that you have a complete understanding of both Poula and myself, since earlier I told you so much nonsense. In the past several days I have spent considerable time with her. The poor thing seems almost haggard. She has been devoting too much of her time to her work.
>
> She has, by the way, explained some of the more fantastic of the legends that have sprung up through the ages about the hyper pineals. Their hatred for garlic, for instance; for some reason they are allergic to it. The story that they emerge only at night; it is because they are more than averagely sensitive to ultraviolet rays. We have laughed together at the thought of the superstitious nonsense that has developed from those two easily misunderstood facts.

The letter broke off here, as though he had written the above at one time, and added the rest later. Pons had groaned once or twice in the reading, now we went on.

> I know now why Poula has appeared so wan. There seems to be almost none of the necessary AB-Rh Negative donors in this area. You would think that London would have a sufficiency. It is an interesting sidelight on the vampire – what a stupid word! – legend that this fact that the hyper pineal must have this particular, and most rare of all, blood types. In the past, their attempts to find a suitable supply must have led them to attack hundreds of victims. If poor Poula could only be successful in her attempts to discover a method of restoring to the hyper pineal the ability to replenish naturally, their own supply.

> I have mentioned to her that I, myself, am of the AB-Rh Negative type, but she told me she had already known. Jim had told her of the circumstances of out first meeting, when he had contributed a quart of his blood to me after an auto accident.
>
> She has been looking so terribly thin, so tired and lifeless these last two days. She must need a transfusion badly.
>
> At any rate, this matter is now closed. Thank you, Mr. Pons for your kind interest, and please, of course, mention my silly nonsense to no one.

He had signed the letter, *David Bentley*.

"And he left his gun here," Pons said, so softly as though to himself.

I stirred uncomfortably. "But Pons, this is fantastic. Even granting that Dr. Coty is a... a hyper pineal, she is still in all, a scientist of the highest standing."

Pons stared unseeingly at the wall. "She is *nosferatu*, Parker, and has a mission in life. A mission that involves bringing her fellows into a prominence in the affairs of the world which they have never heretofore enjoyed. No matter how kindly our naive American friend might have found her, I doubt that she would let anything stand in her way when her own survival was threatened."

"But Pons, she is a young woman. A young woman with ideals."

Solar Pons said, slowly, "Parker, as I have said, I spent two days of continual study on the subject in The Hague. I am afraid that Dr. Poula Coty – if I have traced her career as well as I believe I have – is somewhat more than four hundred years of age. I submit, Parker, that this is but the beginning of an adventure, not the end of one. I am afraid that we have already taken on a responsibility willed us by our young American."

"Oh, surely, Pons," I began.

He held up a restraining hand. "I am familiar with the fact, Parker that you have been making notes of the cases in which we have been associated. I now must make this demand, that whatever transpires in this particular case, from this point on, never be recorded in any literary works you may attempt in the future."

"Why... why, of course, it that is your will," I said

"Very well, Parker, and now come. I am afraid the game is afoot! And while, as always, we are on the side of Justice, I am not too sure that our sometimes myopic police authorities will consider us to be on the side of the law!"

THE ADVENTURE OF THE EXTRA-TERRESTRIAL

From the chess problem in which he had been absorbed, Solar Pons slowly raised his head. His fingers relinquished their hold on the knight and he leaned back.

"Yes, as I thought," he murmured, "we are about to have company."

London was lost in fog, a heavy autumnal curtain shutting the city away from our lodgings in Praed Street, and at first there was only the distant hum of diminished traffic that was the pulse of the city, and the several small noises of water dripping; then I heard the low purr of a heavy automobile, traveling a short distance, stopping, then coming forward again.

"Surely he is looking for Number 7," observed Pons with a satisfaction born of the fact that time had been pressing heavily on his hands of recent days. "To whom else would he address himself at this hour of the night? Clearly now," he went on, listening intently, "he has left his car just a few doors away; he has gone up to the door, flashed his torch on the number. No, that is not Number Seven; yet, Number Seven cannot be far away. Now then! He returns to his vehicle – but he does not get in; no, he is too close to the desired address for that – he locks it, and here he is!"

I looked toward the night bell, back to Pons' expectant features, marking his keen eyes, his aquiline nose, his firm, thin-lipped mouth, touched still by his smile, and once more at the bell. On the instant it jangled, Pons stepped to the speaking tube and invited our visitor to come up and in a few moments there was a tap on the door giving to our lodgings, I strode across the room and opened it.

Across the threshold stepped a youngish, black-haired man whose smooth shaven face was partly concealed by horn-rimmed glasses with dark panes. He was clothed in the best fashion and his well tailored suit went far toward hiding his excessive weight. I had an impression of over-indulgence at the table – and possibly at the nightclub.

Pons said, "Ah! a pleasure to see you again, Mr. Norwood. And how is Sir Alexander, your father?"

The newcomer stared at him. "For Heaven's sake, man. It has been twenty years since you set eyes on me. I was a child of five or six. I had expected to have to introduce myself, even to remind you of my father."

Pons motioned him to a seat. "Not at all. The details of the case upon which I worked for your admirable father are still quite clear in my mind. I have always thought of it as the Riddle of Closton Manor. As for recognizing your features, I assure you, facially you resemble your father of two decades ago."

Pons seated himself in his own favorite chair, after settling our guest, and reached for pipe tobacco. "I assume you are here on matters of personal interest rather than on an errand for Sir Alexander."

The newcomer lifted his eyes to me.

Pons said, "Forgive me. Peter Norwood, Dr. Lyndon Parker. Dr. Parker is my valued assistant." He lit his pipe and said through the smoke. "His discretion is as great as my own."

We nodded politely to each other and the young man began his story. "Mr. Pons, my father has a great deal of respect for you."

Solar Pons nodded. "The feeling is reciprocated. Your father impressed me as a man of integrity, and one with an unusual sense of duty and humanity."

I felt that Peter Norwood was not overly pleased with these words from my friend. He hesitated, and then said, "Then you will be sorry to hear that there is evidence that his mind is beginning to slip."

A shadow crossed the face of Solar Pons. "I am indeed. Your words distress me. But then, let me see, Sir Alexander must be in his late sixties."

Norwood nodded. "Sixty-eight." He hesitated again. "You asked me whether my visit was personal or on behalf of my father. Actually, I am on his errand, but in fact I think it should be me you consider your client."

"Ah?" Pons murmured. He made a steeple of his fingers and I could see his eyes sparkle interest.

Peter Norwood pushed out his plump lips in what was almost a pout. "I am going to put this bluntly, Mr. Pons. My father has only a few years to live and he is about to dispose frivolously of the greater part of his fortune."

"You are his heir?"

Norwood nodded. "His sole heir. If in these last few years of his life my father wastes away the family fortune, it is I who will suffer."

"And this frivolous waste?" Pons prompted. "Frankly, Mr. Norwood, it does not seem like your father. Certainly not the Sir Alexander I knew and respected."

"My father is contemplating leaving the greater portion of his estate to a group of charlatans and, to use an Americanism, crackpots. The World Defense Society, they call themselves." Peter Norwood could not control a sneer. He looked from one of us to the other. "You have heard of it, perhaps?"

Pons and I both shook our heads.

"Please elucidate," I said.

"This group and my father, who is a charter member, are of the opinion that there are aliens in London."

"Aliens?" I blurted. "But what could be more obvious? Of course there are aliens in London."

Peter Norwood turned his eyes from Pons to me. "Aliens from outer space," he said. "Extra-Terrestrial." He threw up his hands in disgust. "Men from Mars. Spaceships, I suppose. All that sort of rot."

Even Pons was surprised at this turn of conversation. "And you say that Sir Alexander supports this belief? Why?"

The young man's rounded face reflected his disgust. "He has a fantastic collection of 'proof.' He has devoted the past two years to the accumulation of it. Flying saucers, unidentified objects in the sky. The case of Kasper Hauser. That sort of thing. Stuff and nonsense, of course."

Solar Pons leaned back and closed his eyes. "You say you are on an errand for your father. Please elucidate."

"Actually, it was I who planted the idea in his head," Peter Norwood admitted. "As I have said, father has a considerable respect for your methods, Mr. Pons. I will not deny that he and I have had several heated discussions on this matter. In the midst of the last one, I suggested that since he thinks so highly of you, that he hire your services to investigate the presence of these aliens. As a result of that argument, I am here, ostensibly to employ you in his behalf to seek out these... these men from Mars."

"Ah?" Pons murmured. "But you said I should consider you to be my actual client."

Peter Norwood spread his hands. "I implore you, Pons, to take this assignment. To pretend you actually seek these extra-terrestrials supposedly running wild about London, and then to report to my father that after a thorough search you can find no such aliens from space. Needless to say, I will reward you amply."

I thought I understood his point. "You want Pons to draw up a supposed report of an investigation and present it to your father so that his neurosis will be cured."

The young man shook his head emphatically. "That would be insufficient. My father is not an easily deceived man. The investigation would have to be made, and seriously so, and reported in a step-by-step manner. Otherwise, the old fool will realize he is being duped."

The term old fool has slipped out, but in a way I could sympathize with Peter Norwood.

Pons was in deep thought. I could not remember the adventure that he chose to think of as the Riddle of Closton Manor; it possibly anteceded my acquaintanceship with my friend. But it was manifest that his regard for Sir Alexander Norwood must have been high indeed and that he was now torn by this regard and by the young man's – what to me seemed – understandable position.

"This is not the sort of thing upon which I work," Pons said slowly.

"Of course not," the other agreed. "But any fee you..."

Pons interrupted sharply, "It is not a matter of fee, Norwood."

The young man blinked behind his lenses, but held his tongue.

Pons puffed his pipe in irritation and stared unseeing at the tobacco filled slipper tacked to the mantelpiece. He muttered finally, "I assume your father wishes me to come to Closton Manor to discuss my employment on this project?"

"That was the purpose of my visit, supposedly. To bring you to him so that he might go over the matter with you."

To my utter amazement, Pons slapped the arm of his chair decisively and said, "You may expect me at your home tomorrow afternoon."

Peter Norwood was manifestly pleased. He came to his feet. "You shall not regret this, Mr. Pons. "I'll see that your time – ah, financially, that is – is not wasted."

A muscle worked in the thin face of Solar Pons, but he said nothing in reply to that. It was manifest to us both that the young man assumed that Pons interest was venial and that he had lost caste by his decision.

Pons saw him to the door in silence.

The following day, at ten in the morning, we embarked on the train for Durwood, the nearest village, so Pons told me, to the ancestral home, Closton Manor, of the Norwood family. I had looked up the title in Burke's Peerage and found the baronetcy an ancient and distinguished one originally granted on the field of battle by Richard the First in the Holy Land. More recently, bearers of the title had distinguished themselves in India and the Sudan.

We arrived in Durwood shortly after twelve and proceeded to Closton Manor by dog cart. An elderly, work bent servant had been awaiting the train. After introducing himself as Mullins and stating that Master Peter had sent him, he lapsed into silence which he maintained until we reached the manor.

We entered the extensive and rambling house by the side entrance where we were met by young Norwood himself, and conducted by way of a narrow staircase to the rooms of Sir Alexander.

The old man was seated in a small study which was well stocked with books, pamphlets and aged manuscripts. In fact, the only description would be to say it was overstocked. Great piles of tomes leaned against walls or balanced precariously without support. But in spite of the fact that manifestly considerable study was done in the room, the light was dim, a result of rather heavily curtained windows.

Sir Alexander was an elderly man and he sat deep in an upholstered chair, rapped in a steamer rug as though for warmth. His chin rested upon his chest and his sunken eyes looked at us from over his pince-nez. A thin mustache and beard, both white, and a fringe of white hair seen from under the skullcap he wore, ornamented his thin ascetic face, white within the darkness of his immediate environment.

"Ah, Solar Pons," he said in a cultured, well-modulated voice. "We meet again." His eyes sparkled with a youth his body belied. He held out a hand to be shaken.

Pons said, "A great pleasure to renew our acquaintanceship, Sir Alexander. May I present my friend, Dr. Lyndon Parker?"

It was my turn to shake the proffered hand, and I found it surprisingly warm and firm. First impressions deceived. Sir Alexander, I suspected, was considerably further from his grave than his son had let us believe.

Peter Norwood said, "Would you prefer I leave, father, while you discuss your business with Mr. Pons and Dr. Parker?"

The baronet gestured with a slight motion. "If you don't mind, my boy. I'll see you at tea, if not before."

Young Norwood bowed to us, winking whilst his back was to his father, and excused himself.

After he was gone, Sir Alexander chuckled wryly. "Peter, I am afraid, is of the opinion that I am somewhat around the bend."

Pons settled back into his chair, and reached into his jacket pocket for pipe and tobacco. "Suppose you tell us this from the beginning, Sir Alexander."

The old man's eyes twinkled. "I am afraid I am working under a handicap. I have no doubt that your minds have already been somewhat prejudiced."

I cleared my throat, frankly surprised at his approach. I had expected senility, but found no outward signs of it. Was it possible the man was pulling his son's leg?

Pons said over the flame of his match, "I consider myself without prejudice, Sir Alexander, as you have had cause to know in the past."

A flush touched the old man's face. "Forgive me old friend. If it hadn't been for your toleration two decades ago, I would be a dead man today." He looked away from us a moment, as though seeking a starting point to his narrative.

"I suppose there is no beginning," he said slowly. "This matter has been coming to my attention, piece by piece, fragment by fragment, throughout my adult life. Only recently have I devoted the attention to the problem that it deserves." He hesitated for a moment then said to me, "Dr. Parker, if you please, would you hand me that book on the top of the pile there to your left?"

I was able to reach the book and hand it to him without leaving my chair. Sir Alexander said, "You gentlemen are both familiar with H. Spencer Jones, I assume?"

Pons murmured, "The Astronomer Royal, of course."

The other lifted the book. "You are familiar with his work, *Life on Other Worlds*?"

"I am afraid not," Pons said. I shook my head.

"Let me read you a passage or two." The old man thumbed quickly through the volume. "Here, for instance."

He began reading. "'With the universe constructed on so vast a scale, it would seem inherently improbable that our small earth can be the only home of life.'" He skipped over some pages. "And here: '... It seems reasonable to suppose that whenever in the universe the proper conditions arise, life must inevitably come into existence. This is the view that is generally accepted by biologists.'"

He began to look for some passages.

"Never mind," Pons said. "I accept what you offer. That is, I accept the possibility – if not the probability – that another life form might be present somewhere in the universe. Let me say, Sir Alexander, that it is an extensive universe in which we reside."

The old man chuckled. "It is indeed. Please, Pons, pass me that magazine there on the floor to your right. No, not that one. Yes, that is correct."

He took up the magazine and thumbed through it. "Ah, here. This is an article by young German, Willy Ley, a chap more than ordinarily interested in the prospects of man's conquest of space. Here we are: '... We are justified in believing in life on Mars – hardy plant life. The color changes which we can see are explained most logically and most simply by assuming vegetation.' He skipped some lines, then went on, 'Of terrestrial plants, lichen might survive transplanting to Mars and one may imagine that some of the desert flora of Tibet could be adapted. At any event, conditions are such that life as we know it would find the going tough but not impossible.'"

The elderly baronet broke off and looked at Pons questioningly.

My friend puffed deeply on his pipe and said, "I submit, Sir Alexander, that the presence on Mars of lichen, and the possible presence on some far distant star of even intelligent life does not mean that alien life forms are roaming the streets of London."

The other was visibly becoming excited by the discussion. He leaned forward. "Ah, but my dear Pons. Do you not see the point? When you grant the existence of life elsewhere than on Earth – no matter how primitive – you must admit the possible corollary."

I scowled and said, "I am afraid I have missed something."

Sir Alexander turned to me excitedly. "Don't you see? If there is life elsewhere in the universe, we must suppose one of three things. It is either less advanced than we; as advanced as we; or it is more advanced than we are.

Pons chuckled. "That about covers everything, Sir Alexander."

"Of course. Now please understand that already here on Earth man is beginning to reach for the stars. The Willy Lay I quoted from is an example of the hundreds and, indeed, thousands of young men who see exploration of the moon in the comparative near future. They see exploration of the solar system, not far after, and they dream of eventual travel to the stars.

"If we grant the possibility of intelligent life elsewhere, then we must also grant the possibility that it is further along the path toward conquest of space. Our race, gentlemen is a young one. Our fellow intelligent life forms might have several millions of years of growth behind them."

Neither Pons nor I had an answer to this. In my case, there was just too much to assimilate.

Sir Alexander pounded the arm of his chair for emphasis. "If man is already laying plans for exploration beyond his own planet, why should not our neighbors in space have already taken such steps?"

Pons said, "You have made a good theoretical case for the possibility of alien life forms, and their desire to reach beyond their own worlds. But you have said nothing definite, thus far. Thus far, it is all in the realm of hypothesis. You have some concrete proof, Sir Alexander?"

The old man tossed the magazine to a cluttered desk and pursed his lips. He said, "I have never shaken the hand of an extra-terrestrial, Mr. Pons."

I laughed aloud. "I should hope not," I said.

He raised his white eyebrows at me. "Perhaps one day I shall, Doctor. Who knows?" He turned back to Pons. "For literally centuries men have been sighting strange flying objects. Long before the Wright brothers, unidentified flying objects, saucer shaped, cigar shaped, ball shaped, have been seen by reputable witnesses. The American Charles Fort recorded literally hundreds of such sightings."

"But, Sir Alexander," I protested, "the man is commonly regarded as a fool, a fanatic, if not a charlatan."

The white eyebrows went up again. "By whom, Dr. Parker? I suggest that his enemies so regard him. And those who have raised our still immature science to the pedestal and cry wrath against all who do not worship. But there are many tens of thousands of persons who regard Fort as a keen brain capable of revealing the shortcomings of many of our so-called scientific beliefs."

"I have never bothered to read him," I said, possibly a bit snappish in tone.

Pons said, "You have other... *ah*... evidence?"

The old man motioned to his room, cluttered as it was with a thousand manuscripts, newspapers clippings, books and pamphlets. "For years I have been gathering data which in many respects duplicates that of Charles Fort. Accounts of strange sightings both on land and sea. Accounts of strange people seen, strange animals, impossible phenomena."

I was becoming impatient. "And you believe them from some foreign planet?"

He frowned at me. "Don't misunderstand, Dr. Parker. I assume no definite position as yet. I have not formed an opinion. But I do want to know. Frankly, I am willing to place the greater part of my fortune at the disposal of the World Defense Society if it can be proven to me that there is danger of invasion of our planet by aliens. Thus far, the evidence presented has been insufficient to convince me." He turned to Pons. "That is why I wish your services. I have great confidence in you. If there are aliens in London, as my associates in the World Defense Society would have it, I wish to know. If they are dangerous to our society, I wish to be foremost in the defense."

He looked down at his aged body. "Unfortunately, my age prevents my services if other than a financial manner."

Pons came to his feet. He said, "I'll take the assignment, Sir Alexander, under one condition."

The old man's eyes pierced him. "And it is?"

"I guarantee that I will investigate to the best of my ability. However, if I find to my satisfaction no evidence of such aliens, you must pledge to drop the World Defense Society and your interests in alien life forms."

The old man sank back into his chair and remained silent for a long time. Finally he said, his voice low, "Very well, Pons. I trust you."

There had been practically no conversation from Pons on the train either to and from Closton Manor. Indeed, it was not until that evening when we were seated restfully before the fire that he discussed the case with me.

Over a steeple of his fingertips he peered at me quizzically. "What are your opinions on this matter, Parker?" he asked. "I assume you have formed opinions. I, frankly, have not."

I shrugged deprecation. "Sir Alexander seems an admirable enough man but I am afraid that he has..."

"Managed to slip around the bend, eh? The expression he, himself used, as I recall."

"Unfortunately," I said. "I feel sorry for the young man. Frankly, I think his only recourse is to the courts unless you are able to convince his father to forego this fantastic hobby."

Solar Pons said slowly, "I am of the opinion that Peter Norwood has anticipated you, Parker. And I am afraid that he is of the opinion that I am pulling chestnuts from the fire for him."

"Eh?" My face must have mirrored my lack of understanding.

"I submit, Parker, that if young Norwood attempted to have his father committed merely on the grounds that he collected books and magazine articles on a rather fanciful subject, he would be rejected by the courts. However, if he could prove that his father had... ah... squandered money by hiring a detective to investigate the presence of extra-terrestrials in London, then I am of the opinion that few courts of law would do other than turn the affairs of the estate over to our young friend."

I was frankly shocked. "Then you believe that young Norwood is deliberately provoking his father along these lines in order to hasten the date of his inheritance?"

Pons said, "Manifestly, Parker, Sir Alexander is in excellent health, considering his age. He might well live another five years."

"At least ten," I muttered.

"It is understandable, then, that Peter Norwood might be a trifle impatient for the title and the estate."

I became agitated. "Then why, Pons, did you accept the case?"

My friend shrugged his irritation. "Confound it, Parker, can't you see? If I had refused, the boy would have gone elsewhere. There are private investigators in London who would gladly have cooperated with him. At least, I have Sir Alexander's interests at heart."

I said slowly, "I am not too sure but that the boy is right. Perhaps his father has slipped mentally to the point where he is incapable of handling his affairs. After all – aliens from space. I ask you, Pons!"

Solar Pons squirmed in his chair. "Do you think I haven't considered that factor, Parker?"

He closed his eyes and leaned back deep in thought and I retreated to my book.

Approximately ten minutes later, and without opening his eyes, Pons said, "Parker, if there are aliens from space in this city, why should they have picked London? Why not Moscow, Paris, Rome, New York, and Tokyo?"

I smiled and tried to enter into his mood. "Perhaps they are in those cities also."

He shook his head. "No. Let us grant, for the sake of our discussion, that such aliens *are* present. And let us grant that they are in London."

"Very well."

"Manifestly, they are keeping their presence here on Earth a secret, for motives of their own. If this is their policy it becomes obvious that they must limit their number."

"Why so, Pons?"

"Because it would be considerably more difficult to keep the presence of an hundred aliens from the attention of we earthlings, than it would one or two. I am of the opinion that if there are extra-terrestrials on Earth, it is only a very small number."

I nodded, finding some amusement in my friend's mental exercises.

"That sounds plausible."

"Why then," he said, "are they in London rather than elsewhere?"

I looked at him in surprise. "But that is obvious. London is the largest city in the world. You might say, the capital of the world. If these extra-terrestrials are investigating Earth and mankind, here would be the place to start."

He opened his eyes and twinkled them at me. "Your loyalty and patriotism overshadow your ability to appreciate statistics, I am afraid, Parker. In the first instance, London is no longer the largest city in the world. New York is."

I began to sputter, but he held up a hand. "No. New York is actually considerably larger than is commonly granted. Political boundaries falsify her size. Actually the city overflows into Connecticut and New Jersey and far up into New York State, but these sections are not counted in her population. She is also the commercial center of the world and by far its largest port. In the second instance, it is Washington which has become the political center of the world. London has lost that position, if we British like it or not."

I was miffed. "Very well, then, you answer the question. Why should they choose London rather than New York or Washington?"

"There could be only one reason, Parker, and I am sure that it gives us our starting point for investigation. I speak of the British Museum."

"I admit, Pons, that I don't follow you," I said.

His eyes twinkled again. "Parker, London may not be the population leader, nor the political head. But if I were another worldling interested in making a thorough study of this planet, I would go to the British Museum, for, without doubt, it does hold more information, more data, on this planet than any other library or museum. I submit, if there are aliens in London, investigating our customs and institutions, they are doing it in the British Museum."

He came to his feet, yawning mightily. "And it is there, my dear Parker, that I shall begin my investigation tomorrow."

"Then you plan to go through with this, to make the motions of investigating the presence of space aliens?"

"Indeed I do, Parker. Pray recall I gave my pledge to Sir Alexander."

I saw little of Solar Pons in the next few days, but it was manifest that he was taking his task seriously. And that, in itself was of considerable surprise to me. On two different occasions I found him leaving our rooms in disguise. On both occasions he winked at me, but vouchsafed no explanation and no description of his progress.

On the fifth day, shortly after a breakfast at which he had encouraged no conversation pertinent to the case of Sir Alexander Norwood, Pons asked to borrow my exposure meter, a device I had acquired but recently, after having received a rather complicated German camera as a birthday gift from a near relative. He returned it that night, and requested that in the morning, if I was able, that I locate Alfred, the captain of his group of street gamins which he was amused to name his Praed Street Irregulars, and have him at our rooms at noon.

The mystery of his activities was beginning to intrigue, indeed to irritate me, and I went out of my way to find young Alfred, a lad of ten or thereabouts. Nor did I fail to be present myself upon Pons' arrival promptly at noon.

He clapped the boy on the back, bade me a cheery afternoon, and came immediately to the point. "Alfred, my lad," he said, "do you think you might find three other boys for an assignment this afternoon?"

Alfred had been standing, his arms akimbo, his bright eyes flashing, before Pons. Now he touched his cap and said, "I think so, sir. Right away, Mr. Pons?"

"Right away, Alfred," Pons said, "Scamper along now."

The boy was gone in a rattle of shoes upon the stairs and Pons beamed after him.

"And how," I asked, "goes the investigation of the men from Mars?"

He turned to me, his brows high. "Why do you think them from Mars, Parker?"

"Eh?" I said "Who?"

"The extra-terrestrials," he said impatiently. "Why do you think they are from Mars rather than, possibly, Venus or even some other star system?"

I was taken aback. "Really, Pons," I said. "I was jesting you know."

"Oh," he said, thrusting his hands in his pockets and striding to the window from which he gazed impatiently down upon the street.

Although burning with curiosity, I didn't break the silence again. Finally he said, "Parker, do you realize that an alien intelligence, far in advance of our science, would be most difficult to detect, if he so chose to make himself?"

"I fancy he might be," I agreed, encouraging him.

"I have thought of but one chink in such an alien's armor," he admitted.

"A chink, Pons?"

"It would seem to me that he would be prone to utilize some of the advantages of the advanced gadgetry of his science when it came to tedious effort."

"I am not sure I follow you."

He turned and faced me. "For instance, if such an alien were employing himself at making records of some of the books and manuscripts in the library section of the British Museum and found that to utilize the cameras of our culture he must carry heavy volumes a considerable distance in order to obtain sufficient light, I can see where he would be sorely tempted to use a camera, or similar device, of his own culture – one that would photograph in an impossibly poor light."

"Good Heavens, Pons!" I ejaculated. "You borrowed my light meter this morning."

"Ummm," he admitted. "Parker, there is a... ah... person daily appearing at the museum who has been photographing pages of certain volumes in the library. According to your light meter, and according to the most advanced works I could find on photography, there is no lens now manufactured that could take such photos in the light he was using, considering that his shutter speed must be sufficiently fast for him to hold his camera in hand."

Before I could assimilate his words, there was a rush and a clatter on the stairs coupled with Mrs. Johnson's indignantly raised voice; the door was thrown open without ceremony and young Alfred burst into the room followed pell-mell by a trio of grinning urchins. I wondered, once again, why our long suffering landlady put up with us.

"Here we are, Mr. Pons!" cried Alfred, closing the door and marching up to him followed by his companions, who ranged themselves in a row.

"So I see," replied Pons. "It is a mystery to me how you can manage to act so quickly." He brought four guineas from his pocket and came to his feet. "These shall be yours," he said, "for what should be a simple task for such active young men. I want you to follow a rather elusive man from the British Museum to his lodgings."

"Yes, sir," Alfred said. "We'll do it."

"I am sure you will," Pons told him, his eyes twinkling. "And where the most cautious of persons might suspect an adult, who is going to keep his suspicious eye on a shouting, playing lad? And now, boys, let us be off to assume a strategic point near the Museum entrance that our quarry usually takes so that I can point him out to you."

"I don't suppose," I said, possibly a trifle wistfully, "that you need further assistance?"

"Not today, Parker," Solar Pons said, "But thank you."

They were gone. Pons quietly, the boys' feet clattering down the stairs.

I heard no more of the case for three days, and then, suddenly, it reached its conclusion.

We were seated early in the evening in our usual places, I with book in hand, Pons tinkering with his .455 Webley, a weapon with which he was remarkably accurate as I have had occasion to witness.

"Ah," he murmured finally, "our friend Peter Norwood is here for his report."

Even as he spoke, I could hear a knock at the door and faintly Mrs. Johnson's voice. In moments there was the sound of feet on the stairs and a knock.

I opened the door and welcomed the young man in, for indeed it was he. His face was slightly flushed, undoubtedly from a surfeit of good food and rare vintages, for it was barely past the supper hour.

He looked to Pons. "How long is this to take?" he said, almost belligerently. "How long does it take to cock up a reasonable story for the old man?"

Pons had not arisen from his chair. He said, mildly, "I sent my report to your father this morning, Mr. Norwood."

"Ah." The other blinked at him, momentarily taken aback. "Well," he said, reaching for his pocket, "I suppose there is nothing more than to pay you off." There was a contemptuous overtone in his voice.

"That will be unnecessary," Pons said. "There will be no fee, in this case. But if there had been, I should have submitted it to Sir Alexander, your father. It was he who employed me, after all."

Peter Norwood scowled his incomprehension. Evidently he began to smell a rat for his eyes narrowed and he growled, "What did you report, Pons? Though, I warn you, it will make no difference."

Pons took a sheet of paper from an inner pocket. "This is a carbon of my report to your father," he said. He read in a clear voice, "'My dear Sir Alexander: This will convey to you my belief that your interest is well founded. And that your hobby, that of investigating the possibility of the existence of life forms on other planets and/or in other star systems, is an intelligent one. I have not found conclusive proof of the presence of such aliens in London, but I have uncovered sufficient data to indicate that further investigation by yourself and the group with which you are affiliated would not be amiss. Signed, Solar Pons.'"

Peter Norwood glared at Pons. He snapped, "I suppose you think that you have thwarted me by this... this piece of lying nonsense."

Pons nodded. "That is my opinion, sir."

"You realize," the young man snapped, "that no court in the land would fail to commit..."

Pons was shaking his head, his eyes flashing fire. "The matter will never come to court, sir. I warn you now. This case has taken a full week of my time. I repeat, I warn you, if your father is brought before the courts in an attempt on your part to secure management of his affairs, I shall reveal your own secret."

Solar Pons could not have been more effective if he had struck the young man across the face. Peter Norwood staggered back, obviously deeply hit; his flushed features turned pale, his eyes revealed their fear.

Solar Pons nodded. "Yes, my time was not wasted, Mr. Norwood. I have no intention of making a report on the subject to your father not to, shall we say, others who might be concerned. But pray remember that this information shall be with me next week, next year, and ten years from now. I bid you take heed – and now, to take your leave."

Without another word the young man staggered from our rooms. "Confound it, Pons," I blurted. "This whole thing escapes me. I am in the dark. What secret of young Norwood's were you able to ferret out?"

Pons chuckled. "Come now, Parker. We have here a young man obviously the victim of his sensual vices. He is desperately in need of money, in spite of what must be a considerable allowance in view of his big cars, and his fine clothes. You know my methods. Utilize them!"

"You mean... ?"

"I mean that I haven't the slightest idea what the young charlatan's secret might be. Excessive gambling, a young woman, or whatever. But I would lay a heavy wager that there is such a secret, or even more than one, that he feels he cannot have revealed."

I chuckled, seeing the humor of the situation. "But my dear Pons, that report you submitted to Sir Alexander. Do you think it well to encourage him in his delusions?"

Pons had found his pipe and loaded it. "I submit, Parker," he said, "that in the first instance, it is a harmless hobby that will fill the hours for an old man whose mind is still keen and interested."

"And in the second instance?" I prompted.

"In the second instance," he said deliberately, "my report was written in good faith. I assume you have deduced from my activities that I located an individual at the museum who was making an extensive collection of photographs of periodicals, books, and pamphlets."

I nodded.

"Very well," he continued, "with the assistance of my Praed Street Irregulars I was able to trace him to his rooms. Eventually I was even able to search them during his absence."

I leaned forward, my interest manifest. "And what did you find?"

"Nothing," he said.

"Nothing? You, Solar Pons, found nothing?"

Pons had lit his pipe and now waggled the extinguished match at me. "Negative evidence is not without value, Parker. The man's – and I use the term man with reservations – apartment was devoid of any records, personal effects, or anything whatsoever which might give a clue to his identity."

"A spy," I blurted. "Did you notify the C.I.D.?"

"A spy for whom?" Pons asked. "It is too late for the C.I.D., by the way, our bird has flown."

"A spy for some foreign power..."

"I'll accept that," Pons nodded. "Very foreign."

"... some power such as Russia, or Germany. Possibly even the United States or France. Each nation has its quota of intelligence agents."

Pons' expression was wry. "I submit, Parker, that none of the nations you name need sneak into the British Museum for such information as is there. It is open to the public which includes the members of the diplomatic corps of these nations."

The truth of his words was self-evident. "But who then?" I blurted. "What was this spy photographing? What was he investigating?"

Pons said slowly, "I admit, Parker, that if there is intelligent life elsewhere in the universe and that if it has been keeping it's presence secret – for whatever purpose – then it would be particularly interested in checking upon our own attempts to achieve space travel."

My face must have been blank.

Pons went on. "He was photographing all books, all periodicals which dealt with rocket experiments, progress toward space travel, man's efforts to reach the moon and the other planets. And his interest was quite catholic. The publications were not only in English, but in German, Russian, French, and Italian as well."

I was speechless.

Pons said, through a cloud of smoke, "It shall be interesting, Parker, to keep up with the progress of Sir Alexander's group."

A Sherlock Holmes Adventure

Originally published in
The Baker Street Journal
July 1946 (Vol.3, No. 1)

THE ADVENTURE OF THE CIRCULAR ROOM

It was a wild, windy night in April of a year in the early nineties when the diabolic affair of the circular room was brought to the attention of Sherlock Holmes. I had been engaged in compiling my notes from which these narratives of my friend's experiences are fashioned in an effort to elucidate his extraordinary methods, and this task had taken all the leisure moments of that day, for my medical practise had not yet grown to such a degree that I had no free time during the afternoon. Holmes was at work on his since-published commentary, designed as a companion piece for Dr. Hans Gross's remarkable *Criminal Investigation*. He had just put his notes aside, and had reached for his violin upon the mantel, when he heard the sound of hoofbeats on the road beyond our lodgings in Baker Street.

"Who could be seeking our lodgings on such a night as this?" I asked, hoping I had correctly interpreted the slowing-up of the hoofbeats.

Holmes had already stepped to the window and drawn aside the curtain, to look down to where the street-lamp shone before the building.

"A young woman of great determination, to dare such weather. Wind and rain, Watson – Oh, to be in England now that April's here! – But she is coming up the steps, and her brougham waits."

Our bell pealed insistently.

Holmes stood with his head cocked a little to one side, listening. He had permitted the curtain to fall back over the window, and stood with his hands in the pockets of his dressing-gown. "Ah, Mrs. Hudson has not yet gone to bed. She has not long since put on her bedroom slippers and her robe. There she is at the door."

In a moment Mrs. Hudson's heavy footsteps came creaking up the stairs, followed by lighter steps, which, however, came with no less assurance. Mrs. Hudson knocked on our door, tried it, and opened it apologetically. "A young lady to see you, Mr. Holmes."

"Show her in, by all means, Mrs. Hudson."

Mrs. Hudson stepped back, and there walked into our quarters a firm-eyed young woman whose dark hair was molded severely about her head under a small toque of an inexpensive fur. She paused just past the threshold, her waterproof thrown back over her shoulders.

"Do sit down, Miss..."

"Manahan."

"Miss Manahan. I trust nothing has happened to your patient?"

"So do I." She gasped. Then she smiled, and her rather severe face broke out into most attractive features. "I have heard of your methods, Mr. Holmes. That is why I came to you."

"It is evident that you are a trained nurse, for your cuffs show under your jacket, and there is a small iodine stain on your finger, though there is no wound there. You have come to consult me about your patient?"

Miss Manahan sat down, having given me her waterproof to hang up.

She clasped her hands, bit her lip, and looked faintly uneasy.

"I do hope I am not doing the wrong thing, Mr. Holmes, but I have such a strong feeling about this that I could not put it off any longer."

"I assure you, I have every respect for a woman's intuition."

"Thank you. You make me feel more right about coming here, though I am sure I do not know what Mr. and Mrs. Davies would think if they knew."

"They need not know. But pray let us hear your story, Miss Manahan."

Thus urged, our attractive visitor composed herself, sat thinking for a moment as if to choose a point of departure, and then began. "Mr. Holmes, I have been out of work for some time, and quite by accident I chanced upon an advertisement in the *News of the World* a fortnight ago. I have it here." She took it from a little bag she carried in her pocket, and handed it to Holmes, who spread it on the table so that I, too, could read it.

> *WANTED: A capable young woman with professional nursing knowledge to serve as companion for elderly lady. Applicant should be prepared against distressing circumstances. Good remuneration. Please apply to Mr. Wellman Davies, in care of this paper.*

Holmes handed it back without a word.

"I made application, and three days later I received a letter asking me to call at a house in Richmond, just out of London along the upper reaches of the Thames. I found the house to be of recent construction, very pleasant and rather modern, set on the shore of the river in commodious surroundings, and occupied by Mr. and Mrs. Wellman Davies, who had in their care Mr. Davies' elderly aunt, a Mrs. Lydia Thornton, who had only recently been released from an institution for mental health, and was still in an uncertain state to the extent of needing a companion with some knowledge of professional nursing.

"Mrs. Thornton proved to be a genteel lady approaching sixty years of age. She had been confined, she confided, for seven years, during which time her nephew had very kindly managed her affairs, and finally, when her condition had improved, she had been released, so that she might come to live in the house the Davies had built for her with funds which the executor of her late husband's estate allowed them at her request. My patient was very unsure of herself, still; following her husband's death, she had gone through a mental breakdown not uncommon to people of middle age; she was difficult at night, but by day, generally, she was so normal that it was hard to believe in her mental state."

"It is often so," I put in.

"Yes, and I soon discovered that she was the victim of alarming hallucinations. She was convinced, for instance, that her late husband called to her to come to him. She heard his voice in the night, and told me about it quite matter-of-factly, as if it were nothing at all strange. That, I believe, is common enough in such cases."

"Is it, Watson?" Holmes looked at me.

"Yes, indeed. The woman has plainly come to accept it as a part of her existence."

"Pray go on, Miss Manahan. I fancy you have something more to tell"

"The hallucination which seems to me the strangest of the lot is one which so profoundly disturbs my patient that I fear for her mind, and I am sure she will eventually need to return to confinement. I discovered it on the second morning after I came, though I was not wholly unprepared for it; both Mr. and Mrs. Davies had very considerately and delicately told me that Mrs. Thornton might 'break out' at any time, and I must not be too distressed or alarmed, for her 'seizures' did not last long. Nevertheless, I was alarmed at Mrs. Thornton's initial 'seizure.'

"I occupy the adjoining room to Mrs. Thornton's, which is a lovely, circular room at one corner of the house, constructed to afford a view of the grounds, the summerhouse, and the Thames there. On the morning in question, I had not yet risen, when I heard my patient scream; then my door was flung open, and she came into my room wide-eyed with fear, and trembling, laboring under the amazing hallucination that her room had been changed, that she was being preyed upon by outside forces – for she had gone to sleep with her bed facing the windows, as usual, and had awakened to find herself and her bed facing my room.

"I persuaded her to return to her room with me, and we found it just as I had last seen it when I left her on the previous night. I thought this a most amazing hallucination, and I found it recurrent – sometimes nightly for a while, and then not occurring for two or three days at a time. I could understand her auditory hallucination about her dead husband's calling to her, since I could believe in the psychological basis for this; but the more I considered this hallucination of hers about her room, the more puzzled I became.

"At the same time, I began to be aware of something strange in the house. I cannot describe it, Mr. Holmes, but it was an impression that grew upon me. I cannot understand it, either, for I have been very well treated, not only by my patient, but also by Mr. and Mrs. Davies and their single servant, a woman who comes by the day from the vicinity. As my patient's hallucination persisted, my own impression about the strangeness of the house grew, and several times I found myself being regarded with something akin to alarm by Mr. Davies, who looked away when I saw him looking at me. This has been going on for approximately a fortnight; I am unable to put my finger on anything wrong, Mr. Holmes, yet I know there is something wrong there."

She was still, expecting Holmes's questions. Holmes sat touching the lobe of one ear with his long, bony fingers for a few moments in silence; then he asked whether our client had correlated any facts in the matter. "Did the occurrence of your patient's outbreaks or 'seizures,' as you call them, coincide with any household event apart from them?"

"I think not. It is only that on the day before her first seizure, she was visited by her sister-in-law, who said something which upset her very badly. In the early dawn of the next day she had her first outbreak."

"Ah! Has her sister-in-law visited her since then?"

"Three times, Mr. Holmes."

"And afterward?"

"She had those outbreaks."

"According to your narrative, however, she also had such outbreaks on mornings which did not follow visits by her sister-in-law."

"Yes, Mr. Holmes."

"Neither Mr. nor Mrs. Davies offered any explanation of these seizures?"

"No, Mr. Holmes. They were very much distressed by them, and hoped that I would not mind too much, for they had looked forward to bringing Mrs. Thornton back to a normal existence, and wanted, at all costs, to avoid the necessity of sending their aunt back to the asylum."

"Do you know what form her insanity took?"

"I believe it was manic depression which came as a result of her husband's sudden and rather shocking death; this took place during her delayed climacteric. The situation is not uncommon."

Holmes flashed a glance at me.

"Yes, that is right. Those years are very difficult, and any untoward shock may bring about disastrous mental breakdowns."

Holmes touched his fingertips together in a characteristic gesture, and closed his eyes. "With what does Mrs. Thornton occupy herself during the day?"

"She reads, or I read to her. She plays solitaire; sometimes I play with her. Once or twice she has evinced a desire to play chess, but she always tires and is unable to finish a game."

"How does she strike you as a chess player?"

Miss Manahan was somewhat startled by the abruptness of Holmes's question. "She is not a good player."

"I fancy that is in part due to her mental instability, wouldn't you say so, Watson?"

I agreed.

Holmes's eyes flashed open and fixed upon Miss Manahan in a long, keen stare. "Have you yourself sought any explanation of why your patient should labor under the extraordinary delusion that her room and bed, as well as her own person, are at the mercy of malefic forces?"

"No, Mr. Holmes, I have been unable to do so. My knowledge of mental cases is limited."

"What would you say of this, Watson?" asked Holmes.

"It is highly unusual. In most such cases there is usually a well-hidden source for all hallucinations and illusions, and once it is discovered and exposed to the patient, the cure is often forthcoming. Mrs. Thornton's illusion is most extraordinary."

"Surely, Miss Manahan, you have your patient's case history from the institution where she was confined?"

"Certainly, Mr. Holmes."

"You have studied it?"

"Of course."

"Very well. What then of her previous record?"

"In what respect?"

"Manifestly in regard to the particular hallucination to which you refer."

"There was no previous record of its occurrence."

"Ha!" exclaimed Holmes, sitting upright in his chair and regarding Miss Manahan with that peculiarly benevolent expression which he always bestowed upon his clients when his interest was aroused. "Surely even insanity has a pattern, Miss Manahan?"

"There are many kinds, Mr. Holmes."

"Yes, yes – but you yourself have grave doubts, is it not so?"

"Yes, it is. But, Mr. Holmes, Mrs. Thornton is very convincing in her agitation. She struggles so hard not to believe in her hallucination, and each time we return to the room to find it as it was before, she breaks down in tears; that sorrow is genuine, Mr. Holmes, and it is most terribly distressing. I am appalled by it; I was impelled to come here by it; I cannot understand what is happening; I admit I have had little experience with mental cases – but, Mr. Holmes, if ever I saw a woman who is fighting very bravely and very hard to escape her mental prison, that woman is my patient. I admire her very much, I admire her courage, and it is heartbreaking to endure her horror and terror and her final grief, as each time she is brought to face the room unchanged in every respect."

"You have come here on your own account, then?"

"Entirely. I want so to help her, if I can, and if somehow her sister-in-law is responsible for the pattern of events, I want to know what to do to prevent my patient's being so dreadfully upset."

"What do you suggest?"

"Mr. Holmes, it is Thursday, my day off. Tomorrow night Mr. and Mrs. Davies are leaving to visit some relatives in Edinburgh. If it is possible, could you come out to the house at 23 Linley Road and yourself speak to Mrs. Thornton?"

"At what time are your employers leaving?"

"They are planning to take the seven o'clock from Victoria."

"Very well. We shall be at the house at approximately that hour, or as soon thereafter as possible."

Miss Manahan rose. "Thank you, Mr. Holmes."

I brought her waterproof, helped her into it, and showed her to the door.

Holmes was sitting in an attitude of deep contemplation when I returned.

"What did you think of the young lady, Watson?"

"Most capable and conscientious."

"With spirit, imagination, and levelheadedness, moreover. Miss Manahan clearly suspects a nasty business, and I have no doubt she is correct. Is that not a most curious hallucination of Mrs. Thornton's?"

"I have never had any clinical experience with anything even remotely similar."

Holmes chuckled. "Allowing for the fact that your clinical experience is somewhat limited, I fancy that states the case well enough. What explanation could you, as a medical man, have to offer?"

"I have not seen the patient, Holmes."

"Come, come – do not stand on ceremony. I am not asking you to prescribe."

"Well, then. I should say that some sudden dislocation in time or space could account for it."

"If, for instance, the sister-in-law had imparted to the patient a piece of very shocking information?"

"Possibly."

Holmes closed his eyes. "And what did you make of her dead husband's voice calling to her?"

"Very common in such cases. The relation between the shock of his death and her initial collapse is very clear."

"Dear me! How insistent we all are upon simplifying even the most remote aspects of human experience! It has been well said that perhaps it is we who are insane, and the so-called insane who are sane. What a proposition! – eh, Watson? And yet, how dreadfully logical! The case of Mrs. Thornton fascinates me out of all proportion to its importance, for its evidence of the depths of depravity and despair of which the human mind is capable."

"'Depravity' is not the word."

"I beg your pardon, Watson. Let us just settle on 'decay,' then. I fear poor Mrs. Thornton is close to the brink, and our client is rightfully loath to see the poor lady go over it again. Would that more young ladies in the nursing profession were possessed of such conscience!"

The house in Richmond was indeed an attractive one, viewed as we saw it in the early twilight of the following evening. It was a building of one storey, low and rambling, with a quaint round corner crowned by a colorful turret; clearly it had been built by someone of imagination with a good sense of harmony, for even its trim in white and blue was pleasing to the eye. It was set, moreover, on a gentle slope toward the Thames, in spacious grounds which had been landscaped, and the summer- or tea-house Miss Manahan had described was set in the midst of a scant grove halfway between the house and the river.

Mrs. Thornton was plainly the most genteel of ladies. She was dressed in a white dress, with a few frills, and wore a velvet band about her neck to support a cameo. Her eyes were bird-like, and her appearance elfin. Holmes and I were introduced to her as friends of Miss Manahan's, and the old lady seemed quite pleased to meet someone new.

For a little while Holmes talked generalities in his most garrulous vein. Both Miss Manahan and Mrs. Thornton easily fell into his mood, and it was with something of a grave change in manner that Holmes introduced the subject of the late Mr. Thornton.

"I understand you have lost your husband, Mrs. Thornton?"

She seemed somewhat startled, but responded readily enough. "Yes, that was eight years ago – no, nine it is now, I think. It was sudden."

"Quite a shock to you?"

"Yes, a severe shock." She smiled. "It took me some time to get over it. I am afraid we poor women are not as strong mentally as we are physically."

It was Miss Manahan who next undertook to change the subject, by making mention of her patient's sister-in-law.

"I am afraid Miss Lavinia is not very kind," said Mrs. Thornton hesitantly. "If she could only know Wellman and Pauline as I know them."

"They are very kind to you, Mrs. Thornton?"

"If it had not been for them, I would still be – I would still be in the asylum." She said this bravely, though with obvious effort. "When it seemed that I was improving my condition, Wellman was notified, and he would not rest until he had secured my release. He had my authority to build this little house for me, and we are all living here very cozily together. I do not know where I should be without Wellman; he has always managed my affairs, and it is distressing that my sister-in-law should say the things she does." She looked toward the window suddenly and, with an expression of dismay, cried out, "Oh, it is coming up fog!"

"We'll draw the curtains, never mind, Mrs. Thornton," said Miss Manahan reassuringly. Then she turned to Holmes and asked casually whether he would like to see the house before Mrs. Thornton retired.

"If Mrs. Thornton would not mind."

"By no means, Mr. Holmes. I am quite proud of it. I worked over every detail of it with Wellman when it was under construction, and it is almost like my own creation! Do you go, too, Dr. Watson; I can keep quite well by myself for so short a time!"

Thus urged, I followed Holmes, whose interest, of course, was Mrs. Thornton's bedroom, the spacious chamber in the rounded corner of the house. This was, as Miss Manahan had said, a singularly attractive room, with a small bed set almost in the center, and facing toward the windows which opened upon the lawns sloping toward the river. A dressing-table stood over against the wall to the left, and to the right, immediately next to the door leading into Miss Manahan's room, stood a little case filled with books. A comfortable rocking-chair of recent manufacture, a little table, and several other chairs were distributed about the room, into which opened three doors – one to a bath jointly shared by Mrs. Thornton and Mr. and Mrs. Davies, on the left, one to Miss Manahan's room, and one into the hall that ran along the building there, separating the bedrooms from the drawing-room, dining-room, and kitchen on the side of the house facing the road.

Holmes stood for a few moments in silence, gazing about the room. "This is the way the room has always been?"

"Yes, Mr. Holmes."

"And when Mrs. Thornton has her seizures?"

"She describes it in various ways. She says she has awakened to find herself facing the door to the hall, with the bookcase over against the windows; or again, facing the Davies' room, with the dressing-table against the windows."

"You have never observed anything which might give her cause or reason for such hallucinations?"

"No, Mr. Holmes."

"Have the Davies offered any explanation?"

"Yes. They felt that perhaps the fact that the room was unusual in that it was circular was at the bottom of her hallucination, and they offered to exchange rooms with her; but she would not hear of it."

"Ah! Why not?"

"Because she felt she must fight this out by herself."

Holmes looked at me with a strange gleam in his eyes. "Surely that is remarkable insanity, is it not, Watson?"

"Most remarkable."

He smiled and began to move around the room; he looked casually at the dressing-table, the bookcase; he examined the windows and opened the door to the bath, muttering to himself as he went along. "Hm! Bath in pale green. Very neat... They have certainly given her the best view of the river," adding over his shoulder to Miss Manahan, "You will have to draw the curtains all the way, for the fog is growing thicker every minute. I can hardly make out the summerhouse." Then he got down on his knees and examined the bed and the floor, crawling around in a manner which puzzled and amused our client, for he was careless, as always, of his clothing, and he picked up all manner of lint, hairs, and the like, for only a few small rugs were laid on the floor, and the rest of it was bare,. though not highly polished. He was occupied at this for some time before he rose to his feet, dusted himself, and confessed himself finished.

"There are then two bedrooms beside this, and two baths?" he asked.

"Yes, Mr. Holmes."

"A drawing-room, a kitchen, a dining-room – and what else?"

"A little room for storage, and two closets, with a pantry. That is all."

"No basement?"

"Only a small cellar for fruit directly under the kitchen."

"Ah, well, I shall just look around."

So he did, much to my amazement, even descending into the small, square concrete cellar under the kitchen. When he came up again he looked extremely thoughtful and somewhat perplexed.

"We can return to Mrs. Thornton now," he said.

Upon our return, darkness having fallen, Mrs. Thornton bade us goodnight and retired to her room, accompanied by Miss Manahan. Holmes lit his pipe and sat with his long legs stretched out before him, looking quizzically over at me with his keen eyes.

"Did not Mrs. Thornton strike you as a most unusual mental case?"

"Indeed she did."

"I watched you with some interest, Watson. The expressions of your features are informative. I submit you did not believe Mrs. Thornton at all deranged."

"Well, it is true her entire manner is that of one who has recovered from a mental lapse."

"Is it not, indeed! I fancy very few patients would have the courage to speak so openly and frankly of their troubles."

"Oh, some of them do nothing else."

"Ah, yes, the hypochondriacs. But you did not think Mrs. Thornton one."

"No."

"You felt that her conduct was inconsistent with her seizures? Come, is it not so?"

"Well, yes, I admit I did. But of course, the trouble with such mental cases is that the patient always seems perfectly normal, and it is difficult to tell which is the real psyche, to put it in those terms – the woman we saw or the woman she is overnight. I thought her comments about the sister-in-law most indicative."

"That it was Miss Lavinia Thornton who was at the bottom of her trouble?"

"I think there can be no doubt of it. I believe we should pay the lady a call and hear what she has to say."

"Oh, I fancy we can avoid doing so," said Holmes with assurance. "I know what the lady has to say."

"Surely you have not seen her already?"

"I have had no occasion to do so. Mrs. Thornton told us."

He left me to puzzle this out for myself, and went back into reflective silence, puffing at his pipe from time to time, and crossing and re-crossing his legs. He got up presently and suggested that, in view of Miss Manahan's present occupation, we might just walk about the grounds a bit.

We left the house and found that the fog had indeed grown thick. It was evident, however, that Holmes wished to see the summerhouse before we returned to our lodgings, for it was directly there that he walked, with an uncanny instinct for its direction from the house. It was, like the house, of wood, but with a little stone terrace around it, and a stone floor; it was not locked – indeed, it seemed to have no lock – and Holmes made his way inside. Like most structures of its kind, it was obviously designed chiefly for use at lawn or garden parties, or for reposing on a summer's day, made up, as it was, of a single large room, with quaint, rustic benches and a table to match. Holmes used his lantern to examine the walls and floor.

"Are those not large stone blocks, Watson?" he inquired thoughtfully.

"Yes. Though I have seen larger."

"It is a substantial floor."

I agreed that it was.

"Hm! It does not seem to you that there is anything noteworthy about it?"

"Nothing beyond the fact that it is a very workmanlike job. If ever I decide to leave Baker Street, I shall have to look up Mr. Davies' builder."

"Well, there is surely no time like the present. Perhaps Miss Manahan can find it out for us."

We returned to the house, where we found our client awaiting us amid some wonderment as to where we had gone. Holmes explained that we had walked on the grounds, and then asked whether Mrs. Thornton had gone to sleep.

"Not yet, Mr. Holmes."

"Ah! Would you be so good as to ask her two questions for me? Whether, if she knows the name of the builder of this house, she might be kind enough to let my friend Watson here have it? And whether her late husband's executor can easily be reached by telephone?"

Miss Manahan looked at him somewhat strangely, but immediately departed to do as he requested. She came back in a few moments with both questions answered; the builder lived in London, not very far, as it turned out, from Baker Street; and, as for the executor, he was no longer active, since her husband's estate had naturally now been turned over to her, and her nephew was taking care of it for her.

"Now there is just one more thing," said Holmes. He produced from his pocket a piece of ordinary chalk. "After your patient has gone to sleep, let us just try an experiment. Take this chalk and draw a small line down any portion of the wall, across the narrow molding between wall and floor, and out onto the floor, constructing a line of approximately a foot in length, as inconspicuously as possible."

She took the chalk with an absurd expression of bafflement on her attractive features. "I am afraid your methods are quite beyond me, Mr. Holmes."

"Oh, there is nothing at all mysterious about my methods, Miss Manahan, believe me. They are all too simple. We have been proceeding all along on the theory that Mrs. Thornton's tale is a fabrication born of hallucination out of her mental condition. Let us just now proceed from the opposite pole. Mrs. Thornton's tale is either true or not true; that is simple logic. We shall have to discover the answer to the riddle ourselves, for plainly she cannot help us."

I could not help adding a question of my own. "Would it not be appropriate to learn whether or not Mrs. Thornton's sister-in-law has visited her recently?"

Miss Manahan responded at once. "It is strange that you should ask, Doctor. Miss Lavinia called this morning."

"Ah, and I fancy the result of her call was the same as before?" put in Holmes.

"Yes. Mrs. Thornton was left much distressed."

"Well, I daresay we can do no more here. How long, by the way, are Mr. and Mrs. Davies planning to be gone?"

"They expect to return Sunday night."

"Capital! That will give us every opportunity of solving this little mystery. I trust your night will not be too difficult a one, Miss Manahan, but if any trouble should arise, pray do not hesitate to call on us, no matter what the hour. In any case, I hope you will send us a wire in the morning and inform us how Mrs. Thornton spent the night."

"I will do so, Mr. Holmes."

We bade our client good night and made our way back to the nearest conveyance into the city. Holmes was singularly silent, with a foreboding frown on his forehead, and he walked hunched up, his chin sunk into the folds of his coat.

"What do you make of it?" I asked.

"A devilish business, Watson. It goes against my grain."

"Ah, you have a theory, then?"

"On the contrary, I have the solution."

"Impossible!" I cried. "I have been with you every moment."

"Ah, yes, physically. Nothing is ever impossible with quite your vehemence, my dear fellow."

More than that he would not say.

In the morning Miss Manahan, instead of using the telegraph, came to see us in person.

She had a sorry tale to tell, for Mrs. Thornton had suffered a most difficult night. It had begun, as on other occasions, with the conviction that she heard her husband's voice calling to her, but last night there was an additional note in that the poor distraught lady had fancied her husband had begged her to leave this earthly plane and join him, and this had kept her awake for more than an hour at approximately midnight. In the early hours, everything had gone as usual: Mrs. Thornton had come into Miss Manahan's room crying that "they" had changed things again, "they" were after her, as always. When they had returned, the room had been just as it should be.

I listened attentively to Miss Manahan's recital, and when she had finished I could not prevent myself from identifying the poor woman's type of delusion. "Paranoidal delusions," I said, shaking my head. "I'm afraid it is all up with her. She will get progressively worse."

"And the chalk mark, Miss Manahan?"

"I believe it was just as I made it."

Holmes chuckled delightedly. "Aha! I detect a note of hesitation in your voice, Miss Manahan. Come, come – what is it?"

"Well," she laughed nervously. "I'm afraid I am beginning to have hallucinations, too, Mr. Holmes. I did think the mark was a little off kilter, but I guess I must have drawn it crookedly; I did it in a hurry, and did not want to wake my patient; but when I first saw it this morning, I did get somewhat of a surprise."

"Ah, no doubt. I fancy we shall be over in your direction tonight, Miss Manahan. Can you put us up?"

"Why – I think so."

"Expect us then. We shall arrive directly after dinner." He turned to me when she had left. "It is as I thought, Watson. We shall have to lose no time putting an end to this diabolic game."

Fog rose again, as on the previous night, when we set out for Richmond, and Holmes made no secret of his elation, saying that he preferred not to be seen in the vicinity of 23 Linley Road, and generally acting in a most mysterious manner, which he said nothing whatever to explain. Nor did he volunteer any explanation to Miss Manahan; he asked at once to see her patient, the gentle Mrs. Thornton, and when the old lady came, he sat down next to her, took one of her frail hands in his, and spoke most cajolingly.

"Do you know, Mrs. Thornton, I have become most interested in your trouble. Unlike Miss Manahan, I am beginning to believe that your room actually is changed, just as you described it to Miss Manahan to be."

I thought that this blunt approach might be harmful to the patient, and was hard pressed to interfere; but I knew better, and Mrs. Thornton's reaction was one of bewildered interest, as if at first she had not understood that Miss Manahan had spoken to us of her hallucinations, and secondly, as if she were pleasantly surprised to discover someone who did not dismiss her hallucinations for what they were.

"Will you give Dr. Watson and me an opportunity to look into the matter?"

"Why, certainly, Mr. Holmes." She looked hesitantly at Miss Manahan, and was reassured by the young woman's confident smile.

"Then for tonight only I want you to share Miss Manahan's room, and permit Dr. Watson and myself to occupy your own. I assure you we shall look into the matter with fairness and impartiality."

For only a moment the old lady hesitated. Then she began to tremble, biting her lip, her emotions aroused. "I am afraid – I – it's no use. It is nothing anyone else sees, or hears – nothing. Oh, Mr. Holmes, if only you could!"

"Let us just see," replied Holmes calmly. "Surely there is no harm in trying."

In the end, Mrs. Thornton gave in. Thereupon, Holmes and I retired at once to the patient's room, though not before abjuring both the ladies to carry on for the remainder of the evening as if they were quite alone in the house.

Once in the room, Holmes drew the curtains and turned up the light.

He took a magnifying glass from his pocket, found the chalk mark Miss Manahan had made, and came to his knees to examine it.

"Ah, our Miss Manahan is not perfect in observation. Look here, Watson."

I took the glass and held it over the angle of the chalk line.

"I submit that Miss Manahan could not have drawn that line in such a fashion. There is a clear, if fractional break, between the wall and the floor. Or let us say, rather, between the edge of the molding and the floor."

"Yes, that is all very true," I conceded, "but what is the explanation?"

"Ah, it is the obvious one, surely." He pocketed his glass, took out his penknife, opened it, and slipped its blade beneath the molding; he moved it freely about. "Does not that suggest anything to you?"

"The molding appears to be attached to the wall rather than the floor."

"Ah, well, that is very often done." He moved along the wall five feet and again passed his knife-blade between the molding and the floor. "I fancy that is the rule." He got up. "Hm! Now let us see. We shall not go to bed, of course, but let us rig up some sort of dummy to occupy Mrs. Thornton's place. I fancy we shall want to be out of sight of that bathroom door, for, unless I am greatly mistaken, it plays its own small part in this mystery."

I looked at the door. "I am in the woods, Holmes. How can you possibly make such an assertion?" I strode over, opened the door, and looked into the bathroom.

Holmes observed me with manifest patience. "Let us say that you make yourself comfortable on the floor behind the door as it opens. I myself will find a place behind the bed." As he spoke, he began to arrange Mrs. Thornton's bed with a roll of blanket and a pillow to simulate someone sleeping there. Having finished this, he turned out the light, crossed to the windows, and threw up the shades, together with the central window, which was the largest; this, despite the fog, he opened halfway. In the adjoining room, meanwhile, the ladies were preparing for bed.

"Now, then, Watson – not a sound. Whatever you hear, say nothing; whatever happens, do nothing until I give you the word."

"If you would give me a hint, Holmes..."

"We shall see devil's work tonight, Watson, unless I am much mistaken."

He said no more; so I composed myself to snatch as much sleep as possible.

Some two hours passed in absolute silence, when there came to my ears the faint sound of a whispered voice. It seemed to rise from somewhere in my immediate vicinity, and, as I listened, it increased in volume.

"Lydia! Lydia!" it cried. "Come to me. Come over. All is pain where you are. Only here will it end in joy again. Lydia! Lydia!"

A man's voice – or was it a man's voice? It had a hollow, funereal sound, and I felt my skin prickle, as if something of the fog flowing into the room through the open window had penetrated my flesh. It was horrible, it was grotesque, it was damnable.

Then I heard Holmes stir, and in a moment he raised his own voice in a remarkable quavering cry that might have been Mrs. Thornton herself replying. "Frank? Frank? Where are you, Frank?"

"Come over to me, Lydia. Come. It does not matter how you do it, only come. We can be happy again over here." Then the voice faded as it had come, diminishing altogether in a last whispered, "Lydia!" urgent and compelling.

Holmes waited a few moments before coming quietly to my side and whispering into my ear. "I fancy that is somewhat more than an auditory illusion, is it not, Watson?"

"Good God! I begin to understand!" I answered. "It is damnable. But why – why?"

"Wait yet a little. It is far from over."

In two hours time, everything happened as before, I had dozed off and was awakened by the voice calling once again. This time Holmes did not come to my side, though a low clucking sound he made after the voice had ceased assured me he had heard.

Then all was silence again, and so it remained until dawn.

It was then that I became conscious of a tremor in the floor of the room where I sat. I was about to call out to Holmes when his cluck of warning stopped me. And then the entire floor began to move, slowly, almost imperceptibly. I had hardly time to assimilate this before Holmes's urgent whisper reached me. "Keep behind the bathroom door." I crept backward along that weirdly moving floor, revolving slowly, soundlessly, until the dressing-table was indeed before the windows lining the east wall of that room, and the bookcase over before one door. There was now light enough in the room to see it as Mrs. Thornton must have seen it, and it took no imagination to understand how horrified and terrified the poor, stricken lady must have been at this sight, and how much more to come back into the room and find it as it should be.

As soon as the movement stopped, Holmes twitched the folded blanket and pillow from the bed, gave vent to a low sobbing moan, and, hastening across the floor to the door leading into Miss Manahan's room, he opened it and slammed it shut. This accomplished, he raced silently around the room to where I crouched, one hand warningly grasping my shoulder.

On the instant, the door to the bathroom was cautiously opened, someone looked into the room, and then immediately the door was drawn noiselessly shut once more.

"So!" whispered Holmes. "That is dastardly work indeed, Watson. And one alone could not do it, no!" He peered around one edge of the window nearest us. "Ha! there is the signal. Come along."

He darted to the open window, crawled out, dropped to the ground, and ran off into the now rising fog. I followed close upon his heels. Without hesitation, he ran to the summerhouse and entered it.

The rustic table had been moved aside, and in the center of the floor gaped an opening through which light flowed upward. Holmes walked catlike to the edge of the opening and looked down. I peered over his shoulder. There below was an extraordinary sight. A man was bent at some kind of great instrument, whose shafts passed into a tunnel leading in the direction of the house we had just left, and before him, attached in some fashion to the machine at which he worked with such quiet persistence, was a perfect miniature, walls and floor, of the room we had just quitted, and, as he worked, the miniature floor slowly shifted its position, righting itself.

"Good morning, Mr. Wellman Davies," said Holmes in a scornful voice. "I fancy you will have no further occasion to carry on your devil's work."

At the sound of Holmes's voice, Davies whipped around. His hand reached out for a spanner which lay nearby, but Holmes's hand was quicker; he showed his revolver, and Davies, a short, benevolent-looking man with pale grey eyes and a clipped moustache, whose nose showed signs of eyeglasses having been worn, hesitated, and glared at us in baffled rage.

"Come up, come up, Mr. Davies. We have yet to take your wife. How did you find your friends in Scotland?"

"In reality," said Holmes in the brougham on our way back to Baker Street through the first morning sun to penetrate the night's dense yellow fog, "the problem offered no other solution. Indeed, Mrs. Thornton, poor unsuspecting soul, told us all herself. What had Miss Lavinia, her sister-in-law, to say that would upset her? Why, could it be other than criticism of, and warnings about Mr. and Mrs. Davies? Surely not, for Mrs. Thornton said, you remember, 'If she could only know Wellman and Pauline as I know them.' Alas! poor woman!

"The fundamental problem was, of course, that of the circular room. Either it was changed, as Mrs. Thornton said, or it was not. Miss Manahan and Mrs. Thornton herself were convinced that it could be nothing but an hallucination. On the contrary, I proceeded from the assumption that something was wrong with that room, and I sought for evidence that it was so. Obviously, the walls were fixed, but the floor did not seem to be. When the space between the molding along the wall at the floor and the floor itself was manifest, it was clear that in some fashion the floor was constructed on a large turntable. I thought there might be a clue in the basement; but there was no basement beyond that concrete-walled cellar. Hence I sought the summerhouse, and it was immediately apparent to my eye that the large stone blocks concealed a trapdoor. The assumption was obvious that that diabolic business was carried on from there. An accomplice was clearly indicated, and who else but Mrs. Davies? It was she who made sure that Mrs. Thornton had fled her room, and signalled her husband in the summerhouse so that he could return the room to its normal appearance, which he was enabled to do by means of that small-scale model geared to the original.

"It was Davies, of course, who imitated her dead husband's voice from the bathroom. Obviously, they did not go to Scotland, but crept back to the house to carry on their fell game, and the reason for that blind seemed inherent in Miss Manahan's story; she told us, you will remember, that Mr. Davies had begun to look at her with apprehension, as if he feared she might leave them; it was just the opposite; he realized that Miss Manahan was not obtuse, and might begin to suspect their involvement in the matter; so he and his wife absented themselves, for the purpose of establishing to Miss Manahan's knowledge that things occurred in their absence, never dreaming that Miss Manahan had already consulted us.

"And the motive for this horrible plot to drive that poor lady into hopeless insanity was surely obvious, too; Davies had control of his aunt's money, and he did not want to relinquish that control. She was wealthy; he was not. He had already squandered some of her money on this house, and if he could succeed in so breaking down the poor lady's mental health that she could be confined once more, or in driving her to suicide by that bogus haunting of her with her husband's voice, his squandering might never be uncovered, and he would remain permanently in control of her late husband's estate, for it had been placed in her hands, and she had given it over to Davies to manage. A callous, diabolic business, long premeditated. I shall see to it that Mr. and Mrs. Wellman Davies get their just deserts."

Assembling the greatest detectives all together

Covering the full range and history of detective fiction.
From Zadig, *The Moonstone*, and Dupin through Sherlock Holmes, Loveday Brooke, Montague Egg, Lord Peter Wimsey, *The Thinking Machine*, Father Brown down to Solar Pons.

H. Rider Haggard
MR. MEESON'S WILL

Melville Davisson Post
MASTER OF MYSTERIES
THE COMPLETE UNCLE ABNER COLLECTION

Jack London
THE ASSASSINATION BUREAU LTD.

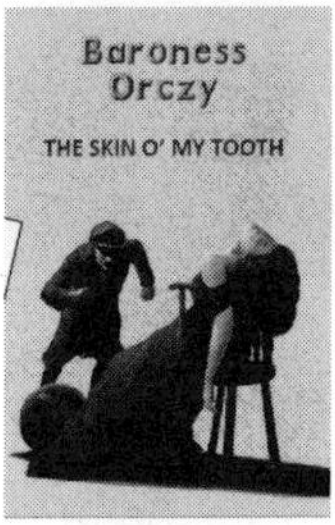
Baroness Orczy
THE SKIN O' MY TOOTH

Earl Derr Biggers
SEVEN KEYS TO BALDPATE

Horace Walpole
THE CASTLE OF OTRANTO

Sexton Blake
THE SEXTON BLAKE COLLECTION
VOLUME 1

Francis Beeding
THE HOUSE OF DR. EDWARDES

A. E. W. Mason
AT THE VILLA ROSE

Fergus Hume
THE MILLIONAIRE MYSTERY

Donald Henderson
A VOICE LIKE VELVET

Richard Hallas
YOU PLAY THE BLACK AND THE RED COMES UP